GLADIATRIX

Russell Whitfield lives in Surrey with his wife and daughter. His lifelong interest in Ancient Greece and Rome inspired him to write *Gladiatrix*, his first novel.

GLADIATRIX

RUSSELL WHITFIELD

MYRMIDON

Myrmidon Books Ltd
Rotterdam House
116 Quayside
Newcastle upon Tyne
NE1 3DY

www.myrmidonbooks.com

Published by Myrmidon 2008

1 3 5 7 9 10 8 6 4 2

A catalogue record for this book is available from the British Library.

ISBN 978-1-905802-09-8

Set in 11/14.25 Bembo by
Ellipsis Books Limited, Glasgow
Printed and bound in Great Britain by
Mackays of Chatham Ltd, Chatham, Kent

For my mother, who I miss every day.

L ysandra would never forget her first time.

Alone, she walked through the darkness of the passageway towards the sun-filled amphitheatre.

As she drew closer to the arena, she became aware of the sound from above – a rhythmic, thrumming cadence that began at the periphery of her consciousness. Distant at first, it became hypnotic as a siren's song, permeating the stone around her, penetrating her to the very bone.

Lysandra battled to keep her churning emotions in check. Fear flowed through her veins and, for a moment, she faltered. Yet part of her surged with the desire to face this most terrible of challenges. It flared only briefly but burned hot enough to sear away her terror. From the darkness, she stepped into the harsh light of the arena.

The roar of the crowd was a living thing as it assaulted her and she staggered beneath its violent intensity. Row upon row of the screaming mob surrounded her, the amphitheatre stuffed full, as if it were a massive god gorging upon base humanity. Her vision swam as she registered innumerable faces, twisted and distorted, their mouths wide open with howls of lust and anticipation.

A fetid stench rose from the freshly raked sands, filling her nostrils with the reek of blood mingled with the excrement of slaughtered animals. The *venatores*, wild beast hunters, had been at their work that day, butchering hundreds of creatures for the delight of the crowd. Her stomach lurched, raw nerves screaming at her to run, to flee this Tartarus made flesh, but again she fought down the urge.

The baying of the frenzied mob increased in its intensity. Her eyes narrowed as she gazed across the arena; emerging from the tunnel that faced her own was another woman.

Her opponent.

Lysandra was only vaguely aware of an arena slave rushing up and thrusting two short swords into her sweat slick hands, as she focused on her adversary. She realised that the combatants must have been chosen for their physical differences. Whereas she was tall and slender, her foe was short and solidly built, her limbs chunky. To Lysandra's Spartan eyes, she looked downright vulgar. Huge, udder-like breasts heaved beneath her white tunic, threatening to burst forth from their confinement. This study of Gallic typicality was crowned by straw-coloured hair, the final contrast to the raven-black tresses of Lysandra's own. There were but two similarities: the weapons they bore and the certain knowledge that, in scant minutes, one of them would die.

The Gaul turned towards the dignitaries' box and raised her right arm in salute. Lysandra, though unused to arena etiquette, emulated her. She had spent her whole life in ritual observance and made the gesture with confidence. Not that it mattered. The richly clad Roman whom Lysandra assumed to be Sextus Julius Frontinus, the governor and procurator of Asia Minor, did not bother to acknowledge them, his attentions clearly focused on the dusky charms of the slave girl by his side.

Lysandra turned towards her opponent. The two women faced each other, the sea green eyes of the Gaul locked with her own.

For interminable moments, they stood, their emotions mirrored in each other's gaze, and Lysandra felt a sudden, sharp regret at their plight. Though they were not foes of their own volition, Lysandra knew she could not stay her hand. Her eyes hardened with the resoluteness to survive and she saw the other woman nod as she too came to this realisation. They raised their weapons.

For a few heartbeats, all was still. Then, with sudden violence the Gaul attacked and the strangely beautiful sound of iron striking iron sang out as Lysandra met her assault. The Celtic warrior screamed and cursed as she laid in, imbibing rage-fuelled courage. There was no order to her attack, just a constant flurry of hacking blows, dealt with all the strength the stocky body could provide. She was like an avalanche, rolling forward, crushing everything in her path.

Lysandra knew she must be as mist. Most of her life had been spent preparing for combat: a ritual training to be certain; a ceremonial skill never meant to be called upon. But now, in the stark reality of mortal threat, this hard-learnt preparation came to the fore, and her body responded instinctively.

It was as if her opponent was moving underwater. As the Gaul initiated an attack, Lysandra's own blade moved to deflect the blow. *Do not meet force with force*, she told herself as she weaved away from the onslaught. Her refusal to engage in a slogging match seemed to encourage her foe, who redoubled her efforts. The Gaul's feet churned up sand as she pursued Lysandra across the arena, slashing and cutting at thin air. As the chase wore on the crowd erupted into a chorus of boos and cat-calls, demanding more action.

Sweat now plastered the Gaul's yellow hair to her forehead and darkened the sheer white tunic to gauzy grey. Lysandra saw her shoulders heaving with exertion as she evaded another attack. The Gaul paused momentarily, gasping for breath. It was obvious that she was weakening but, more, her confidence had drained and the insidious worm of doubt was now eating at her fighting spirit. Gamely, she raised her swords, and a sudden rush of fire filled Lysandra's veins. *Now*, her instincts screamed at her. *Now was the time.*

She countered.

Her blades whirled, blurring in their swiftness as she mercilessly turned defence to attack. Her opponent's parries became frenzied with awful suddenness as she back-stepped, swords moving frantically to deflect the onslaught.

Lysandra pressed in harder, the Gaul only stopping her now at the last possible instant. She increased her efforts, engaging in a final, furious exchange of blows with her desperate opponent. As the impact of blade on blade jarred her arm, she felt the last strength leech from the barbarian and smashed through her guard.

There was no remorse: just a wondrous, beautiful exultation as she felt the other woman's flesh yield and part as she rammed home her blade. The Gaul made a choking sound, huge gouts of blood vomiting from her mouth and the gaping wound in her chest. Lysandra dragged the blade out and, using her own momentum, spun about. Her sword caught the staggering woman on the neck, severing the head from her body; it arced skywards, the eyes and mouth wide open, frozen forever in shock and pain. The headless body stood wavering for what seemed like an eternity before, with an almost reverential slowness, it toppled backwards and crashed to the sand, blood spreading out behind the gaping neck like a crimson pillow.

With chilling abruptness reality crashed back down upon Lysandra, the roar of the crowd cascading over her, drenching her in a waterfall of dissonance. It was a bizarre tableau: the corpse still twitching at her feet and, approaching her, a tall man, clad as Charon, the ferryman of the dead, bearing a hooked staff. Slowly, and with a degree of ceremony, 'Charon' retrieved the Gaul's head, then attached her torso to the staff. At the same

4

formal pace, he retreated, dragging the body behind him.

Lysandra backed away, then turned and made her way towards the tunnel, her thoughts a confused morass of elation, guilt and relief.

II

Lysandra stared disconsolately through the bars of the moving prison, watching the arid Carian landscape roll by with mind-numbing slowness. Nothing broke the monotony of the view, save for a few hardy shrubs, the odd dusty hillock and the occasional traveller heading towards the city.

The cart had been bouncing along for some hours, leaving the sprawl of Halicarnassus far behind. Certainly, what she had seen of the streets as they left the city had impressed upon her the size of the place: compared to her home *polis* of Sparta, it was gigantic and somewhat vulgar. That, she considered, was to be expected of Asiatic Hellenes, who were all fawning imitators of the Romans as far as she was concerned. Not that she knew any personally, but then stories were not told if there was no substance to them.

She was one of seven prisoners in the carriage, but Balbus's train snaked back a good deal further, and she could only assume that she had been placed with the *lanista's* latest 'acquisitions.' The others in the cart were all of barbarian stock and unable to speak Latin, let alone her native Hellenic. However, this did not stop them from babbling in their own incomprehensible tongues, the sound of which set her teeth on edge.

After her bout in the arena, Lysandra had been shuffled unceremoniously to a cell to wait out the day's entertainments. Admittedly she had been fed and even given a perfunctory examination by a surgeon to see if she was injured. Her state of health established, she was locked away in the dark and forgotten until it was time for Balbus's caravan to leave. She had tried to ask questions as they dragged her towards the waiting prison cart but, having ascertained that she was now the 'property of Lucius Balbus,' any further enquiry was met with a barked order to remain silent, followed by a sharp slap around the face when she persisted.

Physical pain was something she had been taught to endure since childhood, but the blow served to remind her of her new status. She was almost physically sick when the word came unbidden to her thoughts.

Slave.

And worse, an arena slave – the lowest of the low – hardly more than an animal. She had become a part of the most derided echelon of society. It was almost too much to bear, but she consoled herself with the knowledge that, as soon as the owner of the troupe found out who she was, this ridiculous situation would be fully rectified.

A tap on her shoulder broke her reverie and Lysandra turned to see a red-haired barbarian offering her a chunk of bread. This dubious gift was clutched in filth-begrimed fingers and she was tempted to slap the hand away; yet the smile the woman gave her was genuine and she realised it would be petulant to refuse the offer. She hoped her returning smile did not look too much like a grimace and took the proffered loaf. The woman gave her a sisterly pat on the arm and returned to sit with her companions. Lysandra went back to her brooding but was inwardly grateful for this act of solidarity.

They journeyed for several days and, to her surprise, they were given food at regular intervals. The fare was of excellent quality: a stew of meat and barley, superior to any Lysandra had previously tasted. In fact, their captors seemed at pains to keep the women in good health, which was contrary to much of what she had heard about the life of a slave. Aside from the lice that had infested all of the captives, the trek was, if not pleasant, at least bearable.

Indeed, communication had, to some extent, sprung up between Lysandra and her barbarian companions. Through some faintly comedic pantomiming she had learned that the red-haired woman was named Hildreth. She and her fellows were of the Chattian tribe, which Lysandra identified at once as Germanic. The Chattians were well known throughout the Empire; their warriors had been giving the emperor's legions hell along the Rhenus River for some years.

Hildreth, of course, had not heard of Hellas; even when Lysandra referred to her homeland as Greece in the Roman manner, the tribeswoman responded with a shrug and a shake of her head. Lysandra thought it pointless to pursue this any further. Geography was going to be far beyond their level of comprehension. Instead, she concentrated on teaching the Germans rudimentary Latin. Unfortunately, the reputation barbarians carried for an innate slowness of wit was not unfounded and she persevered only to occupy her time rather than from any real desire to educate them.

Soon, however, the prison cart was alive with the sound of harshly accented Latin cries such as 'sky!' 'tree!' and 'stone!' which quickly graduated to such statements as 'I-do-not-speak-Latin-can-you-speak-German?'

It was all good fun at first, but inevitably the hilarity that the lessons produced amongst the tribeswomen attracted the attentions of Balbus's guards, who admonished them to keep the noise down with much threatening and brandishing of stout clubs to ensure the message got across.

Nevertheless, Lysandra found the diversion had worked. Time slipped by easily enough so that it was a shock to her when she spied a long, walled structure in the distance; unmistakably, this was their final destination.

An expectant hush fell over the prisoners as the caravan wound its leisurely way towards the construction. As they drew closer, Lysandra reckoned that it was akin to a miniature Troy, so soundly were the walls constructed. The ponderous wrought-iron gates swung open, and the caravan passed beneath an arched sign that proclaimed that this was *Lucius Balbus's School of Gladiatrices*.

Lysandra leant forward, her hands gripping the iron of the bars of the cage as they entered the *ludus*. The place was a hive of cacophonous activity, teeming with women involved in various martial exercises. The clack of wooden weapons filled the air, mingling with shouted orders from the trainers and cries of both exultation and exasperation. It was a familiar scene and, despite her circumstances, she found it strangely comforting.

The doors to the cage rattled open and the guards beckoned them out, shouting an order in their guttural barbarian language. Lysandra could sense the horror flooding through the group.

'Take your clothes off and throw them there,' a guard repeated, this time in Latin. Lysandra shrugged: in Sparta, all exercises were conducted *gymnos*, nude; the body was something to be proud of after all. She complied, glad to be rid of the filthy tunic.

Her companions followed her example reluctantly, and she was at once aware of their issue: evidently, in Germania, the body was *not* something to be proud of. Bereft of their clothes, the tribeswomen were an absurd-looking group. True, she herself was fair skinned, but these women had an almost pale-blue aspect to them. Heavy breasts hung from too-white torsos and such a shock and variety of pubic hair was revealed. Lysandra had to bite her lip not to laugh. Manlike tufts she had seen under their arms on their journey to the *ludus,* but the complete Germanic nude was comedic in its hairy extreme.

'You speak Latin.' The guard's statement interrupted her critique of the tribal form. She eyed the man, and found him to be short, squat and somewhat ill favoured. Not a barbarian, but close enough, he had the look of a Macedonian about him. She drew herself up.

'Yes. And evidently better than you.'

The man was nonplussed: he gaped at her for a moment, his mouth falling open; the others quietened, as stunned by the arrogant response as he was. The atmosphere was heavy and uncertain for a moment before one of the men fell about laughing at his companion's embarrassment. The reaction spread and the guards hooted and guffawed at her audacity. The Germans looked around, unsure of what was happening.

The Macedonian shook his head. 'You're lucky I don't beat you black and blue,' he said, but the previous mirth undermined his threat. 'Let's get you and your barbarian pets cleaned up.' He motioned for them to start walking.

As the group moved away, the guard noted that the Greek's flippant mouth had landed her in trouble before. Though from the front she was beautiful and flawless, her back was marked by a latticework of pale scars.

They were led the length of the training compound, giving them an opportunity to take in their surroundings. As the exterior suggested, the *ludus* was more of a walled town in miniature than a prison. Squat stone huts were set all along one side of the massive training area, which Lysandra assumed to be the slave quarters – her quarters, she thought sullenly. Opposite these were opulent villa–style houses, set much further back from the noise and dust. Fountains and statues were evident, and Lysandra made a gesture of acquiescence as she passed an image of Minerva, the

Roman name for the goddess Athene. The far end of the *ludus* was dominated by a large bath house and it was there she and the barbarians were taken.

The guards ushered them through the entrance and passed them into the care of several slave women, the eldest of whom was a severe-looking German who announced herself as Greta. Fortunately, some of the other attendants spoke Hellenic and hearing the music of her own language lifted Lysandra's mood somewhat.

They were taken to a side room that contained several buckets of evil-smelling liquid and little else. Greta instructed the women to massage the odoriferous stuff into their heads. There was a vague tang of naphtha in the mix and Lysandra reasoned that, though disgusting, the concoction would rid her of the lice that had been her travelling companions for the past few days. In any event, it was preferable to having her head shaved.

Greta ordered the women sluiced down with warm water before taking them to the building's main functional room. Lysandra's lips turned upwards in pleasure as they moved into the baths proper. The pool was large and, to her surprise, scented. Wisps of steam meandered from the surface, making the air humid and heavy. She needed no urging, and made purposefully towards the water.

Hildreth and the others hung back and harsh words in German were exchanged between her and Greta. Greta, though obviously a slave herself, seemed to have carved her way to a position of some seniority in the self-contained world of the *ludus* and evidently tolerated no defiance. Yet Hildreth had a dangerous look to her as well: certainly, she was not a woman to be trifled with. Lysandra paused and cocked an eyebrow at one of Greta's scrubs.

'What are they saying?' she asked.

The girl was young, perhaps six years junior to Lysandra's own nineteen. Tiny in stature, her freckled, elfin face was dominated

11

by huge brown eyes and framed by a mop of unruly dark curls. She shrugged her skinny shoulders.

'I don't know for sure, but I can guess,' came the response. 'The barbarians are fearful of bathing.' She risked a slight smile. 'They think that they will get the chills and die!'

Lysandra sniffed loftily. 'Ignorant savages,' she muttered and plunged into the pool without further comment. True, she had come to look at the barbarians in a slightly less derogatory light after their journey to the *ludus* but her low opinion of them *was* appropriate. They were like overgrown children: stupid, scared and superstitious. And, she thought to herself, their dubious companionship was something that had been forced upon her. In any normal circumstance they would not have warranted even her attention, let alone her time.

Thoughts of the Germans drifted away as she revelled in the sensation of the hot water on her skin. After the filthy days on the road, the pleasure at cleansing herself was immense. She rolled luxuriantly in the bath, letting the heat open her pores and wash the mire of sweat and dirt from her body.

She swam under the water for a while, before letting herself float to the surface and drift lazily to one of the sides. Arms and shoulders resting on the lip of the pool, she watched as the Germans lost their struggle to remain dirty. Reluctantly, one by one, they lowered themselves into the steaming water, crying out with shock at the unnatural warmth. Their fear, however, was soon conquered as the perfumed heat did its seductive work, relaxing cramped muscles and purifying the skin. Greta tossed a bag of sponges among the delighted and cooing tribeswomen. A visible scum began to form around them as their vigorous scrubbing started to shift years of ingrained dirt.

Lysandra stayed well away, but any hopes she had of idling in the water were quickly dispelled as Greta's long-experienced eye adjudged that her countrywomen were sufficiently bathed.

Clapping her hands together briskly, she ordered everyone out of the pool.

The tiny slave girl with whom she had spoken earlier approached her. 'You must come with me,' the girl said. Similarly, each of the new captives was now being led away by one of Greta's contingent. After bathing, Lysandra was feeling relaxed and, despite her current circumstances, better than she had in weeks. As such, she was not inclined to question.

Her diminutive guide took her from the bathing area proper and into a side room. Here, a towelled bench lay prepared.

'I'm Varia,' the girl offered.

'Lysandra.'

Varia indicated the bench, instructing Lysandra to lay front down upon it. 'Just relax,' she said, pouring a liberal amount of sweet-smelling oil onto her charge's back and shoulders. Her small hands deftly worked the unguent into her skin, the surprisingly strong fingers kneading and working any remaining tenseness from her muscles.

She almost purred with pleasure under Varia's ministrations as the massage continued. She could not help but wonder at this sort of treatment, a fact she mentioned to the young slave. Certainly it was not what she had been led to believe a chattel's lot to be.

'Ah,' Varia replied as she now worked her magic on Lysandra's legs. 'It will get harder all too soon. There are certain standards to live up to,' she added matter-of-factly. 'All the gladiatrices here are very well-trained.'

Lysandra murmured her understanding, her nostrils flaring slightly, catching the aroma of wax in the air. Varia was speaking again. 'So it is not all massages and bathing. And some of the trainers can be very cruel. I can see you've had a cruel master before.' The slave's fingertips traced the ridges of the scars on her back.

A sharp tearing sound from the adjacent cell followed by a

scream of agony interrupted any answer Lysandra was about to give. She started and looked enquiringly over her shoulder.

'Waxing,' Varia responded to the unvoiced question. 'It lasts longer than shaving, but the first time is very painful for the barbarians.'

Lysandra found herself in absolute agreement. True, she had been trained to ignore pain, she could not help but feel grateful that the waxing was an ordeal she would not have to face. A once-over with a bronze razor would suffice for a civilised woman such as she.

In much better form after the unexpected indulgences of the bathhouse, Lysandra emerged wearing the light tunic that had been provided for her, enjoying, despite her circumstances, a lightness of heart she had not felt since her ship was wrecked. Hildreth and the tribeswomen joined her, their gait indicating that the attentions of the waxing cloth had left them somewhat tender. Greta bade them form a single rank and remain silent.

After some minutes one of the trainers, the one she knew went by the name of 'Stick' approached the line of women. Lysandra noted his eyes scrutinising them. She had seen the look before in her youth: Stick was assessing their fitness with a glance, seeking a fire in the eyes that might suggest a woman had promise.

'Welcome to your new home,' he said in his high, nasal voice. As he spoke, Greta translated for the German women. 'You are slaves… chattel… less than human. Forget that you were once women with lives beyond these walls.' He grinned nastily. 'It will only make this more painful for you.' He began to pace up and down the line of women, swinging his eponymous vine staff. 'Your sole purpose in life is to provide high-quality entertainment for a very demanding public. You will be trained to this end: to fight and kill, and to face your death in a civilised manner.

'You will obey me and the other trainers at all times. Remember, you are but slaves and it is your lot to serve the demands of your masters.' Stick drew to a halt in front of Hildreth. Slowly and deliberately, he slid a brown, callused hand under the hem of her tunic and fondled her between the legs. He cackled as the tribeswoman flushed scarlet for shame, impotent fury burning in her eyes. Stick withdrew his hand and made a show of breathing in her scent. 'Whatever those demands happen to be,' he added. As an aside, he nodded and winked at Hildreth. 'Very nice.'

Clearly Stick had now warmed to his theme. 'Obey us in all things, and your lives here may even become pleasant. Disobey, and you will find that I can make your existence so terrible that death will seem a merciful release. Train hard and learn well... and you might survive long enough to buy back your freedom.' He glared at them and shook his head. 'But by the looks of you, I doubt it. Most likely, I'm wasting my time and you will be choking on your own blood after your first bout. We had better get to work, curse your eyes! Begin running. Circle the *ludus* until I tell you to stop.'

The women turned and began to run. As Lysandra stepped up, Stick placed the vine staff on her chest. 'Not you, Greek. The *lanista* wants to see you.'

Lysandra regarded the wiry little Parthian, with a mixture of amusement and contempt. 'That is good,' she said. 'For I want to see him.'

Stick held her gaze for a moment; then he slammed the butt end of the vine stick viciously into her solar plexus. The breath rushed out of her and she doubled over in agony. Stick shoved her to the ground and thrashed at her back with the staff, landing several powerful blows. As she reeled in shock and pain, the Parthian grabbed a handful of her hair and dragged her face close

to his own, his bulbous eyes glittering with fury. 'Lose that attitude, my lovely, or you and I will fall out, yes?' He hurled her
back to the ground and brandished the vine staff in her face.
'Now, the *lanista* would like to see you.'

Lysandra glared hatred up at her tormentor. Spartan honour
– *her* honour – demanded that she rise and smash the leering,
ugly face to a pulp. For a moment only, her mind coursed with
bloody fury and she tensed, ready to spring up. Then as quickly
as it had been lost, her control returned. She let the rage drain
away and forced herself to nod in acquiescence. Time enough
for revenge when she had been set free, she told herself. Then
the filthy scum would be made to suffer for this insult to her
person.

Stick wore an impassive mask as he gestured towards Balbus's
quarters indicating that she follow him. But the encounter had
unsettled him. When he looked into her eyes he had seen arrogance and disdain, as well as complete lack of fear. In that moment
he realised that he had not seen the like of this girl in all his
years in and around the arena. He had hit her hard – hard enough
to knock the fight out of most men. But the Greek had not been
cowed and something other than fear had stayed her hand. The
look on her face told Stick that, on another day, he would have
had to put her down permanently.

The house of Lucius Balbus was the most opulent of all those
Lysandra had noted when she first entered the *ludus*. Set farthest
back from the training area, it was clean, white and richly decorated. Several large statues of Roman deities, and also a few local
divinities, were represented in the flower garden that led to the
abode proper. The centrepiece, of course, was an image of the
emperor, Domitian. Painted and garlanded, it was a trifle over-
done to Lysandra's austere eye.

Stick glowered and left her in the care of a youth at the

17

entrance to Balbus's house. He was perfumed and pretty, his pale blue chiton far shorter than her own. The boy's blond hair was outrageously coiffured and oiled, framing a plump, sultry, almost petulant face, a face that was used to having its whims granted.

'Greetings,' he lisped in Hellenic. She recognised the Athenian accent at once. 'I'm Eros.'

'Of course you are.'

Eros sniffed disdainfully and indicated that she follow him inside, tutting as her bare feet left dusty prints on the immaculate marble.

The two made their way in silence through the house to a somewhat cluttered office area. The untidy sprawl seemed out of place in the otherwise sumptuous surroundings. 'The master, Lucius Balbus, is expecting you.' Eros flounced off, his disapproval evident in every step.

Lucius Balbus had long since acquired himself a niche in the entertainment market of Halicarnassus as *the* supplier of novelty acts for the great and frequent games of the province – the only *lanista* who specialised in the training of women for gladiatorial combat. Others dabbled and had women in their stables, but he alone could lay claim to a school comprised solely of female performers.

If he was honest with himself, Balbus had not expected his latest acquisition to survive; to fight as the *dimachaera* – the two-knife girl – required long months of training and this Greek had been with him less than seven days. She had been a timely arrival. His regular fighter had come down with a stomach illness, rendering her unable to perform – leaving Balbus with the unthinkable prospect of a forfeited fee. The *editor* of the games would have been most displeased if the scheduled bill was disrupted at the last moment and was well within his contractual rights to hold back the coin on a no-show.

But Balbus had always been lucky. With a sense of fondness and reverence for Fortuna he pondered the events that had brought the new girl to him. As his caravan had travelled up the coast to Halicarnassus, his evening meal had been interrupted by Stick, excited and demanding to be seen. Grudgingly, he had consented.

'Balbus, we are saved!' Stick had announced as he rushed in. 'The boys and me went riding down the beach to see if there was anything worth having washed up from the storm.' Stick's bulging eyes shone with excitement. 'We found more than flotsam, Balbus!'

'Spit it out, Stick!'

'A girl, Balbus! We found a girl! Rightly, there *was* a ship caught in the storm. The wreckage was all over the beach.' He leant forward dropping his voice to a whisper. 'But it was a *Legion* ship, Balbus, there were swords, *pila*, standards...' He trailed off, seeking the right words. 'Everything!'

Balbus was not a man to miss an opportunity. 'I trust you and the boys arranged to have the loot brought back to the caravan?'

Stick had looked insulted. 'Of course.'

'So what of some Legion whore,' Balbus had wanted to know. 'I take it you've had your fun ploughing a well tilled furrow? I don't see how this 'saves' us.'

'This is the thing,' Stick said. 'Some of the lads *were* going to take her. But she fought like a demon. Grabbed a *gladius* from the wreckage as they got close and set on the two nearest her. Poor Tiro and Gideon... he shook his head with exaggerated remorse. 'She finished them both like that.' He snapped his fingers.

Balbus sat up from his reclined position. 'She what?'

'I'm telling you, Balbus, this girl is a natural, better than anything I've seen. No one was going to try to fight her alone on foot after what she did to those two. We ran her down from horseback and tied her up. All the while she fought like a Fury.'

'You wouldn't be exaggerating, Stick. I'd hate that,' Balbus had warned.

'I promise you…' Stick had put his hand on his heart. 'She can replace Teuta in the two knives; we won't have to forfeit our fees!'

'A consolation for the loss of Tiro and Gideon?' Balbus asked ironically.

Stick got to his feet. 'I never liked them anyway,' he had said, and left him to his thoughts.

Lucius Balbus counted himself no fool and had taken Stick's claims with a healthy degree of scepticism. Tiro and Gideon were often in their cups and perhaps an armed, desperate woman could just about have dispatched them with apparent ease. But now, this 'Lysandra' had impressed him in the arena, dispelling his doubts the moment she put up her blades. She fought with skill that went beyond natural talent; that she was trained – and trained well – was all too obvious. Strategy, timing and stamina had all been evident in her bout with the Gaul. The girl intrigued him and, for that reason alone, he had ordered her to be brought to him at the earliest convenience.

He heard Eros usher her to his office yet she wavered by the door, looking over shoulder at the retreating servant. He was irritated by her disregard for his position: a slave should not keep her master waiting. 'Come in.' His voice caused her to turn back. Seated at the far end of the scroll-lined office, behind an ornate wooden work desk, he watched her approach with a critical eye.

Though ascetically pleasing, she did not possess the charms of the gladiatrix favoured by the predominately male fans of the female spectacle. For one, she was too tall, tall enough to look most men directly in the eye. Her hair, black as night, contrasted sharply with the white, almost alabaster skin. Her breasts were firm, yet were not of the size that was currently preferred by the arena connoisseur: the Northern European women were all the rage, voluptuous, savage and dangerously desirable. But it was her eyes that held him, the ice-blue gaze intent and alert. No, he thought, this one possessed the beauty of marble sculpture, serene and distant – an acquired taste for a refined palate.

'I am pleased this misunderstanding is over,' she said, interrupting his train of thought. 'I can see that you are a wealthy man. I shall need to borrow some funds to return to Sparta.' She raised a hand, cutting off the astonished *lanista* as he made to speak. 'Never fear, Lucius Balbus; the Temple of Athene is not without means, and you will be reimbursed.'

Balbus gaped at her. 'I beg your pardon?'

The girl smiled at him, her expression condescending. 'I need money to get back to Hellas… Greece as you Romans call it. My sisterhood will send you the amount in full when I return home.'

'You are a priestess?' Balbus faltered, unused to having the initiative in conversation taken from him. He was astounded by the girl's arrogant assumption that she would be released merely because she desired it. Indeed, her very manner indicated that she was going through some sort of formality.

'A *Mission* priestess, Lucius Balbus.'

She said it with some pride, though the *lanista* had not the faintest idea what she might mean. He had, however, sufficiently recovered his wits not to show her his ignorance. He eased his large frame back in his seat, folding his fingers over his belly, gathering his thoughts. Balbus had dealt with similar situations: often, these religious types believed that their devotion to whatever gods they prayed to provided indemnity from slavery. They found out all too soon that none were exempt from servitude to Rome.

'I'm afraid it is you who has misunderstood.' He paused, letting that sink in, gratified by the change in her eyes. Evidently, she had not expected this response and it had put *her* on the defensive. And that was precisely how Lucius Balbus preferred his relationship

21

with his merchandise. 'Whatever you may have been, you are no longer. Under Roman law, you are my property. My slave.'

'I am no slave!' Lysandra cut him off, taking a step forward. Balbus had to use every fibre of will not to jerk back. He was no coward, but had seen the Greek in action and had a more than healthy respect for her skills. He forced a smile.

'Your former status does not protect you' – he made a show of looking down at his paperwork, as if seeking a previously scribbled note – 'Lysandra,' he finished. 'I have bought and sold priestesses, princesses and even queens. All have equal rights in the eyes of the *lex Romana* – that is that slaves have no rights.' He could see her floundering. She was, after all, still young, and inexperienced; despite the tough exterior, he could tell she was not yet out of her teens. 'Besides… whoever or whatever you claim to be you are simply detritus washed up by the sea. Two men are dead – my property. As far as the witnesses are concerned you are simply a murderess. The arena is your fate one way or the other. But if the praetors put you there you'll simply be butchered without a chance to defend yourself.'

Balbus could only imagine what the psychological blow of becoming a slave did to a person, especially those that were used to commanding respect, such as a priestess must. But he was wise enough to know that if he pressed too hard at an early stage, he could shatter their spirit. He had seen tribal women, the sight of whom would unman the doughtiest legionary in battle, reduced to sallow husks when their slavery was too keenly impressed upon them. A woman with no fighting spirit was a poor investment.

'Look,' he said, his tone lighter, more placating *and*, he thought, almost… *fatherly*. 'This life is not as bad as you may think.' He ignored the cynical lift of her eyebrow. 'I called you here to ask where you came by your extraordinary fighting skills, but that is self-evident,' he hedged, being aware that certain religious sects trained their priestesses in ritualised combat. Given the Spartans' legendary martial history, it seemed reasonable to assume that they would most likely indulge in such practices.

'You have fought and survived your first bout with ease,' he went on, noting a flash of pride on the ice of her eyes. He made an expansive gesture. 'I don't live in all of the houses you see here. The barracks are for new girls and poor fighters. My best fighters, those of my top tier, live in luxury.' An exaggeration of the truth perhaps but then after the filth of a barracks cell, even one of Balbus's modest houses would seem like Nero's Golden Palace.

Lysandra's expression was derisive. 'You would seek to blind a Spartan to slavery by offering her opulence?' Balbus winced internally. This one seemed to have an answer for everything. He tried a different tack.

'A good fighter receives gifts from the public. An excellent fighter can soon become very rich.' He paused. 'Rich enough to buy her freedom.'

Lysandra pressed her lips into a thin line, showing her irritation. 'You are selling what is mine by birth.'

Balbus shrugged. 'It's a small hope,' he said. 'But it's a hope. That's all I can give you.'

There was a long moment of silence then.

'My sisterhood would buy my freedom from you if I were allowed to write to them,' she said finally. Warmth flooded through the *lanista* as he detected, beneath the parochial accent, a pleading desperation in her voice. It came unaccustomed to those proud lips, he fancied. There was nothing like impressing his will upon another, watching the evolution from free-woman to slave, slave to gladiatrix. No matter how many the mill of the arena churned up, there were always new slaves, new challenges. Watching the proud ones like this Spartan capitulate gave him the greatest pleasure.

Balbus feigned consideration of the idea but had dismissed her words as soon as they had passed her lips. The fact was, any hope of ransom must ever be denied the fighters. The knowledge that there might be a route to freedom outside of winning it by the sword would be disastrous – not only for his *ludus* but also the business as a whole. That is why the Oath existed; of course, he knew this new batch had not yet taken it, but that would happen in time.

'I can't do that,' he said, with just the right amount of regret. 'Were I to agree to your request, I would have to do the same for everyone. My days would be utterly consumed by hearing petitions from people claiming ransoms could be raised for them, my business would suffer and the result would be the end of all I own. I *am* sorry,' he finished with a lie.

He watched, studying the girl's reaction to his words. She was unused to guile, and her emotions were written all over her face, plainly read by an eye as canny as his. Confusion, anger and then the feral look of a trapped animal, each in turn left its mark. The lines of physical age had not yet begun to show on the alabaster features but life's experience had now begun to weather the girl's soul. 'Go and begin your training,' he said, becoming abrupt and dismissive. 'You are good, but there is still much for you to learn.'

She stood a little taller then, a sudden arrogance in her eyes. 'From these amateurs of yours?' she hissed. 'Hardly.' Without waiting to be dismissed she turned about and marched from the *lanista's* presence.

Balbus watched her go with a mixture of amusement and curiosity. The gods had been kind to him of late. His girls were gaining in popularity all the time and the fight proceeds grew more and more lucrative. The Greek would be an excellent addition to his stable, a real money-spinner. He would find out more about his new acquisition's religious order. Girls like this Lysandra kept his interest piqued and his enthusiasm fresh. One could, he thought ruefully, become jaded all too quickly in this business. He laughed aloud suddenly and, rubbing his hands together, called Eros to him.

IV

She would not cry.

It was not the Spartan way. Tears stung her eyes, threatening to well forth, but she gritted her teeth against them. Her jaw set, she emerged from Balbus's villa and made her way back to the training area, thankful only that her bravado had not failed her before the *lanista*. She could not give in to despair. She had to face her fate with courage and the discipline instilled in her since childhood – so she reasoned in her mind but her heart cried out, demanding that her emotions be released.

She fought a desperate battle against herself, drowning in the cacophony of the *ludus*. All about her women whirled in the violent dance of combat, their features blurred behind the opaque veil of her tears. She took a breath to steel herself but, in that moment, the dam of her self-control burst. She fell to a crouch, her raven hair hanging about her face and gave in to the pain. Tears rolled unchecked down her face, each shuddering breath cutting her heart to shreds.

How could she have been so wrong? The face of the *lanista* filled her mind's eye, his words mocking her with their awful truth. She had been so sure, so confident that regaining her freedom was simply a matter of formality; that Balbus, a civilised Roman citizen, would respect both her and her calling. Had he not adorned his *ludus* with images of the gods?

In that moment she knew that Balbus's piety was a facade; the only god he worshipped was money. He made no distinction between civilised Hellenes or savage barbarians – to him they were all simply profit-making flesh.

Slavery.

The very word was an anathema to all that was Spartan, all that she was. With his grim pronouncement, Lucius Balbus had stripped out the very essence of her being, making her an aberration in her own eyes.

To cry was to disgrace not only her Spartan heritage, but Athene herself. Yet now, freed from the shackles of her will, her anguish tore through her with savage claws. In silent desperation she clutched her arms about herself seeking, childlike, to soothe the pain. How long she stayed this way she could not tell, conscious only of her own black despair.

'Here.'

Dimly, she became aware of a gentle touch on her shoulder. She raised her head, her vision still blurred by tears, to look upon the most beautiful creature she had ever seen. Through her misted eyes, Lysandra could not make out if the woman were a mortal or a muse of Apollo come to spirit her away from this place.

Her hair was of the finest spun gold, straight and fair, her skin kissed to delicate bronze by the Carian sun. The flawless countenance was perfection beyond that of any described in Homeric hymn; impossibly beautiful, she moved gracefully, as if she were the remnant of a dream. She knelt before Lysandra and daubed her face with a cool, damp cloth, wiping away the bitterness of her tears. She smiled then, and the light of the world shone in her peerless blue eyes.

'It will go hard for you if they see you cry,' she said. 'Don't give them the satisfaction.'

Lysandra nodded her thanks and was about to speak when a shadow fell across them.

'Eirianwen!' It was Stick. The wiry Parthian did not attempt to hide his leer as he looked down at the two women. 'Is this new slave in tears already?'

'No,' Eirianwen stood. 'She was hit in the face by my back-swing,' she indicated a wooden practice sword lying nearby. 'She's dazed that's all.'

'Dazed is it?' Stick leant over and grasped Lysandra's chin, turning her face from left to right, as would a vet with a sick animal. She resisted the urge to slap his hand away, knowing she must play the part Eirianwen had set for her. 'She looks alert enough to me,' he said, releasing his grip with a disdainful push. Lysandra found anger taking the edge from her grief. She rose to her feet.

Eirianwen shrugged. 'Maybe I'm losing my touch.'

Stick gave his whinnying cackle. 'I doubt that, Silurian,' he said. 'Get back to work.'

The blonde woman nodded, retrieved her sword and began a set drill. Her movements were swift and precise, her strikes executed with speed and power. Despite herself, Lysandra was shocked that her beautiful benefactor was, in fact, from a barbarian tribe of the most savage ilk. The Silurians dwelt in far off Britannia and had been only recently conquered by Sextus Julius Frontinus. Evidently, the current governor of Asia Minor had brought some captives with him to his latest post and sold them on.

'What are you staring at?' Stick interrupted her reverie. 'Five laps of the *ludus* and then join me with the other chattel!'

It was an order and, though issued by the repugnant little Parthian, discipline and training responded. Without thought she

28

took off at a steady run, threading her way through the crowded training area, her long legs eating up ground with easy rapidity.

The simple familiarity of running calmed her nerves somewhat, but she could not shake the emptiness that had overwhelmed her. As she began her circuit of the *ludus*, its very perimeter defining her new imprisonment and new status, she struggled to come to terms with her misfortune: casting her mind back, she searched for some past deed that may have offended the gods and caused them to scourge her so.

It seemed a lifetime ago that she had left the sanctity of the temple, high on Sparta's acropolis, to begin her Mission and yet fewer than two years had passed. It was rare for one as young as she had been to receive this honour yet, in the harsh environment of the temple she had excelled at all trials, both physical and mental. The High Priestess had deemed her worthy, and she was not one to make swift decisions. Calling the old woman's face to mind brought a harsh stab of pain to Lysandra's breast. She wondered if she would ever see her again, or any of those Sisters with whom she had grown up.

She pushed the vision aside: it would do little good to think of what now was lost to her. Instead she recalled her pride and her certainty that the old woman had judged her well. She had been, after all, far ahead of any of the girls in her age group. In fact, Lysandra had considered that she was superior in both learning and physical prowess to most of the priestesses in the temple but this was a fact she felt would have been churlish to overstate. In the Spartan way, she had allowed her actions to elucidate.

Lysandra had left the temple with a definite plan in mind: most of her predecessors on the Mission had confined their duties to mainland Hellas and other centres of civilisation; she had thought this short sighted in the extreme. What use, she had asked herself, in spreading Athene's Word to those that were already familiar with Hellenic religion or its inferior Roman derivative?

29

Yet, for all their lack of culture, the Romans *had* conquered much of the known world – save Sparta, a fact that she had to re-iterate *ad nauseam* to the uneducated – and Rome's legions breasted far-flung frontiers. Away from the epicentre of civilisation, she could pass on her teachings to Gauls, Illyrians, Pannonians and the many other barbarian races that made up the imperial provinces.

As she ran, she recalled her first meeting with the Legate in command of the Fifth Macedonian Legion with fondness. It was, she knew, not unheard of for women to travel with Roman Legions. However, a woman working in an active capacity was a different matter entirely. At first, the Legate tried to dismiss her out of hand, just as she had expected. Nonetheless she cut a fine figure in her hard-earned scarlet war cloak and with a plumed Corinthian style helmet tucked under arm she clearly impressed him.

Though rhetoric was rarely practised in Sparta, her priestesses were usually schooled to convey religious oratory and Lysandra applied this learning to put her case to the Legate. Not only could she take the auguries and provide spiritual guidance to his soldiers, she told him, she was also skilled in rudimentary medicine.

It was this that had convinced him. A good commander's first concern is for his soldiers, and any assistance in the hospital tent was not something to be dismissed out of hand. Admittedly, he had been somewhat grudging with his consent, but he had acquiesced.

Her small tent was billeted with the Sixth Century, First Cohort and their reaction to her presence was surly at best. To most soldiers a woman was good for one thing only, yet her position as a priestess of the Virgin Athene protected her from any amorous advances. A lusty bunch they may have been but soldiers were superstitious enough not to risk displeasing the fickle gods.

It had been a hard task to win them over but Lysandra, already used to the brutal life of the priestesses' *agoge*, had not shirked her duties. She rose at dawn with the men, exercising when they did and even lending a hand to dig the palisades on occasion.

The willingness to get her hands dirty had initially been treated with derision by the tough, cynical legionaries and thereafter became a matter of amusement. One middle-aged soldier, Marcus Pavo by name, always seemed to take special care to tease her. Once, she recalled, he had commented that her 'tits were small enough to fool any recruiter into thinking she was a boy'. Lysandra responded that she had seen him emerging from a swim in the Parapamis River and was sure that he too was still a boy, judging by his 'equipment'. That she bore their jibes with good humour and responded with her own laconic wit in time caused men of the Legion to regard her as a sort of mascot. Their acceptance had meant more to her than she cared to admit; she had become one of them, a trusted augur and priestess and even friend to some, Pavo among them.

Then, on a routine voyage across the Hellespont, the storm came: Poseidon's wrath had dragged the entire century to the bottom, choosing to spare only her. Pavo had tried to swim out to her – to save *her* before his own exhaustion overtook him. His desperate gasps for help as his armour pulled him under still haunted her dreams. In this violent twist of fate, the Earth-Shaker had stripped a priestess of his hated sibling Athene of her friends, her freedom and her dignity. In saving her life, he spat in her eye; Lysandra would rather she had perished with the rest than have to live the life of a slave.

She began to slow her run, realising that she was almost at the end of her laps. Her reverie had turned as black as her circumstances. Lysandra cast a glance at the statue of Roman Athene once again, and wondered why she had been consigned to this cruel fate. The serene marble face gave no answers.

V

They were pushed hard.

From dawn till dusk, the new captives were subjected to a punishing regimen of callisthenics that left them stumbling exhausted into their tiny cells at the day's end. Here they were shackled and left till cockcrow, when the drills began again. Though she prided herself on her physical fitness, Lysandra found the savage regime challenging. The day began with laps of the *ludus*, alternately jogging and sprinting; this type of exercise was known to make the lungs bigger and the legs stronger. A light breakfast followed, for those who could keep it down, and then the real work of the day began. The novices were not given swords to work with because, as Stick constantly reminded them, their bodies had to be strengthened first. And that would take several weeks.

They hung from bars, pulling with their arms until their chins touched the wooden pole from which they were suspended, or lay flat on the ground, sitting up each time Stick barked the order. Many such simple exercises were repeated over and over.

Lysandra and the Germans had been merged into a much larger group of women, other recent acquisitions to Balbus's *famillia*, and all were put through their paces under the exacting eye of the trainers. Many faltered and were encouraged to greater exertions with the aid of the vine staff or birch rod. It was not only Stick responsible for these arbitrary thrashings; the trainers were rotated on a regular basis and Lysandra came to distinguish between the harsh-but-fair and the unfairly harsh.

There was Nastasen, burnt black as coal by the hot sun of his savage Nubian homeland. A huge man, his body thick with cords of muscle, he had strange, wiry hair growing in wild locks. He had taken an intense dislike to Lysandra for reasons unknown to her. She bore his animosity with stoicism, speaking little and working hard. Yet Nastasen still took delight in administering the lash to her, even though she was confident of her own excellence. She took some satisfaction from receiving her punishments in silence, knowing that her refusal to be moved would frustrate him.

Most popular amongst the barbarian women was Catuvolcos, a young Gaul given more to haranguing the women than beating them. His gladiatorial career, Lysandra learned, had been cut short by a sword thrust to the knee. Catuvolcos went easy on them most of the time, especially the tribeswomen, with whom he shared a kinship.

Titus the Roman, middle-aged and tough as a leather cuirass, was an exacting taskmaster, not shy with the whip when it was called upon, but not over-zealous. Unlike the other trainers Titus was not a former gladiator but an ex-soldier and a free man who had never tasted slavery. He was also old enough to have had his fill of inflicting pain for its own sake. Lysandra realised that he was out to instil discipline and toughness in his charges, not to break their spirits. Those of the women who could speak Latin swiftly dubbed him 'The Centurion'.

It quickly became clear to Lysandra that there was a distinct cultural divide in the large group of newcomers. The barbarians, be they German, Gaul, Briton or from farther-flung tribes beyond the Euxine, went about together.

Then there were many women of the South and East: Egyptians, Syrians, Ethiopians and their ilk. They set themselves apart from the rest, babbling incessantly in their staccato tongues.

Lysandra found herself amongst Romans, Italians, Sicilians and even some Hellenes. Unfortunately, none of these were Spartan and, though they tried to converse with her, she found in their inane talk yet further proof that Sparta was indeed the greatest *polis* in all Hellas. She was courteous to them, but she had nothing in common with these seamstresses, these wives who, before the *ludus*, knew nothing of toil and hardship.

In time, none spoke to her at all.

In the pitch black of her cell Lysandra prayed nightly for deliverance but Athene was deaf to her entreaties. She knew why: she was a slave, and the goddess would not condescend to succour one such as she. Beyond the beatings, beyond the daily toil of the *ludus*, this was the pain she found hardest to bear. To a Spartan, admission of suffering, even to oneself, was the gravest dishonour. Yet, in the darkest hours, she began to wonder if she could consider herself Spartan at all.

The crash of the cell doors being flung open brought Lysandra to wakefulness. She sat up on her pallet and stretched, wincing as the recent stripes on her back pulled slightly. In time the door to her own prison was unlocked to reveal the huge form of Nastasen, his grinning face full of contempt.

'Why is it your cell stinks worse than any of these other animals?' he sneered.

Lysandra got to her feet and shrugged. 'Perhaps because the stench you leave in here never seems to fade.'

The big Nubian took a menacing step forward. 'You must like me taking my rod to your back. Maybe a different rod in a different place might teach you some respect,' he said, fondling himself lewdly.

'I'm sure Balbus would have something to say about that, Nubian.' As Stick had demonstrated on their first day, it was apparent that groping and debasing comments were tolerated, but there could be no question of the trainers forcing themselves sexually on the women. This, she had overheard, was a simple economic consideration: pregnant gladiatrices could not fight.

Nastasen grunted, his dark eyes gleaming. 'Get outside, you Greek bitch, and be thankful I don't make an example of you.'

Lysandra could not resist. 'Another one?' she said blandly, arching an eyebrow.

The Nubian's temper snapped and, with a growl, he advanced on her. Lysandra dropped back into a fighting stance, determined to cause at least some damage to the big man. He had initiated this away from the *ludus* and she considered it a personal issue.

'Nastasen!' Titus's gruff voice sounded from outside the cell. The Nubian paused, his eyes still fixed on Lysandra. 'Leave it and assemble the novices.' His demeanour broached no argument.

Nastasen hesitated, then turned sharply away, shouldering past the grizzled Roman. The older trainer shook his head. 'Come on, Spartan. Get moving.' Lysandra nodded and followed him out to the training area.

The women had been drawn into rank and file and Lysandra swiftly found herself a place next to Hildreth. She had not spoken to the German since their first day at the *ludus* but had noted during the exercises that her fellow captive had coped well.

'Good morning, Lysandra, how are you today?' Hildreth's Latin, though weirdly accented, seemed to be improving.

'I would be better if I were out of this place,' she responded. Hildreth looked blankly at her. Lysandra tried again. 'I am very well, Hildreth, how are you?'

The German smiled broadly. 'I am very well.'

Lysandra resisted the urge to grin. Instead she faced the front and waited for the daily grind to start.

With Stick, Nastasen and Catuvolcos standing to one side, Titus began to pace up and down the front line, pausing every so often to scrutinise one of the women. This went on for some time but he turned to address them all at last.

'You are, without doubt, the most useless novices it has ever been my misfortune to train. Cripples would perform better. If you think your training has been tough so far, it is nothing compared to what lies ahead.' He glared balefully at them, daring them to groan, but was greeted only by silence. All the women knew that to voice their displeasure was to invite a thrashing. Satisfied he had their attention, he went on. 'However, that can wait a little. Many of you soft-bodied whores are carrying injuries, either earned in training or self-inflicted through lack of effort.' He held up his vine staff, indicating that a self-inflicted injury was, in fact, a beating administered by a trainer. 'Therefore, it is my decision to give you three days of rest. That is ample time to heal any hurts you pathetic specimens might believe you have.

'In three days, you begin the second and final stage of your training: your training with sword and shield, net and trident, the immortal arts of gladiatorial combat. Only when this is done will you take the Gladiatrix Oath.'

Titus ceased to pace and stood directly at the front and centre of the first rank. 'I have to tell you now that it is not given that you will succeed. If any one of you fails to make the standards set by the trainers, you will be sold on. That might not sound so terrible, you may think. But if you are sold from this place, you will be a slave forever. Whether you toil with your hands at the loom, your back in the mines, or your *cunnus* in the whorehouse, you will end your days as slaves and your children will be born slaves.

'The arena offers you a way out. An opportunity to fight for

36

and earn your freedom. In the weeks to come you must prove to me that you are worthy of this right. That your yet unborn children are worthy to be free. You compete not only against your own pain but against each other.' He paused for a while, letting that sink in. 'That is all.'

Titus watched as the novices hesitated a moment before breaking up into their usual groups. The tall Spartan priestess, of course, turned on her heel and separated from the pack. He shook his head. It seemed she had everything she needed to be a ruthless and skilled fighter. But Titus could sense that the fire that somehow managed to burn behind her ice-coloured eyes was being doused little by little.

Varia struggled under the weight of the damp sheets, her thin arms shaking with the effort of carrying so many. *Stupid*, she thought to herself. She could not manage so many. Her efforts were inspired by fear; Greta drove her scrubs as hard as Nastasen drove the fighters. She had tried her best to complete her quota of work but there was always so much to do. The slave girl tried to pick up her pace but, so doing, overbalanced the precariously stacked cotton.

She fell, the sheets landing with a thud in the dust. Varia bit her lip, tears of frustration and not a little fear welling up in her eyes. Greta would be furious. Frantically, she began gathering the ruined washing when a shadow fell across her. Without even having to look, she knew it was Greta. The German always seemed to know when she had failed; was always on hand to chastise her.

'You stupid little fool!' Greta shrieked, kicking the sheets away from Varia's scrabbling hands. 'It's all ruined! I'll tan your worthless hide!'

Varia cowered, holding her hands over her head, waiting for the stinging blows to land. 'I'm sorry, Greta, I'm sorry!' she cried, her voice breaking as her tears spilled forth, desperate, but knowing that mercy was not in the German's nature. She waited, her eyes squeezed tight shut. There was a sharp snap of flesh on flesh, but no blow landed. Slowly, she turned her head to see why Greta had spared her. She could scarcely believe what she saw.

Greta struggled, her wrist gripped in the hand of a tall goddess; a goddess who had come to save *her*. The bulky German tried to pull away but could not break free. Varia brushed the tears from her eyes and saw that it was Lysandra, one of the novices. Her heart leapt. Never before had anyone intervened on her behalf!

'There will be no punishment today,' Lysandra said, releasing her grip contemptuously.

Greta's eyes bulged, a mixture of fear and fury. 'You take your own beatings well enough, Spartan. And never once have I seen you lift a finger to defend your fellow arena fodder.' She drew herself up. 'This is not your concern.'

'Beating hardens a warrior against fear and pain.' Lysandra sounded as if she were reciting a well-learned phrase. 'This girl is no warrior.'

'It is still not your concern,' Greta recovered herself somewhat. 'She has failed in her duties, and must be disciplined.'

'I have just made it my concern.' Lysandra's voice was low and calm. But Varia trembled somewhat at its sound. 'I would hate for us to argue, Greta.' She took a step forward and Varia swelled with glee as her tormentor gave ground. 'I require this girl's services,' Lysandra went on, her eyes fixed upon Greta's. 'The wishes of the fighting women go beyond any paltry domestic concerns of yours.'

Greta snorted and turned to go. Her stamping feet had not taken her more than two yards when Lysandra called her back. Scarlet faced, she turned about.

'You have forgotten the sheets,' she indicated the crumpled laundry. Fuming, Greta gathered the ragged pile and stormed off.

She had got a little further this time before Lysandra spoke again. There was ice enough in her voice to cause Greta to stop in her tracks. 'If you take vengeance on this child for my actions, I will kill you.' It was stated so calmly, so quietly, yet it was the more chilling for its utter blandness. The tension drained out of Greta, and her shoulders slumped in defeat. She nodded once, and walked away.

Varia waited till Greta was out of earshot and then turned to face Lysandra. There was a strange feeling in her chest, a warmth felt never before as she looked upon her rescuer. She was so tall, so beautiful – so *magnificent!*

'Thank you,' she whispered. 'Thank you for helping me.'

Lysandra's lips curled in the slightest of smiles. She extended her hand and helped Varia to her feet.

'I *do* have need of you,' she said. Varia nodded and she smiled too, her heart overflowing with gratitude.

VI

Lysandra led Varia to the school's infirmary. As there had been no bouts during the recent weeks of training, the small compound was virtually deserted save for a few fighters with minor injuries. She reasoned that would soon change once her fellow novices began to feel the strains and cuts of their morning exercise. She was determined to get ahead of everyone else.

The chief physician, an irrepressible old satyr of a man named Quintus, looked up as they entered his small office to the rear of the main hospital.

'Ah, the Spartan and young Varia,' he said mildly, putting down his stylus. 'What can I do for you today?'

'Myrrh,' Lysandra answered shortly.

'It's expensive stuff, Lysandra,' he grunted. 'Nevertheless, I've seen them take the lash to you more than they should.' He got to his feet. 'Just take your clothes off and I'll apply some to your wounds.'

Lysandra cocked her head to one side. She had heard all about Quintus and his roving hands. 'Just give me the myrrh.'

Quintus made a disgruntled noise in the back of his throat, but moved to a side room to find the balm. There was much clattering of ceramics and cursing but, after a short time, the old man emerged with a small pot. 'Here.' He slapped it into Lysandra's outstretched palm. 'Not too much at a time.'

'I am well aware of how the salve is applied,' she replied loftily, and exited the small room without another word, Varia in tow. Quintus watched her retreating back and mimicked her last words to himself soundlessly, a sour expression on his face.

From the infirmary, Lysandra went straight to the baths. Ignoring the warm water, she marched purposefully to the cold pool, tossed her tunic to one side and plunged in.

The water was not as cold as she would have liked but would suffice for her purposes. This was an often-used practice in the priestesses' *agoge*. After receiving punishment the girls would bathe in the icy waters of the Eurotas River to take the swelling from their painful injuries.

Slowly, she felt her body becoming accustomed to the chill of the pool. She stayed still, not wanting to give her muscles cause for any warmth. She glanced up, and noted Varia's aghast expression.

'What *is* the matter with you?' she asked

'You must be freezing,' the girl responded.

'Cold is a feeling,' Lysandra said, reciting the lessons of her youth. 'You feel hot, you feel cold, you feel pain. All such things are merely a state of mind.'

'I wish I could be like you.' Varia's voice was awed.

'Naturally,' Lysandra agreed. It was, she thought, unsurprising: having been used to barbarians, Romans and lesser Hellenes, the young slave could not fail to be impressed by a true Spartan. This thought caused her mind to take a bitter course. She was a slave, and therefore a true Spartan no longer. She hauled herself from the water and sat on the side of the pool, her feet paddling.

'Pat my back dry and apply the myrrh to my cuts,' she ordered sharply, wondering if she had made the right choice in aiding the child. It was an act of charity that would doubtless have ramifications. This, she thought, is what I have come to. Impressing children and bullying washerwomen. A fine end for a Mission Priestess.

Varia did as she bade her, gently administering the salve. Lysandra breathed deeply through her nose as she felt the sting lift from the lash marks on her back.

'Is that enough?' Varia asked.

Lysandra flexed her shoulders, feeling only a slight pull on the wounds. 'Yes. That is good.'

'I'll get you a clean tunic,' Varia said, evidently delighted that she had done well. She ran off without waiting for a reply but returned quickly, clutching a scarlet chiton. 'Here.' She thrust the garment into Lysandra's hands.

She held it for a moment before slipping it over her head, almost grinning at the irony of Varia's choice. She had not worn the red of Sparta since the shipwreck and here, of all places, she found herself sporting it once more. She felt unworthy, but was not mean-spirited enough to demand another tunic from her newfound companion.

'What would you like to do now?' Varia enquired.

Lysandra was at a loss. From *agoge* to Temple, through to the Legion and even here, her life had been dominated by routine and work. Free time was an unfamiliar commodity. She shrugged. 'I do not know. Perhaps we could watch the senior women at their training?' It was all she could think of.

Varia seemed pleased with that but then the child looked at her with such adulation that Lysandra was certain that she could have suggested sitting in a cesspit and the youngster would have been more than pleased to accompany her. A weakness in the Roman character was the need for companionship, it was certainly one that she herself did not suffer. She was only providing the child with company as an act of charity, she thought to herself. Yes, that was obviously what had prompted her action to assist the girl in the first place. Varia was the one in need, not she. She needed no one.

The two made their way to the training grounds; Lysandra's earlier assumption had been correct – there was indeed a large queue leading from Quintus's surgery. The women were in good spirits, evidently delighted at their free time. No doubt the afternoon would degenerate into a drunken festival, she thought with disdain.

The training area itself was mostly unoccupied as news of the 'holiday' spread. Titus had clearly decided to relax the regime for all the women in the *ludus*. This made sense to Lysandra: it would only serve to create rifts if one group was seen to be given privileges another was not. Soon, only two women remained training. She turned to Varia.

'The blonde woman I know.' She pointed to the beautiful Eirianwen. 'Who is the other?'

'That is Sorina of Dacia,' Varia responded. 'She is *Gladiatrix Prima*. Eirianwen is *Gladiatrix Secunda*.'

Lysandra watched the auburn-haired woman move and was impressed. The Dacians had been a matriarchal society back in the time of King Theseus, a thousand years before. It was them and their Themiskyran kin whom Homer had dubbed the Amazons in the *Iliad*. Their culture had changed little since the days of Troy, she knew – yet that was the way of barbarians. They were happy to ignore progress and civilisation in favour of their unstructured, disordered lifestyle.

But, by the Gods, this one could fight. 'A true Amazon,' she murmured.

'Yes,' Varia said in response to Lysandra's whispered comment. 'Sorina was the chieftain of a powerful tribe in her homeland. She was a great war leader, and speaks of those days often. We

Romans defeated her in a battle and she hates us for it. She calls our cities "cancers on the Great Mother",' the girl added.

Lysandra nodded, not really listening. She was engrossed in the violent dance Sorina was sharing with Eirianwen. Their wooden swords blurred as the two women attacked and countered with savage ferocity. She was so engrossed that she did not see Catuvolcos approach. The handsome Gaul had his reddish hair tied back and wore only a loincloth, showing off his well-muscled body. He carried a wine sack, which he passed to Lysandra as he sat next to them on the ground.

'You're in the shit,' he commented as she took a sip.

'How so?'

'For aiding your little friend here.' He indicated Varia. 'Greta has complained to Nastasen about you and he means to set an example.'

Lysandra shrugged. The Nubian took perverse pleasure out of inflicting pain. 'That would make a change,' she commented blithely.

Catuvolcos chuckled, gesturing for the wine sack. 'You're not afraid of him, are you, Lysa?'

Lysandra stiffened at his familiar use of her name in the diminutive. 'Spartans fear nothing,' she said.

'Do you have a book of these things you say? It seems to me that you have an answer for everything, but no answers that are truly yours. Don't you ever speak from your heart?'

She regarded him haughtily. 'I speak when it is necessary to do so. A Spartan does not talk for talking's sake. Our sparing use of words is so admired it has been adopted into common parlance.'

Catuvolcos gestured, indicating her to continue.

'*Laconic*,' she said. 'This word comes from Lakedaimonia, the area of Hellas where Sparta is situated.'

'You must be very proud.'

'Obviously,' Lysandra chose to ignore Catuvolcos's attempt at

44

irony. 'It is impossible to explain to one who is not Spartan what it means to be Spartan.' There was, she knew, little sense in sharing with the trainer her conundrum regarding her worthiness to claim this heritage.

The trainer let it drop. 'Titus has decided that the novices should mingle more with the veterans. There will be a festivity of sorts this evening.'

Lysandra sniffed. 'Enjoy yourself.'

'You know, Lysa, things would go better for you here if you tried to mix more with the other women. You're not the most popular of the novices.'

Lysandra wondered why he was trying to draw her into conversation. Despite the fact that he too was a slave, the *ludus* had a quasi-military structure and he was her superior. Such fraternisation between ranks was often bad for discipline. Then again, he was a stupid barbarian and could not be expected to understand such concepts as authority and its effects upon morale. 'I am not here to be popular. I am a slave. A performer with only one purpose – to kill for entertainment.'

Catuvolcos turned serious. 'You have a chance to earn your freedom doing it, girl. But that is not my point. I think you should come to this gathering. You might even enjoy yourself.'

'And I think you should not be speaking to me. If you are so concerned about popularity, it would be better if I were not seen associating with a trainer.'

Catuvolcos looked as if he had been slapped around the face. 'Suit yourself,' he said tersely, getting to his feet. 'I have intervened on your behalf with Nastasen because I thought he had been too hard on you. I can see I made a mistake; you deserve everything you get. There is a difference between pride in one's heritage and blind arrogance.'

'Philosophy from a barbarian?' Lysandra sneered. 'I am stunned.'

Catuvolcos stalked away, his face florid.

Lysandra watched him go. She did not feel at all pleased with herself but to accept his advances would have shown her to be weak. She frowned, feeling as though she could have handled the exchange a little better. She turned her attention back to the training ground but Sorina and Eirianwen had ceased sparring and were now performing stretching exercises to warm down their muscles.

'You were very rude to Catuvolcos.' Varia was fiddling with the hem of her tunic. 'He was just trying to be nice.'

'So?' Lysandra snapped. 'Am I supposed to swoon with joy? I have no desire to go to a party. A *party*?' She laughed, a harsh, brittle sound. 'In this place? It is an absurdity.'

'People say that life is what you make it. I don't like it here, but it is all I know and I try to be happy when I can.'

Lysandra got up. 'First philosophy from a barbarian, now from you. Life is what we make it, Varia? I think not, for it was no choice of mine to be here. This place has taken away everything that I was. I cannot make the best of it as you say. It is different for you, you know no better.'

Varia looked up at her, closing one eye as the sun shone in it. 'I know that I am glad you are my friend.'

Lysandra was about to tell the child she was no friend of hers: that she needed no friends, and the girl would be better off just leaving her alone. The words did not come.

'I would be happy if my friend went to the party,' Varia added. 'If only to show Catuvolcos he was wrong about you being too proud.'

Lysandra folded her arms across her chest, tapping her chin with her index finger. 'There is wisdom in what you say,' she conceded. 'It would be wrong to let him think that his outrageous accusation was correct.'

'So you'll go then?'

Lysandra nodded. 'Yes. I think I will.'

VII

Night had fallen over the *ludus*, replacing the harsh burning heat of the day with a pleasant, balmy warmth.

Lysandra could hear the sound of laughter, muted by the thick stone walls of her prison, as women passed by her cell on their way to Titus's gathering. The celebrations had to be in full swing by now as the hour had already grown late. She sat on her cot, forearms resting on her knees, hands idly toying with the laces of her sandal. She had one on already; all that remained was to put the other on her foot and join the festivities.

Lysandra hesitated, deciding if she would go through with it. After all, she was not interested in drunken revelry and she asked herself over and over if the opinion of Catuvolcos mattered. She decided it did not, but then reasoned that it would be churlish not to attend. She placed her foot into the sandal and tied the laces.

She stood, put her hand to the door and froze. Perhaps it was not such a good idea. Had Catuvolcos not said she was unpopular with the women? It could be that excess of wine amongst her detractors could lead to cattiness and possibly worse.

She told herself that she was being ridiculous. No one would even notice her presence or absence; it had been weeks since anybody had passed even a cursory comment to her outside of what was necessary in training. She decided she would stay long enough to be noticed by Catuvolcos, thus proving him wrong, and then she would leave.

She yanked the door open before she could change her mind.

The training ground had been transformed in the hours she had spent in the silence of the cell. At the far end, nearest the baths, many tables had been arrayed, moved from the dining area to the grounds to provide more room for the women. She glanced up at the walls and noted that they were thick with guards and a heavy detail had also been placed around the armoury. A barricade of sorts cordoned off the area where the gathering was being held. Despite Titus's magnanimity he was evidently taking no chances with security. She patted down her hair self-consciously and made her way towards the barricade.

Stick, Catuvolcos and several guards were standing by a small gap in the makeshift construction. She felt the Gaul's eyes upon her as she approached.

'Halt!' said one of the guards. She recognised him as the Macedonian she had spoken with on her first day in the *ludus*. He stepped forward and instructed her to lift her arms, giving her a rudimentary search.

'Is all this really necessary?' She directed the question at Catuvolcos.

He looked at her with an odd expression on his face. *Obviously still bearing a grudge*, she thought. Then he grinned at her, which only served to annoy her further. She hated to be mistaken in her assessment of another's mood.

'Yes, Lysa, it is,' he said.

'Will you stop calling me that!' she snapped. 'My name is Lysandra.'

'Less of your lip, bitch!' Stick cut in. He drew his vine staff.

'Show some respect or, by the gods, I'll beat it into you!' He bristled when Lysandra regarded him as if he were something she had stepped in.

'It's all right, Stick,' Catuvolcos soothed. 'The women have a free night – and so do we, more or less. Let's not have any unpleasantness.' He turned his attention back to her. 'There are over a hundred women back there.' He jerked his thumb towards the gathering. As if to punctuate his words, there was a scream of raucous laughter. 'Most of them are trained killers and some are feuding with each other. The search is just a precaution. You know what women are like. Can't take their liquor and then they get tetchy. So we can't risk someone smuggling in a weapon, that's all.'

Lysandra sniffed, considering that reasonable. 'Like as not, you'll be proving your doubtless titanic capacity for wine at the earliest opportunity.'

'Not a chance. We're not allowed back there. I told you, we can't afford to let the women get their hands on weapons of any sort, you know what I mean?' He moved his eyebrows up and down several times. 'You all find me irresistible, and when the grape takes hold of a girl, she wants to get romantic with me.'

'I find you more irritating than irresistible,' Lysandra told him.

Catuvolcos clutched his hand to his heart and feigned a stagger. 'I'm crushed!'

'Very amusing,' she commented as she made her way past him; she did not fail to notice Stick's malevolent glare. Moving off to the feast, she heard the wiry Parthian berating Catuvolcos for being too familiar with her but the Gaul's response was lost to her in the general hubbub of the revels.

The gathering was in full swing, with many women already slumped over the trestles, the worst for drink. An assortment of food had been laid out, which had been attacked with gusto. There was the usual barley stew but Titus had arranged meat for

49

the festivities to satisfy the barbarian women. The smell of roasting pork and lamb wafted from many spits, the sweet smoke spiralling into the night sky. The mood was buoyant, with laughter and songs sung in a myriad of languages. She picked out smatterings of the words here and there and the subjects were not to her liking, referring to either lost love or the joys of sexual intercourse, neither of which she had experienced. Indeed, she prided herself that she had never given in to such emotional or physical weakness.

Lysandra kept to the periphery, making her way to one of several wine casks that were stacked about the training area. She poured herself a cup and looked around in vain for water to mix with it. She shrugged and sipped the strong liquor, wincing at its full-bodied taste. She started as a hand landed forcefully on her shoulder.

Lysandra whirled about – only to be confronted by Hildreth. The German was holding a jug of beer, the foamy moustache she sported mute evidence that she was drinking the vile stuff straight from the container.

'Hello, Lysandra!' she shouted boisterously in Latin. 'How are you today?'

'I am very well, Hildreth. How are you?' This, Lysandra mused, was fast becoming a ritual between them.

'I am very well!' Hildreth laughed. 'I am –,' she looked up, trying to think. 'How do I say it? Ah, yes. I am drunk as a sack!'

The Spartan arched an eyebrow. 'I can tell,' she said dryly.

'*What*?' Hildreth hollered.

Lysandra had noticed that when the barbarians could not understand a phrase or could not make themselves understood, they thought that shouting would convey their meaning. She tried again. 'Yes, you are.'

Hildreth laughed and clapped Lysandra on the shoulder, causing her wine to slosh over her hand. The German failed to notice and stumbled off, singing a song in her own rough language. Lysandra watched her go, a slight smile playing about her lips. Hildreth, she conceded, was a good enough sort. For a barbarian.

She wandered aimlessly among the revellers for some time, enjoying the celebratory atmosphere. Despite her earlier outburst to Varia, she was impressed by Titus's concession of a feast. Letting the women gather in such a manner was excellent for morale and relieved the pressure of the daily toil in the *ludus*. She stood apart from the others, watching their ribald antics with amusement. Women stumbled about, a score of dances from different nations taking place around the compound. Lysandra rather thought that the *ludus* itself was like the Roman Empire in miniature: different creeds coming together in servitude to Rome. She congratulated herself on her own astuteness.

She saw Eirianwen walking towards her from the crowd. The beautiful Silurian raised her hand in greeting and Lysandra cast a glance behind her to see whose attention the gladiatrix was seeking. There was no one.

Eirianwen smiled as she drew closer; she wore a tunic of white cotton and Lysandra was surprised at how so simple a garment could emphasise her beauty, clinging to her hips and accentuating the curve of her breasts. Lysandra had always been proud of her height, but now, in front of Eirianwen, she suddenly felt ungainly and clumsy.

'Greetings.' Eirianwen's voice was light, almost musical it seemed to Lysandra.

She took a healthy draft of her wine to moisten her suddenly dry throat. Why was the barbarian affecting her in such a manner? Perhaps she was a sorceress, who was skilled in enchantments – like Calypso who so befuddled Odysseus. She dismissed the thought as quickly as it had come. More likely she was feeling the effects of the un-watered wine. 'Eirianwen.' She nodded.

51

'You are alone,' Eirianwen observed. 'That is not the way things should be on such a night.'

'Oh, I am quite fine,' she said, and drained her cup.

Eirianwen cocked her head to one side and Lysandra marvelled at the way the light of the torches reflected on her blue eyes. 'Nonsense,' she said and held out her hand. 'Come.'

Mutely, Lysandra let Eirianwen lead her through the throng, her mind whirling. She felt as if she were walking on air, her heart beating fast in her chest; the flesh of her fingers tingling at Eirianwen's touch.

The Silurian looked over her shoulder and smiled. 'Here we are.' She indicated a table, releasing Lysandra's hand. Several other women were sitting together, including Sorina, the *Gladiatrix Prima*. 'Sit,' Eirianwen bade her.

Two of the women shuffled up on their bench to make room and the Spartan sat between them. Eirianwen moved to sit opposite her. Wordlessly, she refilled Lysandra's cup.

'Greetings, friends,' Lysandra said formally. A chorus answered her. 'I am honoured to join you,' she added, raising her cup in toast to the women. The honour was of course theirs, for it was doubtful that they had ever been in the presence of a Priestess of Athene – a former priestess, she corrected herself.

'You're the Spartan,' the woman next to her said. 'Eirianwen reckons that you have potential. Only veterans may sit at this table,' she added.

'Lysandra *is* a veteran,' Eirianwen interjected. 'Though she has not yet taken the Oath she has already fought and won her first bout. That gives her the right.'

The woman shrugged. 'I'm Teuta,' she said. She was dark haired, her almond-shaped eyes and flattish features betraying her as either Illyrian or Pannonian. 'That's my real name. In the arena, I'm called Thana. Maybe you've heard of me?' This last was said with not a little amount of hope.

'The Illyrian goddess of hunting,' Lysandra identified, ignoring the question. 'A good choice of name.' She had learned that arena fighters were given or chose names from legend. It made them recognisable to the crowds and added drama to an event – or so Titus believed. 'You all have such impressive titles.' She glanced around the table.

'Yes,' Teuta said before anyone else could answer. 'Eirianwen is called Britannica. Soucana over there,' she gestured to a fair, shorthaired woman, 'is Vercengetoria.'

'Yes,' Soucana shouted, evidently a little the worse for wear. 'Scourge of Caesar, I am named for the hero of the Gauls!' The other women cheered good-naturedly.

'And Sorina is Amazona, correct?' Lysandra inclined her head at the Gladiatrix Prima. She kept her expression neutral but was shocked at how old the Dacian was. The tanned face showed signs of time's march. She must be well past thirty already, Lysandra thought. 'Your given name carries history, does it not?'

'That is so, Spartan,' she agreed. 'I am from Penthesilea's line.' She too kept her face expressionless.

Lysandra's lip curled. It was in the barbarian nature to lie, making extravagant claims as to their linage. Penthesilea was the Amazon queen who was slain by Achilles. That none in the entire *ludus* had the benefit of Spartan education was indeed fortunate for the aging warrior, or this probable falsehood would have been called into question long ago. The Amazons of old never took husbands for life, so it was impossible to say who was from whose line. And they were incapable of writing anything down, so they could make up whatever nonsense they liked. She refrained from making an issue of it, however, for it would have been impolite. Instead she changed the subject. 'This is certainly not what I expected from slavery.'

'It is a better life than most can expect,' Eirianwen said. 'Though we are slaves, we are valuable to Balbus. It makes sense

53

for him to see that we are treated well.' She paused, looking straight at Lysandra. 'The trainers are very harsh at the beginning,' she said. 'This is done to break the spirit of the weaker ones, to see who cannot take the pressure. If a woman breaks in training she will die in the arena.'

Lysandra nodded. It was so in the *agoge*.

'To train a fighter costs a lot of money,' Eirianwen went on. 'We have good food, good physicians and, if we survive long enough, a decent place to live.' She gestured to the houses set far back from the training grounds.

'You sound like you are getting to like it,' Sorina cut in, her voice harsh.

'I hate it,' Eirianwen responded. 'But what would you have me do? Waste away in grief or accept my lot and hope to win my freedom one day?'

Sorina spat on the ground. 'Roman bastards. At best they will see you dead. At worst they make you one of them. I will never be corrupted.'

Lysandra watched the exchange, realising she had finished her wine. Feeling somewhat light-headed, she refilled the cup and was pleased to find that the bite had gone and now the liquor was going down much easier.

'I am not corrupted,' Eirianwen said. 'Really, Sorina, you should not burden yourself with so much hatred.'

'How can you say that?' Sorina drained her own cup. 'Did Frontinus not defeat your tribe, slay your warriors and cast the others into slavery? What now of the Silures, Eirianwen? What of your land? Is Britannia not showing the signs of the Roman disease? Growths of stone infecting the fields, roads like swords cut through the heart of the Great Mother. Pah!' She threw up her hand in disgust.

Eirianwen cast her eyes down, and shook her head. 'You speak the truth, Sorina, but I do not hate the Romans for what they have done. They did not invent war, or its consequences.'

'They are raping the world!' Sorina's voice was heavy with wine-induced malice. 'They call it civilisation, but it is an abomination. Let them live in their towns of stone, but do not force the freeborn to do likewise. Since the First Days, the Dacians have ridden free on the plains, beholden to no Emperor, no *man*.' This last was said with utter contempt. 'Then the Romans came, burning and killing the innocents of my land. When the tribes rose against them, we fought hard and well. Well enough to force them back across the Danube. They were afraid.'

There was silence around the table at her outburst.

'Actually, they were not,' Lysandra said. All eyes turned to her. 'Really, Dacia is not worth the effort in manpower to placate.' She shook as she cleared her throat, annoyed that her words were slurred slightly. She knew the wine was taking effect but she found that she did not care and poured herself some more. 'There is nothing there of value, is there? Except slaves,' she said as an afterthought, gesturing to Sorina. 'It would take a long and costly campaign to subjugate such a wide territory, which is why there have only been minor Roman operations there.'

'When I am finished in this place, I will gather the warriors of the plains, and bring them to war against the Romans!' Sorina said vehemently.

'And you will be crushed.' Lysandra shrugged. 'No barbarian army can stand against disciplined troops.'

Sorina got to her feet, swaying slightly. 'Who are you calling a barbarian, you arrogant whore?'

'Anyone who cannot speak Hellenic is a barbarian.' Lysandra stated the obvious, letting Sorina's insult pass. 'It is the sound of your language... like sheep... baa, baa!' She laughed at this. It was an ancient truism, but never failed to bring her to mirth.

'Peace, Sorina.' Eirianwen put a calming hand on the older warrior's arm as the Amazon's face darkened in anger. 'The drink is in us all. Let's have no more of this talk.'

Lysandra was about to speak again but decided against it; she did not want to distress Eirianwen. Sorina sat, but would not let the matter drop. 'How can you be so sure of a Roman victory?' she asked.

Lysandra ran her hand through her hair. She looked around and saw a long wooden ladle on the ground by a pot of barley stew. She stumbled up, retrieved it, and returned to the table. 'Here.' She tossed the implement to Sorina. 'Can you break that?'

'Of course,' the Dacian responded, snapping the wood with ease.

'Now take the two halves and break them at the same time.' This time, the task was much harder but the Amazon persevered. With a loud crack, the staves broke. Sorina triumphantly met the Spartan's gaze. 'You are very strong,' Lysandra observed. 'Now break the four.'

Sorina cast the wood to the ground in disgust. 'That would be impossible. What are you trying to prove?'

'Simple. That is how civilised people fight. In close units, you see. For the Hellene or the Roman, personal valour is honoured but discipline and training count for much more on the battle-field. A barbarian fights for glory, charging to battle, swinging a big sword round his head... her head, in this case. And achieves what? On foot, she needs space around her to wield her sword, lest she kill the compatriots by her side. Instantly, she is outnumbered three to one, for civilised troops lock shields and fight as a unit. On horseback, she charges into a hedge of spears and swords. And dies.'

'You talk a good fight, Spartan,' Sorina said. 'For one who has never set foot on the battlefield.'

'Have it your own way, Amazon.' Lysandra found that for once she did not wish to pursue an argument. Better to end the conversation. 'You are just like every other barbarian. Too proud and too stupid to learn from your betters.'

Sorina sprang across the table, crashing into Lysandra. The two women fell to the ground, rolling over several times. Sorina emerged on top and slammed her fist into Lysandra's face, sending a sharp message of pain through her wine-fogged head. A few onlookers saw the brawl erupt and called to their fellows. Soon a crowd had gathered around the two struggling women and began chanting rhythmically, 'Fight, fight, fight!'

Lysandra thrust her hips upwards, causing her furious assailant to overbalance and topple forwards. She rolled away and sprang to her feet but the liquor had made her clumsy and she stumbled. Sorina was charging towards her, spitting hate, and it was only by long-learnt reflex that Lysandra was able to lash out with her foot, catching the onrushing Amazon in the pit of the stomach. Sorina doubled over in pain and Lysandra moved in quickly, seeking to grasp her foe's head and smash her face to pulp with her knee. But Sorina's reaction was swift: she lunged forwards, butting her shoulder into Lysandra's midriff. Jerking upright, Sorina carried Lysandra with her, flipping her skywards.

She crashed painfully to the ground, cracking the back of her head as she landed. Head spinning, she staggered to her feet, barely in time to meet Sorina's attack; the Amazon's fist connected with the side of her face and Lysandra responded in kind, her own blow snapping back her opponent's head. She surged in, but suddenly, she was being dragged back, as was Sorina, cursing and kicking.

Eirianwen had hold of the furiously struggling Gladiatrix Prima. 'That's enough,' she shouted. 'Sorina, enough!'

Teuta grasped Lysandra around the middle, lifting her from the ground and heaving her away. 'Gods, Spartan! Leave it!' Lysandra ceased to struggle and the Illyrian let go, dumping her unceremoniously onto her bottom.

The crowd around the fracas had dispersed as quickly as it had gathered. Lysandra touched her cheek ruefully, feeling a large bruise beginning to swell up. She puffed out her cheeks, trying to clear her head, which spun both for the wine and the forceful blows landed by the Amazon.

She looked up to see Sorina standing over her.

They regarded each other in silence for some moments, then the older woman extended her hand and pulled Lysandra to her feet. 'You fight well,' she acknowledged.

'As do you.'

'But not well enough.' Sorina turned away before Lysandra could respond. Feeling somewhat foolish, she made to leave, but Eirianwen stepped up to her.

'Don't worry. That will be an end to it for tonight,' she said. 'Come. Let's have another drink.'

VIII

Sorina awoke, her head thick and pounding. Her mouth was gummy, her eyes full of sand. Sitting up, she groaned as her stomach lurched. Teuta lay next to her, snoring softly, her arm resting across her eyes. Sorina smiled and swung her legs out of the bed. Their lovemaking had been unrestrained and passionate, a perfect end to an entertaining evening. She had even enjoyed the fight with the arrogant Spartan.

She made her way to a full-length bronze mirror, a gift from one of her supporters. Leaning close, she saw that Lysandra had blackened her eye. Three years ago and she would have put her down before she had had the chance. She stepped back and regarded herself. Her body was still lean and tight, her breasts still firm. But that belied the passage of years. Thirty six was no age to most in the Empire, with their doctors and medicines. But on the plains of Dacia, her home, she would be classed as an older woman now.

Six years, she mused. Had it really been six years since her capture and imprisonment? Six years of death in the arena, six years of slavery. She looked around her room. She had more than most freeborn Romans could ever hope to possess: a house, wealth, the adoration of the mob. She dimly recalled accusing Eirianwen of getting used to Roman luxuries the previous evening. For a moment she wondered if the accusation was in fact her own conscience speaking. Was she too becoming what she hated? She shook her head and dismissed the thought.

Without her liberty it was all fool's gold. She had long since given up believing Balbus's lies that she would one day buy her freedom. There would never be enough money for him. She knew there were only two chances for her: to be freed during the games by a benevolent *editor*, impressed enough by her prowess to deem her worthy of the wooden sword; or escape. She had come up with many plans, but none seemed feasible. And if she were caught escaping, the penalty for runaway slaves was a slow, agonising death by crucifixion.

She slipped a tunic over her head and made her way to the baths. The training area was a hive of activity as the domestic slaves cleared the debris from the previous night's celebration, looking none too happy that they had had no part in the revels. But, she thought to herself, a banquet was small reward for those risking life and limb on the sands, something the scrubs did not have to bear.

She was unsurprised to see the baths virtually empty. The entire *famillia* would no doubt be sleeping off the effects of the evening. Only Eirianwen, a famous early riser, was there enjoying her routine swim. Sorina disrobed and slipped into the pool, not wishing to disturb her friend until she had finished her laps.

She watched with pleasure as the Silurian's perfect body sliced through the water. Eirianwen was a living embodiment of the universal mystery, a balance of opposites. So beautiful and yet so deadly. She had been at the *ludus* merely two years and had already slaughtered her way to become *Gladiatrix Secunda*. Sorina prayed that they would never be matched against one another. But she knew Balbus. If the price was right they would be compelled to meet on the sands and only one would walk away. She saw Eirianwen swimming towards her and the smile she gave her served to break her melancholy.

'I didn't expect to see you here,' Eirianwen said in the language of the Celts. Though their two lands were separated by many thousands of leagues, their tongues were surprisingly similar. Eirianwen had learned enough of Sorina's native Getic and they conversed in a jumble of both.

'I thought a dip might clear my head,' said Sorina.

'You *did* overdo it.'

'It was that sort of evening. Good fight too,' she commented. 'I should have taken her earlier.'

'You don't like her, do you?'

'There is nothing to like.' Sorina threw up her hands, trying to put into words what she felt in her heart. 'These Greeks and Romans revel in their achievements but what have their kind brought to the world? The cancer of stone, and the fire of war. Was not the greatest of all Greeks, Alexander, a conqueror, a slayer of nations? The Romans have their Caesar and have made him a god. Lysandra is a child of this culture and she represents everything I despise.'

Eirianwen sighed. 'She is just a woman, like you and me, Sorina. She has no wish to be here either.'

Sorina's laugh was sour. 'Have you seen her train? She loves it. It is as if she has been doing it for years. Even the beatings she takes. It is like a contest to her. And yet I sense she is still not giving it her all.'

'Perhaps it is the Greek mindset,' Eirianwen offered after some thought. 'Perhaps she too is trying to make the best of her lot.'

'You sound like a Greek. *Mindset!*' she mimicked. 'Next you will be talking philosophy.' She used Latin for the word, as there was no Celtic equivalent.

'Maybe I am becoming a little too *civilised* for my own good, Sorina!'

'I am sorry for what I said last night,' Sorina said earnestly. 'I was drunk.'

'As were we all; beer makes bad talk sometimes.'

They rested in companionable silence for a while, enjoying the shared feeling of sisterhood with each other. Neither had set foot in the other's land, yet the blood of the Tribes stretched over oceans. Truly, it was an empire greater than that forged by the Romans, for it was made whole by kinship, not carved by the sword. Sorina knew the Tribes would endure when the Romans and their stone cities turned to dust. The Earth Mother would not permit their atrocities forever. Indeed, just over ten years since, she had spat her defiance at them, and turned their great city of Pompeii to molten rock. It was a warning the Romans failed to heed, and it would bring them low.

'Why did you bring Lysandra to our table?' Sorina asked after some time.

Eirianwen did not respond immediately. 'I don't know,' she said. 'There is something that draws me to her. I cannot say what it is.'

'Perhaps you should take her to your bed and get whatever it is out of your system.' Sorina laughed. 'Can you imagine it?' the Dacian hooted. 'She's as dry as a bone, that one!' She wiped her tears of mirth away, noticing that Eirianwen had not joined in the laughter. 'What's the matter with you?'

'You probably have the rights of it, Sorina. She'd be affronted at the mention of bedding someone. But I don't feel comfortable mocking her.'

Sorina snickered. 'Sweet on her, are you?'

'Of course not,' Eirianwen said quickly. She seemed to lose herself in thought for long moments, and when she spoke again, her voice was low. 'But there is *something* about her, Sorina. I know it.'

Sorina sobered. Eirianwen's father had been a Druid, a religious leader of the Britons, and in his blood ran the power of that mystical brotherhood. Some of his magic flowed through his daughter, of that she was certain.

'I feel that our paths are intertwined,' Eirianwen said. 'Yours, hers and mine. The Morrigan has had a hand in this.' Sorina made a sign to ward off evil at the mention of the dark goddess of Fate.

Eirianwen blinked and came back to herself. 'Fate is her own mistress, Sorina. She will do what she will, and we must follow. Come,' she clambered out of the water. 'Let us find some food.'

Sorina nodded, her thoughts still on Eirianwen's mention of Morrigan Dark Fate. A Druid's daughter would not say such things unless the Sight had come through her. That Eirianwen *was* able to say it was testament only to her youth. Fate was nothing to the young, she thought ruefully. Whilst the body still possessed youth and strength, even the gods themselves could be challenged. Only in the later years did one realise that the greener days would soon turn to autumn.

She looked upon Eirianwen's faultless, youthful body as she made her way to dry herself. Then she too heaved herself out of the water, her mood sombre once more.

IX

Never in her life had Lysandra been so ill. She had awoken in her cell, face down on the floor, her face and hair crusted with her own vomit, with no memory of how she had got there. It had been all she could do to claw herself on to her cot where she had lain for some hours unable to move. Her stomach churned, her hands shook and it was as if Hephaestus himself were using her head for an anvil.

Her mood was as sour as her stomach. It was, she told herself, just further evidence that she was unworthy to call herself Spartan. Were Spartans not famed for their sobriety, disdaining strong drink and rich food? Yet there she had been, drunk as a sack with the barbarians.

And then there was the fight.

Although trained from childhood in the *pankration*, the Hellenic art of unarmed fighting, Lysandra had failed to win against an old woman. She could blame the drink, blame the fact that she had been unprepared for the assault, but the stark truth of the matter was that she had failed. Failed her Sisterhood, failed her Spartan heritage and failed herself.

She was lost.

The goddess had turned her face away from her, of this she was now certain. She was destined to die a slave, an ignominious end witnessed by a slavering mob. Perhaps she was unworthy of even facing death with a sword in her hand. She might fail in meeting Titus's exacting standards and be sold on from the *ludus*.

The sun was at its noon zenith by the time Lysandra felt well enough to even contemplate leaving her cell. The first order of the day was to clean herself and then to clean the cell. As she scrubbed the floor she could not help thinking that this was the sort of work she was destined to do from now on.

The bell for the afternoon meal was sounded and the women gathered for a bowl of brown barley. Lysandra sat with the Hellene women, embarrassed to face either Eirianwen or Sorina: Eirianwen, because she had broken the law of hospitality by causing an argument with her friend; Sorina, because the woman was her better in combat. Though no final blow had been struck, the young Spartan knew the truth of it. The thought surprised her as it came to mind. Never before had she admitted another's superiority to her own. She left her meal unfinished and returned to her cell, and decided to remain there till the usual regime recommenced the following day. She had no wish to speak to anyone.

Dawn had cast a pink hue to the sky as the women assembled in their usual places, their shuffling feet kicking up a haze of dust. None could contain their curiosity at the transformation that their area of the training ground had undergone. Straw mannequins had been set up at regular intervals, as had wooden crossbeams, from which swung many sandbags. Set at a parallel to this was a long 'avenue' with sandbags on both sides. Wooden practice swords were stacked up ominously, a mute testament that the most exacting part of the training was about to begin.

Titus strode up, flanked by Catuvolcos and Nastasen, each of them carrying a bucket and stave. They set these down and Titus gave the women plenty of time to take in the new surroundings before speaking.

'You all know what is at stake.' His gravelled voice sounded harsh in the dawn. 'Your last hope of one day attaining your freedom rests upon how well you learn what we are about to teach you.' His eyes swept down the lines as they shifted slightly.

Nastasen stepped to the front. 'Lysandra, come forward!' he barked.

Lysandra's lip curled and she glanced at Hildreth who stood next to her. The red-haired German smiled tightly in sympathy.

'Take off your tunic!' His teeth showed up impossibly white against his ebony face as it split into a cruel grin. As Lysandra made to comply, the Nubian leant close to her. 'I'm sorry,' he whispered. 'I know you love to display yourself for me but I haven't got the time to pleasure you now.' She did not respond, looking resolutely to the front as she tossed her tunic to the ground.

'You are going to learn how to fight and move with skill.' Nastasen indicated the pile of swords. 'In time it will become instinctive to you. But always remember that there are but three rules to gladiatorial combat.' He stooped and retrieved a stave from one of the buckets, its sponge tip was coated in red paint.

'First rule.' Nastasen pointed the stave towards Lysandra. 'You get an instant kill on the red. Here, here.' He daubed a liberal amount of the fluid between her breasts and at the hollow of her neck. 'Always remember, go for the red first. Because if you don't your opponent will.' He replaced the red stave and picked another. This time the tip was blue.

'In the blue you get a cripple,' he said. He smeared uneven lines down Lysandra's pale arms and thighs. 'Second rule. Go for the cripple before the slow kill. Here is the slow kill on the yellow.' He swapped staves once again. 'Here, here and here,' he said as he drew across her stomach and sides. 'Remember, a slow kill might have enough left in her and kill you before she dies. With a cripple, you know you've got her if you keep your distance and wear her down.' He thrust a towel at Lysandra. 'Clean up, get dressed and get back in line!'

As she returned to her place, Catuvolcos now took his turn, casting a wry glance at Nastasen. He shook his head whilst the black giant's eyes were not on him, causing some of the women to grin in response.

'Go and get yourselves a sword each and make it quick!' he said. This done, he regarded them for a moment. 'Yes, heavy, aren't they?' Some assented with a nod. 'These are called *rudis*. They're twice as heavy as any iron blade you'll ever carry – so when it comes to the real thing, your weapon will feel as light as a feather. Watch, and copy me. This is the basic thrust.' He lunged forward with the weapon. Raggedly, the women complied. 'Pathetic,' he said. 'Try again…'

Titus watched as the Gaul took the novices through a fundamental drill, assessing their moves. His eyes were drawn to the Spartan and the fiery-haired German, Hildreth. These two moved with a practised ease, the exercises familiar to them. Yet he saw a disconcerting look in Lysandra's eyes as she worked. Increasingly, she was becoming more detached. He knew that she could fight, that much Stick had told him, and the fact that she had been trained was evident. Yet as each day passed, her effort, her will to continue, seemed to be leeching away from her.

'What do you think about Lysandra,' he said to Nastasen. 'You seem to have beaten the fight out of her.'

Nastasen grunted. 'She is an arrogant bitch. She looks at each of us as if we are but dirt beneath her feet.'

Titus looked straight at him. 'Stick said she knew how to fight, Nastasen. If she deserves a beating, then administer one. But from now on you leave your hatred of her away from my training ground. I don't need damaged goods. Is that clear?'

'Of course.' The big Nubian shrugged, trying to assume an air of nonchalance, but Titus could see the rage seething behind his eyes. Thrashing the haughty Greek gave Nastasen altogether too much pleasure.

'Go and work with the veterans today,' Titus said. Nastasen nodded and made off without another word.

Catuvolcos kept the novices working hard, teaching them the rudiments of swordplay. 'Everything starts and stops at the same time,' he repeated over and over, attempting to commit this to their memories. 'It's no good to strike, *then* move in. Everything starts and stops at the same time. The body moves as one.'

As the Gaul looked after the overall drills, Titus moved amongst the novices, correcting stances and form with a word here and there, often punctuating his remarks with a swat from the vine staff.

His eye fell upon Lysandra as she performed Catuvolcos's commands. Her movements were perfect but he could tell her mind was elsewhere. He walked up and slapped her on the rump with his staff. 'Come, Spartan! Keep your mind here, not in the clouds!'

The strange ice-coloured eyes flicked towards him for the fraction of an instant. 'My name is Lysandra,' she said, her voice strangely subdued. 'Not Spartan.'

'Put some effort into it, girl.' He ignored the statement. 'Concentrate on your task at hand.'

Lysandra frowned and continued, putting more vigour into her movements. Titus could tell that the increased effort was a façade. He shook his head and moved off, bawling at one of the Germans.

★   ★   ★

For Lysandra, the day passed slowly. The exercises were tiresome for her, and the hours passed in a haze as she moved from one drill to the next, not really hearing anything that Catuvolcos said. It was enough for her to catch a glance of his initial demonstration to ascertain the pattern the work would follow.

There was no honour in this she told herself. It was a waste of time. At least in the Temple her training had been in worship of the goddess. Bringing Sparta to mind caused her to flush with shame; she was a slave, and unworthy to console herself with daydreams of a home that was no longer hers.

She was just Lysandra now.

They were drilled unceasingly each day, the trainers becoming ever more critical of their efforts, demanding perfection from each movement. And as their skill increased, so their exercises became more complex. From merely standing and executing strikes they advanced to moving forwards, backwards; they were taught to change the angle of their attack; to turn with speed and efficiency.

From striking empty air they moved to the sandbags. The trainers would set the heavy canvas sacks swinging and the novices were to strike the moving targets.

'It's simple,' Stick bawled at them. 'Hit the mark or be hit yourselves.' A miss would result in a sharp blow from his vine staff. Even as Stick hurled abuse supplemented by physical threat, Catuvolcos played accompaniment to him, constantly exhorting the women that 'Everything starts and stops at the same time. You must flow around your opponent. Lose the tension in your bodies.'

As the weeks passed the novices learned quickly, even gaining the grudging approval of Titus. From hitting the sandbags, they advanced to running the gauntlet, weaving their way through the wooden avenues as the canvass bags were swung at them. Satisfied with their coordination, Titus gave the order that they were ready to move on to the more complex combination drills, using the sword and shield in concert.

They were given the *scutum*, the shield common to the Legions of Rome. As Lysandra hefted the unfamiliar item, she noted it was much lighter than the Hellene *hoplon* she was used to. The *scutum* was tall, protecting one's own body, whereas the round, bowl-shaped *hoplon* was designed primarily to defend the person to one's left in the Hellene phalanx.

It made sense, she thought to herself. The ancient Hellene phalanx was a massed formation, using the spear as the primary weapon of attack. The legionary relied on the sword and thus needed more personal protection. In single combat, she knew, the weight of the *hoplon* would prove more of a hindrance than a help.

Catuvolcos bade them form lines in front of the straw mannequins. 'This,' he told them, 'is your enemy. You must see this in your mind. Strike hard and fast, as you would against a real opponent.'

Lysandra stood behind Hildreth. Having seen the German perform her drills, she knew that the redhead was an accomplished swordswoman.

'Treat *that* as your enemy?' Hildreth called out in her thickly accented Latin, gesturing with her sword.

Catuvolcos nodded, and at that Hildreth took off at a run towards one of the straw men screaming, 'Death to the Romans!' which provoked scattered laughter from the barbarian tribeswomen.

Hildreth's wooden blade whistled as it cut through the air in a broad strike, hitting the mannequin's head, causing hanks of straw to explode skywards. Not content with decapitating her inanimate foe, she bashed her shield into it, hacking down with her weapon in a frenzy.

71

Catuvolcos laughed. 'Brutal, but effective, Hildreth! Good work. The Roman is dead!' The barbarian women cheered at that, and even the Romans among the novices grinned wryly. They understood that the derision was not directed at them personally but rather at those who ruled the empire that had enslaved them.

'Lysandra!' Catuvolcos called.

Lysandra set her shield and held her sword close to her right hip, its tip pointing upwards at a precise angle. The shield covered her body from eye to knee as she marched deliberately towards the mannequin. When she was only five paces from the mark she suddenly accelerated and the sword thrust out like a viper, the point sinking three inches into the breast of the straw man.

She glanced at Catuvolcos, who merely nodded once, and she returned to the back of the line. It was pointless to charge wildly into the fight, she knew. Slashing strokes with the sword may look more impressive, but her 'opponent' was as dead as Hildreth's and she had expended none of the effort the German had. It was an example of the difference in their *psyche*, she supposed.

As the sun began to set, Catuvolcos called halt to the day's proceedings, instructing the women to stack their gear and go for their evening meal. He watched Lysandra, who as always detached herself from the main group, engaging in none of the chatter and camaraderie that the shared learning of new skills had built up among the women. He too had noticed a change in her over the past weeks. The arrogance had gone from her walk and, whilst she performed all exercises and drills adequately, there was a slump in her shoulders. He decided to call her to him, telling himself that she needed his counsel.

'Your training is progressing well,' he said as she approached. She nodded briefly while he found himself becoming distracted by the way the sun had cast a reddish gold tint to her pale, beautiful face. He cleared his throat. 'Well, but not as well as you could do.'

'Have I failed in any of the tasks you have set me?'

'No. But neither have you excelled,' he said quietly. 'We know that you are a trained warrior, Lysandra. Where is your fire?' Catuvolcos felt his throat catch as she smiled at him, realising that this was the only time he had seen her do so with genuine feeling, her face bereft of the usual ironic, sneering cast.

'I have nothing to fight for,' she said.

He took a step towards her – too close, he knew, but he could not help himself. 'Your dignity, Lysandra. You are fighting for your dignity. Soon you will begin your first mock contests and you'll be judged on them. Those that fail will be sold on. You will become a slave. A *true* slave. Here, at least there is some semblance of freedom, some chance at regaining a life.'

'Dignity.' The cruel mask hardened over her face once more. 'I have none. This place has stripped it from me. It is better that I go to a life of drudgery than continue on here. Can you not see that wielding weapons is making a mockery of me? I have dishonoured my people,' she added softly. 'No Spartan would submit to slavery. I am Spartan no longer. Without that, I am nothing.'

'You are wrong, Lysandra' Catuvolcos began, but she jerked her chin up, her pale eyes locking with his, causing the words to die on his tongue.

'Good evening to you, Catuvolcos.' She turned and walked away.

He watched her as she made her way to the kitchens, his heart in turmoil. It was only then that he realised that it was the first time he had heard his name spoken from her lips.

The brief conversation with Catuvolcos stayed with Lysandra over the next days. Again she wondered why the trainer was concerning himself with her. Certainly, there were other women more in need of his guidance. This became even more evident when the trainers had them begin sparring sessions.

Weeks of hitting sacks and straw mannequins was one thing, but putting the lessons into practice against a living opponent was a somewhat different matter. For her part, Lysandra found her mind not really on the task at hand, hating the mockery of herself that she had become. Her opponents were trying hard, but their attacks were slow and clumsy to her experienced eye and she was able to dispatch them with a 'killing' strike almost at will. Long years in the *agoge* had taught her body to respond, even if her heart was not in it. Hildreth too, she saw, was cutting a swathe through all set against her. The German was evidently enjoying herself, whooping and shouting with each victory.

In the midst of one of Hildreth's celebrations, Titus gave the order to cease work. The women stopped, confused. It was nowhere near the noon break and they had only just begun to work up a sweat. Even the veterans had stopped their training and were making their way over to the novices' area. They sat on the ground, watching as some of Greta's women brought up some chairs and several long benches. More of the scrubs, including Varia, were marking out a ring in the sand with ropes – Lysandra estimated it was about twenty feet in diameter.

She saw the little slave pause in her work to wave at her, and she inclined her head in greeting. They had seen and spoken to each other often during the second period of the training and the child had come to regard Lysandra as a confidante of sorts. If she was honest with herself, Lysandra enjoyed the girl's company too, as it was a diversion from her own thoughts.

'Today will be different,' Titus shouted. 'Today you will fight for the crowd.' He indicated the veterans. 'And you will be judged.' Even as he said this, Lucius Balbus, approached with Eros, his catamite. The *lanista* sat on one of the chairs and Titus continued. 'You are fighting for more than practice from now on,' he said. 'You are fighting to stay in this *ludus*.' The women gasped. This was unexpected. They had had no time to prepare themselves for this test.

'Those of you that perform well in this arena,' he gestured to the roped area that Varia and her fellows had marked out, 'will stay and take the Oath. Those of you that slacken will be gone. We are looking for effort,' he went on. 'Fight well and, even in defeat, you may be spared.' He thrust his fist towards his chest. 'That is the sign for the *missio*, meaning you will have survived. This,' he thrust the fist out, his thumb held horizontally, 'in the arena would mean death. Here, it means you are to go to the blocks. In defeat, to entreat mercy, you turn to the *lanista* and hold up your finger. It is his decision if you go or stay. He may be influenced by the veterans if they think you will be worthy to take the Oath. That is all. First to fight will be Decia and

Sunia.' The two women looked at each other, stunned by this pronouncement. 'Next will be Thebe and Galatia. Stay warm,' he advised them.

On stiff legs, the first chosen stepped up. Nastasen placed helmets upon their heads and moved away.

'Begin!' Titus's voice was sharp. The women moved together, and the cheering started.

Lucius Balbus settled comfortably into his seat, and took a sip of wine from his goblet. Eros stood behind him, holding a shade over his head to shield him from the sun. Balbus always enjoyed these contests: it was good to see first hand which of his acquisitions were worth keeping and which were a bad investment. Experience had taught him that giving the women time to prepare for these bouts was detrimental to their performance. It was better to thrust the news upon them before they had time to dwell on it and allow nerves to set in.

The first two combatants had begun awkwardly enough but, roared on first by the veterans and then their fellow novices, they laid into each other with gusto. Their high-pitched cries of effort punctuated the air, mixed with the clacking of their wooden blades as the two attacked and countered. After a furious flurry of blows, Sunia struck home with a vicious thrust to Decia's sternum, knocking the wind from her. She fell back, tearing the helmet from her head, gasping for breath. Balbus had already made up his mind: the two had fought well and, as soon as the girl's finger went up, he signalled the *missio*.

The watchers cheered and the next two women made their way the fighting area.

Lysandra watched the combats with a sick feeling of dread welling up inside her. Now, it became apparent why she and Hildreth had not been paired together before. The trainers had planned it all along. They had kept them back, knowing that they were the superior warriors amongst the novices.

Despite the heat of the day, Lysandra felt a cold sweat break out on her brow. Her stomach churned and, on inspection, she found her hands shaking. It was one matter to defeat those who had never held a sword before setting foot in the *ludus*; but a blooded killer like Hildreth was a different proposition entirely. Her spat with Sorina had proved that all her training was nothing compared to the hard-won savvy of a battle-tested warrior. Her own desperate struggle with Stick's men on the beach, and the subsequent bout in the arena of Halicarnassus was the only real experience she had. It was nothing compared to the years Hildreth had spent battling the Romans on the borders of her savage homeland.

At least, she thought, she would go down to a foe who would finish her quickly. From then, it would be up to the Fates where she ended up. She glanced about, her eyes seeking Hildreth in the throng of novices. The German was looking directly at her, her eyes alive and sparkling. She too had guessed they would be paired against one another. Her fierce smile told Lysandra that she was relishing the opportunity to test herself. She looked away quickly, unwilling to hold her gaze, and instead let it fall on those women who Balbus had already singled out for the blocks. Soon, she knew, she would be among them.

The day wore on and the novices fought with a passion that overcame their inexperience. Lysandra realised that, for all their loathing of slavery, many of them believed what Titus had told them to be true. To live and fight for freedom was preferable to an existence that held no hope of such. For them, perhaps it was acceptable, for the sword and shield were new to them. They had not disgraced themselves or their ancestors the way she had done.

The girl next to her nudged her and she glanced up once

more to see Titus looking at her expectantly. 'You and Hildreth are to fight next,' the girl told her. 'You'd better get your kit.'

Balbus rubbed his hands together as Lysandra took her place on the fighting area. He had wanted to see more of his prized new slave in her training but administrative matters had kept him busy of late. She was, he thought, a fascinating creature. Eros, at his behest, had gone through the library, searching for any histories of the strange sisterhood of which the girl claimed to have been a member but there had been nothing. It all added to her mystery.

And then there was the German, Hildreth. A handful, he had been advised, but then she was one of those warrior women that so terrified the legions on the frontiers. The forthcoming contest promised to be of excellent quality.

At Titus's barked command, the duel began.

Hildreth exploded into action, leaping to the attack, her wooden blade hammering into the Spartan's shield. Lysandra backed off under the assault, occasionally hitting back with a strike of her own, but Hildreth was relentless. The German ploughed onwards, giving her foe no respite; the watchers roared her on, screaming for the quick kill.

The women's shields crunched together and Hildreth lifted her sword, thrusting over the top of Lysandra's *scutum*, catching the taller woman on the shoulder.

'Just a wound!' bellowed Titus. 'Continue!'

Hildreth backed off, catching her breath, and Balbus leant forwards in his seat. He had seen Lysandra in the arena and knew she liked to let her foe tire before she herself took the initiative. But no such attack came, the two merely circled each other warily, each moment that passed lending Hildreth more confidence.

Balbus flinched as one of Greta's young scrubs screeched high-pitched support for Lysandra. He cast an annoyed glance at her, but she did not seem to notice. Hers was a lone voice, he realised; all the cheers were for Hildreth. Urged on by the crowd, Hildreth yelled and attacked once again, bearing down mercilessly on her foe.

'What's the matter with her?' Balbus asked Nastasen.

The big Nubian raised his eyebrows. 'She's not as good as Stick said,' he declared, glancing apologetically at the Parthian who was seated next to Catuvolcos behind the *lanista*. 'Sorry, but she's nothing special. And there's the proof.'

'She's sick today,' Catuvolcos cut in. 'Running a fever.'

'She looked well enough this morning,' Nastasen said with a wolfish grin. 'I don't think she's good enough. All talk and little return. I recommend the blocks for that one.'

'You know nothing,' Catuvolcos spat. Balbus raised a hand abruptly, cutting the argument short, and returned his attention to the contest.

She was too fast. Hildreth was too fast. Lysandra found she could not breathe properly in the oppressive, full-faced helm. Her chest heaved and sweat ran into her eyes continually, blinding her. It was all she could do to raise her shield and deflect the lightning-quick strikes of the German. She tried to dig deep, to retaliate, but it was useless: all her attacks were battered contemptuously aside, giving her no respite. The German was too good and Lysandra could feel herself tiring swiftly.

She saw the strike coming but could not defend against it. Hildreth's sword crashed into the side of her helmet and Lysandra's vision was filled with a bright, white light. She felt herself stagger and tried to raise her shield but she was hit again.

Lysandra blinked and pain exploded through her, as Hildreth rammed her sword into her abdomen. She doubled over, bile rushing to her throat. The wooden *rudis* fell from her hand, the sound of it hitting the ground strangely loud in her ears. There was sharp pain at the back of her head and the world tilted crazily before turning to black.

Balbus's mouth was agape. The Spartan lay prostrate on the ground before her triumphantly screaming foe.

'*Habet, lanista*,' Nastasen said. 'She's had it.'

This could not be. Balbus himself had seen the woman in combat and knew her worth. This was not the same gladiatrix that had so consummately dispatched her foe in Halicarnassus. She was a shadow of that, her movements stiff and disjointed, her attacks feeble.

He felt a clutching at his calf, and looked down to see the child slave that had been screaming for Lysandra. She was on her knees before him.

'Master, please.' The girl's eyes were full of tears, her voice anguished. '*Missio*, I beg of you. She is the best, I swear it.'

'Get off my foot.' Balbus shook his leg as one would to dislodge an over-affectionate dog. The girl released him but would not relent. 'Master, spare her!' She was cut off as Stick leapt up from his bench and clouted her around the head.

'Get away, Varia.' He kicked her in the rear, sending the little slave sprawling.

Titus approached, shaking his head, his lips tight.

'Well, Titus,' Balbus demanded archly. 'How do you explain that?' He pointed furiously to the unmoving Spartan. 'Your training methods have blunted this girl.'

Titus flinched, his eyes narrowing at this maligning of his skills. It was Nastasen who had beaten the girl, but he was the head trainer, and thus ultimate responsibility for a fighter's performance lay with him. Yet he knew that the Spartan's failure had little to do with the Nubian's bullying. It went deeper. '*Lanista*,' he said respectfully. 'Something has changed the girl. I cannot say what. I know she has it in her to make good, but she has lost her fire.'

'She was lucky that first time,' Nastasen said. 'Look at her now. Lose her,' he advised Balbus. 'She's damaged goods. Anyone can see that she doesn't have it in her.'

Balbus felt the eyes of all upon him, awaiting his decision. On this showing, she should go. Could he have been wrong about her? After all, anyone could be lucky in the arena. Many times he himself had seen a superior fighter taken down through sheer bad luck. Perhaps it had been so with Lysandra's first opponent. Perhaps her poor performance had flattered the Spartan too much. He raised his arm, ready to deliver his final judgement.

'She feels the gods have abandoned her,' Catuvolcos said quietly.

Balbus paused, recalling his first conversation with Lysandra. She was rather straightforward and unimaginative in her manner, he thought. Perhaps a crisis of faith might cause this display. He weighed up her performance in the arena against what he had just seen. Could he afford to lose her?

'One last chance,' he said quietly, and thrust his fist towards himself, indicating the sheathing of a sword. '*Missio!*'

He got to his feet and whirled away. He was aware of an angry muttering amongst both the veterans and the novices. He realised it would not be seen as fair to free one who had performed so poorly and yet send more worthy fighters to the blocks. To show favouritism could cause havoc in the *ludus* if the women thought one of their number was receiving good treatment that they had not earned. He glanced at the women already condemned, who looked on sullenly. Some of them were no-hopers, extra mouths to feed, and that meant more overheads. But he had made his own bed. He turned back.

'I understand from Catuvolcos that there is an illness amongst the novices,' he called loudly, causing the hubbub to quieten instantly. 'I was unaware of such before the day's contests. This might be a reason for your pathetic displays today. However, I am not an unreasonable man.' He glared at the women, silencing any contradiction. 'I shall not be so lenient again.' He raised his arm to the condemned. '*Missio!*' he said.

A cheer erupted from all the women, veterans and novices both. As one they rose to their feet, whooping and shouting, for none enjoyed the sight of those they had come to know being expelled from the *ludus*. As he walked away, they began to chant his name, showing their appreciation of his clemency.

He jerked his head in Lysandra's direction. 'Have her taken to the infirmary.'

XII

Balbus had a slave wake him before dawn the following day and bring him a hot cup of mint tisane: the *lanista* found he could not face the day without his morning brew. Even so, rising at such an unearthly hour was far from pleasant. He sipped the herbal infusion, his hand idly playing with the sleeping Eros' golden hair. The youth stirred and opened his eyes blearily.

'Must you go?' he mumbled.

'Business is business.' Balbus said gently. 'I want to ride to Halicarnassus and I know how you hate horses. I shan't be gone long.'

'Just make sure you are not.' Eros's hand moved under the cotton sheet, stroking the *lanista's* thigh and began moving inwards languidly. 'You know what you'll be missing.'

Balbus felt himself jerk in response, swelling into life. He chuckled. 'I have appointments,' he said, placing his cup to one side. 'I must get going.'

'Feels like I've got you going already.' Eros disappeared beneath the covers.

Balbus sighed, and gave in to the delicious warmth as Eros took him in his mouth. Time enough for business later.

It took a day and a half for Balbus and his bodyguards to ride to the city of Halicarnassus, leaving the *lanista* somewhat saddle sore. Still, for all that, he usually enjoyed his time on the road, finding that the occasional foray away from the comforts of home had an invigorating effect.

Balbus loved the city. As he and his guards stabled their horses, he recalled with fondness his early days in the place that had made him his fortune. Living on a small inheritance, he had invested wisely and had made enough money to buy a share in a small but profitable inner-city *ludus*. From there, he had never looked back. He reminded himself to make a donation at the shrine of the goddess, Fortuna. Balbus was always careful to honour her, as she had always looked out for him.

The horses stabled, Balbus booked himself and his entourage into a reasonably priced tavern on the outskirts of the city before going about his business. There were accounts to be settled, supplies to be purchased and a dozen other minutiae that had to be taken care of. Of course, he could delegate tasks, but Balbus prided himself on his business acumen and knew that, whilst Fortuna may have a hand in his success, hard work and the personal touch provided its own reward.

It took some hours to attend to these matters and it was mid-afternoon by the time Balbus felt that he could indulge himself in a trip to one of Halicarnassus's excellent public baths. He let the busy cosmopolitan atmosphere wash over him as he threaded his way through the crowded streets. Many of his social standing preferred to travel in a litter, but not Balbus. He had no wish to miss out on the vibrant hum of the city by being encased in a box. And he was big enough to admit to himself that he enjoyed the occasional recognition his work as a successful *lanista* afforded him.

As always, the baths were crowded, but not overly so. Balbus liked to visit the more exclusive facilities that, in his view, were well worth the extra expense. There was a time for frugality and a time for extravagance. No use in wealth if one could not enjoy it, he told himself as he languished in the deliciously warm waters. He had lolled luxuriantly for some time, eyes closed, senses soaking in the perfumed air, when his relaxation was interrupted.

'Greetings, Lucius Balbus.'

The *lanista* opened his eyes, recognising the voice at once. 'Septimus Falco,' he said, smiling. 'Greetings.' Falco was a young man, not yet in his thirties but, like Balbus, he had made his fortune early in life. They were long-time business associates, the glib younger man a promoter of some repute in Halicarnassus.

'Are you here on business or pleasure?' Falco asked him.

'A little of both, of course. Do you have anything for me?'

'Always, Balbus, always. You'll be pleased to hear that Fat Aeschylus is making another bid for government, this time as *aedile.*'

Balbus chuckled. Fat Aeschylus was an Asiatic Greek with more money than sense, who had been trying to buy his way up the political ladder for more years than Balbus cared to remember. An accepted part of political manoeuvring was to provide games for the public in an attempt to secure votes from the plebs. Unfortunately for Aeschylus, the plebs were happy to enjoy his entertainments, but were well aware that he was not taken seriously enough to be considered a viable candidate for office. Aeschylus however, was a fan of female combat in his games and Balbus was his preferred supplier. And, if his bid for the office of *aedile* were successful, it would mean that, alongside supervising public works, Aeschylus would also be responsible for sponsoring the games for the province. 'Good news for all of us,' the *lanista* said, nodding.

'Indeed. But this time Fat Aeschylus is going to the expense of hiring another *lanista* to provide women to fight. He feels that he can offer the plebs more by pitting one school against another.'

Balbus was scandalised. 'That's absurd,' he said. 'My fighters have always provided him with excellent quality.'

'Of course,' Falco soothed. 'He's just looking to increase interest in his spectacle and you can't really blame him. You know how fast the mob gets jaded; and you have to admit, it's highly ostentatious. The teams of women together with male fighters – that makes four schools.'

Balbus mulled that over. He considered it a professional slight, but he had no intention of missing out on the business. He would overlook any bruises to his pride as long as his purse was not similarly dented.

'I understand that you have recently acquired some new stock, Lucius.' Falco was always well informed. 'How are they shaping up?'

'Extremely well,' the *lanista* responded. Even if some of the latest novices had been extremely poor, Balbus was not about to give any impression other than a good one. 'As you know, I have an excellent eye for quality merchandise and my recent purchases are no exception.'

'Yes, I saw your new girl at Frontinus's recent games.' Falco's gaze became feline. 'The *dimachaera*. She was impressive.'

'Oh, her.' Balbus grinned at his young countryman. 'Very dangerous, that one. She's from Greece.' He paused for effect. 'Sparta, in fact.'

'Really?' Falco's eyes lit up. Like most Romans he was enamoured with tales of ancient Sparta and its illustrious Three Hundred. Already, in his mind's eye, he was probably creating scenarios where he could use her famous background to the most profitable advantage. 'We could use that to increase the interest in her.'

'That's what I thought.' Balbus was pleased that Lysandra had caught the other's imagination. On no account was he going to let the promoter know that the Spartan was proving troublesome. 'Anything to get them going. You know how cynical the mob can be about new fighters,' he finished smoothly.

'Tell me about it.' Falco's sigh was world-weary. 'It's a problem always being one step ahead of them, they demand new diversions every games, it seems.'

'Falco, I must be away. I have matters to attend to.' Balbus said, inwardly wishing that he could spend more time idling with the younger man. 'You'll be in touch about Aeschylus's forthcoming games?'

'Indubitably, my friend. If he has the money, I'll put on a show none will forget in a hurry. I might even get him voted in this time.'

'I doubt that.' Balbus laughed, and lifted himself from the pool. Even though they lied to each other all the time and often cut each other short in profits, he had a genuine affection for the flashy promoter. 'Take care of yourself, Falco.' He tipped a finger to his brow.

'You know me, Lucius.' Falco kicked out into the water. 'I always do!'

Balbus left the baths with a specific purpose; there was, after all, a twofold objective in his visiting the city. Having concluded the usual business earlier in the day, he now made his way to the Greek quarter. Certainly, there was a large population of Asiatic Greeks throughout Halicarnassus, but the suburb he was headed for was renowned as a hive of expatriates from the 'old country.'

Balbus could not resist a smile as he made his way into the quarter. Having visited Athens in his youth, he instantly recognised the essential *Greekness* of the place. Togas had been replaced by *chitons* and the clean-shaven Roman fashion had no place here; most of the men wore beards, oiled and curled. On every corner there was a debate of some sort going on, philosophies being exchanged, politics being argued.

He stopped by a street-side vendor to enjoy a cup of wine. The man tried to fleece him in the typical Greek manner but Balbus rebuked the fellow flawlessly in his own language.

'I thought you were a tourist,' the wine vendor apologised.

'Afraid not.' Balbus's answered lightly. 'Tell me, my good man, is there a Temple of Athene hereabouts?'

'Athene?' The vendor scratched his ear, and examined the residue before answering. 'I thought you Romans called her Minerva? *She* has a temple in the city.'

Balbus did not take offence at his abrupt manner; Greeks were famous for their xenophobic attitude. 'I promised a Greek –' he stopped and corrected himself, knowing that the Greeks preferred to be addressed in their native terminology, 'a *Hellene* friend of mine that I would make an offering for him while I was in the city,' he lied smoothly. 'He insisted that I make his devotion in a Hellenic temple of the goddess.'

The vendor sized him up for a moment. 'Yeah, there's one down the street. Not much of a temple, though. More of a shrine.' He gave Balbus the directions. In return, the *lanista* flipped him a coin, which vanished with preternatural speed.

Balbus found the shrine with no difficulty. It was a small building but, as with most Greek architecture, it was quite beautiful. He made his way inside, pausing a moment to let his eyes adjust to the comparative darkness within. Incense hung heavily in the air, giving the interior of the shrine an ethereal atmosphere. At the far end of the room was an altar behind which was a tall statue of Athene, resplendent in her armour and war helm. Her presence dominated the room and Balbus bowed his head in acknowledgement. Like most Romans, he had a healthy respect for the religions of foreign lands.

'Can I help you, brother?'

Balbus saw a priest approaching him from behind the statue. The man moved with an assured grace, his arms and chest were muscular, giving him more the look of an athlete than a cleric.

'You are the High Priest here?' Balbus asked in a reverential whisper. It always felt wrong to him to speak at normal tenor in a place of worship.

The Greek's rugged face creased into a grin. 'I am the *only* priest here, brother. Though I think those in Athens might take issue with me if I affected myself with so a grand title as High Priest.'

'Yes, I should think so.' Balbus returned the smile, finding the man's gentle manner putting him at ease. 'Is there somewhere we might talk? I have some questions that I feel you might be able to help me with.'

'Of course.' The priest indicated that Balbus follow him. He lead the *lanista* back towards the statue of Athene, behind which was a set of steps leading down to a small door. 'This room is set aside for such purposes,' he explained as he unlocked the door. 'As you can understand, people wish to discuss matters with a priest that they feel they can discuss with no other.'

The temple's anteroom was small and comfortable. There were couches on which to recline, between which lay a small table, decked with fruit and a jug of watered wine.

'I am called Telemachus,' the priest said as he sat.

Balbus introduced himself but if the cleric had heard of him he gave no indication.

'How may I help you then, Lucius Balbus? Do you wish to commune with the goddess? To beg a divine favour?'

Balbus poured a small measure of wine for himself and the priest. 'Not exactly,' he said. 'Tell me, Brother, have you heard of Athene's Temple in Sparta?'

The priest laughed aloud, so surprising Balbus that he spilled wine down his toga. 'I certainly have,' Telemachus replied after a moment. 'A very strange place indeed. Why do you ask?'

There was, Balbus knew, a time and a place for lies. Any good businessman knew when to cast the dice in honesty, or weigh them to fix an outcome. The *lanista* felt that there would be no point in trying to deceive Telemachus. Also, it would be impious in the extreme to lie in a temple. 'I am the owner of a school for gladiatrices,' he said.

'Oh.' Telemachus sat up on the couch. 'You are *that* Lucius Balbus! I did not want to say before. I have seen your women on occasion, they are very entertaining.'

'That's always good to hear.' Balbus was somewhat taken aback but was ever the professional. 'I did not think the priesthood would approve of the games.'

Telemachus's smile was disarming. 'Athene is not only the goddess of wisdom, *lanista*. War is also her dominion.'

'Ah yes, of course.' Balbus nodded. 'The thing is,' he said, 'one of my newer charges is a former Priestess of Athene's temple in Sparta.'

'Indeed?' Telemachus motioned him to continue.

'I was hoping you could tell me a little of this sect and their ways, Telemachus. My Spartan has it within her to be a famous gladiatrix, but of late she has seemed out of sorts. One of my trainers mentioned to me that she — Lysandra is her name — feels abandoned by the gods. I thought you might know how I could counsel her through this difficult time.'

'The Spartans are a strange breed, *lanista*. Nowhere is this more evidenced than in the sisterhood your Lysandra was part of. As any learned person knows, Sparta's history is steeped in military stoicism and covered more or less with glory.

'This excellence on the battlefield was not attained cheaply, however. From ancient times, even up till today, Spartan youths from the age of seven are compelled to attend the *agoge*, the Spartan upbringing. It is not dissimilar to a *ludus*, in its atmosphere and purpose. The difference being, of course, that the Spartans are training their youth for defence of the state, not for the pleasure of the crowd. Their women also are duty-bound to compete in athletic contest, in order that they beget strong sons.'

'Athletics?' Balbus brushed absently at the spillage on his toga. 'That would not explain Lysandra's brilliance with weapons.'

'Well, Sparta's Temple of Athene is an oddity.' Telemachus nodded. 'Let me explain. Some three hundred years ago, the Epiran warlord, Pyrrhus, invaded Lakedaimonia, the Spartan heartland.'

Balbus nodded; all Romans knew of Pyrrhus. He had inflicted many defeats on the fledgling Roman city-state, but his victories had been so costly to his own men, it had given rise to the derisive phrase 'a Pyrrhic victory'.

'Then, as now,' Telemachus went on, 'Sparta's heyday had passed and, in truth, she was nothing more than a minor Hellenic *polis*. Pyrrhus wanted to be the first conqueror to walk in triumph through her streets. As you know, the city of Sparta has never fallen to a foreign power – Alexander chose to ignore her and you Romans chose to make her a client state. But in those days, the memory of her grandness was still fresh in men's minds and the Epiran decided that he would be the one to take the city.'

Balbus was enjoying himself. He loved a good yarn and the Greek, like most of his countrymen, liked nothing better than the sound of his own voice.

Telemachus drank some wine before continuing. 'Typically, the Spartans decided that they could fight him off, despite being overwhelmingly outnumbered. They retreated behind their city walls and prepared for a siege.

'Pyrrhus did not disappoint them and hurled his men at the defences, seeking to swamp the Spartans by sheer weight of numbers. At first the tactic seemed to be working. However, it was at this time that a Spartan Princess called Archidamia went to the women of the city and led them to the walls to fight alongside their menfolk.'

Balbus was scandalised. A Roman woman would never be allowed to pick up a sword and fight. That was man's work, and women had no business interfering in the business of men. Admittedly, he had Roman women in the *ludus*, but that was different. They were slaves, not Roman citizens.

The priest smiled slightly at the *lanista's* expression. 'Against all odds, the Spartans crushed the invasion force, inflicting huge casualties on the Epiran army. This great victory had to be due to the intervention of the gods. Athene is the patron of Sparta as well as Athens, Lucius Balbus, and the triumph was attributed solely to her. As thanksgiving, the Spartans set up a new religious sect to honour her. It had a typical Spartan twist, however. They set up an *agoge* for Priestesses on their acropolis, replacing the more traditional temple with a fortress.'

'They have a *ludus* for children. For girls?' Balbus could scarcely credit it.

'Worse than a *ludus*. Your charges are adults. That the Spartans subject their children to this regimen is inhuman. I cannot describe to you how horrific the *agoge* is in its practices. It goes beyond mere religious and physical training, friend Balbus. These children walk barefoot in winter snow, are mercilessly beaten for any transgression, real or imagined, given so little food that they are forced to supplement themselves by stealing. Indeed, such thievery is encouraged, for it shows resourcefulness. But the penalty for being caught is terrible, for it is seen as failure.'

The priest paused in his narrative, letting Balbus assimilate the information. The *lanista* was shocked that such antiquated and barbaric practices went on in Greece, supposedly the font of civilisation.

'All the while, they are being schooled in military doctrine,' Telemachus continued. 'They spend years studying weapons and tactics in this crucible of discipline; of course, it's antiquated and highly ritualised. Indeed, Sparta is the only place in the world where one can still see an ancient hoplite army, albeit one formed solely of women. This is done, ostensibly, to answer any future call of Athene to bring the women of the city to arms. In addition, it is their religious and secular education. You will find your Lysandra eminently well schooled, my friend.'

'So, if Lysandra has been trained with weapons since childhood, why then is she not performing?' Balbus asked.

'Ah ha!' The Greek smiled, and tapped his nose. 'The heart of the matter. For centuries, Spartan power was based on the subjugation of her neighbouring state, Messenia. The Spartans put the entire population to slavery. To a Spartan, the enslavement of another race is a proud part of her heritage. But to make a slave of a Spartan ...' He shook his head. 'You have made your Lysandra everything she despises. You have taken away that which makes up her *psyche* and she is as lost as a babe. For all their prowess, all their training, these priestesses are very flat in their thinking. All Spartans are, but they especially so. Things are very simple to them, and they can rarely find a middle ground as more cultured people can. To her, as you say, it appears that the goddess has turned her back, abandoning her to the most shameful, the most ignoble fate a Spartan can imagine. It is no wonder she cannot function.'

Balbus felt utterly defeated. 'She has the potential to become my greatest asset,' he said. 'Are you saying there is no way to convince her to fight,' he patted his chest, 'from her heart?'

'No.' Telemachus drained his cup. 'I think perhaps I could find a way to convince her.' As he poured more wine, he sighed. 'But unfortunately, my work is here, and I cannot afford to leave. The people around here are not rich and the votive offerings barely cover the expenses of the shrine.'

'I see.' Balbus smiled, now on familiar ground. 'Of course, I can understand that. If you can find it in your heart to take a short leave of absence to aid this poor child, I would be extremely grateful, both to you personally and to the goddess herself. Though earthly things cannot compensate for the good work you will do, I am sure that my provision would be such as this temple has never known before.'

'The goddess loves a generous man, *lanista*,' Telemachus said. 'Shall we say twenty thousand denarii?'

Lucius Balbus balked inwardly at the sum but reasoned that Lysandra had come to him for nothing and so perhaps this was the gods' way of balancing the scales. She was a rare piece of merchandise – young, fit and already trained. She would have cost a lot more if he had bought her on the open market, that much was certain. 'Twenty thousand, friend Telemachus,' he agreed.

XIII

Nastasen should have felt elation but there was only a strange sense of emptiness. In his mind's eye, he saw the scene played out many times. The Spartan whore facing the German, her staid movements, her clumsy attacks, her woeful defence. And her humiliating defeat. His heart had leapt for joy when he had seen her topple to the sand, utterly beaten. But that joy had passed too quickly to be replaced by the injustice of it. *He* should have been the one to break her. The night-borne silence of his room mocked him as he twisted the strands of hemp inside an earthenware jar before lighting the ends from a nearby lamp. As soon as they started to glow, he put down the lamp, leaned over the mouth of the jar and inhaled deeply.

He had hated her from the moment he laid eyes on her: the arrogant swagger in her walk; the supercilious mien she used when she spoke to any and all, including himself. He, Nastasen, son of princes, from a line of warriors famous when the Spartans were still herding goats in their rough little corner of Greece. So, she had proven she could take a beating; but any fool could do that. For all her talk, all her disdainful manner, she had been found wanting. It was all bluster.

And that had disappointed Nastasen.

He had wanted to bring her down at her peak when the arrogant bitch had felt she had come to the height of her powers. She had been resilient to the vine staff, but there were other ways of breaking the spirit. *He* would have *fucked* some humility into her.

His lips closed around the cone of smoking hemp, seeing her struggling beneath him, begging him to stop as his greater strength, his power, overwhelmed her. Savouring the look on her face as he forced himself into her, hearing her agonised scream as her tender flesh tore open to receive him.

He grew hard at the thought of it.

Visions swam in his mind as the opiate took hold of him, images of the delicious cruelties he would inflict on her; cruelties only a man could mete out to a woman. He lay back, his skin tingling and, almost unconsciously, he began to stroke himself, gasping at the drug-heightened pleasure of his own touch. There was Lysandra, proud and arrogant, as he, Nastasen, came to her, tearing the clothes from her body. He laughed at her shock, and laughed again as his great fist smashed into her face. He was bearing her down, holding her wrists to the ground as he pushed between her splayed legs. Splayed like a whore's. And the unimaginable pleasure of that first, bleeding violation…

He gripped himself tightly, cutting off his impending orgasm, his heart pounding, sweat coursing over his body. Sitting up, he blew softly on the smouldering hemp until the ends glowed brightly. Why just imagine he asked himself? Had she not done enough merely by despising him? She deserved to be punished.

The drug coursing through him, he allowed his initial arousal to wane but he still felt a heavy, urgent desire to spend his seed.

The Spartan would be his receptacle.

Catuvolcos was worried, both for Lysandra and for himself. He had seen many women come to the *ludus* and had inured himself to tender feelings towards them. Balbus was a good master, providing women for his trainers in order that they would not be driven to distraction by the gladiatrices with whom they were allowed no intimacy.

But this was different, the Gaul realised. He *felt* for this cold, beautiful woman in a way he had for no other. Every time he closed his eyes she was there. He ran his hands through his coppery hair, trying to purge his thoughts of her, knowing it was useless.

He had felt sick with fear when she had fallen to Hildreth, desperately anxious at the fact that the blows had been to her head. He had seen what could happen with the head wound, the wound that sucked the soul but left the body alive. He had interrogated the physician, Quintus, as to her condition and, though the old man had assured him all was well, Catuvolcos's worries were not assuaged. In truth, he felt he had persisted too much in his inquiry: Quintus had thought it strange that he be so concerned over the fate of a single fighter.

He knew he had to see her for himself, just to be sure. He had had experience on the battlefield; he knew the signs of the head wound that caused damage deep inside. Quintus was competent, but Catuvolcos feared that he may have missed a vital sign. He was no longer young, and could have made a mistake.

The hour was late but, even so, getting to the infirmary would be a risky undertaking. He was confident that he could pass off a nocturnal wander around the *ludus* as a need for fresh air or even just a fancy. But if he were seen entering or leaving the infirmary, there would be questions asked and Catuvolcos would have no answers. The best course of action was not to arouse any suspicion by being seen out of his quarters. That would take skill, a hunter's expertise, and he possessed that in abundance. It was risky but, he decided, a risk worth taking. Just to see her.

Exasperated, he slapped his palm to his forehead. What was he thinking? He could not afford to care about Lysandra; it was fraught with danger for them both. If anybody discovered his feelings, both of them would be sent to the blocks. He would lose his chance of freedom and rob her of the chance to win hers.

A sudden fear gripped his heart. *What if she does not survive?* his own voice whispered in his mind. He could not live with himself if he let that happen. His tongue licked dry lips. He *must* see her. He did not give himself a chance to think the matter over: his decision made, he stole from his quarters, shutting the door quietly behind him.

The night was still and humid, the air heavy with the promise of thunder. The chirping of nocturnal insects was loud and somewhere an owl called its hunting song. Above, the clouds swept across to hide the face of moon, and Catuvolcos felt that the gods were with him.

His eyes scanned the walls of the *ludus*, seeing the silhouettes of Balbus's hired guards, some pacing, some lounging on their spears. It seemed that they had relaxed their vigilance somewhat in the absence of the *lanista*. He paused, his body alive with the thrill of apprehension. There could be no going back.

Catlike, he crept through the darkness, keeping to the shadows, his movements slight and slow. Stealth, he knew, required patience and care; speed counted for little. He slipped between the houses inhabited by the school's top fighters, Titus and Balbus's higher ranking servants, moving only when he was sure he was unobserved.

To reach the infirmary he had to circumnavigate the training area. Cutting across it would be quicker, but to cross open ground, even in the dead of night, was to invite discovery. With painful slowness, he skirted the sands of the training ground, passing the locked cells of the gladiatrices. As he moved, he checked again to see if the guards were watching. They were not. Even from this distance, he could hear the sound of chatter and scattered laughter. He smiled grimly, imagining what Balbus would have to say about their slovenly behaviour.

He made it past the cells and the scrubs' quarters without incident. As he made it to the massive bathhouse, he breathed a little easier. His goal was in sight.

The door to the infirmary was ajar.

Catuvolcos leant around it, his senses alert to the slightest movement or sound from inside. There was none. He let go a breath he had not realised he had been holding. He slipped into the infirmary. Once inside he paused for a few moments letting his eyes adjust to the gloom. It was at that moment that the moon goddess pushed away the curtain of clouds that obscured her face. A dull light flooded into the infirmary and Catuvolcos's heart stopped in his chest. Illuminated clearly at the back of the room, was Nastasen.

Naked save for his loincloth, he stood over the only occupied bed in the infirmary. Catuvolcos did not need to see the light of the moon on her pale features nor the hair that shrouded her pillow like a silken black sea to know that it was Lysandra who occupied that bed. The Nubian had not moved. He merely stood like a Promethean statue, staring down at the sleeping Lysandra.

'Nastasen!' the word escaped Catuvolcos before he could stop himself.

As if awaking from a dream, the Nubian looked up slowly. The strange locks hanging about his face and the feverish gleam in his eye gave the gigantic trainer a demonic aspect. Nastasen held his finger to his lips, and moved slowly away from Lysandra's bed.

As he approached, Catuvolcos could smell the Nubian's sweat and, beneath his loincloth, the vestiges of his arousal showed plainly. He felt his face grow hot as his blood burned with anger. The thought of Nastasen's hands on the Spartan sickened him.

'What are you doing here?' Catuvolcos realised his whisper was harsh and too loud.

'What are *you* doing here?' Nastasen's voice trembled with a nervous tension. He seemed to be on the border of hysterical laughter.

'I saw you come in here and wondered what you were up to,' Catuvolcos lied.

Nastasen inhaled deeply, causing his massive chest to expand. 'I needed some medication,' he whispered. 'The hemp, Catuvolcos. I know that Quintus has a supply and I am running low.'

'Does he keep it by Lysandra's bed?'

'She called out in her sleep.' The Nubian shrugged. 'It caught my attention and I stopped to look at her.' He paused, the hugely dilated pupils regarding Catuvolcos. 'What do you care, anyway? You seem to be sweet on this girl. Saying she's ill when she performs badly. And now, out in the middle of the night, just turning up where she happens to be.' His face split into a smile, his teeth starkly white against the ebony of his flesh.

Catuvolcos swallowed. 'Don't be stupid,' he said, hoping his intonation was glib. 'Like I said, I saw you and wondered what you were up to.' The Nubian nodded.

'Join me in a snort or two, Gaul?'

Catuvolcos was appalled that Nastasen had even suspected his true motivation for being in the infirmary. He cursed himself a fool for putting himself in this position, but now he had no choice other than to accept the Nubian's offer. Not to do so would give the black giant time alone, time to think about what had transpired. Catuvolcos hoped that a night on the hemp would dull his fellow trainer's suspicions. Forcing himself to smile, he nodded wordlessly and turned away, leaving the infirmary on cat's feet.

He did not see Nastasen glare hatred at his back.

XIV

Lysandra awoke slowly, aware instantly of the dull ache in her head. She felt nauseous and disorientated, as if all the strength had been leeched from her body. Blinking, she realised that she was in the *ludus's* infirmary, a fact reinforced by the sudden appearance of Quintus by her bedside. The surgeon pulled up a stool and sat, putting a cup of water to her lips. She was parched, and tried to gulp the cool liquid down but Quintus pulled the cup away, tutting.

'Not too much, my girl,' he said. 'It will make you sick. Just small sips.' He offered her the cup again. She took it from him and nodded.

'You're lucky,' Quintus said. 'You have a thick skull.' Lysandra shot him a venomous look, but the surgeon grinned at her. 'It didn't crack at least,' he went on. 'Whether what you had in there has turned to mush is still to be seen however.'

'Thank you so much for your observation, Hippocrates,' she muttered, handing the cup back.

Quintus shrugged and then winked at her. 'My bedside manner does leave something to be desired,' he said. He rose and poured her more water from a pitcher. 'How are you feeling?'

'Sick,' she responded. 'Dizzy and weak.' It was senseless to lie to a physician.

Quintus made a noise at the back of his throat. 'You've had a concussion,' he said. 'It occurs, obviously, when a blow is received...'

'I know what a concussion is,' Lysandra cut him off. 'I am not an idiot.'

'Hippocrates recommends trepanation as a treatment,' the surgeon retorted dryly. He smirked as Lysandra's hand flew to her head, seeking a hole. 'But I did not think your condition serious enough to warrant it.'

'That is reasonable,' Lysandra agreed, her own lips twisting in an answering grin.

'You should smile more often, Spartan. You are pretty when you do so.' He held up his hand, cutting off any response. 'You must stay here and rest, at least for a few days. You cannot risk further injury to your head, it's not safe.'

'It does not matter,' Lysandra told him. 'I am to be sold, as I am fully aware that my performance was not up to standard. I doubt if my next owner will require me to fight for him.' Her tone was bitter and self-reproaching.

'I'm afraid you don't get away from here quite that easily. It seems as if Balbus has given you another chance. None of the women are to be sold.'

Lysandra was about to respond, when the door to the infirmary opened. Varia peered into the room and, seeing Lysandra sitting up, she squeaked with delight and bounded towards the bed.

'She's been here every free moment she's had,' Quintus whispered before announcing more loudly, 'I'll be in my office!'

'Lysandra!' Varia skidded to a halt by the bed, her face wreathed with smiles. 'It is good to see you awake! I knew you would be well.'

102

Lysandra smiled back at the youngster, and held out her hand. Tentatively, the little slave reached out and clasped her fingers with her own. 'It is good to see you too, Varia,' she said. 'The face of a friend is the best sight when one has woken from a long sleep.' Lysandra realised that this was the first time she had called the child her friend. It was the first time she had admitted it to herself. Varia beamed at her.

'You are not to go to the blocks,' she said.

'So Quintus tells me.'

'Isn't that wonderful?' Varia was enthusiastic. 'We can be friends forever,' she added with childish hope. Lysandra did not respond, unwilling to dampen the girl's spirits. In her heart, she knew that nothing had changed, that she had lost the will and desire to fight. Her next bout would carry the same result.

Varia chatted on, oblivious to the dark turn in her mood. She spoke of a child's matters: that she had adopted a kitten she had found, an offspring of one of the cats that so plagued the kitchens.

'I've called her Sparta, after your home,' Varia confided. 'I know she will grow to be the best hunter of mice ever.' Lysandra nodded and smiled, hoping that she kept a bitter cast from her face. Varia continued in a similar tone, updating Lysandra on the gossip from the recent bouts, but much of what she said was lost to her. Lysandra's thoughts turned to what her future held.

Balbus had arranged to meet the priest at daybreak and was pleased to find the man punctual. The *lanista* had ensured his business matters were closed and, as promised, had made an offering at Fortuna's temple. He wanted to be on his way, and Telemachus too seemed eager to get their journey started. For some reason the priest had brought with him several leather buckets, each full of scrolls.

'I don't think we'll be on the road long enough for you to read all of those,' Balbus commented.

Telemachus grinned at him. 'I like to be prepared for all eventualities.' Balbus grunted, and the little group got under way.

The *lanista* found the priest to be a witty and engaging travelling companion, the journey becoming increasingly enjoyable as they went. Telemachus had what seemed to be an endless supply of stories and fables with which he regaled Balbus and his guards. The Greek had no shortage of the more ribald tales too and the men laughed long into the night at his retellings of the myths with his inimitable earthy slant. Interspersed with the stories, Balbus told the priest what he knew of Lysandra: how she had been found amidst the wreckage of a destroyed ship and of her self-proclaimed title of Mission Priestess.

The days passed quickly, thanks to Telemachus's incessant chatter, and soon the *ludus* came into sight. Balbus always felt a sense of pride as he approached the complex, knowing that he had built up his empire with his own sweat.

'Impressive,' Telemachus acknowledged.

Balbus spread his hands, affecting a modest expression. 'Things can always be better, but we are in profit and that's the main thing.'

'I should like to bathe and change before I speak to your Spartan,' Telemachus said as they drew closer to the *ludus*. 'It would be unseemly for a priest of the goddess to meet one of her handmaidens covered in road grime.'

'My home is yours,' Balbus said.

Balbus's facilities were excellent, rivalling the city-based baths that Telemachus frequented. After they had bathed and enjoyed a massage, the *lanista* gave him a short tour of the *ludus*. Telemachus was surprised at the good conditions that these fighters lived in. To see inside a *ludus* was an opportunity not often afforded to a common member of the populace, but he had heard that arena fighters were often treated in a shameful manner.

'That is largely a myth,' Balbus told him when Telemachus broached the subject. 'These slaves are expensive to buy, and they only really fetch a good return if they perform well. It's like owning a team of racing horses,' he elucidated. 'One treats one's horses well, gives them the best food, attention and training in order that they will produce results on the day of the race. These women are prized assets, and I should go out of business very soon if by the time they came to fight they were so broken that they were killed in their first bouts. That is not to say I am not an advocate of discipline, but I see little sense in ruining a fighter by oppression. I find that giving the women a sense of worth increases their efforts. One needs spirit to survive in the arena.'

'A wise policy, *lanista.*' Telemachus saw sense in the Roman's methods. 'Talking of lack of spirit, it is about time I saw your Lysandra.'

Balbus rubbed his hands together. 'Excellent. I shall have her brought to the main house and we can interview her there.'

Telemachus shook his head. 'With respect, I should see her alone.'

'As you wish,' Balbus shrugged. 'She is in the infirmary. I shall take you there and ensure that you are not disturbed.'

Dusk had begun to darken the sky as Telemachus entered the infirmary. The Spartan sat on her bunk, staring into space. The priest was at once struck by her beauty as the half light fell upon her. She turned slowly as he approached her and he saw that her eyes were the colour of ice.

'Greetings, Lysandra of Sparta, Handmaiden of Athene, Priestess of the Mission,' Telemachus raised his hand. 'I am Telemachus, and I too am in her service.'

The Spartan cocked an eyebrow. 'Greetings, Athenian.' Telemachus resisted the urge to grin both at her rustic accent

105

and her instant recognition of his own. 'Have you come to take me from here?'

'No.' Telemachus sat at the foot of her bed. 'That is not within my powers, and even if it were, I would not.'

'So you have come to gawp at me?'

Telemachus ignored that. 'I have brought you some books.' He placed the buckets on the bed. He could tell that she was interested, despite herself. 'Homer, of course, and Herodotus. Xenophon, Caesar, Gaius Marius, and other manuals of tactics. I know that the Spartan Priestesses covet such reading.'

'Indeed.' Lysandra pulled one of the scrolls out and inspected it. '*The Gallic Wars*,' she read aloud. 'To what do I owe all this, then?' She snapped the scroll closed. 'Are you merely concerned for one of the Sisterhood who has fallen on evil times?'

Telemachus scratched his beard. It had been a long time since he had spoken with a Spartan and he had forgotten how blunt they could be. 'No. I am here because Lucius Balbus asked me to speak with you. There are concerns that you are not performing here as you should.'

Lysandra's smile held no humour. 'He is disappointed that I am not worthy to fight and die in the arena. A pity. But the fact that I am here is ample proof that Athene has turned her face from me. It is better that I am sold, for I have done nothing but dishonour my Order and my people.'

Telemachus fixed the girl with a cold stare. 'You should be ashamed of yourself.' He could tell that this had taken her aback. 'You call yourself a Spartan? It is not the Spartan way to hold oneself locked in gloom and self-pity.'

'What would you know about it, Athenian? You have no right to come and speak of matters of which you have no comprehension.'

'I know enough to see that you are right when you say you dishonour your Order. You dishonour the goddess by your refusal

106

to accept the gifts she has given you. Instead you sit and sulk like a petulant child.'

'Gifts!' Lysandra exploded. 'To consign her Priestess to slavery is a gift? I think not.'

Telemachus got to his feet. 'Look about you and think to where you came from. Your life in the Temple has been dedicated to what? The practise of martial skills in honour of the goddess!' He threw up his hands. 'And what a waste! To what end do you learn these skills? To parade on the festival days in hoplite panoply before once again shutting yourself off from the world in your little temple.'

'It is not the Spartan way to be ostentatious,' Lysandra replied loftily. 'We need no Parthenon, for we worship with our hearts.'

'You are avoiding the issue, Priestess. To what end has your training been? Is it merely to pay the goddess lip service?'

'For a priest, you are poorly educated. Our Order was founded after the invasion of Pyrrhus...'

Telemachus made a sharp gesture, cutting her off. 'Yes, I know all that! Do you honestly think that your Sisterhood will be called on to defend Sparta again? Rome has outlasted all other Empires, Lysandra. The *Pax Romana* keeps us safe, the frontiers are marked, and there is no foreign threat. No,' he shook his head, his expression mocking, 'you practise the empty ritual of combat, harking back to days when Sparta was a great power, not a rural backwater of Hellas.' He had hit a mark by design and was pleased to see anger burn in her eyes. As a Hellene, Telemachus understood the Spartan *psyche* and knew that laying insult at the gates of her *polis* would not fail to move her from the lethargy that Balbus had described.

'It is not for Athenians to speak ill of Sparta. You are nothing but a race of effete snobs.'

'At least we are a race of snobs with some intelligence, Lysandra. You have been given a sign, a True Mission by the goddess, and you are too wrapped up in your own ignorance and disgusting self-pity to see it.'

'A Mission? Do not be absurd. I was abandoned to the Earth-Shaker and left to this −' she gestured around her, 'this *cesspit*.'

Telemachus softened somewhat. 'You have a crisis in your faith, Priestess. It is no wonder, finding yourself in this place. But I, as an outsider and a priest, can see it so very clearly.'

Lysandra looked down and remained silent for a moment. When she spoke, her voice was low. 'I *have* feared she has turned her face from me.'

'I'm not surprised.' Telemachus placed his hand over hers and she did not pull away. He was struck, in that moment, by her youth: she was not yet out of her teens. 'But there is *purpose* in this. The goddess does *nothing* without design, Lysandra. Or do you think it is mere coincidence that Balbus travelled to Halicarnassus to seek me out? To see if I could help you. Odd behaviour for a trader of skins, is it not? Or perhaps it was because he was compelled by a higher power.'

'Why?' Lysandra frowned. 'I fail to see the purpose you speak of.'

'You were a Mission Priestess, Lysandra. Your Mission was chosen by your Order, not by the goddess. And thus it failed. I know how Balbus's men found you. The *only* survivor of shipwreck! And the goddess delivered you. Delivered you to the one place that the skills you learned in her honour could be put into practice. *That* is your Mission, Priestess of Sparta, chosen by the goddess herself. You have been trained from your seventh year to fight for her. She has, in her wisdom, afforded you the opportunity to do something no other of your order has ever done before.'

'I don't understand!' Lysandra's eyes entreated him to give her some meaning to her plight. And Telemachus had been paid well to deliver. It was, he considered, fortunate that the Spartans were amongst the most gullible of people.

'If you fight as you have been taught, you do Athene, your Sisterhood and your *polis* great honour, Lysandra. I cannot know her reasons, but I have read the signs of your situation clearer than you have. Your shipwreck, your being here, has the touch of the Immortals about it. You feel Athene has turned her face from you but it is just the opposite. *You* have spurned *her*, and this is why you feel as you do.'

'I am still a slave.' Lysandra shook her head.

'No,' Telemachus said. 'You are a gladiatrix, and a Spartan. I do not believe Athene would abandon one of her handmaidens to such a fate as this without design. Is it not the Spartan way to make good of hardship, to prove that to endure and win is better than capitulate and die? You have been put in this place to restore honour to your Order and your people, in the Spartan way.' He clenched his fist, not above a little drama. 'By the sword.'

Lysandra did not respond but Telemachus knew that he had got through to her. He stood abruptly. 'Make sacrifice and read the omens, if you need more confirmation. But look always to your heart. In there you will find the divine purpose.' She nodded and smiled at him, her eyes full of a light that had been absent when he had first seen her.

'Yes. Thank you for talking to me.'

'A pleasure to serve a fellow servant,' he said blithely. 'Enjoy your books, Lysandra. And do the goddess proud.'

She nodded. 'I will think carefully on your words, Telemachus, that much I promise.'

The priest left her to her thoughts, feeling a little guilty. He had been paid too well to counsel the girl to a realisation that she could, and perhaps should, have come to in her own time. But Spartans were not renowned for their diversity in thinking and therefore his advice, such as it was, would have rung true with no other save for a Spartan. The truth of it was that the girl had been the victim of unhappy circumstance. Fate was cruel and Lysandra was a mere victim. Yet, he felt he was correct in his tackling of the former priestess's concerns. She, like most of her kin, could fight. It was that skill, that instinct which would serve her best in the *ludus*. The money he had received would do well for the shrine, he told himself. But a nagging guilt at exploiting the girl's circumstances refused to leave him.

XV

The sun was warm on Lysandra's face as she stepped out of the infirmary. The very morning after her conversation with the Athenian priest, Quintus had given her leave to return to her training. This was, she knew, further evidence that Telemachus's words had been heavy with truth.

She had cursed herself for a fool after he had left her to her thoughts. How could she have been so blind? It was all so obvious after the Athenian had cut through the fog of her melancholy. She did indeed feel ashamed of herself for acting in such a pitiful manner, but that was past and there was no changing it. The future was a path not yet set and she now knew that the goddess had given her an opportunity to truly test herself and win honour for them both.

After a speedy visit to the bathhouse, Lysandra made her way to the kitchens to join the others for the morning meal. As she approached, the women around her fell silent until they considered her out of earshot; then they tittered and were probably making barbed comments about her. She felt her face flush, knowing that it was her own inept performance that afforded these inferiors licence to behave so.

111

But the mocking of Lysandra was not the main topic of conversation that morning. There was much excitement, as the new women were soon to take the Oath. They had, all of them, passed their tests and could now be considered gladiatrices proper – though the ultimate challenge would come on the sands, Lysandra knew.

Of course, the training routine had not ceased in the three days she had been absent and Lysandra found that the women had been split into smaller, more specialised groups after Balbus's impromptu contest. Instead of merely practising with sword and shield, the novices had been set to work with the various tools of the gladiatorial trade. The larger, bigger-boned barbarians were heavily armed, fighting in the Gallic style, whereas the slighter women were training as the *Thraex* – the Thracian – clad in only the *subligaculum* loincloths, their torsos bare. These fighters were armed with nothing other than a sword and small shield. Still others were working with trident and net, the *retiaria*.

Titus, Stick and Nastasen prowled amongst them, berating and shouting, demanding more skill and speed. In the midst of one such haranguing, Stick noticed Lysandra standing apart, taking in the scene. He approached, shaking his head, his expression disgusted.

'Well, if it isn't my favourite invalid,' he said. 'Feeling better after our little break, are we?' His brown, calloused knuckles rapped her on the forehead. 'Still working, is it?'

Lysandra ignored the jibe. 'What am I to train with?'

'After your performance, you should train with Greta and the scrubs. I'm not sure you're going to be any use to this *ludus*, Greek.'

Lysandra glared at him. 'If you are going to refer to me in that manner, please address me as *Hellene*, for that is my nation, or *Spartan*. That is what I am,' she said imperiously.

112

'I don't give a shit,' Stick responded. He looked her up and down. 'You're a tall streak, but there's no meat on your bones. I reckon you won't be able to handle the heavy gear.' He jerked his thumb at the women fighting as *secutorixes*.

'That is absurd,' she retorted. 'I am well used to long hours in armour heavier than that.' It was true; the *secutorix* kit afforded the women more protection than most, but the panoply covered only the arms and legs. There was nothing to protect the torso; this would, after all, defeat the object of the games, which was to slake the mob's thirst for blood.

Stick jabbed her in the stomach with the vine staff, just hard enough to make her step back. 'I was thinking aloud, not asking you for your views on the subject, slave. If you want a beating to put you back in the infirmary, just carry on giving me your opinion.'

Lysandra glowered at the insolent little savage, but remained silent, refusing to give him an excuse to hit her.

'*Thraex*, I think,' Stick said after a moment's more consideration. 'You're fast, Spartan, but I think you are not yet ready to train as the *dimachaera*: that is for proven fighters, and that time in Halicarnassus you were merely lucky.' He gave her his toothiest grin. 'So let's get you into a *subligaculum* and see those little titties jiggle.'

'I am not ashamed of my body,' Lysandra sneered. 'I find it quite pitiable that you seek your sordid self-gratification in such a manner.'

Stick's eyes bulged and he raised the vine staff, swinging it across towards her shoulder. Lysandra reacted on instinct, stepping to one side and intercepted his forearm with her own. She twisted her wrist and gripped, pulling his arm down, dragging him towards her. 'There is no need for that, Stick,' she said, her voice calm. She released him and stepped away. Lysandra could see a range of emotions flicker across the trainer's face as he decided whether he was going to take issue with her insubordination. He glanced around but satisfied himself that none had seen their exchange.

'Just get into a *subligaculum*, and get to work with the others,' he grunted.

'Certainly.' She smiled slightly and stalked off, feeling rather pleased with herself.

Stick put Lysandra to work with Thebe, the Hellene girl who had performed first in Balbus's recent trials. Much shorter than the Spartan, she was slightly built, but the months of training in the *ludus* had hardened her body and the evidence of her strength was etched on her naked torso.

'Just take it slowly at first,' Stick instructed Lysandra. 'Get used to the *parmula*.' He referred to the small buckler that offered a Thracian gladiatrix her only protection. 'The important thing is not to wave it about. It's not a fan. Keep it close to your body and deflect attacks – don't try to swat them out of the way.' Stick pantomimed waving his arm away from his body. 'You see. If you do, you leave yourself wide open and you'll get skewered.'

Lysandra nodded and turned her attention to the somewhat diminutive Thebe. She stretched her neck from left to right and spun her wooden sword twice in her hand, making it hiss as it cut the air. Stick shouted at her for showing off and ordered them to be about their work.

Thebe advanced confidently, her expression leaving Lysandra in no doubt that she was being held in contempt. After all, Thebe had won her bout whilst she herself had been dispatched with ease by Hildreth. That, she thought to herself, was the way of the lesser Hellenes – they were all so damned arrogant.

As instructed, Thebe struck out lightly with her *rudis*, letting Lysandra become accustomed to the small, Thracian shield. Stick was quite correct: the *parmula* would take some getting used to. It felt extremely odd, and the natural instinct was to fend off attacks long before they came into range. However, Lysandra felt indeed fortunate that she had been trained to ignore instinct and observe the disciplines of combat.

After a few exploratory exchanges, she nodded at Thebe to pick up the pace. The slight Hellene responded, changing her angles of attack and breaking up their rhythm. It came to Lysandra as they sparred that her *pankration* skills could be applied to wielding the *parmula*. If she treated it as an extension of her hand, rather than a shield proper, then she could block and parry as she would in unarmed combat.

'Come at me,' Lysandra encouraged her smaller opponent. 'At full speed.'

Thebe stepped back, however, and lowered her guard. She turned to Stick. 'I don't think she's ready for this. She could get hurt. Stick, you saw how she fought the other day. She is the only one yet who has ended up in the infirmary.'

Lysandra fumed. If Thebe thought that a few months of training could eclipse a lifetime's worth, then she was sorely mistaken. She was about to explain matters to the girl but Stick spoke to Thebe first.

'Just let her have it,' he suggested.

Thebe shrugged and raised her guard once again. For a moment she was still; then she attacked. Lysandra did not step back as the Hellene girl moved in. Rather she twisted her hips and her feet followed, causing her body to angle away from Thebe's sword. The *parmula* guided the weapon away from Lysandra and she struck home with her own sword, the tip stabbing her opponent painfully on the side of the neck. Thebe dropped to the floor, clutching her hurt.

Lysandra turned to Stick, her eyes alight, her nostrils flared slightly. 'First rule,' she quoted Nastasen. 'You get an instant kill on the red. Always remember, go for the red first, because if you don't your opponent will.'

'I'd call it luck,' Stick said dourly. 'Let's see it again.'

This time, Thebe was more cautious, now aware that perhaps she had underestimated her adversary. She feinted, shuffling in and out, seeking an angle of attack. Lysandra merely watched, conserving her energy, her own eyes probing for weaknesses. Thebe thrust out with her sword but again Lysandra pivoted, bringing her blade down sharply on the other girl's wrist. Thebe cried out in pain, the *rudis* falling from her grasp. With a real weapon, Thebe's hand would have been severed. Lysandra followed up her move by ramming her own sword into her foe's stomach, doubling her over. Softly she placed the wooden edge to the back of the gasping Thebe's neck.

'In the blue you get a cripple,' she referenced Nastasen again. 'Second rule. Go for the cripple before the slow kill. Remember, a slow kill might have enough left in her and kill you before she dies. With a cripple, you know you've got her.' She paused and glanced down at Thebe who had sunk to her knees, the wind knocked out of her. 'As you just saw.'

Stick shook his head. 'Thebe, can you continue?'

Thebe shook her head, tears streaming down her face as her lungs tried to fill with air. She held up her arm, to reveal an ugly swelling on her wrist. Stick's expression became disgusted.

'Broken!' he exploded. 'Damn you!'

Lysandra shrugged. 'It appears that my luck, as you call it, has held out. It would also appear that I am no longer the only one to be sent to the infirmary.' She felt a sense of vindication. Thebe had learned that it could be painful to question a Spartan priestess's ability to fight. She had brought her injury upon herself with her boastful words and Lysandra deemed that she should consider herself lucky it was only a broken wrist she had suffered. Insolence was something she was no longer prepared to tolerate. 'Perhaps

I should train with a more experienced fighter,' she suggested contemptuously.

'Like Hildreth?' Stick shot back. 'You think you can put *her* down?'

'I will put down who ever I am matched against, Stick. Have no fear of that.' She held his gaze, realising that his statement had been designed to test her. By threatening her with a bout against the imposing German, he was gauging if her confidence had truly been restored, for her eyes would give her away if there were any doubt behind them. 'Well?' she said after moment's silence.

Stick looked away, and spat on the ground. 'No, I don't think so. Listen to me. You'll train with the novices, but I warn you. Any more of this,' he indicated Thebe who was now on her feet, 'and I'll have you crucified. You've proven your point.'

'Very well.' Lysandra moved away to join the main throng of women, confident that she would impress upon the novices just who was the superior in the *ludus*.

Lysandra worked herself hard, revelling in her newly discovered resolve. Her opponents were, of course, mediocre, but she could only fight who was put before her. It was all training, she told herself, and substandard opposition allowed her to try out and perfect techniques that could later be used against more competent opposition.

By the day's end, she had left many of the novices sporting bruised bodies and injured pride. This first day had done much to earn her the respect she deserved, and she determined that the proving would go on until she was satisfied.

'You trained well today. *Really* well,' Thebe commented as the Hellene contingent ate their evening meal. The smaller girl was from Corinth and, though that was some distance from Sparta, she was a Peloponnesian and that gave them a vague kinship.

Thebe had made an effort to find her at the close of the days training, and invite her to share a meal; as it was, Lysandra was pleased to accept. Thebe held up her bandaged wrist ruefully. 'Stick was wrong, though. It's not broken, just bruised. And wounding me seems to be the tonic you needed,' she added with a smile. 'You've come out of your shell.'

Lysandra considered apologising for the injury, but decided against it. Better to leave the impression that she was implacable. 'Yes,' she agreed. 'I have found that I have adjusted to life here. It is not the Spartan way to fail at a task. I had felt hard done by to be here, but we must accept the will of the goddess.'

'I'm coming around to that way of thinking,' Thebe agreed. 'You know, that bastard Titus is right. At the end of the day, this is a better life than most have.'

'Too right,' another novice cut in; Lysandra knew her as Danae, an Athenian. 'I thought at first this would be the end of me. I mean, *slavery*!' she laughed aloud. 'Can you imagine it? But I'll tell you this: I'm more free here than ever I was in Athens.'

'How can that be so?' Lysandra arched a quizzical eyebrow.

Danae chewed thoughtfully before responding. 'It's hard for a Spartan to understand,' she offered. 'I know that Spartan girls are allowed to walk the streets unescorted, that they own property, and have a voice in affairs.'

'Of course,' Lysandra said. 'That is only right and proper.'

'It is not so in the rest of Hellas.' Danae shook her head. 'I was married when I came of age and my life consisted of the home and pleasing my husband. That was it. It was rare to see Athens. That is a conundrum, is it not?' she added thoughtfully. 'We Athenians live in the most beautiful city in the world, yet half its people are rarely allowed out to enjoy it.'

'So how do you come to be here?' Lysandra wanted to know.

'My husband was many years older than I. I was married off to him at the age of twelve in exchange for a dowry – which one could say is a form of slavery in itself. We women are bought and sold for money even in life outside the *ludus*.' She paused and her expression became melancholy. 'Things went well enough at first, but soon he became intolerable.' She held up her cup. 'Wine was his master. When he was drunk, he would beat me and do unspeakable things.

'I bore it from my twelfth year to my eighteenth, but some things are unendurable. He came after a night of dicing and drinking – I think he had lost a purseful of money – and started on me. I fought back for the first time and he fell. Smashed his head open.' She snapped her fingers. 'I was convicted of murder and sent to the blocks. One of Balbus's agents liked the look of me, and here I am,' she finished.

'Surely you cannot have been convicted at trial for that,' Lysandra said. 'You acted in self-defence.'

'Trial?' Danae looked about at the other women's knowing faces. 'Where did you get the idea that women are entitled to trial, Lysandra? We have no rights, no say.'

'It's true,' Thebe agreed. 'This place offers a woman freedom outside of what she can get in normal life. Men run this world, Lysandra, but this *ludus* exists outside of that. We may be slaves to Balbus, but we do own our lives here. I am coming to understand that now. They might call us slaves but we are free in our hearts. That is what Titus meant behind all his bluster and his threats.'

'I'd like a piece of him,' another woman cut in. 'And you know what piece I mean.'

Thebe turned, astonished. 'Titus!' she exclaimed, laughter in her eyes. 'Penelope, that's disgusting. He's so… old.'

Penelope, a chunky fisher girl from one of the Aegean islands shrugged. 'I'm drying up in here,' she complained.

Lysandra flushed, her embarrassment plain on her pale features. This was certainly not a fit topic for discussion. She was about to turn the conversation to another area but Thebe spoke first.

'But that Catuvolcos.' Thebe sighed. 'Now *he* looks like he could really go at it.' She made an obscene gesture. 'That big chest and those muscular arms. And I reckon there's a cornucopia of joy under his *subligaculum*. A shame he only has eyes for Lysandra though.' She nudged Danae's knee under the table with her own.

'I am sure you are mistaken.' Lysandra was scandalised at this kind of talk. 'He took a professional interest in my skills.'

'He's taken an interest in sheathing his sword in a Spartan scabbard,' Danae said, laughing. She put on a high falsetto voice. 'Lysandra, Lysandra, I love you. Oh, Lysandra…' Danae moved her bottom on the bench seat, thrusting it back and forth. 'Ohhh, you are so wonderful, Lysandra, you are so good!'

If Lysandra had flushed before, she was scarlet now. This banter was outrageous. The women at the table fell about themselves laughing, sparing her further taunting. She did not feel anger at the jibes, for they were plainly made in good humour and without malice, but they did underscore the differences between herself and this uncouth band.

They finished their meal in light-hearted spirits and Lysandra had to admit to herself that, whilst she maintained a certain aloofness, she was pleased that she had allowed them to include her in their group. Certainly, these crass, ill-educated souls could only benefit from being in her company. It was not enough that she show them her prowess in fighting; she must also be pre-eminent in all other matters. Teaching them some decent, Spartan manners would certainly be beneficial she decided.

As she bade them good evening to return to her cell, she wondered where they had got the absurd notion that Catuvolcos had some sort of interest in her outside that of her training. She had had advances from men before, but had always shunned them. It was forbidden for a Spartan priestess to engage in congress with a man.

Lysandra stripped off her tunic and lay on her cot, staring into the blackness. Obscured by the heavy door, she could hear the now familiar sounds of the *ludus* preparing for slumber: doors slammed shut; women called endearments to each other before sleeping; the guttural male voices of guards and trainers hurried them to their cells. She found herself straining to hear Catuvolcos's lilting accent among them.

She could not help but bring the Gaul's face to mind. He was, in his barbaric way, handsome. And, as Thebe had pointed out, very muscular. The way a man should be. Lysandra felt a warmth in her stomach as she thought of him then. Self consciously, she ran a hand over her breasts, trying to imagine it was Catuvolcos touching her. Her nipples hardened at her caress and her skin became hot, tingling with a delicious sensation. Her hand crept guiltily to between her thighs and she began to stroke herself, her mind swimming with images of flesh on flesh. She moaned softly in the dark, biting her lip lest anyone hear her at this iniquitous self-pleasuring. She let her mind drift, swimming in images of desire. But as her passion heightened it was not Catuvolcos she saw. Her climax burst through her with powerful suddenness at this realisation, the chains of her well-learned restraint breaking as wave upon wave of joy flooded through her.

She lay still, her heart pounding. As the glow of her orgasm faded, the image in her mind did not. As she drifted into sleep, the face behind her eyes was Eirianwen's.

XVI

'Well, well, well,' Sorina grunted as she and Eirianwen pulled themselves up on the chin bar.

'What?' The Briton was trying to blow a sweat-slicked strand of hair from her mouth.

'The Spartan has woken up.' Sorina released her grip and dropped to the ground, flexing her wrists and fingers. 'Look over at the novices.'

'You've made me lose count,' Eirianwen complained, she too letting go. She tilted her head, her eyes following the Amazon's gaze. Through the throng she picked out the raven-haired Lysandra sparring with a German novice. Her moves were assured, economical and, Eirianwen noticed, dangerously quick. 'She's toying with her,' she murmured.

'Aye.' Sorina nodded. 'That she is.' She winced as Lysandra felled her opponent with a vicious strike to the stomach. 'See that? She fights like a Roman. Rarely swings the blade, stab, stab, always stabbing.'

Eirianwen shrugged. 'It takes discipline but lacks power. I couldn't do it. The sword is an art, not…' She looked at Sorina, gesturing.

122

'Science?' the Amazon finished for her in Latin.

'Yes.' Eirianwen smiled. 'She is good, but she will never understand the spirit of combat. A Roman and Greek trait.'

'Having a breather, girls?' Catuvolcos's voice cut through their conversation.

Sorina glanced at him. 'We were just admiring Balbus's pet Spartan.' She jerked her chin as Lysandra began to assail another German.

'Lysandra?' Catuvolcos turned too fast, craning his neck to see across the crowded training area. He flushed when he turned back, noticing the arch gaze of both women upon him. 'I am glad to see she is on her feet,' he muttered.

'Your concern is too keen,' Eirianwen said. 'Your eyes betray you.'

Catuvolcos cleared his throat. 'I don't like to see a good fighter finished by the head wound. It would have been a waste.'

Eirianwen gave him a meaningful look.

'Shouldn't you two be working?' The big Gaul began to bluster. 'There is a spectacle coming soon,' he added. 'Rather sweat now than bleed later! Come, to the swords with you!'

Sorina moved off, but Eirianwen regarded Catuvolcos, suddenly angered for reasons she could not understand. 'You should stay away from her!' she snapped, and followed Sorina.

They made their way to the armoury, Sorina expressing a desire to fight as the heavily armed *secutorix*. To complement her, Eirianwen chose the net and trident of the *retiaria* as the two styles were often pitted against each other.

'What do you think?' Sorina asked as the Briton assisted her with her armour.

Eirianwen snorted. 'He's pining for Lysandra,' she said. 'It's written all over his face.'

'That's typical of men,' Sorina spat. 'They're always thinking with their pricks.'

123

'I think it might be a little deeper than that as far as he's concerned,' Eirianwen muttered.

'I doubt it. All men are pigs. They only want one thing, and to get it they will run in circles. Once it's been attained, they revert back into swine. Besides,' she flexed her arms, testing the tightness of the leather protection Eirianwen had tied in place. 'The *lanista* will have his balls for breakfast if he tries anything with her. Catuvolcos knows the rules.'

'You've never had much time for men, Sorina.' Eirianwen put her hands on her hips, admiring her handiwork.

'Of course not. I am Chieftain of the Horse Clan. We take men only to replenish the tribe. Once their purpose is served, what use are they? I certainly wouldn't want one lying around *my* tent, farting and scratching himself all day long.'

Eirianwen retrieved a wooden trident and hefted it. 'There is more to men than scratching and farting,' she said, laughing. Sorina's mock dourness had broken her own fit of pique, she realised.

'Yes.' Sorina's voice was solemn, but her eyes sparkled with mirth. 'They think both actions are amusing and look for approval when they do it.'

Eirianwen shook her head. 'Come!' she said, waving the trident lightly at the older woman. 'Let us see if these are some pricks you *can* handle.'

Sorina grinned at the quip and picked up one of the heavy shileds. The two women moved away from the armoury and all banter between them ceased. Combat was not a game. The time for friendship was over. The Amazon raised her wooden sword, indicating she was ready, and Eirianwen moved in to the attack.

At the day's end, Titus and trainers called the novices together. As they assembled, Lysandra noted Catuvolcos watching her, but she looked away quickly, the jibes of her Hellene compatriots still fresh in her mind. The trainers had set up a small table behind which sat Eros, Balbus's catamite. The youth had a stylus in his hand.

Hildreth sat on the ground next to her. 'Hello, Lysandra. How are you today?' she ritualised. Lysandra grinned tightly at her, not knowing how Hildreth would act towards her now that they had fought.

'I am well, Hildreth. How are you?'

'I am very well. My Latin is well. How is your head?'

'Still on my shoulders, apparently,' Lysandra muttered.

'What?' Hildreth shouted.

'My head is well, thank you.'

'That is good,' Hildreth grinned, a little condescendingly for Lysandra's liking. 'You fought shit.'

Lysandra grimaced; of course Hildreth's Latin was learned by hearsay, but there was no need to resort to vulgarity. 'Yes, you are correct, I did.'

'Never mind,' the German punched her on the arm – too hard. 'We all have shit days.' Lysandra nodded, and turned away, rolling her eyes. She did not need to be reminded.

'Shut up, all of you!' Titus bawled. Instantly, all chatter ceased. Responses to orders, Lysandra noted, were now becoming second nature to the women.

'Penelope,' Lysandra heard Thebe whisper from somewhere behind her. 'It's your boyfriend. Look how handsome he is. And so mature.' There was some tittering, and Penelope's response was so obscene it boarded on the blasphemous.

'Your training is coming to an end,' Titus's harsh voice rang out. 'The *lanista* has secured a contract for this *ludus* to fight in the forthcoming games in Halicarnassus.' He paused, his hard eyes sweeping over the women. 'You are to perform as an under-event, a match against another school. That means you will not have to fight each other.'

Hildreth nudged Lysandra, her expression plainly confused.

'We are to fight for real,' Lysandra explained in a whisper. 'In the arena.' Hildreth's smile at this news was triumphant.

'Many of you are barbarians with unpronounceable names,' Titus went on. 'The mob doesn't like that. The world is Rome and you must have a name that is familiar to the people. Something they can cheer. You will choose a name that is suitable. If you cannot, one will be given to you.' The women got to their feet, an excited buzz of conversation rising amongst them.

'But first,' Titus shouted, causing them all to fall silent, 'there is one matter to be attended to.' He raised an arm towards the veteran's compound and, at his gesture, a procession of the top-tier fighters, headed by Lucius Balbus himself, made their way towards the assembled novices. Each person carried a torch, the flames bright orange in the night air. Smoke curled from the brands, oily and thick. Balbus stepped away from the procession to stand before the novices. Lysandra was embarrassed to find her neck craning to see if Eirianwen was amongst those women in the parade that had followed the *lanista*. She was, and Lysandra blushed when she met the Briton's eye. She was sure, however, that Eirianwen gave her what she read to be an encouraging smile.

'Novices!' Balbus's voice caused her to look away. The Roman was wearing a pure white toga of the finest quality. 'You have trained hard. When you came through my gates, you were but women. Now, through our skills and your own sweat, you have become something more. More even than most men can hope to be. You are strong. You are fast. You are deadly. I tell you this: in all the Empire, from misty Britannia to the desert sands of Arabia, there are no warriors more dangerous than those trained here. Some of you wore swords before you came to me; look now to your hearts and answer inside – are you not better than before? And those of you who were used to women's work, look now to your hearts and answer inside – would you return to that life?' The *lanista* paused, letting his words wash over the assembled women. Lysandra was impressed and found herself being caught up in the excitement of it all. Balbus certainly knew how to win a crowd.

'You will now become part of a sisterhood, a sisterhood forged in blood, stronger than iron. But this sacred thing demands an Oath. A terrible Oath that you must serve. Women of the *ludus*, will you serve this Oath?'

As one, the novices raised their hands, and cried out their acceptance. Even Hildreth had picked up the gist, Lysandra noted.

'Repeat, then, after me.' Balbus voice carried over them. 'I swear, by my gods, that I will fight with honour. That if it is my time to die, I will meet my death with the same courage and honour by which I live my life. That I will observe the Laws of my *ludus*, to suffer myself be whipped with rods, burned with fire or killed by steel if I disobey.'

The last intonations faded, and there was a heavy silence in the wake of the Oath, broken only by the crackling of the torches. 'Woman!' Balbus shattered the stillness. 'You are now Gladiatrix.' At this, the veterans began to cheer, and the cry was taken up by the newly made warriors. Lucius Balbus nodded to them and turned about, leading the veterans away with him.

Lysandra frowned, despite the women's enthusiasm. She wondered if the Oath was binding. Certainly, many of her fellows would not speak such a thing unless they were made to in these circumstances. As they began to line up to receive their fighting names, Lysandra recalled the conversation with Danae and the Hellene women. There was, she realised, a sense of belonging here for many of them, much as there was in the Temple of Athene.

The Oath was, as Balbus had said, terrible. Conversely, they were swearing to do what had already been ingrained. They already obeyed and had already been 'whipped with rods,' for transgression. She noted that the women seemed to walk taller now, carrying themselves with assurance and pride. Lysandra realised how adroit the *ludus* system was. If the Oath had been spoken at the beginning of their training, many would have feared it. As it was, with their new skills, the women would take it as a challenge. More, they would think it a code to live by, a source of spirit and honour within the cadre. She smiled to herself; it was probable that only she among them was intelligent enough to recognise these things.

Lysandra waited her turn in line, already decided on what name she would chose. Thebe, Danae and Penelope were in furious argument as to who would be Heraclea, after Heracles, the greatest of Hellene heroes. It took some time for the queue to shorten. Hildreth stood before Lysandra and she overheard Eros assign her the name Horatia, after an ancient Roman hero who had defended the Roman borders against the invading Eutruscans. Lysandra thought it ironic in the extreme that this name should be given to one who had been captured raiding Rome's extremities herself.

'Well?' Eros looked up as Lysandra stood before him.

'Leonidia,' Lysandra said instantly. It would be an honour to carry the name of the most famous Spartan king. She could not avoid the eyes of Catuvolcos who stood with the other trainers now. He smiled slightly at her and she blushed.

'Can't,' Stick cut in. 'We have a Leonidia. She's a veteran, fights as *secutorix.*'

'Oh.' Lysandra was crushed momentarily. 'Spartica, then.'

Titus threw back his head, and roared with laughter. 'I don't think the public would take to a fighter named after a man who led gladiators in revolt. It might offend their sensibilities.'

'I *am* from Sparta,' she argued. 'It's as good a name as any.'

'I haven't got all night,' Eros sighed, looking up at Titus.

Titus regarded her, eye to eye, and smiled suddenly. Lysandra was surprised at its warmth. 'You have it in you to be great.' He paused, coming to a decision. 'Achillia. It suits you.'

'Achillia,' Lysandra repeated, trying on the name as one would a new *chiton*. She was satisfied; the female form of Achilles, the greatest warrior of antiquity. 'Achillia,' she said again.

'Go on.' Titus jerked his head. 'Next!'

Lysandra walked away, feeling somehow different, as if something inside her had changed. She realised that, coupled with the Oath, gaining a name under which to fight had divorced her from her old life totally. It went beyond merely satisfying the public's demand; it was a psychological tool. It would be Lysandra who trained and lived in the *ludus*. But come the day of the fight, it would be Achillia who walked onto the sands of the arena.

XVII

The train included around twenty women from the *ludus*. As they were herded aboard the prison carts, Lysandra noted that the majority of this number had been taken from the novices. Evidently, Balbus wished to try out his new stock under the most testing of circumstances and would doubtless be hoping that the weaker ones were culled early.

The women were grouped together by rank and nationality. Lysandra found herself in one of the rearmost carts, along with Hellene women. As she settled onto the straw-covered floor, she saw Eirianwen making her way to the front carriage. The beautiful Silurian stopped and walked up to the Hellene cage.

'Good luck to you,' she said. The comment was made to the group, but her eyes did not leave Lysandra. She smiled in response, her heart beating wildly, full of guilt over her illicit fantasies involving the tribeswoman. Eirianwen's eyes lingered on her a moment longer and then she was gone, vanishing into the crowd of fighters.

'You've made a friend,' Danae commented as Lysandra settled back in the corner of the cart.

'We have spoken once or twice,' Lysandra acknowledged carefully. 'She is affable enough for a barbarian.'

'Dangerous too.' Danae affected a sagacious expression. 'An excellent fighter.'

Lysandra gave her a half grin. 'We are all dangerous fighters, Danae.'

Soon after, the carriage lurched and the caravan got under way. Conversation was sparse for a time, which pleased Lysandra. She had asked for and been given permission to carry her bucket of books with her on the journey to Halicarnassus. As the train wound its painfully slow way towards the city, Lysandra certainly had no desire to reacquaint herself with the featureless, sun-blasted Carian landscape, and so she entertained herself by reading Gaius Marius whilst the other women chatted amongst themselves. However, as the sun reached its zenith, the initial gossiping ceased.

'What's that you're reading?' Thebe wanted to know.

Lysandra grimaced, as she hated to be interrupted whilst she was studying. She bit down a waspish response to the intrusion and looked up. 'A manual of tactics,' she answered shortly.

Thebe wrinkled her nose. 'How dull. Why would you want to read that?'

Lysandra sighed and placed the scroll in her lap. 'At the temple, we were taught tactics as well as martial skills. Gaius Marius was a military genius and his book makes interesting reading.' Danae did not look convinced. 'I have Homer in here, if you would like to read that,' Lysandra offered.

'I don't read very well,' Danae said. 'You know, I did when I was a child, but my husband made me stop. He said reading was for *hetairai*.'

'That is absurd,' Lysandra snorted. 'Reading is not only for courtesans!'

'I can't read either,' offered Thebe. As she spoke, the other women nodded in agreement.

'I suppose if you have never read, books are unimportant.'

Lysandra turned her eyes back to her scroll. Despite her intention to raise the general level of education amongst the women, at this time she was more interested in reading for herself. There was a heavy silence in the cart, broken only by the groaning and creaking of the wood. She looked up once again, and saw all eyes upon her. She sighed. 'Do you want me to read to you?'

The women nodded.

'Well,' Lysandra said, 'this book details the structure and tactics of the Roman army from *contubernalis* to a legion entire.' Faces fell at this comment. 'But I suppose you would rather hear the *Iliad*,' she added. Again, every head nodded. She rolled Marius up for digestion at a later stage. Leaning back, she closed her eyes, as she knew the text by heart. '*Sing, O goddess, the anger of Achilles son of Peleus...*' she recited, her voice lifted in song.

For the rest of the journey, Lysandra narrated the great works to the women, deciding that oratory was perhaps the best way to introduce them to literature. It was not tiresome, as she enjoyed singing. A good voice was prized in the Temple of Athene and Lysandra reckoned hers to be of excellent quality. As she sang she offered silent thanks to the goddess for endowing her with so many gifts.

These tales helped the days pass quickly for the women but, as they drew closer to the city, Lysandra noted that there was less chatter amongst her companions, a tension and gloom falling upon them. The caravan halted some two miles from the walls of Halicarnassus and the guards began to pitch camp. As the sun was still high in the sky this seemed ridiculous in the extreme, a fact Lysandra pointed out to the Macedonian guardsman she recognised.

The guard paused as he walked past her cage, and grinned at her. 'Have you any idea of the hubbub the arrival of a gladiatorial *famillia* causes?' he asked her.

'Obviously not.' Lysandra gave him her most imperious stare. It was demeaning to seek knowledge from such an imbecile.

'Well…' The Macedonian stooped and plucked a blade of grass to chew on. Lysandra thought it befitting as it gave him the appearance of a hayseed, which all Macedonians were. 'It's mad,' he said after some time.

'Your powers of description are epic,' Lysandra sneered.

Irony was above the man. 'What I mean is *the people* go mad. It's like the Emperor himself has arrived. Causes all sorts of traffic chaos, as you can imagine. People crowding round the carriages, nothing can move for hours. You're new, you've never seen the furore – they absolutely love gladiators. And gladiatrices,' he added quickly. 'So we go in at night.'

'I see.' If that was the case, then it was wise to avoid attracting undue attention. There was nothing worse than people acting in a disorderly manner.

'We cover the carriages in cloth, too, just to be on the safe side.'

'How considerate.'

'See you then, Lysandra.' The man smiled, and she noticed with distaste that he had a gap in his front teeth. He ambled away, still chewing his stalk of grass.

Lysandra relayed the reason for their journey's interruption to the other women. She told them the tale of Orion the Hunter to while away the time, and soon the day dimmed to twilight. With little else to do, the women laid out their blankets, seeking to catch a few hours' sleep. Resting when the carts were on the move would be impossible.

'Thank you for the stories,' Thebe said as she lay down.

'It was nothing.' Lysandra sounded slightly lofty, even to herself.

'It kept our minds busy, at least. We are all scared, aren't we? Of the arena. Of what might happen.'

'Spartans fear nothing,' Lysandra intoned, her response instinctive.

Thebe snorted derisively. 'Horse dung. You know, Lysandra, none of us believes this impassive act you put on. You're like us and we are all scared.'

Lysandra sat up, coming to a decision. These women were not as she. Despite what they thought, they needed leadership and were incredibly fortunate that she was among them. Again, she realised the truth of Telemachus's words; indeed, there was a divine purpose to her being here. 'Gather round,' she said.

The Hellene women formed a circle, cross-legged. They could hear the soft sounds of the guards' chatter, the crack of the fires lit around the caravan and, somewhere, the mournful sound of a flute being played. In the dim twilight, Lysandra fancied that this must be akin to the eve of the Battle of Thermopylae, when Leonidas had gathered his warriors about him.

'Listen to me,' she said. 'Fear is a thought, not a feeling. It exists only up here.' She tapped her head. 'Forget fear. It stiffens the limbs and numbs the sinews, and if it takes a hold of you, all that you have learned in the *ludus* will be for naught. You all know that I was a priestess, trained since youth to fight.' She paused, looking around the dim, frightened faces, holding each gaze for a few moments. 'I can tell you this. I have seen you train, and all of you could hold your own in the Temple of Athene.' This was a blatant falsehood but Lysandra considered it a necessary one. These words had the desired effect and she felt a measurable lapse in the tension around her.

'My experience tells me that the training we have received from Stick, Catuvolcos and yes, even Nastasen, is excellent. It has been hard and gruelling, and often cruel. But this is necessary. To forge the superior fighter from flesh, flesh needs to be beaten hard. Your training has made your responses natural to you. Remember: fighting, from single combat to the clash of mighty armies, is not an art. It is a science. It has its theorems, its truths, its applications. In the end, superior tactics will always win out against brute force. Your lessons, well learned, will keep you all alive and send your foes to Hades.'

'Do you really think so, Lysandra?' Penelope, the fisher girl, whispered.

'I know it to be true,' Lysandra said softly, nodding her head, once again meeting the eyes of the women around her.

'It is the arena, Lysandra,' Danae stated grimly. 'The people we are to fight are unknown to us. We may be killed.'

'We may,' Lysandra agreed. 'But only if it is our time and nothing can alter that. But certainly, we shall not fail because we were afraid,' she added scornfully. 'We will fall only if the gods have marked us to die, and then we shall fall in their honour. But I do not believe that will be so. I believe we will cut down our enemies like wheat before the scythe.' She fell quiet, letting her words sink in, allowing the women to mull over what she had imparted to them. 'Sleep now,' she ordered. 'And think not of what the future will bring. Trust in the goddess.'

Lysandra broke the circle and moved back to her corner, throwing the blanket over herself. One by one, the others lay down, seemingly calmed by her words. She smiled slightly as sleep crept over her; if there was any doubt as to who was pre-eminent among them, it had now been dispelled. Come what may, she knew that they would now regard her as leader and that, soon, others would too.

It was right that this should be so.

They entered the city quietly, the caravan winding its way through the narrow streets of Halicarnassus. The night air had turned chill and not a few of the women, roused into wakefulness by the movement of the carts, shivered quietly. Time crawled by slowly in the netherworld between dusk and dawn, but eventually the train reached the great arena and, with almost military precision, the women were ensconced in purpose-built gaols, which were situated around and beneath the arena complex. The cells were large and, the women were surprised to discover, comfortable. Certainly the accommodation was preferable to the tiny cells they slept in at the *ludus*. Exhausted by the uncomfortable journey, they fell into slumber. A few of Lysandra's compatriots stayed awake, chatting into the night, before she admonished them to sleep. It would, she told them, be a testing day to come.

Nastasen and Stick roused them much later than was usual, and hustled them into a large courtyard; they were ordered to strip their dirty tunics and were sluiced down with water. The morning was already warm and the cold water served to revive and invigorate.

'Not as good as a bath,' Nastasen laughed. 'But we have to have you looking your best for the parade.'

'Parade?' Lysandra glanced at Danae, who shrugged.

'Not that you'll be leaving for some time yet. Obviously, the people have come to see the male fighters. You women will walk behind them.' Lysandra caught sight of Sorina, who spat on the ground at these words. Nastasen began to walk down the line of women, thrusting clean clothing into their hands. 'One size fits all,' he said. 'We've even brought your sandals so your delicate little toes don't get stubbed.' The Nubian gave Lysandra a greenish tunic which she held up critically.

'Do you have a red one?' she asked.

Nastasen stopped in his tracks and turned back. 'Why?' he said after some time, his dark eyes glittering.

'Spartans wear red, Nastasen.'

The trainer seemed to mull that over. 'Do they, now?' He jerked his chin, indicating that Lysandra toss the green tunic back to him. 'Fucking Spartans!' he muttered and continued doling out his supply of clothing, leaving Lysandra standing naked.

It took some time but, with Stick's aid, all the women were given new attire, save Lysandra who was left without. Though there was no shame in nakedness, she knew that this action had been taken to humiliate her and she felt it keenly.

'You see,' Nastasen swaggered past her, his voice loud. 'Our Spartan here didn't like my choice of tunic. That's too bad.' He turned and leered at her. 'Still, I will not be called unreasonable.' This caused derisive laughter from all those women who were not in his direct line of sight. The enmity between trainer and fighter was well known amongst the *famillia*. 'So our Spartan will walk the streets naked. *Gymnos*,' he added in Hellenic. He stepped in closer to her. 'Unless you want to give me something to change my mind,' he whispered, his big hand reaching out to stoke her thigh. His nostrils flared as Lysandra flinched at his touch and he moved his hand upward.

'Do not.' Lysandra's voice was cold.

'I think you might like it,' Nastasen grunted, stroking her sparse pubic hair beneath his fingers.

It was too much. Lysandra felt her temper snap, and she lunged forward, her forehead smashing into the trainer's face, feeling the satisfying crunch of bone as his nose shattered. Nastasen bellowed in pain and staggered back clutching his face, blood pouring from between his fingers. The women cheered enthusiastically at this rebellion.

'I'll *kill* you!' the Nubian hissed, drawing his vine staff. Lysandra moved from her rank, finding herself eager for the confrontation. Nastasen screamed and lunged at her, the vine staff hissing through the air. Lysandra stepped back, avoiding the wild swings, and countered by lashing out with a kick, catching the rage-blinded trainer in the midriff. But the strike did not slow the powerful warrior. In a rush he was on top of her, his great weight bearing her to the ground, the vine staff at her throat. 'Now!' he screamed, spittle foaming on his lips.

Lysandra could not move, Nastasen had her pinned, immobile. She tried to thrust her hips up to dislodge him, but his weight was too great. Blood pounded in her ears and white sparks began to burst in front of her eyes.

Suddenly, his hands left her and she rolled away, retching and choking. She looked about, seeking the trainer, and saw that he too had fallen to the ground, holding the side of his face. Catuvolcos was there, his own vine staff in his hand. Somewhere she could hear Stick screaming for the guards.

'Leave her be!' Catuvolcos shouted, stepping between her and the Nubian. Nastasen surged to his feet and was about to advance on his fellow trainer. The prison guards had come running and, though none could match either Catuvolcos or Nastasen in size and strength, they were of sufficient numbers to drag the two apart.

Stick was furious, hopping from foot to foot. 'What do you think you are doing!' He was beside himself. 'You stupid bastard!' This he levelled at Nastasen. Still held by the guards, the Nubian roared and tried to break free. That was enough for Stick. 'Bind him!' he ordered the guards. There was no way to subdue the huge warrior, save for the most basic: the guards began to rain blows down on their captive, knocking the fight from him before hurling him to the ground and slapping manacles into place.

Catuvolcos broke free of his own captors and rushed to Lysandra's side. Gently, he lifted her head from the ground, cradling it as softly as he would a child's. 'Are you all right?' he said, his green eyes full of concern.

'I just wanted a red tunic,' Lysandra croaked, gingerly rubbing her throat.

'Get away from her!' Stick aimed a kick at Catuvolcos's rump. The Gaul turned angrily but Stick held up his hand. 'Don't! We have enough troubles now.' At this he began screaming at the guards to get both Nastasen and the women into cells.

'I am uninjured,' Lysandra said. 'Really, Catuvolcos, I am well.' Catuvolcos smiled gently at her, and helped her to her feet. When they stood, he did not let her go, seemingly reluctant to break the contact of her skin on his own. 'Thank you,' she said simply.

Stick thrust them apart. 'What the fuck is this?' Catuvolcos began to speak, but the Stick cut him off. 'No, I don't want to hear it. Get out of here, Catuvolcos! I mean it.' The Gaul glowered at him but moved off. 'And you…' Stick turned to Lysandra, placing his vine staff on her chest. 'You've caused enough trouble. Come with me!'

Lucius Balbus steepled his fingers and regarded the naked Spartan standing before him. Stick had taken the precaution of having her arms and legs manacled and she appeared very much the defiant warrior captured.

'She head-butted Nastasen,' Stick said. 'She's a troublemaker, Balbus, and well you know it. This sort of defiance can spread and, before you know it, we'll have a riot on our hands.'

Balbus motioned Stick to silence. 'Why?' he asked her directly.

'He was trying to touch me. In my private place. We are not whores, *lanista*, and I resented his familiarity.'

'One of the guards says that you refused to wear clothing offered you, Lysandra. Is that not so?'

'It is so,' she agreed. 'I asked Nastasen if I could wear a red tunic. I did not think that this would be an issue. It is the colour of Sparta.'

Balbus leant back in his chair, looking up at the ceiling. It was a trifling matter, but Titus had told him of the Nubian's dislike for Lysandra. A simple request that should have had no consequence had now escalated into a brawl between trainer and gladiatrix. Proud Lysandra and stupid Nastasen. By rights, he should have the girl crucified before the entire *famillia* for her insubordination.

Should, but could not. She had just cost him twenty thousand denarii, and he could not simply nail that investment to a chunk of wood to watch it wither and die. Aside from which, Falco's promotion had billed her on the under card as Achillia of Sparta and Lysandra was quite correct: everyone knew that Spartan warriors wore red. Balbus's head throbbed. He could not even punish her, as she was to fight on the morrow and would certainly be killed if fresh lash wounds hampered her. He toyed with the idea of pulling her from the contest and replacing her with another but quickly dismissed it. He *had* to see if the girl was worth his indulgence.

He turned his gaze to Lysandra once again. 'You will fight tomorrow,' he told her. 'On return to the *ludus*, you will be given twenty lashes for your disobedience. Guards!' Two of his men came trotting at his call. 'Take her to her cell!' he ordered. 'And get her a red tunic!'

Stick sat down opposite the *lanista*. 'I don't know what to do about her,' he said when Lysandra had been led away. 'I think Nastasen was asking for it, though. He detests her.'

'And you do not? You are free with the staff when it comes to her. And groping the women is one of your prime humiliation techniques.'

'I detest everyone, you know that. As for the other, that only happens at the beginning, to let them know they are property.'

Balbus inclined his head in acquiescence. 'And Nastasen?'

'I had him put in a cell to cool down.' Stick shrugged. 'He took a bit of a kicking but I think it's his pride that will be more bruised. It's Catuvolcos that is my concern.'

'How so?'

'He has a thing for Lysandra. I think he cares for her.' This last was said with distaste.

Balbus sighed heavily. Indeed Lysandra was close to becoming more trouble than she was worth. 'Has he been with her?'

Stick's cackle was lewd. 'I doubt it,' he said. 'I don't think she has anything to get into, if you know what I mean. Might as well try to prod a statue. But the way Catuvolcos acts towards her I can tell he's carrying a torch. We don't need that, *lanista*. There will be more trouble between him and Nastasen over her and next time I might not be around to stop it.'

'Stick,' Balbus said heavily, 'these are problems I don't need the day before a spectacle.'

'Maybe we *should* put her on the blocks.'

Irritated, Balbus waved this away. 'What's done is done. She stays for now, Stick, but the punishment stands. I want you to keep an eye on Catuvolcos, however. He's too soft on the women as it is, and if he's getting sweet on one of my possessions it'll be him that goes to the blocks.'

It was an artificial freedom, but it was freedom nevertheless. For the first time since her capture Lysandra looked upon the world without confines. There were guards, to be sure, but no walls enclosed her and it was liberating to see as far as her eyes would let her.

The Macedonian guard had told her that the arrival of a *famillia* caused a furore but she had been unprepared for the public hysteria that accompanied their parade through the city. The *editor* of the games had hired several troupes which, though not unprecedented, was certainly a rarity. As such, the interest aroused was spectacular.

The day had become blistering hot, but even the scorching eye of Helios had not deterred the people from thronging the streets to catch a glimpse of their favourites. Thousands of citizens lined the route of the parade, pitching and roaring against the thin dam of legionaries who had been assigned to crowd control by Halicarnassus's urban praetor. Still, despite the throngs, Lysandra was able to catch small glimpses of the city. To her eye, Halicarnassus had a jumbled look to it, the original architecture of the Carians improved upon by Hellene expatriates, and this in its turn ruined by inferior Roman styling. The great Mausoleum, named for the ancient Carian King, Mausolos, was the city's centrepiece and a beautiful building, to be sure. Yet it looked sadly out of place amidst the muddled array of architectural styles. It was, she thought, a place at odds with itself.

Lysandra knew that the women fighters commanded nowhere near the interest that the men aroused, but it did not seem to be so as she marched with the others. Each step of the way, she was deafened by shouts of both encouragement and derision as the crowd saw the fighters they had wagered on – or against. Like the others, she carried a placard bearing her name, and her arena tally – one victory. Thus, the devotees had a name for a face, and they gave voice to their raw feelings. As well as this, Lysandra heard many marriage proposals on her walk and countless other more intimate suggestions.

She was not the only one to be subject to such interest. At the front of their column, Eirianwen was hailed as a goddess. It was not surprising, Lysandra thought. Certainly, the Silurian would have aroused envy in Helen of Sparta herself. There were calls for Sorina as well: many times the *victrix*, she had her own solid core of devotees. It was exhausting, but exhilarating. The adulation of so many people was a heady wine, so much so that Lysandra barely reflected on her confrontation with Nastasen. She would bear her punishment and try to put the incident behind her.

The parade ended at the great arena where the traditional pre-games feast for the competitors would be held. The custom was ancient, affording the fighters a last sip of life's pleasures before the inevitability of combat. Lysandra thought it ironic that this pleasure was to be taken on the very sands that would taste the blood of many of the revellers. Yet, the *editor*, Aeschylus, had spared no expense and the fare laid out was lavish. Trestles had been arrayed in neat rows, almost groaning with the weight of food and wine. Fruits and sweetmeats, many of which Lysandra could not identify, were in abundance and the air was heavy with the delicious tang of cooking meat. Barrel upon barrel of wine and other alcoholic drinks were also in evidence and it was to these that most of the fighters headed.

Lysandra was amazed to see that the sponsor had even gone to the expense of providing musicians. Flute girls wound their way through the tables and though their tunes were rarely in harmony, the shrill discord somehow seemed to suit the revels. Much thought had also gone into security. Each school had a clearly marked area to keep any over-eager or over-liquored competitors from settling their arranged disputes before the day of competition. Though segregated, the male gladiators were also present, a fact that delighted Penelope.

The Hellene women had found a free table and had gathered together as was now their custom.

'I'm telling you,' Penelope enthused, chewing on a chicken leg. 'It's been my bleeding time for days. I'm going to get some action tonight if it kills me. No risk fun.'

'It might kill you,' Danae commented. 'You know it's forbidden.' The Athenian wrinkled her nose as she bit into a stuffed dormouse, which, they had been told by one of the Italian girls, was a popular Roman delicacy.

'I don't care.' Penelope shrugged. 'Just because most of you are happy with a licking, doesn't mean it's satisfying me. You've been snacking for months. I want the whole meal – meat and vegetables.' The women fell about laughing and Lysandra found that this last comment brought a slight smile to her face.

'More wine?' Thebe reached for a carafe. Lysandra's hand snaked out, and slapped her away. Thebe flushed angrily.

'Do not be foolish, Thebe,' Lysandra admonished.

The Corinthian gestured to Eirianwen and her coterie, who were indulging in the foul-tasting beer that they craved. 'They're drinking and we should too.'

'They are barbarians!' Lysandra snapped haughtily. '*We* are Hellene. It is enough to take wine in small quantities, with water, especially tonight. I would not see you with a sword in your guts because your head was heavy with wine.' She felt slightly hypocritical saying this, as it was well known that she had been carried insensible from the gathering at the *ludus*. None saw fit to bring that up, however.

At the end of their repast, Lysandra excused herself and made her way to Eirianwen's table. She nodded at Sorina, who regarded her coldly as she sat. For her part, Eirianwen's eyes were somewhat glazed from imbibing her vile liquor.

'Lysandra.' She grinned. 'It is good to see you!' Her enthusiastic embrace caused Lysandra to stiffen a little. She was unused to affection and the barbarian habit of constantly touching one another was unsettling.

'I came to wish you luck.' Lysandra's eyes swept around the table. 'All of you.'

Sorina took her cup away from her lips. 'We don't need it,' she said shortly. 'We are not novices like you and your friends.'

That was typical of barbarians. Sorina could not be held accountable for her rudeness, she knew no better.

'Thank you, Lysandra.' This was from the Illyrian *dimachaera*, Teuta. She raised her foaming cup in a toast.

'You are all drinking,' Lysandra noted the obvious.

'Of course, do you want some beer?' Eirianwen smacked her lips. 'It's Egyptian, the best.'

'No, thank you. I do not think it is wise to drink heavily before a combat.'

'Ha!' Sorina ejaculated. 'This from the veteran of one combat and the model of sobriety. Forgive me for not bowing to your great experience.'

'Have I done something to offend you, Amazon?' Lysandra asked carefully. She would not cause another brawl between them.

'You don't matter enough to have offended me, girl,' Sorina sneered. 'You and those others,' she gestured to the Hellene women, 'are just fodder for the arena. It's a rare novice that lasts. And you don't have what it takes.'

'You're drunk.' Lysandra's own voice was harsh. 'But there is no need to insult me.'

'Of course I'm drunk. To be drunk before battle is to honour one's gods. You should know that, being a priestess and all.'

'We do not honour Athene by falling around in a stupor. It is foolish to fight with a thick head.'

'You trust your goddess, yes?' Sorina placed her cup on the table between them.

'Naturally.'

'Then if you are marked to die it will make no difference if you are drunk or sober, will it? For a priestess, you have remarkably little faith.'

Lysandra stood, her frame rigid. 'I came to wish you well, but I will not play the whipping girl to a drunken old hag who swims in liquor and past glories.' She stalked away before Sorina could respond. She breathed out, forcing the anger from her body. Suddenly, she had a headache, and decided to retire for the night.

The cell of course was empty, the other women making the most of the freedom the revels offered. She removed her sandals and sat on her bunk, pulling her knees up to her chin, her thoughts turning inevitably to the morrow and what it might bring. She did not fear the coming of daylight. Rather she felt a keen sense of anticipation. The Athenian priest had been right when he had challenged her. A lifetime of training served no purpose unless that training was tested. What use was the sharpest sword if it were left in its scabbard? How could one truly know the mettle of the blade save for matching it against another? That she would defeat her enemy was undoubted and all would know

145

that it was a Spartan who was *victrix*. The thought warmed her and she smiled slightly to herself.

The cell door opened, causing Lysandra to start from her reverie. She turned sharply to see Eirianwen silhouetted in the half-light. She was holding a carafe idly in her hand, her face turned away as she addressed the guard. A few words were heard exchanged with the unmistakable clink of coin changing hands. Eirianwen moved into the cell, shutting the door behind her.

'I brought you some wine,' she said simply. Without waiting for an invitation, she made her way to the bunk and sat opposite Lysandra.

Lysandra felt her mouth go dry and butterflies flitted insanely deep inside her. Her hands suddenly became cold and damp, her heart beating a little faster. 'I am not drinking tonight,' she said, embarrassed at her feelings.

'Nonsense!' Eirianwen handed her the carafe. 'I have mixed it three parts water, one part wine as you Greeks like it.'

Lysandra smiled at her, finding it easy to forgive her Latin usage. Normally, being referred to as Greek was offensive to her but, from Eirianwen's lips, it was not so. 'Well,' she said, shrugging, 'why not?' She felt the tribeswoman's eyes upon her as she drank and found she could not meet her gaze.

'You mustn't mind Sorina,' Eirianwen said softly. 'She is spiteful when in her cups. I came to apologise for her. Lysandra, you may think of us as barbarians but we too have our rules of…' she looked up to the ceiling, gesturing.

'Etiquette,' Lysandra finished for her.

'Yes!' Eirianwen snapped her fingers. 'Etiquette. Sorina was rude, but she is drunk. She will regret her words in the morning.'

Lysandra passed her the wine. '*In vino veritas*, Eirianwen. She holds a dislike for me.'

'She dislikes all Greeks and Romans… No,' she shook her head, 'she dislikes what Greeks and Romans represent. Civilisation,

146

the Law of Man, straight roads and philosophers' words. All this is against the Earth Mother. It is unnatural and it is wrong to go against the way of the goddess.'

'I *am* a Priestess of Athene,' Lysandra noted. She kept her tone gentle, and was surprised to find she was not affronted by Eirianwen's theology.

'*Ath-e-ne*,' Eirianwen repeated the unfamiliar word. 'That is so Greek.' She laughed somewhat tipsily. 'It is the civilised way to put everything in a box. Ath… ene is only an aspect of the Great Mother. As is your Juno, Venus and all those others.' She used the Roman names for the goddesses, but, Lysandra realised, they were all she would have heard.

'It is not the night for theological discourse,' Lysandra said after a moment's thought. Eirianwen's views were somewhat offensive and patently incorrect. She was, however, unwilling to put this to voice. She cast her eyes down and her gaze fell upon the Silurian's feet. They were small, much more so than her own, and exquisitely beautiful. She swallowed. 'We should focus on tomorrow and the trials it will bring.' Eirianwen shuffled a little closer to her on the cot. She leant towards the Spartan, so that their faces almost touched.

'Are you afraid?' she murmured.

'Spartans fear nothing.' Lysandra's habitual response was a whisper. She looked up, her gaze locked with Eirianwen's and she found she could not break it.

'But you are trembling.'

'No I'm not…'

Her words were cut short as Eirianwen's lips found her own. The kiss was soft and Lysandra's mouth yielded to its caress. The trembling inside her melted away at the Silurian's embrace, fading to a warmth that she had not felt before. She felt herself drifting, surrendering to bliss. Eirianwen's mouth brushed slowly downward, paying exquisite attention to Lysandra's neck, causing her body to tingle.

Somewhere, at the back of her mind, Lysandra knew she must put a stop to this before it went too far. Certainly, she knew her sisters at the temple often practised Sapphic love, considering it was not a breach of their vow. In the *ludus* too, all the women released their tensions in such a manner. But never before had she been prey to the weakness of her flesh – that she should succumb to her lust so easily shamed her.

But even as she thought this, she found her arms lifting above her head, as Eirianwen pulled her tunic gently from her. She sat before her, naked and suddenly shy of her body in a way she had never been before. She made to cover her breasts with her arm, but Eirianwen's hand intercepted her movement. Looking into her eyes, she placed her fingers on Lysandra's shoulders and ran them lightly downwards. Lysandra's lips parted in anticipation as Eirianwen's touch drew closer to her almost painfully erect nipples.

'You are beautiful, Lysandra.'

These words caused a lurch in Lysandra's heart and she reached out tentatively to touch the tribeswoman. Eirianwen lowered her head, her lips seeking the swell of the Spartan's breasts. Lysandra let her head fall back, succumbing to this delicious ministration, her whole body, her whole being becoming alive with sensation. She heard herself sob with pleasure as the warm wetness of Eirianwen's mouth closed over her nipple, drawing it in, tongue rolling over it with maddening intensity.

When she drew away, a moan of disappointment escaped Lysandra's lips. But then she looked up to see Eirianwen lifting her own tunic to reveal such magnificence, such faultless beauty that Lysandra thought she would weep. She had thought the large breasts of the Celtic women unattractive but, as her eyes drank in the sight of Eirianwen's flesh, she knew that she had never seen anything as lovely. A fierce desire seized her and she pulled Eirianwen close, seeking her lips with her own. They kissed, and

Lysandra felt a delerious passion flood through her, so strong that it threatened to break her heart.

Then, almost imperceptibly, Eirianwen pushed her onto her back and moved up her body. She lay on top of her, her breasts swaying tantalisingly close to Lysandra's mouth. She lifted her head to taste the proffered bounty and tried to do as Eirianwen had done to her, alternately teasing the areola with her teeth, then paying soft attention to the delicate bud of her nipple.

'Am I doing this right?' she whispered urgently, suddenly fearful. 'Is it good for you?'

Eirianwen laughed softly. 'Don't worry,' she said, easing her body lower so that Lysandra could reach her without lifting her head. 'You are wonderful.'

They lay like that for some time until Eirianwen began to journey downwards, tracing her tongue ever lower. Lysandra stretched out her arms, tensing the muscles in her shoulders as she felt the tease of teeth on the soft flesh of her inner thigh. Her lover's lips moved slowly, maddeningly inwards, only to brush over the wetness of her sex and then continue onwards. She bit her lower lip and her hips began to move slowly, not of her volition. Eirianwen continued her game, tormenting her with the promise of the ecstasy to come.

'Eirianwen, please…'

She was silent then, as Eirianwen relented, kissing the wet warmth of her nether lips. Lysandra gritted her teeth, the tendons in her neck standing out in thin cords, her hands clawing at the blanket. Eirianwen moved her tongue languidly up and down her now soaking furrow, making love to it with her mouth.

Lysandra was lost in joy; sweat pearled all over her body, warming her, then cooling her. She cried out as Eirianwen found the sensitive apex of her sex, her tongue circling it, tasting it, each pass more wonderful than the last. She reached down, her hands finding the spun gold of Eirianwen's hair, twisting it in her fingers. Lysandra felt a pressure, soft at first, on the flesh between her sex and her anus. Eirianwen's tongue moved faster now, her finger pressing rhythmically, more urgent and firmer than before.

Fire began to burn in Lysandra's stomach, spreading out to consume her entire body, a breathtaking pressure building inside her. She became rigid, every muscle in her body tense as she teetered on the brink of an unknown abyss. Eirianwen's finger moved lower, resting on the bud of Lysandra's anus for a moment, before sliding it into her. Her mouth opened in a silent scream, her body threshing and twisting in a paroxysm of lust as this last act sent her tumbling helplessly over the precipice of ecstasy. A sound was loud in her ears, and she dimly realised it was her own cries of pleasure. Wave upon wave of agonising bliss burst through her, years of restraint exploding free in a cleansing fire. As it subsided so it began anew, each time taking her higher, before finally leaving her quivering and spent.

Her chest heaved with exertion, hair damp and plastered to her forehead. Eirianwen moved up and smiled, her lips glistening. As they kissed, Lysandra tasted herself there and felt no shame. Eirianwen kissed her cheek, her neck, before she herself lay back, her legs parting. Her small hand began to stroke herself and, for a moment, Lysandra was mesmerised.

'Well,' Eirianwen's voice was gently teasing, breaking her gaze, 'I think I deserve something in return.' She pulled Lysandra to her and soon it was the sound of the Silurian's cries that filled the room.

XVIII

Eirianwen left after some hours, though Lysandra entreated her to stay. She had the strangest sensation in her heart, unfelt before. It was as if there was now a physical need within her to have the Silurian close by her. But Eirianwen would not be moved and, with soft words and kisses, she left her alone.

Lysandra lay back on her bunk, forearm across her forehead, her body still tingling with remembered passion. Never before had she felt such abandonment, such lust. It was unseemly to act with such wantonness, but she was suddenly aware of why people so craved the sexual act. She smiled wryly as she realised that it was certainly preferable to self-pleasuring.

The door to the cell swung open with abruptness, and Lysandra looked around sharply, hoping against hope that Eirianwen had returned but was keenly disappointed when her Hellene companions struggled in. They were, despite her admonishments, a little the worse for drink, but at least none were wildly in the clutches of Dionysus.

'I'm telling you,' Penelope enthused as she entered. 'It was like a baby's arm holding an apple.'

'Spare me the details.' Thebe waved her away, but Penelope would not be stayed.

'Massive.' She sighed happily. 'Big balls on him like a bullock, big muscles. A real man.'

'What was his name?' Danae wanted to know.

'What's in a name?' Penelope shrugged and made her way to her cot. 'I was only interested in one thing and I got it. Had me moaning like the lowest whore in an instant.' She glanced over at Lysandra who had sat up. 'I'm sorry,' she said. 'Did we wake you?'

'No.' Lysandra found that even this ribald commentary could not disturb her languid mood. 'I was awake. You found what you were looking for, I take it.'

'Too right.' Penelope peeled off her tunic and scrambled under her blanket. 'I'm telling you, Lysandra, the man was a stallion. There was nothing he didn't do! I feel like I've given birth to a pony, you know what I mean?'

Lysandra shrugged and smiled. 'No, but I'll take your word for it.'

'You look as if you're in remarkably good spirits yourself,' Thebe observed as she too got into her bed. 'Have you been drinking?' She indicated the carafe left by Eirianwen.

Lysandra flushed, knowing all to well her happy disposition had nothing whatsoever to do with wine. 'No, not really. Just a cup to help me sleep.'

There was no more conversation, as the women lay back to slumber. As each waited for Morpheus to claim her, they spared a thought for the coming of the morning.

None were afraid.

They were awoken at dawn by Catuvolcos. He was in his customary good spirits, bantering with all the women, but his gaze fell often to Lysandra and softened as it did so. Seeing his eyes upon her, she grinned slightly. He bade the women leave the cell to prepare for the games and made to speak to her as she passed him.

'You look fit,' he said. 'And ready.'

'That I am, friend,' she said, and moved on. She hoped her emphasis on this last would dissuade him from caring too much. She must let him know where he stood in her affections. He was merely a friend; her heart had only room for Eirianwen.

With quiet efficiency, the women were moved to the underground corridors that lead to the arena. The bustle of slaves was all about them, and they were anonymous amidst the hubbub.

Lysandra made her way to the Gate of Life to observe the arena. As the women were accorded inferior status, they had no part in the inaugural ceremony; it was considered enough that they had been paraded once. The male fighters however, were marching around the circumference of the arena to the cheers of the adoring masses. Behind each man, slaves bore his weapons and armour and a placard bearing his name, his fighting style and arena tally. As each gladiator passed by the dignitaries' box, a burly slave with a large horn to amplify his voice bellowed out the words on the placard – the great majority of the audience could neither read nor write. Much was made by the betting fraternity of this segment of the spectacle, those with a canny eye seeking any weakness in a fighter's gait.

There was a great buzz as it was announced that Sextus Julius Frontinus, the governor of all Asia Minor, was present. The man himself rose from the dignitaries' box close by the sands to acknowledge his applause. Lysandra thought that his acclamation was enthusiastic enough to be real. Evidently, the governor was a popular man.

'A butcher,' Eirianwen's voice sounded in her ear.

Lysandra turned, her face lighting in a smile. 'Eirianwen.' She tasted the name on her lips. 'You have no love for Frontinus, I take it?'

153

Surreptitiously, Eirianwen's hand reached out and touched Lysandra's waist. 'No,' she said. 'He is the conqueror and enslaver of the Silures. I hate him.'

Lysandra nodded, not sure what to say. She could understand her resentment, of course, but how else were barbarians supposed to be civilised unless by the sword? Certainly, they would not willingly embrace the enlightened path. In war, there were always victims of circumstance but this was for the greater good. Even as the thought came to mind, Lysandra's faith in it was shaken. Somehow, it seemed wrong to her that Eirianwen had been enslaved. She *was* a barbarian yet there was much beauty in her. 'Forget about him,' she offered, for the want of anything constructive to say. 'Concentrate on your match. You must be safe.'

Eirianwen smiled her beautiful smile. 'Oh, my match will not be for some days yet, but all will be well. Britannica is a fearsome warrior.' She referred to herself by her arena name.

Lysandra laughed. 'Britannica has competition. Achillia the Spartan will be more famous.'

'Achillia the Spartan is soft underneath her armour,' Eirianwen said, and winked. 'I know all her vulnerable parts.'

Lysandra desperately wanted to kiss her then, but held back, aware that there were too many eyes about. She saw Eirianwen wanted it too, but they stepped apart. 'Good luck, Eirianwen.'

'And to you.' Eirianwen paused. 'Spartan.' With that she turned away, and was gone.

Lysandra watched her until she was lost in the crowd before turning her attention back to the arena where elaborate, forest-themed scenery was being set up.

'You scratched your itch then.' Sorina's tone was scathing.

The more experienced gladiatrices had gathered together in a large cell. Well used to the arena itinerary, they had long since

154

lost the desire to watch all the proceedings. Eirianwen looked up from tying her sandals, and nodded.

'Indeed. But I think the itch will not go away.'

'Pah!' Sorina spat. 'She is a Greek, and they are worse than Romans. I will not have one of the tribe consorting with those animals. Use her body, druid's daughter, but that must be as far as it goes.'

Eirianwen got to her feet, her blue eyes blazing. 'You might be chieftain in this place, Sorina, but you do not own me.'

'No,' Sorina said. 'I do not. Balbus does, and he is from the same type as *her* who you now are so eager to pleasure.'

'Your hatred has made you bitter. I take my joy where I can find it, and I find joy in Lysandra.'

'Oh, *Lysandra*, is it? Not Spartan. Not Greek.' Sorina shook her head in disgust. 'You should be ashamed of yourself!'

Eirianwen burned with the desire to lash out at the older woman but tribal custom forbade it; Sorina was the chieftain and her word was law. She shook her head and sat down, her attention fixed on her sandals.

'I hope she dies,' Sorina said. 'Then perhaps you will remember where your true loyalties lie.' She stalked out without another word.

Lysandra was joined in her watching by Hildreth.

'Hello, Lysandra, how are you today?' The German spoke their ritual greeting.

'I am well, Hildreth, how are you?'

'I am well,' Hildreth responded gravely, her eyes turning to the sands. A bizarre tableau was being played out, as a dozen or more horsewomen plunged through the staged forest scenery.

'What is this?'

'Criminal executions,' Lysandra said. 'Those women on horses are hunting men in the 'forest'. It is an unusual turn for the games, I think.'

'How so?'

'Usually, there are wild beast hunts followed by criminal executions. It seems as though the *editor* has decided to mix the two. By all accounts, Hildreth, these games in which we make our first marks are special and unusual.'

'They are excellent riders,' the German noted.

'They are from Thessaly. It is in the north of Hellas. The people there are noted for their horsemanship.'

Hildreth grunted appreciatively as one of the Thessalian women speared a hapless youth to encouraging applause from the thickening crowd. 'You are ready for your fight?' she asked, her eyes not moving from the arena.

'Of course.' Lysandra's reply was haughty. Hildreth's consistent arrogance about their first encounter was becoming insufferable. That she had fought badly was one thing, but that Hildreth was acting as if she were somehow superior was patently outrageous. She turned her attention back to the drama being played out in the forest.

One of the Thessalian horsewomen had been taken down by a group of the 'prey' and the men were extracting a grisly revenge on her prone form, hacking into her with her own sword. The woman howled for aid and was derided by the crowd. With a final slash, however, one of the condemned chopped the rider's head from her neck cutting her cries short. The prisoners exulted, but their joy was short-lived as other mounted warriors, alerted by their now fallen comrade, galloped into view.

Lysandra was shocked as the men were dispatched like so many animals; it offended her that they were scarcely given a fighting chance. No matter what their transgressions, it seemed barbaric in the extreme to butcher them so. Perhaps, at times, Sorina's view of Rome was not so awry.

'Don't fight shit again!' Hildreth said, interrupting her thoughts. 'It is for real out there,' she added as another of the unfortunate prey in the forest was skewered.

'I will not, of that I can assure you,' Lysandra replied tersely. She spun on her heel and left Hildreth to her watching.

Lysandra returned to find the Hellene women. They sat in silence, each lost in thought. She thought to say some encouraging words but held her tongue. Perhaps they needed this time to reflect, to steel themselves for the coming trials. With little else to do, Lysandra sat, and her mind turned to Eirianwen. She shook her head, irritated with herself. She too had to focus on her combat. It was not the Spartan way to err towards distraction. Despite her feelings for the tribeswoman, she must cast her from her mind. She once again considered that she was blessed: Hellene by birth, Spartan by the grace of the Gods as the saying went. Only a Spartan could have such control of her emotions, she knew. It was what made them superior to all others.

Stick emerged from the gloom of the catacombs, his ugly face twisted in a grin. In his hand he carried a bucket of oil. 'It's almost time,' he said. 'The executions are about to finish.' This pronouncement caused a stir among the women. 'You had better start to get ready.'

'Who is to fight first?' Thebe wanted to know. There was a crack in her voice that Lysandra recognised as the beginning of fear.

'Why, our Spartan, of course,' Stick said. He set down the oil and left with a small wave.

Lysandra smiled tightly, and pulled her tunic away, tossing it to Danae. The Spartan rolled her head, loosening the muscles in her neck, casting all thought from her mind. Victory lay in prepared-ness, in training. The mind must be given over to reaction, not thought. Thus, she performed her callisthenics without being aware of her routine. Her body began to sweat and her muscles relaxed – she felt no tension as she worked, her mind clear and prepared.

She stooped and took a handful of the oil Stick had left them and slicked it through her hair, scraping the raven locks back severely. As if by unspoken order, Thebe approached and tied back her hair. The Corinthian took some oil, and began to work it into the scarred muscles of Lysandra's back, whilst Danae came forward and, kneeling, began to apply the unguent to her legs and torso. As the two worked on her, Lysandra found that the application of the oil was somehow cathartic. It was as if with each pass of her companion's hands she was less Lysandra and more Achillia, that the unguent was somehow an armour that protected her true self from the arena fighter that was Achillia. Danae and Thebe stepped back admiring their handiwork, nodding appreciatively at Lysandra's body gleaming slightly in the torch-light. Clad only in the *subligaculum* loincloth, her pale skin gave her the appearance of a marble statue.

'You are as ready as you'll ever be,' Danae said.

Lysandra stepped forward and, flanked by Thebe and Danae, made her way towards the Gate of Life.

'Don't be afraid,' Thebe whispered as they walked. 'All will be well.'

'Do not be absurd,' Lysandra murmured. 'Spartans fear nothing.'

'Well, I'm afraid.' Thebe was waspish. 'How can you be so calm?'

Lysandra glanced at her. 'Because I know I am going to win.'

They stopped by the entrance to the Gate, and looked out upon the crowd. It was mid morning and the arena was not yet full, but there was throng enough to make a massive noise.

'It *is* sort of exciting,' Danae said, ignoring Thebe's baleful look.

A fat, balding man puffed his way onto the sands, and began

158

motioning for silence. He raised the horn to his mouth, and began to shout. 'The first of today's combats is upon us!' he bellowed and was instantly drowned out by the crowd. It took some time, but eventually they quieted. 'The gladiatrices to fight for your pleasure today come from great warrior lands. Far to the north, beyond the land of the barbarian Britons is Caledonia, a place where they eat the flesh of babies and worship evil gods!' This was greeted with a chorus of boos and hisses. Evidently, the *editor* was casting Lysandra's foe in the role of villain. 'Great Governor Frontinus, gathered notables and people of Halicarnassus, I bring you Albina of Caledonia!'

At his words, the Gate opposite Lysandra's own swung open, and a huge woman stepped out. She was freakishly tall, her skin whiter than winter snow; on this canvass she was painted in weird blue designs, spirals and arcane symbols that crawled all over body. Her chest was so corded with muscle that her breasts were non-existent, and thick ridges stood out on her stomach. Her head was shaved bald, giving her an even more hellish aspect. The Caledonian was truly an awesome sight, towering like a colossus as she derided the abuse the crowd hurled.

'What do you think?' Danae said after some moments of stunned silence.

'I think I shall need a bigger sword,' Lysandra muttered, taken aback at the sheer size of the woman despite herself.

'And her opponent,' the fat man was shouting, 'from the great warrior state of Sparta,' he gestured theatrically. 'I give you Achillia!'

The Gate of Life drew open but Lysandra remained inside. It was Achillia who stepped out before the crowd.

To the sound of the trumpets, Lysandra marched towards the centre of the arena, as did the massive Caledonian. She could hear the odd dirty comment at the sight of her near naked body, but this she ignored. That women were made to fight in near nudity was all part of the show and she knew it.

She faced Albina as slaves rushed out, handing the two women buckler and sword. The Caledonian grinned at Lysandra, revealing a savage array of teeth that had been sharpened to carnivorous points. Lysandra cocked an eyebrow at this, her own mouth twisting in a sneer.

The two turned and saluted the governor, who acknowledged them with a nod of his head. This done, they whirled about to face each other. The Caledonian dropped into a fighting crouch. Lysandra remained standing erect. She stretched her neck from left to right and spun her sword twice in her hand, drawing appreciative whistles from the watching mob. Only then did she take an on guard position.

'I'll kill you,' Albina growled, her voice hideously distorted by her sharpened teeth.

'The contest is not won on foul stench and ill-looks. Were that the case, you undoubtedly have the advantage. As it is, I shall carve you to ribbons, you barbarian bitch.' With that Lysandra stalked forward, her face an implacable mask.

Albina did not rush in as Lysandra's first opponent had done. She was no novice and she would not be provoked by harsh words. She allowed herself to be tracked, content to mirror Lysandra's movements, cutting off her angle of attack.

They circled for some moments, neither willing to commit to the strike. Lysandra could hear the mob becoming restless, shouting for some action. *Let them*, she thought. *They* are not fighting a Colossus made female.

Suddenly, without sound or warning, Albina lunged in with a quickness belying her enormous size. Her short sword hissed like a viper as it cut the air, and instinctively Lysandra raised her shield to intercept the blow.

It was like punching a wall of marble, so powerful was the Caledonian's strike. Gritting her teeth, Lysandra hit back, feeling her own blade clatter off the barbarian's shield.

'You are weak!' Albina snarled and attacked anew, driving Lysandra back with a flurry of blows. The Caledonian's greater height gave her an advantage in length of stride and her forward momentum ate up the ground between the two combatants, bringing her ever closer to Lysandra. The powerful northerner rained blows down on her, but she was able to fend them off with her *parmula*. Albina stepped in as Lysandra struck back and the two women locked together, sword on shield.

Lysandra felt her muscles bunch as Albina forced her downwards, straining against the inexorable force of the Caledonian giant. Albina's eyes bulged as she pushed, cords of iron-hard sinew standing out on her pale flesh. Lysandra butted her head forward, trying to catch Albina unawares, but the savage warrior was too canny. She lifted her chin, allowing Lysandra's forehead to slap harmlessly against her chest. She was now blinded by a wall of flesh, her face sliding over the oiled, muscled torso of her enemy. Suddenly, pain tore through her shoulder as she felt Albina's sharpened fangs sink into her. Blood burst from the wound, dripping wetly down her back and chest.

Agony lanced through her body, but the pain gave Lysandra strength and she surged back, shoving the heavier woman away. She scuttled backwards and Albina laughed, a harsh guttural sound. Her sharp teeth were stained pink with Lysandra's blood and thick, scarlet fluid hung from her chin in glutinous strands. The crowd screamed, excited at the sight of first blood, and Albina spat out a whitish clump of Spartan flesh.

It was a sickening sight, but Lysandra ignored it, calling on her training, learnt both in the *agoge* and the *ludus. Ignore the pain. The mind is stronger than pain.*

Her face emotionless, she advanced on her grinning opponent, refusing to allow herself to become angered. In fury lay defeat; she would win through superior tactics and skill. Her blade flashed in the sunlight as she attacked, causing the Caledonian to lose her sneer and focus on the task at hand. Albina struck back and Lysandra let her come on, waiting, waiting, judging the correct moment to strike. She lowered her buckler a fraction and the northerner seized the opportunity, stepping in to cut her head from her body.

Lysandra's foot lashed out, hammering straight up between Albina's legs, smashing satisfyingly into the barbarian's pubic bone, causing her to cry out. Elated, Lysandra pounced, her blade cutting downwards. Albina hastily raised her buckler, catching Lysandra's iron, but the deflection was glancing and the sword bit into her upper arm, causing bright droplets of blood to fly. Albina tried to stab her sword into Lysandra's side, but her shield was there. The blow was still sickeningly powerful, the force of it knocking her off balance. Intertwined, the two women crashed to the sand, rolling over and over, each trying to gain the advantage.

Both gladiatrices scrabbled to gain a grip on the other, but their oil-slicked bodies would not allow purchase. As they writhed against each other, Lysandra felt her hold on her shield break and it was lost to her as they fought on. With a desperate effort, she scrambled on top of her foe, her blade spinning round in a dagger-like grip. She caught Albina's sword arm with her left hand, now free of the buckler, and made to ram her sword into Albina's chest; but the Caledonian, seeing her danger thrust her shield arm straight up before Lysandra could strike, the hide of the buckler slamming into her face with a stunning force.

Dazed, Lysandra fell back, regaining only enough of her faculties to roll away. The titanic Albina got to her feet, her huge chest heaving. Both women were bloodied and sand mired, the grit of the arena floor clinging to their bodies. The barbarian came in, and a furious flurry of blows was exchanged, Lysandra's sword moving like lightning to deflect both blade and buckler, which was at once weapon and defence.

She was fast, but could not avoid a horizontal slash, and the tip of Albina's sword sliced across her belly. She hissed in pain, but no respite was afforded her. Albina's buckler swung round, catching her in the side of the head, slamming her from her feet. Blood pounded in her ears as she crashed to the sand. White spots exploded before her eyes, and the world tilted crazily. Through the haze she saw Albina walking in, her sword raised for the killing blow.

No! It could not end thus.

Lysandra surged upwards, rolling towards the onrushing Albina. The move caught the Caledonian off guard, but even so, she was fast enough to bring her shield down to protect her exposed stomach. Too late she realised Lysandra's gambit.

Lysandra, crouching before her enemy, stabbed downwards with her sword, the blade cutting cleanly through the top of Albina's foot, shearing through bone and gristle, to pin the screaming gladiatrix to the sand. Lysandra heard the dull thud as Albina cast her weapon aside, trying with both hand to dislodge the blade that had transfixed her. Lysandra lurched unsteadily to her feet, holding her hand to her injured shoulder. Around her she could hear the crowd screaming at the sight of her. Albina had ceased her struggle, and instead raised her finger, imploring for the *missio*. Lysandra stooped, and grasped the barbarian's fallen sword, her eyes flicking to the governor's box.

The mob howled with glee, their hands cutting downwards in the motion for the kill. The *editor* had set them against the Caledonian from the start and they were eager for the sight of her blood. That she had fought well was of consequence. Sextus Julius Frontinus was evidently a man of the people; he would not disappoint them. Grimly, he turned his thumb, this one gesture signalling the end of a life.

Lysandra moved behind her vanquished opponent. She felt no remorse. If she had not been victorious, the barbarian would have spared her no such thought. Holding Albina's own weapon in both hands, she brought it savagely downwards, spearing the back of the massive Caledonian's neck, severing her spine from her brain. Lysandra twisted the blade twice as her foe's blood gouted, drenching her *subligaculum* and belly. She heaved and dragged the crimsoned iron free. Like a felled oak, Albina toppled forward and smashed into the earth. The sand around her darkened with blood and shit, as her body defecated in the spasms of death.

For a moment, Lysandra stared, stunned at her action. But then, the adulation of the crowd washed over her in rapturous waves. She heard her own voice scream in triumph as she raised her arms skywards, brandishing the dripping sword above her head. Her eyes swept around the stadium, falling upon the statues of the pantheon. She pointed her bloody blade at the statue of Minerva, the Roman Athene, letting all know in whose name she fought.

This show of piety after such ferocity caused an eruption in the stands and, as Lysandra marched back to the Gate of Life, the masses chanted the name '*Achillia, Achillia*' over and over.

It was the sweetest music she had ever heard.

The Hellene women were dancing about and screaming with joy as Lysandra returned. Danae embraced her enthusiastically, heedless of her wounds.

'You did it, you did it!' she shouted, spinning Lysandra about.

'Well fought, Lysandra!' This from Penelope. Other such encouragements followed and Lysandra was caught in the euphoric flush of victory. She did not feel the pain in her wounds, nor did fatigue weigh at her limbs. Rather, she felt more alive than ever before. Success was heady wine, an addictive narcotic which she knew she must taste again.

'All right, all right, break it up.' Stick appeared, interrupting the women. 'Get yourself to the surgeon,' he told Lysandra. 'No telling what diseases that Caledonian has. *Had*,' he corrected himself. 'And the rest of you,' he brandished his vine staff, 'get back away from here!' Throwing a few half-hearted jibes at Stick, the women began to disperse and make their way to their cell. Stick watched as they departed, his eyes fixing on the lash-scarred back of the Spartan. 'Lysandra!' he called out. She stopped and turned back. 'You fought well.'

Lysandra gave him a rare smile. 'Thank you, Stick. I know.'

The Parthian looked down for a moment, seeming to come to a decision. 'Listen,' he said, approaching her. 'I'll make no secret of it, I urged Balbus to send you to the blocks. But I was mistaken, I think. I know you are talented. But curb your arrogance. It rubs people the wrong way. And more, you've made an enemy in Nastasen and he gets crazy at times.' Stick whirled his finger at his temple.

Lysandra cocked an eyebrow. 'Nastasen is the one who needs to be careful, Stick. If he touches me again, I will kill him.'

Stick sighed. 'You are still a slave. Remember that.'

'Am I?' Lysandra jerked her chin at the Gate of Life, from where the chanting of her arena name could still be heard. She spoke no more but turned on her heel and made off.

Lysandra did not spend long in the infirmary; the surgeons were well skilled and well practised. A bitter-smelling, stinging unguent was applied to her wounds, which were bound swiftly. After a brief instruction to keep the wounds clean, she was given a small pot of the stuff and told to apply it three times a day. Thereafter, she might as well have ceased to exist as far as her jaded carer was concerned. On her way back to the Hellene cell, she encountered Hildreth clanking her way towards the Gate of Life. The tall German was clad as *secutorix*, heavily armoured with helm and shield.

'You fought shit again,' Hildreth commented as she saw Lysandra. 'But at least you won. You should watch me now, you will learn how a true warrior fights.'

Lysandra felt a brief rush of anger. If Stick was going to give speeches about encroaching arrogance, he would do well to direct his comments to the barbarian. She was not about to let Hildreth ruin her good mood, however, so she bit down a catty response, settling for giving the German an expression that was half grin; half sneer. She doubted if the thick-skinned warrior would even notice.

166

The women in the Hellene cell were still chattering about Lysandra's victory as she entered.

'What was it like?' Penelope wanted to know.

Lysandra sat on her bunk. She thought before responding, but the truth was undeniable. 'It was good,' she said simply. 'Of course, I was not afraid before the combat. A little tense perhaps,' she acknowledged. 'But when you are out there...' she trailed off, reliving the battle in her mind. 'I have never felt so exhilarated. It was as if I had finally found a purpose. I will tell you this...' – she met the gazes of her companions in turn, 'you have nothing to fear.'

'You enjoyed it?' Thebe seemed both incredulous and disgusted.

'Yes,' Lysandra admitted. 'I did.'

Further conversation was curtailed as an arena slave appeared in their doorway. He referred to a scroll he was carrying. 'Is there a Heraclea in here?'

All eyes turned to Thebe, who had won the argument to use the august name. 'That would be me,' she said, raising her hand.

The slave nodded. 'Good,' he said. 'I don't know why they can't keep these rosters in some sort of order. I've been running about all over the place looking for you. It's more complicated today, because there are many schools here. You know what it's like. Each show has to be bigger and better than the last. Not that anyone ever thinks about the organisation that goes into this whole spectacle.'

'You were looking for Heraclea,' Thebe broke in as the man paused for breath.

'Oh,' he was evidently disappointed that his captive audience was not willing to listen to more of his problems. 'You must prepare,' he said. 'You are to fight next.'

'Thanks,' Thebe said shortly. She glanced over at Lysandra who grinned at her. 'Well then,' the Corinthian murmured. 'Let's be about it.'

*   *   *

It was only once the combat had begun that Lysandra truly understood why the gladiatorial games were such a huge and compulsive phenomenon to people all over Rome's Empire. It was utterly thrilling to watch two people fight when the stakes were highest. The excitement was, of course, different when one was not participating in the battle, yet it was no less compelling – perhaps even more so. Now she realised why people supported certain fighters, following their careers to the point of obsession. Though she saw herself as reserved by nature, Lysandra found herself screaming encouragement and advice to Thebe along with the others. She parried each cut, winced at every near miss and yelled at each hit that Thebe made.

Thebe was fighting as a *Thraex*, matched against a thin Egyptian *retiaria*, armed with net and trident. It was a contest of speed, both women lightly armed and able to skip over the sands, unhampered by heavy armour and encumbering helm. The contest was disputed with furious rapidity, the women's limbs blurring as each fought to mark the other.

The Egyptian cast her net early in the match, but Thebe had avoided the entangling ropes, and pressed close to the other woman, forcing her to use the trident as a staff not a stabbing weapon, thus negating the advantage in reach the pole arm was supposed to give.

It proved decisive.

In the midst of a vicious exchange, Thebe succeeded in breaking through her opponent's guard, and plunged her sword into the other woman's chest, ending the contest abruptly. The Egyptian fell back, dead before she hit the sands.

The crowd erupted at the clean kill, hailing 'Heraclea' loudly, though, Lysandra noted, not as loudly as they had hailed herself. That was not surprising, she thought, as she knew she was the superior fighter. Still she screamed in delight along with the rest of them.

On visibly shaking legs, Thebe walked back through the Gate of Life, her face ashen.

'Well?' Lysandra asked jubilantly.

Thebe's response was to be suddenly sick.

The contests continued into the afternoon, with Balbus's fighters performing well, suffering no fatalities. As dusk began to fall, torches were lit around the arena, signalling the end of the female combats, and the real business of the male gladiators began. The Hellene women took no interest in this. They had had their fill of excitement for the day, which was exhausting both for those who had fought and those who had watched.

Lysandra had expected that she and her companions would be confined to their cells, but was surprised to find this was not the case. Since the arena and its adjoining gaol complex was heavily guarded by legionaries and hired ex-gladiators, both the *editor* and the owners of the different *famillia's* were content to let their warriors wander about the enclosed areas.

Thebe recovered from her bout of shock with some care and attention from Danae. The Athenian was fast becoming the soft ear for the Hellene women. Whilst Lysandra considered that her own presence was an inspiration to her comrades, she was not as sensitive as Danae to the more emotional needs of the gladiatrices. It was hardly their own fault that they had such weaknesses – not everyone could be Spartan.

With little else to do, Lysandra decided to go in search of Eirianwen. Though the initial rush of victory was beginning to wane, the nearness of death had awakened other needs in her and she knew that the Briton's touch would sate the slow burn of sexual desire she now felt. She threaded her way through the crowded corridors of the gaol, noting that despite the lenience the organisers had afforded the fighters, the male and female competitors had been separated. This would be frustrating to

169

Penelope, she knew, as the fisher girl had not ceased to elucidate all and sundry on the erotic prowess of her gladiator, who, for lack of knowing his name, she had come to call 'Horse'.

'Lysandra!' Catuvolcos's voice rang out from the throng. The Spartan stopped and looked about, seeking the friendly face. The handsome Gaul was shouldering his way through the crowd of gladiatrices, smiling and laughing as he was groped and propositioned outrageously by the women. As a trainer, he was not subject to the segregation rules and that he was walking around bare-chested only added to the attention he was receiving. As he approached Lysandra, she was regaled by insults from the gladiatrices, as they now believed that she was to be the object of the big man's much sought after attentions.

'I am glad you are all right,' he said to her.

'I was never concerned,' she told him honestly. She turned, dragged a drink-sodden barbarian from a stone bench and sat down. The barbarian hit the ground with a groan and passed wind loudly.

'You should be,' Catuvolcos said as he joined her. 'It's not a game.'

Lysandra bit down an angry retort. She was getting somewhat frustrated with being admonished by the trainers. It was not as if she had performed badly. 'I am aware of overconfidence,' she said with a civility that was somewhat less than heartfelt. 'I am also aware of my own abilities and have faith in them. I have been trained since youth for this, Catuvolcos.' He met her gaze for a moment.

'I was worried for you, Lysandra. You are not like those others, you are special.'

She nodded thoughtfully. 'Yes, I have come to think so. Of course, I do not tell the others this: humility is to be admired. However, it cannot be denied that I am indeed fortunate. The gods have gifted me well and it is in their honour that I fight.'

170

'No, I meant you are special to me. I have never felt this way for anyone before.'

Lysandra frowned. She had not thought that he would blurt out his feelings to her. Of course, she realised that he was enamoured of her. She knew her beauty and charisma had had an effect on him but hoped that his discipline would keep him from speaking of his attraction. That he had chosen to mention it was embarrassing: there was a brief moment in the past when she may have considered his advances, but she knew now that had been merely a fancy.

'I have saved money,' Catuvolcos went on. 'Not much, but in a year or two I will have enough to buy us free from Balbus. We could leave Caria and return to Gaul. I would be a good man for you, Lysandra, if you would have me. I am young and strong, and know how to raise cattle, and to build. You would want for nothing.'

'Catuvolcos…' She put her hand on his arm – and saw hope and love flare in his eyes, the beginnings of a smile playing about his lips. This would be difficult, she thought, having had no experience in this kind of arena. 'I do not love you,' she said bluntly. It was the Spartan way, after all. But Lysandra was not prepared for how so simple a statement could affect someone. She could see the pain in his face as she spoke and felt his hurt almost as keenly as if it were her own. 'I am sorry,' she added, trying to be gentle. 'You are a friend to me, a compatriot, a brother in arms. But I do not feel that way about you.'

Catuvolcos looked down and shook his head. 'I should not have spoken so,' he said, a crack in his voice. She hoped he was not about to burst into tears, for such action would make her despise him. 'I have embarrassed you.'

That was true, but Lysandra thought it impolitic to mention. 'I would not be any good as a wife,' she said, trying to make light of what had become an excruciating situation. 'You have heard of Spartan cooking, haven't you?'

171

Catuvolcos shook his head glumly, refusing to meet her gaze.

'Well,' she said. 'In the *agoge* we had a diet of what is called blood soup. It is black in colour, made of pork, vinegar and pig's blood. Once, a visitor came to Sparta and, after tasting the soup, declared that now he knew why Spartan warriors were so eager to die. It is the only food I know how to make and this, I think, would not make you happy.'

'I would eat it every day if it meant we could be together,' he said, which Lysandra felt was rather pathetic. Men, it seemed, were like children: when they could not have what they wanted, they sulked. 'Do not dwell on it, my friend,' she offered. 'I have an affection for you, but it is not love.'

'But this affection can grow.' He turned to look at her then. 'Many times a man and woman are put together in youth and love grows between them. It could be so for us.'

That was enough. 'I said no. If you felt as you say, you would not continue in this manner,' she said tightly. 'My place is here. In the arena. I will not be any man's wife, Catuvolcos.'

She saw his face redden as anger took the place of petulance. Lysandra raised her eyebrows, curtailing any outburst from the wounded Gaul. She did not wish there to be harsh words between them. She got to her feet, and smiled tightly. 'You are a good friend, Catuvolcos. I would put these words behind us, if you would.'

He nodded and shrugged and then looked back to the floor. Lysandra turned away without further comment. She had done what she could to spare his feelings; it was his own fault for coming to her in the first place, certainly she could not be held accountable for his desires. Let him sulk.

She was confident he would get over it in time.

'What is the matter, Sorina?' Teuta offered the older woman a drink from her sack of beer. 'You look angry.'

'I *am* angry,' Sorina snapped, then tilted her head back to let the liquor pour down her throat. 'The Greek lives.' She had watched Lysandra fight from the stalls, and her disappointment was keen at the Spartan's survival. More, she had shown skill and resourcefulness that belied her inexperience.

'You should not let it play on your mind so,' Teuta said gently.

'She will ruin Eirianwen. She will corrupt her.'

'Eirianwen is not a child. She knows well who she is getting into bed with.'

'You cannot see it either! The Greek carries the taint of her 'civilisation,' Teuta. It is disease, and with it she corrupts Eirianwen. And more of us, if she has her way.' Sorina cursed and hurled the beer sack away, where it splashed wetly against the wall.

'I think you are making too much of it.' Teuta baulked at her rising fury, but the Amazon did not care.

'That is just how it works!' Sorina shouted, rounding on her. 'Lysandra's lust for Eirianwen is the beginning of a cancer that will destroy her. The Greek's wickedness will spread to Eirianwen and be passed on to others!' The civilisation of the middle sea was a disease, but a seductive one; Sorina knew this all too well. Its arms would engulf anyone who chose to stray too close, blinding them with comforts, but all the while leeching their freedom. To be 'civilised' here was to be controlled. It infuriated her that no one but she could see what was happening. 'Only I am not blind to Lysandra and her evils, it seems,' she muttered, putting the thought to voice.

'Sorina…'

'Leave me be!' She jerked away from Teuta's outstretched hand. Furious, she stalked off, knowing she had hurt the other, but too angry to care.

Though the corridors of the gaol were crowded, all made a path for her; she was well known outside the confines of Balbus's *ludus* and the other warriors respected her seniority and, more, the look of rage etched onto her face. She wandered aimlessly, the Greek's hated visage swimming before her eyes. For a moment, she seriously considered asking Balbus for a match with her but, as swiftly as the thought came, she dismissed it. He would never agree to such a bout, as Lysandra was only a junior fighter. Exasperated, she looked for somewhere to rest and calm herself. She was surprised to see Catuvolcos sitting nearby on a stone bench. The trainer was clutching a sack of beer, his face wrapped in gloom.

'What's amiss?' she asked as she joined him.

Catuvolcos regarded her with glassy eyes. 'Nothing,' he muttered, handing her the beer sack.

'Come on,' she said, taking a swig. 'You look as if your best friend just died.'

'It's Lysandra,' he moaned, causing Sorina to bristle at the sound of the despised name. 'I love her.'

Sorina sighed, keeping the simmering fury inside. She hated to be proven aright in this, but the Greek's disease had taken hold of another close to her. 'Put her from your mind,' she advised meaningfully. 'She's just a Greek – not one of us, Catuvolcos.'

'It's not about where you come from.' Catuvolcos sighed mournfully, full of beer-induced melancholy. 'When two people meet, sometimes it is just meant to be. I am sure this is the case. Sorina, I have been with many girls but I have never felt this way before.' He tilted the beer sack. 'And I have not even lain with Lysandra. It is just a feeling I have in my heart.'

'She is an evil woman. She is heartless, and I would not see you hurt.'

'No, she's not heartless,' he argued. 'She just has a way about her. She's special, Sorina, and it must be hell being put in a place like the *ludus*. With the type of women that we get.'

'Thank you very much,' Sorina muttered.

'I didn't mean you.'

Sorina forced herself to smile. What she must do was distasteful but necessary if the taint of the Greek woman was to be washed from Catuvolcos's soul. 'I know, I was joking. Much as Lysandra does about you.' She could see that these words had penetrated the boozy fog that enshrouded the Gaul's mind. He sat straighter, and frowned at her.

'Lysandra does not laugh at me, Sorina,' he slurred sternly. 'That she does not love me doesn't mean she despises me.'

'No?' Sorina turned her mouth down as if contemplating this for a moment. 'You are wrong, Catuvolcos.'

'What do you mean?' The big man's bleary eyes focused on her briefly before he again sought solace in the beer sack.

'Well, I don't want to speak out of turn,' Sorina injected just the right amount of hesitancy into her voice, 'but you must know she is only for women.'

Catuvolcos was stunned. 'No,' he admitted slowly. 'I did not.'

'Oh, yes. She and Eirianwen are quite the young lovers. They find your so obvious attentions very droll. It's all over the *ludus*!'

she added vehemently. 'All the women are laughing at you behind your back, because of this infatuation with the Greek. But it is Lysandra who laughs hardest. She has a need in her, Catuvolcos. A need to control others, a need to have them at her beck and call. She finds it most amusing that you, a trainer, should be so smitten by her.'

Catuvolcos lurched to his feet. 'I will speak to her on this,' he declared with drink-inspired earnestness. 'Where is she?'

'With Eirianwen, I should imagine.' Sorina was disgusted with herself but considered that she acted for the good not only of the young Gaul, but of Eirianwen too. She had not lied over-much; Lysandra did indeed have a need to control others, like all of her goddess-cursed race. This was evidenced in her rise amongst her own kin, and now they all deferred to her. 'I wish I could open Eirianwen's eyes as I have yours, but she will not hear of it,' she went on. 'I beg you not tell *her* of my words, Catuvolcos. If she hears I have spoken against her lover, she will be lost to us forever. And Lysandra will ruin her as surely as she tried to ruin you. At least, if she and I are still friends, I have a chance of helping her.'

Catuvolcos grunted his acquiescence, swaying slightly on his feet, eyes staring straight ahead. 'I will find her,' he said, and stalked off, clutching the beer sack.

Sorina watched his broad back disappear through the crowd, her emotions a mixture of self-loathing and satisfaction.

'Did you see my fight?' Lysandra and Eirianwen had found a relatively secluded corner of the catacombs, and were sharing a sack of wine.

'Of course.' Eirianwen smiled. 'I was with Balbus at the time. He is beside himself with glee at your performance.'

'But what did *you* think?' Lysandra pressed, the need for Eirianwen's approval suddenly urgent.

'I thought you were wonderful, Lysandra. Truly, a brilliant display.'

'Really?' Absurdly, Lysandra found herself blushing. Eirianwen leant forward and kissed her softly, her hand briefly caressing Lysandra's face.

'You are a fearsome gladiatrix,' she whispered. They gazed at each other for a moment, when the sheer banality of the statement became suddenly apparent to them both: Eirianwen sniggered and Lysandra's lips turned up in a grin. The Silurian mimicked the blaring of trumpets that always accompanied a fighter's entry to the arena. 'You're so scary!' she added, tears of mirth in her eyes.

Lysandra gave her a soft punch on the shoulder. 'You!' she said, full of mock anger. She paused, gazing at Eirianwen. She was so beautiful, so perfect. Lysandra felt a sudden rush of love. She wanted to say something, but could not. It was not the Spartan way to blurt out soft words.

'It is possible to speak your heart now and again, Lysandra.' Eirianwen's eyes met hers, their deep, blue gaze suddenly so wise and knowing; it was as if her thoughts were an open book to Eirianwen.

Lysandra felt herself colouring again. 'I was just wondering if any of your tribe are as fair as you.' It was a ridiculous question, but she was desperate to please Eirianwen and it was the first thing that came to mind.

'Actually, no one in my tribe is as fair as me,' Eirianwen replied. 'Fair skinned, I mean. The Silures are dark — it's funny but they resemble the Romans more than Britons. The truth of it is, Lysandra, I am not of the Silures at all. I grew up with them, yes, but my father was a druid of the Brigante tribe. The Brigantes are 'typical' of Britannia — tall, blonde and fair. Their queen, a traitor called Cartimandua, submitted to the Roman invaders and became their whore.' Eirianwen's eyes glittered with a malevolence that Lysandra had never seen before. 'It was not the Druid way to treat with Romans,' Eirianwen continued, 'so my father took me far from Brigante lands to the west, where the Silures still fought the Empire. So I grew up as one of them, and it became my honour to call myself Silurian. In the end, my tribe was conquered by Frontinus – but at least we fought to the last. Not like the Brigante filth who capitulated so easily.'

Lysandra wished she had kept her mouth shut as this turn in the conversation had darkened Eirianwen's mood. 'I am sorry for asking such a question,' she said. 'It is just that it is difficult for me to say pleasing words.'

'There is no shame in saying what you want to say, in showing a loved one how you feel. It is unnatural to keep all emotion locked inside you.'

'It is how I have been taught,' Lysandra responded sounding somewhat helpless even to herself. Eirianwen kissed the end of Lysandra's nose, her mood seeming to lighten at once.

'We, none of us, are what once we were. The *ludus* and what we do here changes us. It is a hard place most of the time, Lysandra. There is always a need for gentleness, especially between lovers.'

Lysandra swallowed, her mind racing – she must try again to say something that would evoke her feelings. There was a moment of silence, and then she spoke. 'For some – it is horsemen; for others – it is infantry; for some others – it is ships which are, on this black earth, visibly constant in their beauty. But for me, it is that which you desire.' When Eirianwen smiled in response, Lysandra's heart leapt, but she knew not whether it was from relief or joy.

'Did you make that up?' Eirianwen asked. 'It seems very *you*, with its infantry and horsemen.'

Lysandra hesitated. 'Well... I... well. No, actually, I did not make it up. The poet Sappho wrote it.'

'Lysandra!' Eirianwen laughed. 'You are hopeless!'

'And I suppose you can quote the classics, Eirianwen,' she shot back, but there too was mirth in her voice. The two women embraced, each loving the foibles of the other. When she had spoken the poetry to the beautiful Silurian, Lysandra had felt something inside her overflow, like the bursting of a riverbank. For the first time, emotion coursed through her, unchecked and unabated. It was frightening, terrifying in its intensity. It felt unsafe, maddeningly uncontrollable; but she found that she would not let the feeling go.

They held each other thus for a few moments, before Lysandra broke away. She looked about, and saw Catuvolcos standing not far from where they were sitting. She raised her hand in greeting, but suddenly stilled it as she saw his face. It was contorted, a mix of anger and grief. Slowly, her hand lowered, her head cocking to one side. She opened her mouth to call out to him, but he spat on the floor before him, and stalked away.

'What is it?' Eirianwen turned her head, following Lysandra's gaze.

'Nothing. Nothing at all,' she said. 'Come, the night is still before us.'

XXI

'**Y**ou're such a slut, Penelope,' Thebe said caustically.

The former fisher-girl had been waddling around the cell all morning, regaling her compatriots with lurid tales of her nightly adventure with Horse. The previous evening, the titanically endowed gladiator had invited a friend to share the gifts Penelope was so eagerly bestowing.

Lysandra listened with amusement. It occurred to her that before Eirianwen, she would have been scandalised by Penelope's commentary. Now, she found that with each passing day her soul, and with it her cares, grew lighter.

'Of course, I didn't know what they meant when they said they wanted to do it Greek.' Penelope had obviously decided to ignore Thebe and continued playing to her audience. 'I mean, I *am* Greek!' She shook her head. 'I found out soon enough, I can tell you. I was like the meat between two hunks of bread! I won't have any problems with my movements after that little encounter if you know what I mean…'

'That's enough!' Thebe shouted, hurling a pillow at the island girl who was now gesturing obscenely with her forearm and fist. She retained enough presence of mind to duck the pillow, however.

Penelope sat down with exaggerated gingerness and tossed the pillow back. 'Prude,' she said, and stuck out her tongue.

The women all looked around as the door to the cell scraped open, revealing Stick's skinny silhouette. The Parthian sauntered in, carrying the oil bucket.

'Good morning, ladies,' he said gaily. 'How are we feeling today?'

'What do you care?' Once Danae would have been beaten for addressing him in such a manner but now, as if by unspoken agreement, the women had passed from being novices to veterans and Stick was beginning to treat them so.

'I'm wounded, Danae. Don't you know that concern for your welfare is my highest priority? Yours especially,' he went on. 'You are fighting today.' Danae paled slightly, but nodded, her face resolute.

'But first, Penelope,' Stick placed the oil bucket on the floor. 'Or should I say 'Patrocla, the deadly blade'. Get yourself ready, girl!'

Penelope looked a little taken aback and Stick picked up on it. 'What, did you think it was all going to be watching, feasting and enjoyment? It's time for you to start repaying the inordinate amount you cost us.'

Penelope shrugged, and began to remove her tunic. She paused, and raised an eyebrow at Stick, who chuckled and left the cell.

'I cannot believe that you, of all people, have suddenly acquired modesty,' Lysandra said. Penelope shrugged.

'It's never too late,' she muttered.

Lysandra got up and scooped a handful of oil into her hand. 'Maybe you should save some of this,' she commented, slapping the stuff wetly onto Penelope's buttocks. 'I'm sure you could find a use for it.'

'I'm not sure about this,' Penelope said, her voice obscured by the *murmillo* helmet she was wearing. 'It's not supposed to be funny.' That Stick was making her fight as the 'fish girl' was a huge joke to everyone, the trainer included. The *murmillo* fought in medium armour, the head protected by the ornate, full-faced helmet, the right arm and shoulder covered by the distinctive leather *manica*. The first and best, defence, however, was the large, curved shield that Penelope was hefting about. Her torso was left bare, ensuring that the maximum amount of blood and gore was displayed if the gladiatrix was injured and, of course, revealing her ample breasts for the delight of the crowd.

'Do not be concerned.' Lysandra patted her shoulder. 'You look most threatening.'

Inside the helmet, Penelope flushed with embarrassment. 'I'm sure.'

The announcer was once again going through his tirade, as the Gate of Life opened to the sound of the trumpets. Penelope steeled herself, and passed over the threshold into the arena. She had been matched against another heavily armed fighter, a *hoplomacha*, the only discernable difference between the two being the round shield the other woman carried and the Corinthian crested helmet that she wore. The helmet was of an archaic type, made famous by the Greek hoplite warriors of ancient times. The thick nosepiece and flared cheek guards obscured the woman's face in shadow, and so both fighters were rendered anonymous to the crowd. Penelope guessed by the brown cast to the *hoplomacha's* skin she was of eastern stock, a fact confirmed when she was announced as Draca of Syria. Both fighters received their swords from the attendant slaves and then made their ritual salute to Frontinus. This done, they faced one another, shields raised.

Penelope's tongue was dry as she licked parched lips. Despite her usually bombastic demeanour, she was nervous. And with good reason, she told herself as she advanced towards Draca: only a fool would be complacent when entering combat.

She made herself recall one of the first lessons at the *ludus*, when Catuvolcos had had them charge straw dummies. This, she reasoned, would be a similar exercise. She tensed and lunged forwards, her sturdy legs working at speed, eating up the ground between them. The Syrian, however, was no mannequin, and set herself to receive the charge. The mob screamed in delight as the women collided, their shields crashing together with thunderous report. Penelope's sword flashed down, only to career off the edge of Draca's *hoplon* shield. The eastern woman grunted and struck back, catching her stocky foe with a glancing blow to the side of the head. Though the metal absorbed the strike, Penelope's ears rang from the ferocity of the blow. She gritted her teeth and butted her shield forward, trying to overpower the lighter woman.

Draca was cunning; instead of trying to match force with force, she angled her body away from Penelope's shove, causing her to overbalance. She stumbled forward, and Draca's blade lashed out, scoring a bloody line down her opponent's back. The crowd shouted with glee at the sight of first blood. Penelope cried out as the pain flashed through her but swung her sword about as she passed, trying to keep Draca away. She turned, sweat pouring down her face in the furnace of her enclosed helmet, whirling around in time to see the Syrian coming at her again. A sudden fury possessed her and, screaming a war cry, she hurled herself forwards.

Her iron met the wood of the *hoplomacha's* shield and Penelope redoubled her efforts, hoping to draw the other woman into a slogging match, sure she could overcome her. It was at this moment that the pain faded and the long months of training began to pay dividends. She found herself in a place so pure it was almost blissful: she was at one with her blade; her mind, body and soul in perfect harmony with the combat, revelling in the furious exchange of blows, seeing the moves of her foe before they had been executed. She realised then what Lysandra had felt: that there was a liberty to be found in battle. The exultation, the surging power in her veins made her feel as though she were the War Goddess herself. Now she could see the gaps in Draca's defence and she exploited them, her blade biting into the other woman's shoulder as the Syrian sought to strike back. The mob roared her on, delighted with the recovery from her initial error. Penelope was relentless. She churned forwards, hammering blow after blow onto Draca's shield, forcing her back. With each hit she knew she was sapping the energy of her opponent; the shields were heavy and, under this repeated assault, she knew the slighter woman would tire quicker than she. Inwardly, she thanked Stick, Nastasen and Titus for the relentless regimen they had forced her to go through. She was possessed of a strength that she never knew she could attain, muscles responding again and again, with no burning fatigue.

Draca's ripostes were becoming slower and less frequent as she backed up under the furious assault. Penelope redoubled her efforts, sensing that the other woman was almost spent. She slammed her shield into the Syrian's, knocking her off balance. For the merest instant, Draca's guard was down – and Penelope struck. She lunged forward, her blade screaming towards the throat of the *hoplomacha*.

Draca dropped low, ramming her sword into Penelope's abdomen with savage ferocity. Penelope stiffened and wailed in agony as the iron invaded her flesh, slicing upwards into her vitals. Louder than the roar of the crowd, she could hear the Syrian's triumphant yell of victory. Blood sprayed from the wound, drenching both fighters and she screamed again as Draca twisted the blade, feeling it grate on her ribs. Only then, at the white-hot peak of her agony, did the easterner drag her weapon free, leaving Penelope free to collapse, clutching desperately at the wound. She rolled into a foetal position, retching into the steely confines of the helmet, aware only of pain.

After indeterminate moments, rough hands grasped her and dragged her from the ground. In a final moment of brief lucidity, Penelope realised that she had been given the *missio*.

It was unseemly to show emotion. One must remain implacable at all times, for it was a weakness to show too much concern for another. This was the Spartan way: though camaraderie and love were to be expected between fellow warriors, when the gods decreed that it was a comrade's time to pass, the hour must be met with solemn dignity. But to see Penelope moan and cry on the surgeon's pallet was a trial Lysandra had never gone through before. Penelope's legs kicked in response to her pain and so much blood flowed from her that it covered the pallet and dripped to the floor.

Danae knelt by Penelope's side, holding her hand, whispering meaningless things to her as the surgeon tried desperately to staunch the flow of blood. There was always a bonus for arena doctors should they save the life of an expensive arena slave but, after a brief struggle, he gave up. He looked up at Lysandra, and shook his head slowly.

'Have you no opiate?' she demanded. Whilst the examination had been going on, she could understand why the man had not given her friend a drug for the pain. Such things could complicate medical procedures, but now it would not do to have Penelope go to the Styx crying like a baby.

'Of course,' he said resignedly. 'But I am not supposed to give it to those that are going to pass. It is expensive, and if my master found out he would have me whipped.'

'I understand,' Lysandra said. 'But this cannot be.' She indicated Penelope who had begun to shake uncontrollably, her eyes rolling in her head, her mind eroded by pain. 'Where is it?' Lysandra stepped forward.

'Just there.' The surgeon turned, indicating a shelf that held medicines and salves. He was about to speak again when Lysandra lashed out, her fist exploding into his jaw. The surgeon dropped like a stone and lay crumpled on the floor. Calmly, she stepped over him and retrieved a small pot. She sniffed the contents and was satisfied.

'What are you doing?' Danae was stunned at this sudden violence from Lysandra.

'He is a decent man,' Lysandra said as she returned to the pallet. 'It would not be fair of us to allow him to be whipped for breaking the rules. In this manner, he can merely tell the truth.'

'But *you* will be whipped for hitting him!'

Lysandra pressed her lips into a thin line as she poured the glutinous liquid down Penelope's throat. 'I think the pain I shall bear will be somewhat less than hers.'

They waited for the drug to take effect and, slowly, Penelope's agonised spasms began to abate. As the pain receded behind the veil of the opiate, Penelope began to speak. Her words were strange, as if she were a child, and Lysandra thought perhaps that she was reliving events from her youth. It was appalling to watch. Only that morning, Penelope had been among them, laughing, joking and telling her ribald tales. Now she was just a quivering chunk of meat, breathing her last in a drug-induced stupor. It was a sobering thought.

Danae was weeping copiously, her head resting on Penelope's hand as she held it.

They waited in silence, hoping that Penelope would regain some lucidity, that they could tell her that she was not dying alone. But it was not to be. It seemed as if she drifted off to sleep, but her chest had ceased to rise and fall.

'It is over.' Lysandra's voice was harsh.

Danae looked up, her face haggard. 'Poor Penelope,' she cried.

Lysandra nodded. Inside she felt a terrible sense of sadness at her friend's passing, but she knew that this must not be revealed. Spartans never wept for the slain. With force of will, she closed off that part of herself that cared, hardening her heart. It was strange but, in some ways, she felt somewhat less than human as she did this. 'Come, Danae. We must go now.'

'How can you be so heartless? Our friend is dead!'

'Yes, but that is what she was here for, Danae.' Lysandra tried to be gentle, but the strain of the moment caused her to snap. 'That is what we are all here for. That could be you or me. Do you think the comrades of the woman you killed felt any less grief than you do now? Sooner or later this was going to happen to one of us. I blame myself that I have not prepared you to bear this grief.' Danae was struck speechless for a moment by this last comment.

'As if it is for you to prepare us for such things, Lysandra,' she spat. 'You are no different to us, despite what you might think. You are not our leader. You are merely an arrogant bitch who likes the sound of her own voice too much for my liking. For anyone's liking.'

'Danae…'

The Athenian pressed her hands to her ears. 'Shut up, just shut up!' she screamed. 'I can't stand to hear your voice any more.' She scrambled to her feet and ran from the surgery in tears.

Lysandra watched her go. She knew that Danae was merely lashing out in her grief. Anyone else would have taken her words to heart, but Lysandra was pleased that she was above such things. Now was the time that the Hellene women would need her leadership most. It occurred to her that this more personable, caring side of her nature had been brought out by Eirianwen.

She leant over the corpse that had been Penelope and whispered a prayer for the dead. She did not know if the gods would accept her words but this was a duty she felt she must fulfil. She

187

had no coin for Charon, and hoped that he would understand this, allowing Penelope to pass over the Styx to Elysium.

That was all she could do.

XXII

ysandra decided that there was no time like the present to console the Hellene women. Certainly, they would all be upset at Penelope's demise but it was her opinion that Danae's histrionics would only make the situation worse. Now was a time for cool heads and calm voices, not for funeral wailing. That Penelope was gone was tragic, but a warrior must not only be prepared to meet death but walk with him as a constant companion. The reasoning may have sounded hollow even in her own mind but it was her duty to convey strength to the others.

She made her way through the warren of tunnels beneath the arena, back towards the Hellene women's cell. On her way, she spied Sorina and her entourage walking purposefully to the Gate of Life. The aging barbarian was not clad for battle and Lysandra paused, interested to see which one of the more experienced fighters from Balbus's *ludus* would take to the sands. As they passed her by, her throat caught as she saw Eirianwen among them.

She was totally naked, her body coated in the same strange bluish paint that Albina had used, and her normally lustrous hair was sticking out from her head at all angles. Eirianwen stared straight ahead, her eyes not deviating from the woman in front of her. Lysandra was about to call out but stilled her voice. She did not want to break her love's concentration before a bout.

Her love.

The thought came unbidden but she realised the truth of it. She was gripped with anxiety at the thought of Eirianwen entering the arena. What if she were hurt, or worse? Certainly, it was an ill-omened day; they had lost Penelope, and Lysandra feared that Eirianwen would share the same fate. She must watch the combat and pray for her safe deliverance. She could not bear the thought of having to await the outcome, even though she would not be welcome in the stalls with Sorina's people.

She waited for them to pass her by and had decided to follow on at a discreet distance, when she realised that she should go to her friends. The Hellene women needed her now, but she was torn: her heart told her to follow Eirianwen, to see her safe home; her duty, her responsibility, lay with the Hellenes. Biting her lip in frustration, she hesitated. Perhaps, she told herself, she should wait before seeing the Hellene women. Emotions would still be running high and she should speak when they were calm. That might be the more prudent option – then she could both watch Eirianwen's bout *and* fulfil her duty.

'No,' she said aloud. That was a dereliction. The feelings that urged her to be near Eirianwen were of no consequence. Eirianwen was strong. She had not survived thus far by luck alone and perhaps she would be insulted if she knew Lysandra had been worried over her. After all, she had shown no such concern when Lysandra had fought her own bout.

Lysandra watched the little entourage till they were swallowed by the crowd and gloom of the tunnel before turning about to stride purposefully back towards the gaol.

*   *   *

190

Nastasen looked up, squinting at the light that flooded into his prison. He still ached from the beating he had taken but his fury had burned much of the hurt away.

'Hello, Nasta.' Stick's ugly face greeted him with a grin. 'Are we calm today?'

'Just get me out of here.'

'Balbus should be mightily fucked off with you.' Stick sauntered in, keys jingling. 'I know *I* was. But you're lucky that these games are such a huge event and that he has much to worry about.'

Nastasen nodded his thanks as Stick freed him from his bonds. 'What about the Spartan bitch?'

'You just forget about her,' Stick admonished, waving a finger in his face. 'She'll take a lashing for insubordination and that will be that.'

'Is that all?'

'That's *more* than enough.' Stick retorted. 'It's not her fault that you've taken a dislike to her. Besides, she won her bout and looked good doing it. Balbus isn't going to sell her after that display so you'd better get used to having her around the *ludus*. And,' he went on as they left the cell, 'you put this whole thing behind you. You don't like her, ignore her.'

'She has offended my honour.' Nastasen would not be mollified. Inwardly he burned with the desire to have the girl punished in the most humiliating of ways.

'And you think trying to shove your fingers in her *cunnus* isn't offending *her* honour?' Stick gave one of his neighing laughs. 'You know how uptight she is.'

'You do that to the novices all the time.'

'Only to the ones I know will take it without causing a fuss.' Stick grumbled. 'You're the second person to mention me doing that. Is everyone around here getting soft all of a sudden?' Nastasen did not respond to that. 'Look,' Stick said after a moment. 'It's better for everyone if you just stay away from her.'

Nastasen regarded the little man. He could not let Lysandra go unpunished for drawing his blood, for daring to strike him. She was a woman and such an insult could not be borne. But he was no fool. Revenge would be his, but he must play the crocodile for now, waiting calmly beneath the surface to strike when none expected it. He forced a smile. 'You're right, Stick,' he said, patting him on the shoulder. 'I'm being foolish.'

'Yes, you are.' Stick responded with his buck-toothed grin showing that he considered that matter closed. 'Now then – Eirianwen is just about to fight. Let's go and see our woad-painted savage in action.'

Lysandra could hear the roar of the crowd as she entered the cell. Pressing her lips into a thin line, she tried to cast thoughts of Eirianwen from her mind. She must focus on the task at hand. The women were sitting about the cell, a pervasive air of gloom hanging about them like a shroud. Danae was sobbing inconsolably, rocking back and forth in the arms of Thebe. The Corinthian glanced up at Lysandra as she entered but made no comment.

She drew herself up and took a deep breath. 'I can see that you are all aware that Penelope has...' she groped for the right words, before deciding that laconic was best, '... died.' At this, Danae wailed and began crying aloud. Lysandra glowered, but pressed on. 'That this happened is unfortunate. But not altogether unexpected.'

'I don't think now is the time for this sort of thing,' Thebe said, her comment greeted by affirmative mutterings from the others.

'I disagree,' Lysandra told her. 'This is precisely the time. In retreating into sadness, we do Penelope no honour,' – she made a slashing motion with her hand – 'none at all. We debase her with our grief and,' she scowled at Danae, 'our wailing. All of you have turned your thoughts to the possibility of death. You saw Penelope fall and you think: 'that could be me'. Indeed, it could. But if you fear death and go to fight with that fear in your hearts, you will surely follow her. The superior fighter does not fear Hades. The Lord of the Dead is our constant companion whilst we play this game. Show him no fear, and he will not rush to take you. Cower from him and you will surely die.'

'That's easy for you to say,' Danae sobbed. 'You survived. Poor Penelope…'

'Stop your whining!' Lysandra's voice was harsh. 'You think that it will do any good? Do any of you?' She glared at the women. 'We are fighting for our lives as are our enemies. Do not think of them as merely opponents. They are the *enemy*. Hold the memory of Penelope close if you will, but do not grieve for her. Turn your emotion to hatred. Hate those that killed her; picture her foe, standing over her, laughing at the agonies of our friend. Keep that in mind when you face your enemy. And make sure you send the bitch screaming to Tartarus.'

The women nodded, harsh masks descending over their faces. It was a subtle change but the look in their eyes hardened somewhat and Lysandra could tell they were reliving Penelope's death throes, turning their sadness to cold anger. Thoughts of grief were being forged into those of revenge and hatred for the women of the other schools. Her eyes met Danae's. Like the others, her tears had ceased. Lysandra nodded in satisfaction and left the cell.

As soon as she was out of the Hellene women's sight she made haste back to the arena and the Gate of Life. Above her, she could still hear the crowd howling encouragement to the fighters on the sands. At least, she thought, Eirianwen still lived.

Lysandra squirmed her way through the press of fighters gathered around the gate to watch the match. Her height afforded her a good view of the arena and her eyes widened as she saw

193

Eirianwen. She was drenched in blood and Lysandra's hand flew to her mouth before she realised the blood was not hers.

Eirianwen wielded a one-handed axe with which she was hacking viciously into her hapless opponent, causing chunks of displaced flesh to fly. Even above the cheers, and the terrible screams of Eirianwen's adversary, Lysandra could hear the wet crunch of the iron axe-head crunching through bone and gristle. The stricken woman fell to her knees, bleeding from a dozen mortal wounds, her left arm nearly hanging off at the shoulder. Without even acknowledging Governor Frontinus, the beautiful Silurian grasped her foe by the hair and dragged her head back, exposing the throat. She raised her axe, punching the air in time to the mob's chant of '*Jugula! Jugula!*' drawing out the moment, eking out their pleasure. Only when she had them worked into a fever pitch did she bring the axe down, slicing her opponent's head from her shoulders with a single blow.

The crowd erupted as Eirianwen held her grisly trophy aloft. She was a terrible sight, naked, her hair awry, coated in blood and gore from her victim. She walked across the sands, coming close to the barrier that separated the spectators from the combat area. The mob stilled as she regarded the section before her. Holding the severed head by the hair, she whirled it several times above her before casting it like a hammer into the poorer upper tiers. A fight erupted at once for possession of the awful prize. Eirianwen saluted Frontinus nonchalantly before sauntering back to the Gate of Life.

Lysandra watched her approaching, at once relieved and appalled. This was a side to Eirianwen that she had only glimpsed when the Silurian had spoken of her past – but now she had revealed of her true nature, the savage come to the fore. She herself had taken pleasure in killing her enemy and had drunk in the adulation of the crowd as though it were a heady wine. But Eirianwen had plainly butchered her opponent, making her suffer before she released her to merciful death. That, Lysandra thought, was truly barbaric. However, she reasoned, Eirianwen was indeed from a savage tribe and could not be held accountable for her lack of restraint.

It was a hollow thought, and forgotten at once as the gore-drenched Briton entered the tunnel. Lysandra rushed forwards and embraced her, congratulating her on her win, ignoring the mire that soaked into her tunic. Eirianwen's smile was a white slash against the crimson and blue darkness of her face as she returned the embrace, both women heedless of who saw them.

Lysandra understood now that life was all the more sweet when death waited close by.

XXIII

Day in, day out, the ritualised slaughter of the arena continued. Hundreds of men, women and beasts died for the amusement of the mob, the candidacy of Aeschylus and the ambition of Sextus Julius Frontinus.

The governor of Asia Minor was not a young man, but was possessed of a strength and vigour that belied his age. It was by force of will that he held back the encroachment of time, refusing to retire and reap the benefits of decades in the service of Rome. Frontinus knew that he was not unique in this regard: the Empire was full of such men. How else could Rome maintain her place as the ultimate power in the world?

The governor was a connoisseur of the arena and its spectacles and, though he despised the mincing Aeschylus, he had to admit that the fat man had put on a grand show. His idea of pitting different schools against one another was not exceptional in Rome, but here in the provinces it was almost unheard of and the promotion of the women's game to something more than a sideshow was inspired.

Frontinus, like most discerning enthusiasts, had never taken the gladiatrices seriously. They were a novelty act, a joke. But the women of this Lucius Balbus were deadly in the extreme, their beauty adding a heady intoxicant to their allure. Indeed, as he watched the bare breasts and buttocks cavorting past in their deadly dance, Frontinus found himself shifting uncomfortably in his toga, lest his excitement be all too obvious.

He found himself arriving at the games earlier than usual just to catch all of the women's combats. He was well taken with one or two from Balbus's school, and decided he would grant the man an audience to acknowledge his skill as a trainer.

Thus it was that he welcomed the swarthy, sweating Balbus to the dignitaries' box.

'I am most impressed by your troupe, *lanista*,' he said. 'You have brought a diversity and dimension to these games that may well ensure a political post for my esteemed colleague, Aeschylus.' He indicated the Greek who was sitting close by.

'Your Honour is too kind.' Balbus bobbed his head up and down in deference. 'We do our meagre best, and your words mean very much to a lowly man such as I.'

Frontinus laughed. 'Come, *lanista*. You are as rich as Midas and all know it.' Waving away Balbus's denial before it could be spoken he turned his attention to the arena. 'Who is that girl?' he enquired.

Though Lucius Balbus was overjoyed with his summons he was more than a little nervous. It seemed, however, that his anxiety was without foundation, the governor merely wishing to acknowledge his troupe's skill. And his latest addition.

'That is Achillia, sir,' said Balbus, wincing slightly as Lysandra sliced the hand from the Thracian she was facing. Evidently, Spartan toughness was no myth and he was well pleased with the girl. Wounded in the first days of the games, she had recovered quickly, and as the spectacle entered its second moon, she was ready to fight again. It seemed also that she had forged the Hellene women who had performed so poorly before the games into a close-knit group of killers. The death of the fat fisher girl, whose name he had forgotten, had gone a long way to making the rest of the miserable bunch profitable.

'No, I meant who is she *really*?' Frontinus said. 'Achillia is not her real name, is it?'

'She is a slave, sir, nothing more.' Balbus felt small droplets of sweat break out over his body, suddenly fearful that Lysandra's outlandish Sisterhood had tracked her down and petitioned the governor for her release.

'But she has a name?'

'Yes, my lord, her name is Lysandra.' Balbus swallowed, wondering where the line of enquiry was going.

'And she *is* a Spartan, or is that just a piece of theatre that you have invented?'

Balbus hesitated. He desperately wanted to lie to Frontinus but, if the man knew more than he was letting on, lying to him could be ruinous – and potentially fatal. 'She is indeed, sir. The Genuine Article, so to speak.'

Frontinus acknowledged Lysandra who was standing with her opponent's neck under her blade. He thrust his thumb out, indicating that the Spartan put the woman to death. A one-handed ex-gladiatrix was useful to no one. Nonchalantly, Lysandra slit the Thracian's throat and was on her way back to the Gate of Life before the woman had finished her death throes. 'I want to meet her.' He turned back to Balbus.

'Yes, of course, Excellency.' Balbus felt something inside him fall over. Frontinus had not heard from any Spartan Embassy! The old goat merely wanted to be pleasured by a gladiatrix. That he had chosen one so frigid she could have been made of marble was a situation that the *lanista* could have done without. Why had the old man not chosen someone who would have willingly fucked him senseless? Balbus could only assume this to be a manifestation of the other gods' jealousy at all the favours Fortuna had shown him of late. He gave Frontinus a sickly smile. 'I shall have her sent to you at the end of today's spectacle, my lord,' he added.

'Excellent.' Frontinus regaled him with a smile. 'You may go.'

'You wanted to see me, *lanista*?'

Balbus had had Lysandra conveyed by litter to his rented offices outside the arena. She was fast becoming popular with the mob and could not be allowed to travel openly. He regarded her critically, wondering if she would cause a stir in *his* loins. Despite his preference for men, Balbus had enjoyed females as his bed partners in the past. But, as she stood before him, tall, pale, and undeniably beautiful, he came to the conclusion that she was just not his type. 'Indeed.' He smiled at her in what he hoped was a genuine fashion. 'Please,' he gestured to a couch, 'sit.'

Balbus clapped his hands and ordered slaves to bring wine. If she was at all taken aback by this show of hospitality, she gave no sign. Her cold gaze did not leave him and, though he could not be certain, Balbus thought there was the merest hint of an ironic half-smile playing about her lips. 'You have been fighting extremely well,' he told her as they sipped the local vintage.

Lysandra shrugged at the compliment. 'Of course. I hope to be matched against more competent opponents. These we face currently are somewhat beneath me.'

Balbus resisted the urge to laugh at her casual arrogance. Or, he mused, was it more than mere superciliousness. He had the distinct impression that Lysandra's bluster was heartfelt. 'You underestimate the other schools, Lysandra,' he offered. 'There are some good fighters out there.'

'I underestimate nothing, Lucius Balbus,' she said. 'That is folly. However, I am aware of my own skills and have seen nothing in this competition to trouble me.'

'You have not yet seen Sorina take to the sands.' Balbus wanted to know just what Lysandra thought of his *Gladiatrix Prima*.

'That is not a concern. We will not fight each other in these games. If the gods will that we are to meet on some other occasion, I shall have no compunction in sending your most profitable asset to Hades. But,' she added, 'you have not summoned me here to discuss my opinions on the games.'

'No,' Balbus agreed. There was little point in stalling matters any further. 'The governor is quite taken with you,' he went on. 'He wants to meet you.'

'He is an admirer of gladiatrices? Of women fighters?' Lysandra raised a quizzical brow.

'Well, as you say,' Balbus smiled at her, 'you are extremely good.'

Lysandra seemed to mull that over for a few moments. 'Yes,' she said. 'That would be most pleasant. I fail to see why Frontinus would want a slave at his dinner table, however.' She said this with a sarcastic lilt in her voice.

'Well…' Balbus spread his hands. 'Everybody loves the games. Frontinus is a connoisseur and his position affords him the opportunity to meet the best fighters. You should be honoured,' he added, appealing to her ego.

'Slaves have no honour, Balbus,' she told him mildly.

'Yes, well,' he brushed over that. 'Have a good time.'

Lysandra rose to her feet and made to go to the door. She paused, and turned back to him. 'Balbus… the governor wishes to talk to me. And that is all?'

Balbus sighed. He wanted to lie to her, but he realised that if Lysandra went into the situation unknowing, her reaction to wandering hands from Frontinus could be violent, as she had proven when Nastasen had manhandled her. That would certainly spell death for her, and a mountain of trouble for him and the repercussions. 'You had better sit down,' he said. He watched her return to her seat, wondering how she was going to react to the unspoken truth. 'Lysandra. It may be that he wants more than talk.'

'I will not lay with him,' she affirmed, ice in her voice. 'We are not whores, I have told you this. I am, or was, a Priestess of Athene. It is forbidden for me to be known by a man.'

Balbus had not known that, but part of the girl's enigma was revealed to him; this, then, was why she reacted so to Nastasen's attentions. 'Look, I said it may be that he wants to...' the *lanista* cleared his throat, 'you know. Do it. But maybe not. I just thought I would say something in case he... you know...' Balbus trailed off, feeling somewhat like a mouse under the gaze of a snake.

'In that case, it is impossible for me to attend. Balbus, you must tell him I am unwell.'

'Lysandra, you cannot refuse a summons from the governor.' The *lanista* hated to implore, but the ramifications of snubbing an influential man like Frontinus would be huge.

'No.'

'Look.' Balbus became all business. 'I'll make it worth your while.'

'There is nothing you can offer me that will make me change my mind.' Lysandra said loftily. 'Unless you offer me freedom, which I sincerely doubt.'

'No, I can't offer you that,' he agreed. 'But I can cancel the twenty lashes you are to receive when you return to the *ludus*. And,' he added, 'I can also forget about the complaints from the surgeon that you knocked him out cold to steal drugs for an already dead companion.'

'I am used to the lash, Balbus. It was common to receive it in the *agoge*. Or have you failed to notice how much my back is scarred already?'

'I can also have you and your Greeks moved from the barracks cells into the houses,' Balbus offered, his eyes not leaving hers. She wavered, he could see it. 'And ensure that Nastasen is assigned duties that keep him away from you.' He pressed his advantage. 'In effect, you would be responsible for training the Greek women. Though of course, you would have to muster with the others.

201

You must have seen that the more senior gladiatrices do not have the same regime as you currently do. I can elevate you and your women,' he snapped his fingers, 'like that.'

'*If* I go.'

'Yes. If you go.'

Lysandra got to her feet and commenced pacing up and down her arms folded across her chest, finger tapping her chin. Balbus watched, fancying he could read her thoughts by her expression. Intelligent she may be, but he was the master of making deals, his experience spanning years. She stopped suddenly. 'Very well. I shall go, if you swear that you will not renege on your promise.'

'I swear,' Balbus said at once, raising his hands piously.

Lysandra rolled her eyes. 'You make oaths too swiftly, Balbus.'

'I am a religious man,' he retorted. 'You may not think it, but it is the truth.' Lysandra stared at him for too long and Balbus had to fight down the urge to fidget under her cold, ice coloured gaze. There was something commanding about her, he realised. Guile she may not possess, but nevertheless she would be a formidable woman in years to come.

'I hope matters do not transpire as you have foreseen,' she said quietly. 'But if the lives of my sister Hellenes can be made better by my…' she trailed off. 'By my giving myself to this man, then it shall be done.'

'I hope so too.' Balbus was surprised that he actually meant it. He did, however, feel no guilt that he had bargained with gifts that Lysandra and her women had earned already. Their performances had warranted that they be elevated, but it would have been senseless to let her know that. Better to let her think that her self-sacrifice was duly noble.

And he was pleased that, along with their toughness, Spartan gullibility was no myth either.

*   *   *

Lysandra returned to the amphitheatre, her face a controlled mask. Inside she was in turmoil, her stomach in knots at what she may have to do. But it would be churlish of her to burden the women with her concerns. She desperately wanted to see Eirianwen, to seek her counsel, but there was no time. Balbus had instructed her to go straight to the baths and have herself 'made presentable' for Frontinus, but she felt she must share her news, at least the good part of it, with her confederates.

'What happened?' Thebe was full of concern when she entered the cell.

'It is nothing bad.' Lysandra forced herself to smile. 'In fact, it is all good,' she went on. 'As the best amongst you, I have been asked to attend a dinner tonight held by the governor of all Asia Minor. It seems that Sextus Julius Frontinus is an admirer of mine and the *lanista* is keen to pander to his whims.' Lysandra assumed that Thebe's roll of the eyes and sour expression was pure jealousy; little did the Corinthian know that more than dinner would be on Frontinus's menu. 'The other news,' she continued, 'concerns us all. Balbus is impressed with us and has ordered that, on our return from the games, we are to be elevated from the novice class.' This was greeted by nods and grins from the women. 'We are to be moved from our cells to the main houses. I shall be in command, of course.'

'Command?' Thebe cocked her head to one side.

'Yes. Of our training. As I am best qualified for the task. You people cannot be expected to be as competent as me when it comes to the use of weapons and the application of discipline. I have had the benefit of the *agoge*.'

'Oh, that *is* good news,' Thebe muttered.

'But now, I must go,' Lysandra said. 'No doubt I shall be able to regale you all with a few stories of the Roman high life when I return.' Her sardonic twist was missed by Thebe and the others. They were not as overjoyed as they should be by her news. She supposed that they were a little fearful that they would have to live up to her example when they trained and that would be no easy task.

But for now, she had to pay for the boon.

XXIV

Lysandra hardly recognised herself when they had finished. A small army of slave girls swarmed around her, erasing the Spartan and obscuring her with some other woman she did not know. Her face was painted with chalk and then her cheeks rouged with red ochre. This same substance, but of thicker constitution, was applied to her lips. Khol had been applied to her eyebrows to accentuate them, whilst the lids were decorated with a shadow of saffron. Her hair had been piled on top of her head in what the slave girls assured her was the latest fashion. This arrangement was held together with pins which Lysandra found extremely irritating, maddened by the urge to pull the fastenings away.

They dressed her in a long, white *chiton*, after the Hellene style, her arms bedecked with expensive-looking bracelets. The girls cooed and gasped at their handiwork but, when they held out a bronze mirror for her, she could only comment that she looked ridiculous. Her cheeks burning with the shame of it, she got to her feet to find that she felt almost off balance. Her hair felt as though it were suspended from the ceiling by wires that threatened to pull her off her feet. No one should be subjected to this, she thought angrily.

'I resemble a painted doll,' she complained to one of the girls. 'Perhaps I should attend as myself and not some… flute girl.'

The girl, much to Lysandra's annoyance, merely giggled. 'Don't be silly,' she chided. 'You look beautiful.'

'I look like an idiot.' Lysandra looked into her big, limpid eyes, and saw only confusion. She shook her head in disgust, realising that all these women thought about was hairstyles, makeup and gossiping about who was sleeping with whom. 'Come, feather-brain,' she hissed. 'I must be about it.'

'Featherbrain!' the slave exclaimed, and her compatriots tittered. 'Lysandra, you're so funny.' In her mind's eye, she saw herself glee-fully throttling the imbecilic little slut.

The slave girls escorted her through the gaol, in full few of her fellow gladiatrices who screamed abuse at her the moment she came into view. It must be very amusing to them, Lysandra seethed inwardly, to see someone as respected as she trussed up in such frippery. She thought she would die of embarrassment.

To compound matters, as they drew near the exit, she spied Catuvolcos, sitting with Sorina. The Gaul looked up at her and blinked, squinting through the gloom. She did her best to ignore him but he knew she had seen him.

'Well, well,' he said, approaching her. 'What have we here?' Sorina was at his shoulder, smirking.

'I am attending a banquet with the governor,' she told him. Ever since Catuvolcos had confessed his feelings and had been rebuffed, he had refused to speak to her. Instead he confined himself to harsh glares and mutterings in his barbaric tongue. But she supposed this sight of her humiliation was too good an opportunity for raillery. She decided to get a barb of her own in at his newfound 'friend'. 'Yes,' she went on. 'He has requested the presence of the games' foremost gladiatrix.' She directed her look past him to Sorina.

'A banquet!' Catuvolcos roared with laugher, and she smelt

the foul Egyptian beer on his breath. 'We know what sort of thing goes on at a *civilised* banquet, don't we, Sorina?'

'Indeed,' the older woman sneered. 'Painted like a whore, to be a whore. You'll have so many pricks in you before the night's out, your *cunnus* will be gaping like Helle's pit.'

Lysandra recoiled, stunned at the vulgarity to which the Amazon descended. 'I doubt that,' she spat. 'Unlike you, I don't open my legs for any and everyone who fancies it.' Lysandra was well pleased with herself, having managed she supposed to insult both Sorina and Catuvolcos at the same time. Certainly, she would not play the whipping girl for them. However, the barb was a little too sharp because, with a snarl of rage, Sorina leapt at her.

Lysandra dropped back into a fighting stance, ready to hammer the Dacian into the ground, but Catuvolcos grabbed the furious barbarian around the waist and hauled her back.

'She's not worth a flogging,' he shouted. Around Lysandra, the slave girls screamed and tried to get out of Sorina's way.

Sorina glared pure hatred at Lysandra who merely smirked, considering that it had been the older woman who had lost this encounter. That Catuvolcos had turned against her was, however, hurtful, especially when his amorous feelings towards her had never been encouraged. It was not as if she had led him to believe that she reciprocated in any way other than friendship and his hostility was uncalled for. And evidently, he was enjoying some sort of intimate relationship with Sorina; it was unreasonable of him to act in this manner, especially if he had found consolation elsewhere. But then, he was a barbarian, and what could one expect?

Lysandra made off without a backward glance.

The girls escorted her to a litter outside the gaol. Six strong men were lined up to carry it and eight legionaries stood fore and aft as escorts. Of course, the *lanista* was keen to ensure there were no mishaps with one of his prized possessions. Lysandra clambered into the lush, red-cushioned interior, exhortations to take care of both hair and makeup ringing in her ears.

Trussed up in her finery, she was unable to flop back on the cushions and try to relax. As if that would be possible, she thought to herself. The argument with Sorina and Catuvolcos had taken her mind away from the prospect of the evening's diversions, but now, alone, she had little else to dwell upon. She had to admit that she was somewhat fearful of what the night may bring. She prayed that Sorina's vicious comment was not the truth. She shuddered at the thought of being used in such a manner.

It was not the thought of a man that worried her; this was something she had discussed with Eirianwen. Indeed, she and the Silurian had used the *olisbos* together, and Lysandra considered the act of penetration to be extremely pleasurable. But this was an altogether different proposition; there would be neither tenderness nor care spared for her, she would merely act as the receptacle for another's gratification.

This night her slavery would be impressed upon her more vividly than ever before

Danae had been right when she had said that being a gladiatrix afforded some level of freedom. It was dangerous, to be sure, but Lysandra would by lying to herself if she did not admit that the danger was addictive. Life at the *ludus* was less harsh than her youth in the *agoge*, and afforded her the opportunity to honour Athene in blood. An ancient tradition, perhaps, but she felt her life had purpose.

Admittedly, her noble sacrifice would bring benefit to the women in her care; it was the Spartan way to embrace sacrifice and not to shirk from duty. But inside she was afraid. Lovingly penetrated by the *olisbos* guided by the hands of Eirianwen would be nothing like being held down and raped – for it would be rape – by an aging senator.

It is just the body, she told herself. In some ways it was akin to entering the arena. As the thought occurred – and she clutched at it – she dedided she could face Frontinus as Achillia, rather than Lysandra. For it was Achillia who was slave and gladiatrix, not Lysandra, once-priestess of Athene. If Achillia died in the arena or was treated basely it did not matter. She could, she realised, don the armour of the *psyche* and hold back the taint that rape would bring.

She felt some tension drain from her. Her genius had allowed her to find a solution to a moral conundrum that few others would have been able to solve. That she had the benefits of education and the Spartan upbringing made her fortunate enough to look at a situation logically, and not with histri-onics. Her neat psychological charade would save her honour and enable her to submit without submitting. As she felt the litter being lowered, she allowed herself to smile slightly at her own cleverness.

Lysandra was taken aback as she emerged from her carriage. She had expected opulence but the abode of Sextus Julius Frontinus must surely rival Domitian's Imperial Palace in Rome so impres-sive was it in size and décor. Great pillars of marble supported a structure that Lysandra fancied was easily as large as the Parthenon itself. Grand statuary formed an avenue to the entrance of the main house, the twelve gods and goddesses of the Pantheon stared down at all those who approached the abode of Asia Minor's governor. Fountains depicting dolphins and mythical creatures were interspersed artfully through a huge garden surrounding the palatial residence, the music of water filling the night air with a mystical cadence.

Balbus's men led her toward the entrance, where she was handed into the care of yet another soldiery. They eyed her appreciatively, evidently unaware that she could cripple or kill any one of them if she wished. This vindictive thought made her feel somewhat better about the openly salacious looks and she had to acknowledge a side to her that enjoyed the fact that, in the truest Spartan tradition, she was obviously a beauty.

The men, however, made no attempt to touch her, as they could not know she was a slave; the idiot girls at the amphitheatre must have done an excellent job at disguising her as a Roman freewoman. As they walked through the gigantic atrium, Lysandra could not fail to be impressed by the sheer beauty of the abode. It was only by sheer effort of will that she did not gawk at the marvellously arrayed treasures and murals that surrounded her.

Two grandly proportioned doors were at the opposite end of the entrance hall, attended by a bird-like man of middle years. He smiled at her, and produced a scroll from within a voluminous toga.

'I am Achillia,' she said in her most gracious Latin.

The birdman scanned the list, and shook his head. 'I have but one lady… unaccompanied,' he said, '*Lysandra*.' He looked at her inquisitively, eyebrows raised.

'That is in error,' she told him imperiously, inwardly crushed that Frontinus must know her real name. However, she would not discard her armour so easily. 'You have heard of me, of course. I am the gladiatrix…'

'Yes.' He cut her off. '*Achillia*. A great match against the Caledonian last month! I saw that,' he went on. 'A fabulous show. I recognise you now that I look closer. You know, you can't expect much from scribes.' He took a stylus and altered her name on his scroll. 'There we are.' He grinned. '*Achillia*. I shall announce you as 'Achillia of Sparta' then?'

'As you wish.' Lysandra was loath to admit to herself the thrill she garnered from the man's recognition and deference.

The birdman looked from side to side as if checking to see if anyone was watching him. 'I'm a really big supporter of the games,' he whispered. 'I wanted to ask…' He hesitated, his eyes blinking owlishly. 'Can you write?'

'Of course I can write.' Lysandra was outraged, feeling the blood rush to her already too-pink cheeks. 'Do you take me for some sort of imbecile? Or do you merely think that breasts disqualify one from having an iota of intelligence…?'

'No, no.' He held up his hands apologetically. 'I wanted to ask you if you would sign your name for me.' He blushed as he spoke. 'Well, not for me, really. For my children. They are huge admirers of the games…'

'My name?'

'Yes.' the man offered her a piece of parchment. 'As a souvenir.'

Lysandra was taken aback by the request, but she kept her expression neutral. 'Certainly.' She took the stylus. 'What are their names?'

'Marcus and Lucius,' he said proudly. 'Two terrors, but they are all I have since their mother passed on a few years back…' He trailed off as Lysandra continued to write. Eventually, she handed the parchment back, inwardly thrilled at having been recognised. 'Thank you, lady,' he said, clearly grateful.

He turned and opened the great double doors, and in a voice that belied his slight build bellowed the arrival of 'Achillia of Sparta, famed Gladiatrix of the Games of Aeschylus.'

As soon as he closed the doors behind her, the man looked excitedly at the parchment. 'Marcus and Lucius,' the man read. 'Achillia of Sparta greets you, admonishes you to obey your father in all things. Only through discipline and deference can excellence be attained.' He could not help but smile at the stiffness of the language, and indeed, the message, but he knew that his children would be well pleased. And he also had a tale to tell; it was not often that the famous spared even a look for those such as himself. Stiff she may be, but Achillia of Sparta had won a friend, and he would be sure to tell his fellow aficionados just whom they should be cheering on.

'You're *not* screwing her?'

Stick and Catuvolcos had been long ensconced at the trainers' recreation site and if they were not exactly swimming in their cups they had at least begun to paddle in them. The 'recreation site' was, in fact, a rented warehouse, not far from the amphitheatre. It had the advantage of being cheap enough and spacious enough to accommodate the trainers from the different schools, a good number of whores and a vast amount of wine and beer, all of which were paid for by the various *lanistas* by way of thanks to their training staff.

'No. She's a friend. You know, we of the tribes share a kinship of custom if not of blood.' Catuvolcos's eyes swept around the room. Nastasen was sitting with some friends from the other schools. A motley bunch from all over the empire, it seemed to Catuvolcos that evil followed the Nubian wherever he went. Certainly, Nastasen's band had a dangerous look to them, hard men who enjoyed their brutal work. He caught Catuvolcos's gaze and waved, evidently feeling well disposed – probably due to the copious amount of hemp he and his companions were inhaling.

'That is good,' Stick said sagely. 'Balbus would skin you alive if you were emptying your sack into Sorina. Bad for business.'

'Well, I'm not. And what is it to you anyway?'

'No need to get tetchy.' Stick's eyes became more bulbous. 'I was just worried about you. Everyone knows you were sweet on the Spartan, and now you're spending all your time with Sorina. You just can't go round wanting to hump the flock, my friend.'

'Well.' Catuvolcos took a huge draft of his beer. 'I'm not sweet

212

on anyone, especially Lysandra. She's a bitch and I'm grateful for Sorina for pointing it out.'

'Ah,' said Stick. 'Well, she's becoming a very popular bitch. I saw in the market today that there are Achillia figurines on sale. That's unheard of, this is her first proper games. I can imagine that Sorina...' Stick proceeded to choke on his wine and received a hearty pounding on the back from the big Gaul.

'Go down the wrong way?' Catuvolcos teased. His own capacity for drinking was legendary.

'Look!' Stick pointed. 'I thought that was her for a moment!'

Catuvolcos followed the Parthian's gesture, and his own mouth fell open. One of the whores was serving some drinks, deftly avoiding the grasps of inebriated trainers. She was remarkably similar to Lysandra in looks if not bearing, though she was somewhat shorter and slightly younger, she could have been sister to the arrogant Spartan.

'Must be a Greek.' Catuvolcos scowled, lacing his tone with scorn.

Stick regarded him. 'You're a bit terse, aren't you?' Catuvolcos glowered, but Stick had looked away. 'Oh dear,' he laughed. 'Nastasen has an eye for her.'

Indeed, as the girl passed the Nubian, he lunged forward and grabbed her, pulling her onto his lap. She squealed in fake outrage, making a small, yet obviously provocative attempt to escape. Nastasen laughed and groped the girl's breasts, pulling down her tunic to reveal them. She giggled, her face a mask of seduction, and wiggled her bottom on the trainer's lap. Nastasen pulled her closer to him, his purple tongue licking at her neck, his fingers pulling hard at her small nipples.

Catuvolcos saw the girl – she could not have been more than sixteen – wince at this. It was none of his business, so turned his attention back to his drink. Nastasen, it seemed, liked it rough, but the girl, young as she was, was a whore, and would

213

be well used to satisfying the demands of a paying public. *Much like Lysandra*, he thought: both prostituted their bodies for the enjoyment of men. In Catuvolcos's experience, some women came to love the adulation gained in the arena, the competition and the winning. Lysandra, Sorina had taught him, was such a one. She proclaimed a moral high ground: to be *civilised*. But in truth she was the most barbaric, for she truly enjoyed the killing. For her, it was not survival but pleasure. Even her seduction of Eirianwen was an act, designed to insult the tribal matriarch: the corruption of the woman who would likely succeed Sorina in the tribal hierarchy was indeed something she would revel in.

The girl with Nastasen cried out and Catuvolcos glanced up to see the big Nubian turning her round and lifting up his own tunic. To calls of encouragement from his group he spat on his hand and felt between her legs, grinning as he lifted his glistening fingers to show his comrades. Smearing his now massively engorged phallus with her juices, he spread open her legs, revealing her sex to the gleeful shouts of his friends. Then, settling himself, he rammed himself into her savagely.

The girl screamed in pain as Nastasen penetrated her. This only seemed to excite him more, as he pulled at her long hair, leaning over as he continued to thrust brutally into her. The girl desperately tried to turn her cries of pain into those of simulated lust but Catuvolcos could see at each repeated push from Nastasen her expression twisting in agony. The trainer was talking to her as the debasement continued; the Gaul could see his lips forming obscenities and degradations of all kinds. He was asking her if she liked it, if she wanted more. Through her tears the girl was nodding and encouraged him to quicken his efforts.

His hands were all over her, pulling, and scratching, his hips thrusting hard as he enjoyed her. Catuvolcos was revolted, yet could not tear his eyes away from Nastasen as he pumped unceasingly into the girl's flesh. The trainer's pace quickened and his confederates began to clap faster and faster. The Nubian's eyes were squeezed tight shut as, with a bellow of mingled joy and triumph he came into her. In the throes of orgasm, his teeth clamped down on her shoulder, breaking the skin.

Catuvolcos had seen enough.

'Where are you going?' Stick asked blearily, but the Gaul waved him away. As he made his way towards the couch, Nastasen had pulled out, and was forcing the girl to take his still half engorged member in her mouth.

'Suck it,' he crowed, egged on by the others. 'Suck it after it's been in you, you dirty slut.' He looked about at his companions. 'You have to try this bitch,' he said, languidly moving his hips as the girl's mouth worked on him. Her eyes were closed and Catuvolcos could see her throat working, trying not to gag as the Nubian forced her head further down. 'Who's next?' he laughed. 'Who wants some?'

'I'll be next,' Catuvolcos forced himself to smile. The group of trainers looked up at him, patently surprised that he had the temerity to interrupt their party.

'You?' Nastasen pushed the girl away, eyeing him. 'Yes.' He grinned. 'You want her for the same reason I did. It's just like fucking Lysandra and we both want to do that, don't we?'

'Only so I can imagine treating that arrogant bitch in the way she deserves.' Catuvolcos hoped his manner was glib. He had not realised that Nastasen's hatred and contempt for Lysandra extended so far. 'I might even piss on the slut,' he added, extracting a grin from the Nubian giant.

'Take her, then my fine friend.' Nastasen said with a sweep of his arm. 'You can bring her to us later.'

'I doubt that.' Catuvolcos winked. 'I plan to keep her entertained for hours!' He clamped his jaw, resisting the urge to smash the leering, black face in. 'Come on.' He gestured to the girl, who tried to smile coquettishly. On her tear-streaked features, the expression was almost obscene.

'Have fun,' Nastasen called as he lead her away. Catuvolcos looked over his shoulder and grinned.

XXV

As she entered the *triclinium*, the dining area, Lysandra felt the eyes of guests upon her. They were not the rough supporters of the arena. These were, for the most part, the richest and most influential people of Halicarnassus. It should have been a great honour to be invited to such a soiree but the fact that she was here as little more than a piece of meat galled her. It would, she knew, have been a terrifying experience for an ordinary woman, but she was secure in the knowledge that her fortitude and bearing would see her through the humiliating ordeal. She was Achillia, not Lysandra, she reminded herself.

The *triclinium* was vast, comfortably accommodating the crowd of diners Frontinus had invited. The centrepiece of the room was a wrestling ring, in which two men grappled to the half-hearted attention of the notables. All manner of delicacies were on display and the tang of incense hung in the air, masking the fishy odour of *garum*, the sauce Romans so loved. Dining couches were arranged artfully, allowing the guests to chat with ease, yet spaced well enough to permit slaves to be about their work of pouring and serving without becoming embarrassingly noticeable.

Slaves, Lysandra knew, were to be neither heard nor seen.

Much like the *helots* of old Sparta, they existed merely to provide a service. She had come to realise that, whilst in principle she was a slave herself, she was far superior to the domestic chattel. Her skills and her heritage made this so. Calling a Spartan a slave and her being one were two different things entirely.

Of course, the forthcoming encounter with Frontinus might impress slavery upon a lesser woman but, Lysandra thought suddenly, it was her beauty and presence that had inspired lust in the man. Whilst this was distasteful, it was perfectly understandable. That men admired her was an undeniable fact. Had Catuvolcos not professed his love, and then fallen to depression at her refusal? She had seen, too, the hungry looks from the men in the crowds at the amphitheatre and heard their declarations of love and other more unsavoury suggestions. As she moved into the room, she realised that Frontinus was merely acting in a Roman manner, exercising his power, taking for himself what he wished. It was the way of the Empire, in microcosm.

Her reverie was interrupted as an elderly man stepped up to her, smiling openly.

'Achillia of Sparta,' he said. He was somewhat shorter than she, his face lined by age and the elements. 'I am Sextus Julius Frontinus.'

'Greetings,' Lysandra nodded.

'You are as beautiful as Venus,' he said, using the irritatingly incorrect Roman name for Aphrodite. It was Lysandra's view that if their plagiarism of the Hellenistic pantheon was so blatant, why did Romans bother with the farcical name-altering. 'Or, perhaps Minerva would be more apt,' he went on. 'The warrior goddess come from Olympus to grace us with her presence.'

Comparing her to the goddess to whom she was once a priestess was ironic in the extreme; however, she suppressed a grin at the man's unintended witticism. 'You are most gracious,' she acknowledged, with a tilt of her head. 'I thank you for your words, Sextus Julius Frontinus.'

'Sextus, please,' he smiled disarmingly. 'I find *trinomen* awfully stuffy, don't you?'

'They are a very *Roman* thing,' she responded.

'You have no love for Rome or Romans, I can tell.' Frontinus led her to a section of couches arranged in a semi-circle. Had the governor's intentions been anything other than what they were, this would be a place of extreme honour. 'Your current situation would make that understandable,' he added.

'You are mistaken, Governor,' she said, deliberately using his formal title. She would not cause a scene, for it was not the Spartan way to act without decorum, but she felt no desire to endear herself to the man. 'I admire Rome and view her as a natural, if somewhat crass successor to the Hellenistic ideal.' He raised his eyebrows and gestured for wine to be brought.

'Crass? That could be called rich, coming from a Spartan, my dear. It is said of Sparta that she is the most uncultured city in all Hellas.'

Lysandra sipped her wine, regarding him over the rim of her cup. 'If one thinks of culture as statues, droning rhetoric and the rule of the *demos*, then your observation would be correct. These are Athenian 'qualities,' so called. If one views the precepts of honour, virtue, forthright speech and prowess in war as culture, then you shall find no *polis* more sophisticated than my own.' She was rather pleased with that answer, for Rome was, by nature, a martial society.

Evidently, Frontinus was pleased by it also; raising his cup, he smiled and drank. '*Ave, Victrix*,' he said. 'I can see why you are so dangerous in the arena, for your tongue is as skilful as your blade.'

'I find it somewhat offensive,' a younger man broke in.

'Gaius Minervinus Valerian,' Frontinus introduced him. 'Tribune of the Second Augusta.'

'What do you find offensive, Tribune?' Lysandra asked.

'That a woman has opinions on things that are no concern of hers.'

Lysandra bristled. 'The governor has invited me to his couch, Tribune, and engaged in discourse on matters upon which I have knowledge. I will not sit and bat my eyes, giggling like a fool in the pretence that I have no understanding.' Her eyes flicked towards Frontinus momentarily, as she tried to judge his mood. The governor was watching them both and seemed to be revelling in their disagreement.

'Anyone may be taught a few well-learned phrases, *lady*,' Valerian sneered, 'and Greek *slaves* are much valued for their retention of knowledge.'

'It is true there are few Romans who possess our wisdom.' Lysandra's lips twisted in the slightest of smiles.

Valerian's face flushed in anger. 'I overheard you speak of Spartan battle prowess,' he said. 'If Sparta is so mighty, how then is she merely part of Rome's Empire?'

'Sparta is a client-state, Tribune,' Lysandra corrected. 'But, the answer to your question is Poseidon's will and technology.'

'How so?' Frontinus raised a hand, cutting off further comment from Valerian.

'Poseidon's will, Governor, came in the form of an earthquake. After the war with Athens, Sparta was pre-eminent in Hellas which, at the time, meant pre-eminence on the world stage. But Sparta was never a greatly numerous population and the loss of life by the Earth Shaker's hand, coupled with the numerous wars she fought, was irreplaceable. It was impossible for Sparta to retain her position. Though, as all know, our warriors are the finest to ever grace a battlefield.'

'And technology?' Frontinus prompted. Lysandra had the feeling that to him her display of wisdom was akin to watching a dog speak.

'Technology drives war, governor. The Hellene phalanx was becoming archaic as generals drew more upon the resources of manpower in the country. It was no longer enough to have merely men of landed status bearing arms. Lesser men became lighter infantry and cavalry became more widely used. Philip of Macedon took the phalanx to its next, and natural stage of development, producing the finest military machine the world has ever known. That his son carried his torch to the Persian barbarians is both testament to Alexander's genius and the skill of his father in moulding the army.' Despite herself, Lysandra too was enjoying the conversation. It had been a long time since she had been able to discuss such matters with anyone who would have the remotest chance of understanding her.

'But,' Valerian cut in once again. 'How can you say that the Macedonian phalanx was the finest military machine, when it was consistently beaten by us Romans?' His smile was triumphant; history was the final arbiter.

'Technology, Tribune.' She spoke as one would to a child. 'The phalanx had been adapted continually, as it only had to face armies of similar disposition. Thus, the *sarissa* – or pike,' she translated the Hellenic word to Latin, 'was lengthened to ridiculous extremes. Indeed it became the primary weapon of the army, a task for which it had never been intended.'

Valerian waved this away. 'A gap in your knowledge, lady. The Macedonian pike would grind the enemy before it. How then is this not the primary weapon?'

'The task of the *phalangite* – the pike-man – was to engage the enemy. It was the task of the heavy cavalry to deliver the hammer-blow that ended the battle. Thus it was at Chaeronaea and indeed all of Alexander and Philip's victories.'

'This does not explain the pathetic failure of the phalanx against our Legions,' Valerian declared hotly. 'You evade the point, gladiatrix.'

Lysandra regarded him as though he was something she had trodden in. 'I have already told you, the phalanx that faced Rome was a mere shadow of its former self. Had the fledgling Roman republic faced the army of Philip or Alexander, I think we might have found our roles reversed at this table.'

'You insult me!'

'No, your lack of military knowledge and persistence in pursuing the argument insults you… *Tribune*. Rome's officers ought to know their history: Hannibal and Pyrrhus both brought Rome close to defeat using an inferior phalanx to Alexander's.'

'What an amazing slave you are.' Valerian sneered, gesticulating for more to drink. 'You are a tactician as well as a historian then?'

'Of course.' Lysandra allowed herself to be smug. 'In the Temple of Athene, we are well educated.' She let the word hang, fixing Valerian with her gaze. She hoped she made it plain that she thought him anything but.

'You were a priestess?' Frontinus interrupted, evidently deciding to intervene before the argument degenerated to insult-hurling.

'Yes, Governor.' Lysandra turned her attention back to him. 'Before I came to this, I lived all my life in the auspices of Athene.'

'I have heard of your Order.' Frontinus said, surprising her. 'A very Spartan thing,' he added. 'They train you as they do their men. This then, would explain your knowledge of all things martial, as well your skill in the fight.'

'That is so.' Lysandra affirmed.

'But your Sisterhood has made no effort to find you, to buy your freedom?'

'They must think me dead, and to that life I suppose I am dead too.' She was shocked as the words came from her mouth but realised instantly the truth of them. 'I could not go back now to what I once was. There was a time when my current circumstance gave me a grave dilemma, but a wise man — a priest – told me that I honour Athene in what I do. I am a slave, yes. But what slave, what woman, may honour her goddess in blood and sit at discourse with the governor of all Asia Minor? One of my companions once said that there is a liberation in the arena that no freewoman can know and there is truth in that.'

'You compare yourself to a freewoman, slave?' Valerian sniped from the sidelines.

'I am at the beck and call of no man,' she said pointedly, not taking her eyes from Frontinus. 'I live by my skill and I am extremely good at what I do. My days are not taken with the raising of children or the care of a husband. Instead, they are filled perfecting what I have trained all my life to do. That, to me, is the will of my goddess. In serving her, I cannot consider myself slave.'

'*At the beck and call of no man*? That is not so. For you *are* a slave and I am a Roman. You will decorate my pillow, should I wish it, and then I'll give you a firm enough lesson.'

Lysandra had had her fill: it was one thing to maintain decorum, but the insults had now gone beyond a duel of wits. 'You are drunk, Tribune' she smirked 'and I fear that your teaching would be anything but firm enough.'

Valerian lurched from the couch, his arm poised to slap Lysandra across the face but, even as he moved, Lysandra was on her feet, her eyes burning with a cold fire. The sound of her wine cup smashing on the floor was loud and many heads turned towards the governor's couch. Feeling the eyes of his peers upon him, the Roman officer hesitated and lowered his hand. Turning to Frontinus he bowed stiffly. 'Forgive me, Governor. I must leave your gathering; I just recalled an unavoidable appointment.'

Frontinus smiled coldly and nodded his assent. He kept his gaze on the young officer as he walked away, swaying ever so slightly, before turning back to Lysandra. 'Come,' the governor got to his feet. 'Walk with me.'

She eyed him for a moment, before nodding her assent, but did not take the hand he extended.

XXVI

'This has to stop,' Sorina declared, her eyes fierce.

Eirianwen shrugged, and turned her attention to her drink. 'I don't see what business it is of yours. Clan Chief you may be, but it is my choice with whom I make love.' The two sat apart from the rest of the tribeswomen; the others wisely decided to leave both *Gladiatrix Prima* and *Secunda* to themselves. Sorina had decided that now was the time to confront Eirianwen directly regarding her infatuation with Lysandra. The feeling between the two young women was obviously growing and her own disapproval was not enough to discourage Eirianwen from the relationship. A more direct approach was required.

'I say this not from spite, Eirianwen, but to protect you. It is a disaster waiting to happen. You must see this.'

The beautiful Briton looked up. 'I can see that you are getting old, Sorina, and are growing bitter in the autumn.'

Sorina recoiled. 'Before *she* came along, you would never have spoken to me like that. She is tainting you, Eirianwen. All can see it but you. Even Catuvolcos, who was once besotted by her, has reckoned her for what she is.'

'Catuvolcos is hurt because she rejected his advances. This, as you have often told me, is the way of men. I no longer wish to speak of Lysandra to you.' Eirianwen slammed her cup down on the table, causing the others to look around. 'It is you who have become tainted, not I. Your bitterness is consuming you and you must lay it aside.'

'Do not think to give me advice, whelp,' Sorina warned, leaning forward on the bench. 'You are not ready yet to challenge me for leadership of the Clan.'

Eirianwen sighed, her shoulders slumping as she let the anger drain out of her. 'I have no wish to challenge you, Sorina. I have found some small happiness. How can you begrudge me that?'

'Because it will destroy you, girl. I seek only to spare you the pain that I foresee coming from this. Even now, your Lysandra is with governor Frontinus, drinking and, aye, parting her legs for him. Think on that, Silurian. Next time you put your lips to her sex, think of what and *who* has been there.'

At the mention of Frontinus, Eirianwen stiffened once again, and Sorina knew that her barb and sunk deep. 'Yes,' she hissed. 'I can see your feelings on your face. You are no longer sure, are you? Sure of her, sure of how you will feel about her. I will guess that she'll claim that she went unwillingly. I can tell you this is not so, for Catuvolcos and I saw her – painted and perfumed like a Roman whore. Beneath her veneer of chastity, she is a wanton.' When Eirianwen did not respond, Sorina pressed on. 'But this you know, as does everyone who passes by whatever dark corner you can find for your lovemaking. Her moans and sobs are loud for all to hear. Does she not please you, Eirianwen? She will please this Roman in the same way, with her mouth and tongue, giving herself and enjoying her debasement…'

'Enough!' Eirianwen shouted. 'You do not know her, Sorina. Your words strike me as hard as iron, for I am sick that she must go to *him* of all Romans. But she had no choice. Speak to me no more of this. I have made my choice and you are not a goddess to curse me for it.'

'Then you are not of the tribe.' Sorina's voice was low, but the words were heavy with doom.

Eirianwen went white. 'You cannot do that.'

'I can and I will, unless you cast her aside.'

For her part, Sorina had not meant matters to go so far, but now the awful words were pronounced she could not take them back. She loved Eirianwen but the corruption was deep in her and, as Clan Chief, Sorina could not allow its influence to spread amongst the others. But in that moment, she saw that she had erred greatly. Eirianwen's perfect features began to twist in hatred, the usually soft blue eyes becoming hard and empty.

'Then I *do* challenge you!' Eirianwen hissed. 'Here and now or in the arena. It makes no difference, for the result will be the same.'

Sorina baulked but could not back down; it was not the way of the Tribes to refuse honourable challenge. She cleared her throat, lest her voice crack. 'The arena, then,' she said. 'Balbus would kill the winner if we fought without his agreement. I shall see him and tell him of our intention.'

'Good.' Eirianwen got to her feet. 'I told you, months ago, that her fate, yours and mine were intertwined. Only now do I see the truth of it. Morrigan Dark Fate has decreed this, Sorina.'

'You are sure of your course?' Sorina set her shoulders, looking up at the younger woman from her bench. 'You are willing to die for your Spartan?'

'When the Mother becomes the Crone, the dark days draw close, Sorina. I am still yet the Maiden and your day is done.'

'We shall see.' Sorina forced iron to her voice, though her heart was breaking. 'I have fought many battles, child, against better even than you. They are now fled the flesh, whilst I live on. You will go the same way as those others.'

Eirianwen smiled, but it was bleak with anger. 'Everyone has her day, Clan Chief,' she spat. 'The time for talking is over, then. You and I are done... till we are done.' She turned on her heel without another word and stalked away from her kin.

She walked aimlessly through the corridors of the gaol, her eyes blurred with tears. Sorina's mention of the hated Frontinus had twisted in her guts like the cold iron of a blade.

Eirianwen recalled the coming of the Legions, the fire and sword, and the blood of her tribe. The legionaries were like ants, moving inexorably over the land, swarming over and destroying all that stood against them. The mightiest warriors of the Silures were naught before the slight but iron-disciplined men of Rome. Strength meant nothing against their cowards' organisation; courage futile in the face of such honourless, efficient warfare.

Eirianwen had known Lysandra had gone to Frontinus. The news of it was common amongst the fighters from Balbus's *ludus* but she had had no chance to speak to Lysandra on the matter. The Spartan had been whisked away to be prepared for her meeting and Eirianwen had steeled herself for the worst. But she knew Lysandra and knew that she would not go to the Roman with willing enthusiasm. She was well aware that the inexperienced former priestess had come to love her and, having listened to her incessant talk of Spartan virtue and honour, Eirianwen trusted that, in her heart, Lysandra would remain true even if her body was violated by the governor. It was a sickening thought. Eirianwen had seen Frontinus many times, the image of his lined, weather-beaten face branded onto her mind's eye and the thought of his hands and lips on Lysandra's skin turned her stomach. Sorina had hit a nerve with her and she now harboured a doubt that she could look on her lover in the same light. But she would not discard her at Sorina's say so; she and Lysandra shared too much for it to be so easily cast aside.

Sorina.

Thinking of the Clan Chief caused her fresh pain. The older woman was friend, sister and mother to her, her kin through the blood of the Tribes. When she had first come to the *ludus* it had been Sorina who had allayed her fears, Sorina who had given her the courage to fight on, Sorina who had taught her the tricks of the arena, the skills needed to survive. To win.

Yet Sorina's eyes were skewed when it came to Lysandra. She was not of the Tribes, true, but Eirianwen knew there must be more to the hatred than that. It was blinding, all consuming, and that in itself was an evil. The Morrigan was playing her game, even here in far off Asia, setting those that loved against each other so that another love might survive.

Eirianwen cursed the goddess with all her heart for she knew that Dark Fate laughed at them all.

Catuvolcos took the girl from the warehouse and led her through the dark streets of Halicarnassus. A slight rain was falling, masking the usual rotting odour for the warehouse district. Feeling somewhat self-conscious, he put his arm round her shoulder, feeling her snuggle against him as they walked.

'I'm available for anything,' she said. 'I don't normally take more than one man at a time, but I'm told that I must if the trainers want it. I can also sing and play the lyre, but people hardly ever want that.'

'I'm not going to do anything with you, girl,' Catuvolcos said gruffly.

'Oh.' The prostitute was taken aback. 'You'd like to watch me with others then? Or shall I just put on a show for you?'

'No… no.' Catuvolcos was appalled. 'I just wanted to get you away from Nastasen. He can become strange when he's been inhaling that stuff of his.'

'Yes, opiates do that,' the girl said. 'They prolong the act of sex, but they affect people in odd ways.' She paused, looking up at him. 'Thank you.'

Catuvolcos gave her a slight smile. 'It is well,' he said. 'You are very young, and I doubt that anyone deserves to be treated in that manner.'

'Oh, you get used to it,' she said nonchalantly. 'It's not as if I like it, you know, but we are paid well enough. Well, the owner of the brothel is paid and we earn a little. I am not on the streets and my belly is not hungry. Most of the time.'

'You are hungry now?' Catuvolcos asked, realising that the beer he had drunk had made him ravenous.

'Starving,' she said. 'But I never eat before a party. I could be sick if someone puts it too far…' she trailed off. 'Well, you know what I mean.'

He grunted, knowing all too well. 'I could eat too.'

The girl pulled away suddenly, looking up at him. 'Why are you doing this?' she demanded.

'Because…' He trailed off, looking at her. In truth, she *did* resemble Lysandra but there was a youthful softness to her face the Spartan did not possess, even though only a few years separated the two girls. Certainly, the prostitute was streetwise and accustomed to being used, but her pathetic attempts to feign enjoyment at the degradation that Nastasen had subjected her to had sickened him. Indeed it had wrenched his heart to see so young a girl forced to act in such a manner. He realised he had not answered her question and shrugged with a grin. 'I don't know,' he answered honestly. 'What is your name?'

'Well,' the girl lowered her eyes, toeing the pavement, 'they call me Venus at the brothel. But my real name is Doris.'

'Doris?'

'It's Greek. I'm named after my mother,' she said defensively.

'It's very pretty,' he lied. 'I am called Catuvolcos.'

'Well then, Catuvolcos,' she smiled and offered him her hand, 'shall we eat? I know a few places nearby.'

Catuvolcos encased her tiny hand in his big paw. It felt good, he realised.

Lysandra ignored the sly looks and muttered comments as she followed the Roman governor from the *triclinium*. Everyone who saw knew that she could only be accompanying him for one reason. It was humiliating in the extreme but she was too nervous to be as outraged as she should be.

'These formal parties are such a bore,' the Roman said as they walked through his abode. His voice echoed slightly on the marble walls. 'I must apologise for Valerian. He is a good boy normally but turns ugly with drink.'

'It is of no matter, Governor. I am well accustomed to abuse. I hear it all the time from the crowds.'

'Yes, I suppose you do,' he acknowledged, leading her to a small anteroom. It was well furnished with three couches and a table, draped resplendently in red coverings. Many scrolls adorned the walls and there was a desk and chair set up in one corner near a small window. 'My study,' he said.

'It is very lavish.' Lysandra hesitated as he walked through, easing himself onto a couch. She did not now know what to do and felt vaguely foolish standing in the doorway. Perhaps she should merely disrobe and get the whole sordid business over with quickly. Suddenly, she realised that getting out of the raiment in which she was clad would be no easy undertaking.

'What are you doing there?' Frontinus smiled at her. He poured wine for them both, with his own hand, from a *krater*. 'Please, do sit.' He gestured to the couch opposite his own. Lysandra was relieved. Evidently the time was not now and she would have died of embarrassment if she had cast her clothes aside before the moment was upon her.

'So tell me,' he said as she sat. 'Do you think the *retiarius* superior to the *murmillo*? I am always fascinated by those bouts, as they say so much. Two opposites, each affording the fighting man or,' he inclined his head, 'woman, different advantages and weaknesses. One would have thought the armour of the *murmillo* would afford heavy odds in favour over the net and trident of the *retiarius*. Yet these bouts are always closely fought.'

'I am not trained as a *retiaria*,' Lysandra said after a moment's thought. 'But I should hazard that it takes much skill to fight as one. In my view, skill should prevail over brute force. But, it depends on the fighter,' she added. 'There really are no superior *styles* of gladiator. It is the individual and how he or she applies the training of the *ludus* when in the arena.'

Frontinus continued in this manner for some time, quizzing Lysandra on her knowledge of the games, her opinions on different fighters she had seen and their particular merits. In time the conversation turned to war and strategy as it had in the *triclinium*. Yet Frontinus was not confrontational as Valerian had been. Indeed, she found his discourse engaging and his tactical knowledge superior even to her own. Then again, he had had the benefit of practical experience. In her turn, she queried him, applying his know-how to the gaps in her theoretical training.

For hours, they debated the battle of Cynoscephalae, regarded as the classic legion against phalanx clash, this and the campaigns of Caesar in Gaul, the Marian Wars and more. Frontinus refilled the oil lamp several times and, though they both partook of the wine, sobriety and dialogue not drunken revelry was the order of the night. She found herself almost liking the man. He was witty, engaging, and possessed of an awesome knowledge of all things martial. Lysandra was also gratified that he, the great general, even conceded to some of her points.

The hours passed into the next day and Lysandra found herself growing tired. Nevertheless, she considered it would be crass in the extreme to show this so she continued, matching the old night owl, point for point. But, during a particularly interesting discussion on Leuctra and the Spartan tactics employed there, she could not help stifling a yawn.

Frontinus broke off in mid-sentence. 'Forgive me,' he said. 'The night has almost passed us by.'

Lysandra swallowed, her heart beginning to pound anew. 'Yes, Governor,' she said. The debate had disarmed her, but now she had to steel herself once again for the ordeal to come. At least, she thought, he was not as hateful as she had supposed. She considered that the Roman's lovemaking would in all likelihood be straightforward, and uncomplicated. She counted herself an excellent judge of character and the lengthy conversation had revealed much about him. Though she knew she would not enjoy it, at least it would not be the nightmare rape she had envisioned and, for that, she was thankful. She reached to her shoulder, and began to tug the soft silk of the *chiton* away.

Frontinus sat up quickly. 'Whatever are you doing?' he asked, looking vaguely perplexed.

She blushed furiously. Removing the garment was as difficult as she had imagined. 'You would prefer me to keep this on?' she asked. 'I am sorry, I have never done this before, and am unused to pleasing the male sex.'

'I did not invite you here for *that*!' Frontinus's smile was kindly. 'I will not deny that if you came to me willingly, I would be honoured, for you are extremely beautiful… not to mention intelligent, which is rare amongst women.'

She pulled the *chiton* back into place too relieved at being wrong to be offended by his unconscious arrogance. As she adjusted the dress, she realised it was not she who had erred; Balbus had misled her. Certainly, had the *lanista* kept his peace, she would not have been so fraught with worry. And, she thought angrily,

233

she had now embarrassed herself, due to him. Had she been given the opportunity to judge the situation for herself, the evening would have passed without incident. Now, as it stood, she felt intolerably foolish. She cleared her throat, now thankful for the make up the slave girls had applied. Frontinus would not know that beneath it she was as scarlet as a Laconian war-cloak.

'Why did you ask me here then?'

'Because I admire skill at arms and I think you have the potential to be great.' Lysandra nodded; it was not the first time she had heard this, and she believed it was the truth anyway. 'Certainly, I am an enthusiast of the games,' he went on, 'and my eye is well practised. But I wanted to see if there was more to you than merely a good sword arm. And,' he grinned, 'governor I may be, but like everyone else, I am star struck by you warriors of the arena. And luckily for me, my position affords me the opportunity to meet those I admire.' He raised his cup to her. 'There is indeed much more to you than a good sword arm, Lysandra of Sparta.'

She lifted her own drink. 'An astute observation, Governor,' she said. 'I salute you.' Placing her cup on the table she rose to her feet. 'I bid you good evening, Sextus Julius Frontinus. *Vale*.'

'*Vale*, gladiatrix.' Frontinus smiled and watched her depart. She was indeed a marvellous creature, he decided. The perfect catalyst for his plans, in fact.

234

XXVII

'I won't have it.' Balbus glared at Sorina, his tone heavy with finality. This was not what he needed. It was early morning, the sun only just creeping across the desk in his rented Halicarnassus office and already there were problems to deal with.

'You have no real choice in this, *lanista*,' Sorina responded evenly. 'We *will* fight, regardless. But it is my hope that one of us will survive. And that, in this, you may profit.'

'It's not a question of profit.' Balbus slammed his fist onto his desk. 'It's a question of hierarchy. I'm the owner of this troupe, in case you had forgotten. You can't just go arranging your personal feuds because it pleases you to do so.'

For a moment, sadness flickered across the harsh, weathered features of the Amazon. 'It does not please me to do so,' she said. 'But nevertheless, I must fight Eirianwen.'

Balbus raised his eyebrows. 'I'm sure you two can work it out,' he said placatingly. 'You've always been so close, there must be a way to extricate yourselves from the situation without bloodshed.'

'You do not understand the ways of the Tribes, Balbus.' Sorina sighed. 'This is not a contract we can negotiate, or a court in which we can argue. I have been challenged and that challenge must be answered.'

'This is preposterous,' the *lanista* spluttered. 'What am I running here?' he implored, eyes flying to the heavens.

'I am *Gladiatrix Prima*; Eirianwen, *Gladiatrix Secunda*. These games have brought your *ludus* to prominence. Was Lysandra, a novice fighter, not invited to the seat of the governor himself?' Balbus noted the distaste when she mentioned the Spartan but waved her to continue. 'I admit this match is not planned but it could show you, *lanista*, as one extremely willing to please the crowd… and the *editor*. By offering your two best fighters in a death match you show your generosity, risking your greatest assets. Your gladiatrices have, on the whole, outclassed those novelty fighters from the other schools. The crowd will love it. Think of the money in side-betting alone. And I am sure that you and Falco can squeeze some more coin from Fat Aeschylus for this… spectacle.'

'You have a point,' Balbus conceded, all too aware that avarice was getting the better of him. Then again, he soothed himself, everyone had to make a living. 'I'm not promising anything, mind,' he admonished. 'But if the terms are agreeable, you shall have your fight. Fair enough?'

The barbarian got to her feet. 'Fair enough.' She nodded briefly. 'I thank you for this, Balbus.' She turned to leave.

'Sorina,' he called out as she put her hand to do the door. 'Who should I bet on?'

'I will walk away alive, *lanista*,' Sorina said, her back to him. 'Eirianwen is young, strong and fast. But she is not Clan Chief and never will be.' She left before he could phrase another question, slamming the door behind her.

Balbus sat back heavily in his chair and mulled over the prospect. The barbarian was correct, he could make a fortune from this bout. The aging veteran facing the young lioness; the strength of youth versus the wisdom of experience. It had all the makings of a classic confrontation.

'Nikos!' he screamed, calling a scribe to him. The skinny Greek entered in a rush, looking somewhat dishevelled.

'Master?'

'Get a messenger to Septimus Falco. Tell him that I require his presence with all haste.'

'At once, Master.' He bowed and left, leaving Balbus to contemplate the money he would soon be counting.

Lysandra arose early, filled with a desire to see Eirianwen, but her Hellene compatriots were not sensitive to her needs and quizzed her mercilessly about her evening with the governor. When none of the details were as lurid as had been expected, they soon lost interest. She could not help thinking of Penelope, and this brought a sad smile to her face. The fisher girl would have been most disappointed by the lack of carnal excesses.

'I do not expect you to understand,' Lysandra finished disdainfully. 'We spoke mostly of matters tactical and military. Whilst you are all competent fighters, I fear that such stratagems would be beyond you.' This was greeted by ironic chuckles from the women. This, Lysandra reckoned, was to cover their own embarrassment. She was only speaking the truth.

Nevertheless, when they realised there was no gossip to be had, they let her be and she made her way from the cell. The passageways were mostly deserted at the early hour, the fighters still sleeping off their excesses from the previous evening. Lysandra could not get to grips with the need to drink oneself into insensibility after a bout but she had noticed it was the norm for almost everyone else.

Eirianwen, she knew, was an early riser and, though a prodigious drinker in her own right, she could normally be found in the baths at daybreak. This in mind, Lysandra headed straight for the small facility in the grounds of the amphitheatre, and her heart leapt when she saw Eirianwen sitting by the pool, her feet paddling.

Lysandra moved behind her and sat, her legs scissoring Eirianwen's hips, and wrapped her arms round her belly. Eirianwen started slightly, but relaxed as she kissed her neck and shoulders. 'Good morning,' she whispered, breathing deeply the scent of Eirianwen's freshly washed hair. 'I missed you.'

'How was your night?' she let her golden head fall back to Lysandra's shoulder, but there was an edge to her voice.

'Not what I expected,' she answered quickly, keen to allay any fears Eirianwen may have pertaining to her fidelity. 'The governor is an admirer of the games,' she explained. 'He had no interest in anything else. He merely wished to talk, that is all. I think he is enamoured of us female fighters.'

'A pity he wasn't enamoured of keeping the Silures free. Roman bastard.'

Lysandra bit her lip, desperate to appease her. 'Please do not be angry with me, Eirianwen. I had no choice in this. But I swear to you that nothing happened. We just talked.' There was a silence, punctuated only by the gentle dripping of condensation and the distant roar of the furnace that kept the waters hot. Lysandra pulled Eirianwen closer to her. It was now, she decided, that she must give voice to the truth. 'I love you.'

Eirianwen turned her head, and Lysandra saw with shock that her eyes were red rimmed and cracked. She had been crying. Full of concern, she touched the tear-streaked face. 'What is it?' she whispered, kissing her. 'What troubles you?'

'Love,' Eirianwen said simply. She turned about so they faced each other, and pulled Lysandra to her. For long moments they held each other, aware only of the closeness and comfort that embrace gave.

'What is it?' Lysandra asked again. She felt herself close to tears at Eirianwen's pain, but she forced them away by effort of will. It would be unseemly to cry, she admonished herself. Despite her declaration of love, she still had standards to adhere to.

Eirianwen broke their embrace, and sat back a little, gazing into her eyes. 'I *do* love you, Lysandra,' she said, and Lysandra's heart leapt. 'But this love causes me great pain.'

'But why?' Inside, Lysandra was all in delirium at Eirianwen's words, but she forced herself to calm. There was more to this.

'Sorina…' Eirianwen swallowed. 'Sorina hates you and is displeased by the way we feel. She…' The Briton stopped, tears flooding her eyes. 'She has cast me out of the Tribe.'

That, Lysandra considered, was only a good thing. Perhaps free of the old bitch's influence, Eirianwen could truly learn what it was to be a civilised woman. She could see though that this proscription was hard for Eirianwen to take. 'Perhaps she will reconsider,' she offered.

Eirianwen shook her head. 'That cannot be. For I have challenged her right in this.'

'This is bad news.' Lysandra nodded. 'I am sure none of your kin would vote in favour of our love.' The last word tasted good on her lips. But Eirianwen laughed harshly.

'Vote?' she said. 'This is no *vote*, Lysandra! I am to fight her over you. To the death.'

Lysandra recoiled. 'That cannot be!' she exclaimed. 'It is true that she and I are not enamoured of each other but she is *your* friend. Your Clan Chief!'

'Not when this is over. One of us will die. It must be so. Either she will remain Chief or I will take her place. That can be the only outcome. But either way, I lose. If I die, then it is over. But even if I win, what have I won? The others will have to take me as Chief but I shall ever be an outcast because of my love for you!'

Lysandra took Eirianwen's hands in her own. 'This is an absurdity,'

239

she stated. 'If Sorina has issue with us, then let it be me that takes this burden.' Inwardly she burned with the desire to face the Amazon with her sword in hand, partly because she had come to hate her, but more for the pain she had caused Eirianwen. But the Briton shook her head.

'You are not of the Tribes. And even if you were, it was I who made the Challenge. It is I who must face her.'

'I cannot understand this,' Lysandra said. 'It is the way of…' She halted, nearly uttering the word 'barbarians'. 'The Tribes,' she amended hastily, 'and I have no experience of it. But I do know this. Leaders are the same, whatever their kith or kin. When you defeat her, the others will know that you have taken your rightful place. You said it yourself, Eirianwen. Sorina has grown bitter in hatred.'

Eirianwen's brow creased as she considered her words, and Lysandra fought down the urge to kiss her, which would have ruined the flow of her impromptu oratory. She pressed on. 'Does it matter that my ancestors were Spartan and yours noble folk of Britannia? How can there be evil in two people's love for one another? Especially in this place! Why would she see ill in our happiness?'

'Because we are *not* the same,' Eirianwen whispered. 'What hope can there be for us, Lysandra? Truly? Our chances of getting out of here alive grow slimmer with every bout. And even if we win free, what then? We are two women, a barbarian and a former priestess. Where could we go together that would not bring a thousand troubles on our heads?'

'*Amor vincit omnia*, Eirianwen. Love conquers all things, and there is truth in that. We will win free, and we will be together.' As she spoke, Lysandra felt alive with the conviction of her words. 'I have never known love before. Indeed, I have spurned it, thinking it would make me weak. But when I look into your eyes, I feel such strength… I feel that when I am with you I could accomplish anything. I care not for the scorn of others. I care only that you are by my side and I by yours. Women we may be, but our love goes deeper than any shared by man and wife. For we are *equals*, Eirianwen, and that is a rare thing in this world.'

Lysandra saw hope flare in Eirianwen's beautiful blue eyes. 'You think this could be true?'

'I know so,' she said. This was the first time, she recognised an Eirianwen who needed her. The Briton was older and more experienced than she and Lysandra had been happy to let her take the lead in their relationship. But now, it was the tribeswoman who was lost and, in supporting her, Lysandra felt her own inner strength magnified. 'That this has happened between you and Sorina is a bad thing,' she conceded. 'Life is full of bad things, Eirianwen. But the gods sweeten the bad with the good. Is it ill we are slaves? Yes. But if we were not, how would we have met? And my freedom is small price to pay for what I feel at this moment.'

Eirianwen did not speak but leant forward, kissing her with a soft yet urgent passion. And for a while, the concerns of the world were lost to them.

XXVIII

'Aeschylus wouldn't budge.' Septimus Falco and Balbus were relaxing in their favourite bathhouse, some distance from the arena. *Lanista* and promoter both found it beneficial to discuss matters away from the distractions of the amphitheatre.

'A pity.' Falco wiggled his toes, enjoying the calming heat of the water. 'But, as for me, I can't lose. You see, I didn't exhaust my options.' He chuckled. 'Really, Balbus, you may be dripping in gold, but I have to make a living too! The governor himself has an interest in the bout and will be willing to cough up to see it.'

Balbus's eyes were hooded. 'I thought he was an 'Achillia' devotee,' he said. 'Why would he pay to see the others fight?'

'You must have your head buried in day-to-day papers.' Falco kicked out and floated lazily on his back before continuing. 'Our Sextus Julius Frontinus has become an advocate of the women's game. He's totally enamoured of your Achillia, true, but have you not noticed he is always early for the female matches?'

Balbus's grunt was derisive. 'No,' he admitted. 'I have too much to do. My days aren't taken up with spectating,' he added. 'There are surgeons' fees, bids for slaves from other schools, reports *on* slaves from other schools, correspondence, bet settlements...' he trailed off. 'It's not easy being a *lanista*, Falco. People believe that all you need is a few sesterces and a couple of armed slaves to be a success. But I'm telling you, there is a lot more to it than that!'

'You've turned it into an art form,' Falco commented blithely and was rewarded by a scowl from Balbus. He returned to the side of the pool. 'At any rate, the fight can go ahead,' he said. 'I'm haggling over terms but the governor is already sold on the idea. It's just a question of how much I can squeeze out of him.'

'That,' Balbus smiled, 'is always music to my ears, Falco.'

News of the impending bout between the two tribeswomen did not take long to spread amongst Balbus's fighters and quickly to the other schools at the games. Keeping the fact a secret was impossible, as gossip amongst the slaves of both arena and *ludus* was rife. No sooner had Balbus put the paperwork together, than the news got out, courtesy of the scribes.

For Eirianwen, it was hellish. Having been cast out of the Tribe, women whom she counted friends could no longer associate with her: this was the law. Lysandra did her best to include her, but the Greeks were so different to the women that Eirianwen knew. There had been truth in Sorina's words; the folk of the middle sea were another breed to those of the Tribes. However, they did try to be friendly and, though it went against the grain, Eirianwen was grateful to them, even if she could not allow herself to be taken in as part of their coterie.

It would be difficult enough to take Sorina's place as Clan Chief if she should win the bout and openly consorting with the Greeks as a whole would only cause her kin to despise her. She considered that the tribeswomen might just forgive her in her love for Lysandra, but she could not allow herself to seek comfort with the rest of what her own kind saw to be a rival clan.

She was all too aware of the ramifications of her contest with the Clan Chief. It was much more than two women fighting: she represented change; Sorina the old ways. The older warrior's anger had festered and infected the other women. Sorina looked at things as part of the whole and that could not be applied to individuals. Rome was a cruel empire, but that did not make all Romans evil, nor all Greeks, for that matter. Eirianwen hated *Rome* for enslaving her people, but could not bring herself to judge an entire race on the actions of politicians and generals.

Sorina's constant haranguing would lead to trouble in the *ludus*, of that Eirianwen was certain. If one of the tribeswomen did get it into her mind to cause trouble with the women of the middle sea, they would tire of it sooner or later and retaliate. The entire school would be split and this would make for an intolerable situation. Blood could be spilt away from the arena, which would in turn lead to more death by reprisal.

There was too much death already, she thought. The gladiatrices *had* to fight in the arena, but to follow the path of Sorina would bring the blood from that place into their own lives. Eirianwen could not stand for that.

But could she kill Sorina over it? That was the dilemma. She had spoken out in anger against her, words said by both that now could not be taken back. She could not bring herself to hate the older woman, they had been friends for too long. That they were from different tribes no longer mattered: in the enclosed world of the *ludus* they were kin.

Eirianwen Kinslayer.

The thought was a bitter one, but she knew in her heart that when they faced each other on the sands Sorina would give her no quarter. She must steel herself and bury her feelings. To do

244

otherwise would be to invite defeat. Even then, she feared that the Dacian would be more than a match for her. She was the younger but Sorina had a lifetime of battle behind her, both in the arena and also on the plains of her homeland. There were no ruses Eirianwen knew that Sorina did not, no skill mastered that had not been taught by the Clan Chief.

Despite Lysandra's constant encouragement, she knew that the odds were against her in this. As a Druid's daughter, she was sometimes possessed of the Sight. But this time the Sight would not reveal her fate, the Morrigan had drawn a veil of darkness over the future.

And Erianwen was afraid.

'So my money's on the Silurian.'

Stick and Catuvolcos had returned to their regular night-time haunt, the trainer's recreation site. As always it was crowded and all the talk was of the bout between Gladiatrices *Prima* and *Secunda*.

'I've never seen so much interest in a women's bout,' Stick went on. 'It's incredible. The money changing hands over it is unheard of. Balbus is beaming like Helios himself. How about you, who do you think will win?'

Catuvolcos stared into his beer. 'Hard to say. All the odds favour Sorina but I have a feeling Eirianwen will come through. She has a stronger cause to fight for.'

'Huh.' Stick helped himself to another cup. 'What cause?'

'Sorina fights to preserve what she thinks is right; Eirianwen fights for love. That is the strongest cause.'

Stick gave his neighing laugh. 'You're going soft,' he accused, his bulbous eyes shining with mirth. 'You sound like a poet. Don't tell me that because Lysandra and Eirianwen are tonguing each other's buds you think that they are in love! Come on!' He slapped his thigh.

'Stick, you're disgusting,' Catuvolcos retorted.

'Thank you.'

'But I'm serious,' Catuvolcos went on. 'I've been watching them since news of this broke out. Unbelievable as it may sound, the Spartan cares for her. I did not think she had any real feelings but it seems she has. And what's more, Eirianwen can't stop touching her. Small things, you know, Stick. But these things tell. When they talk, it's a touch on the hand or the shoulder. They are so *close* now.'

'Now that's one party I'd like to be invited to.' Stick licked his lips. 'I keep my sword in its scabbard at the *ludus*, but I'm still a man. That Eirianwen… those lovely big tits… and imagine getting one in Lysandra. That's what she needs, you know. And I'd be the man to give it to her, I'm telling you.'

'Stick, she'd eat you for breakfast.' Catuvolcos laughed. 'She's a head taller than you and better in a fight.'

'I like it rough, anyway,' Stick said, his own face splitting into a grin. 'That's what I mean. It would be like two opposites, one blonde, one dark haired, the soft and the hard…'

'You're turning my stomach.' Catuvolcos could imagine nothing more obscene than Stick in the throes of passion. 'And you need to invest in a whore,' he added. 'Empty your sack, and spare me your fantasies.'

Stick nodded enthusiastically, eyes roving about the room. 'Are you going to join me in some entertainment?'

Catuvolcos shook his head. 'No, I think I'll take a walk.'

'Back to the brothel?' Stick eyed him owlishly. 'To see…' he grinned, 'what was her name again?'

'Doris.'

'Ah yes.' Stick was brimming with suppressed glee. 'Doris. The lovely Doris. You must be spending a fortune there. That's madness, Gaul, because the whores here are all for free. *Lanista's* expenses and all that.'

'Well, I wait till she has finished work,' Catuvolcos said. 'I enjoy her company,' he added, sounding rather foolish in his own ears.

'You mean you aren't giving her one?' Stick roared with laughter. 'Catuvolcos the lover! It's priceless. First Lysandra, now this one. You amaze me.' Catuvolcos scowled, his face flushing with embarrassment, but Stick sobered, smiling slightly. 'Good for you, boy,' he said, for once not chiding or mocking. 'There's little enough to take a man's mind from where we are and what we do. If your Doris makes you happy, then that is a good thing.'

'You think so?'

'At least it has gotten you over Lysandra,' Stick observed.

'That's true. If I am honest, since I have met Doris, I cannot find it in my heart to stay angry towards Lysandra. I was being foolish.' He waved at a slave girl for more beer. 'She could not be a wife to me, nor any man. Her upbringing, and now her life here in the *ludus* has changed her; it would change anyone,' he added quietly. 'Of course, she welcomes the change. Victory to her was an outlet, a vindication of her belief in her own greatness.'

Stick laughed. 'You have to admit, it's rare to come across a woman with that big a head. Do you think all Spartan's are like her?'

'They cannot be, surely.'

'Sorina will take it hard if you reconcile yourself to Lysandra, though.' Stick was again serious. 'Especially now.'

Catuvolcos scowled. As a Celt, he understood that Sorina and Eirianwen must fight. A challenge had been made and must be accepted lest honour be forfeit; but the reason for the battle was *without* honour. Lysandra and Eirianwen's affair was their own and, even as Clan Chief, Sorina had little right to interfere. He had told Sorina so and they had quarrelled over it. 'I wish that it had not come to this, Stick,' he said after some time. 'Eirianwen and Sorina are both good women, but the Clan Chief is blind

247

over the love between Eirianwen and Lysandra. Publicly, she says it is because Lysandra's 'civilised ways' will corrupt the Clan. But the truth is that she is jealous. I feel badly to say this, for Sorina has been a good friend for me in troubled times. But she loves Eirianwen as a daughter and it cuts her to the quick that she has chosen Lysandra. She cannot stand to be second place.'

Stick shook his head. 'And when one barbarian challenges another, neither will back down,' he said sadly. 'One of them will die over it. It seems a waste, Catuvolcos.'

'It is that,' Catuvolcos agreed. 'Sorina is now distraught at the consequences of this quarrel. How can she kill the one whom she had come to regard as daughter? I think that she now regrets her words but there is no going back. If she had closed her eyes, it would not have come to this.'

Their mood had taken a gloomy turn and the two men drank in silence. Perhaps it would not have come to this if Eirianwen had been any other, Catuvolcos thought to himself. So beautiful, so perfect. She was almost a goddess on earth. Her physical attractiveness was matched only by her good nature, and as a Druid's daughter, her knowledge of lore was great. She was the perfect successor to Sorina in so many ways. Save for her love of a Greek woman. 'I had best go,' he said, rising to his feet. 'I must meet Doris.'

Stick seemed to shake off his grim mood. 'I think you're an idiot for not spearing in this pond where the fishes are free. Now piss off and leave a real man to his enjoyment.' Stick tipped him a wink and got to his feet, seeking his diversion amongst the women.

Catuvolcos left him to his enjoyments, walking briskly towards the brothel. Though he had only known Doris a short time, he felt a genuine affection for the young prostitute. That she plied her trade on her back was of no matter to him. He himself peddled flesh, only in a different way. More often than not, his charges would end up dying young or worse, maimed and useless. He shook his head, annoyed that the conversation with Stick had turned his mood bitter. Yet he was able to cast these grim thoughts from his mind as soon as he spied Doris's place of work. She was waiting for him by the doorway, her labours over with for the night. She walked towards him and it made Catuvolcos happy to see that her step was quick.

XXIX

The cell resonated with the shouts of the crowd above. The noise of their rhythmic chanting pervaded the very foundations of the amphitheatre, filling inanimate rock with a pulsing, violent music. Lysandra stood before Eirianwen, applying the oil to her body.

'Sorina always used to do this for me.' Eirianwen's voice was the barest whisper.

'Do not think of her as Sorina. She is not a person now, she is your enemy.'

'That is not the way of the Tribes. Though we meet in battle, we must do each other honour.'

'I am sure,' Lysandra said tartly. 'Time enough for honour when she is dead, Eirianwen.' Her tone softened then. 'You must win this fight. For you. For us.'

'I'll try.'

Lysandra's eyes fixed the deep blue of Eirianwen's. 'You *will*,' she insisted. 'Trying has nothing to do with it. I have known her only a short time, Eirianwen, but well enough to realise that she will not spare her hand in this. If you have a chance, take it. You must cut her down without compunction.'

Eirianwen's smile was dazzling. 'You think to make yourself a trainer, Lysandra?'

Lysandra tweaked Eirianwen's nose, making her laugh, and the heavy mood was broken for an instant. 'Doubtless I'd be better than the imbeciles we have to work with at the moment.' She stepped back, and eyed her handiwork. 'I don't think I've missed a spot,' she nodded satisfied. 'Are you sure you do not want to wear even a *subligaculum*? They have not insisted that you fight naked.' Eirianwen opened her mouth to speak but Lysandra raised her hand. 'I assume it is 'the way of the Tribes'?'

'Yes. One of us will go to the underworld as we came to *this* world. Also, we fight as equals in this manner. No blow will be deflected by armour. We fight, blade to blade, flesh to flesh.'

'A pity it is not a contest of form.' Lysandra forced herself to smile, though her heart was pounding with apprehension. But it would not do to show Eirianwen that she was nervous; she must project a solid image of unwavering confidence.

'What do you mean?' Eirianwen began to flex her shoulders and neck, loosening the muscles.

'If this were being judged on your looks,' she extrapolated, realising that the subtleties of Latin were beyond the Silurian, 'you would certainly have the advantage over that leathery old bag.'

'You're being rude,' Eirianwen said, but her eyes were bright. 'Don't worry about me, Lysandra. I'll fight hard and, if the gods will it, I shall win.'

Lysandra nodded; there was truth in that.

It was deafening.

Lysandra had thought the cheers in her own bouts loud, but the cacophony that greeted the two barbarian gladiatrices as they stepped onto the sands was like nothing she had ever heard. It was greater than a simple roar, it was a constant, unending reverberation that seemed to stem from the very soul of those who watched. Lysandra gripped the bars to the Gate of Life, feeling them vibrate under her fingers.

Her eyes were drawn to Sorina. The older woman's naked body was brown and tough, her muscles defined and hard beneath the skin, whereas Eirianwen had a more womanly look to her. Sorina, like Lysandra herself, was angular and solid but Eirianwen was possessed of gentle curves. This was mere appearance, for beneath the deceptively soft surface, the Silurian was as hard as iron.

They faced each other, raising their blades in salute. Through the din Lysandra heard the high-pitched voice of the *editor*, Fat Aeschylus, giving the order for the battle to begin.

But neither woman moved. For indeterminable moments they stood like two statues, images forever poised to strike a blow that was never to land. The crowd quietened, as if becoming aware of the solemnity of the occasion. Sweat beaded on the bodies of both gladiatrices, their shoulders rising and falling as they slowed their breathing, letting nervous energy transform to controlled aggression.

'Fight!' Aeschylus' voice piped out again, irate at the delay, but the women yet remained still. *Harenarii*, slaves charged with forcing unwilling gladiators to fight, began to move in, clutching red-hot irons in gloved fists. Though silent, the minds of twenty thousand watchers willing the two to close was a palpable thing, hanging heavy over the dead calm sands of the arena floor.

Sunlight caught in Lysandra's eye and it was a moment before she realised that it was the reflected glint from Sorina's blade as it screamed towards Eirianwen. The sound of her sword deflecting the attack broke the overflowing dam and, once again, the arena became awash with maddened dissonance.

* * *

'Aren't your friends fighting today?' Doris and Catuvolcos were sitting in the brothel's small garden. She was eating an apple he had brought for her.

'Yes.' Catuvolcos turned his head in the direction of the arena. The screaming of the crowd could clearly be heard. 'That roar is for them now.'

'Shouldn't you be there, watching?'

'I'd rather be with you.' Catuvolcos said. It was partially true, but there was more to it than that. He could not bring himself to watch Eirianwen and Sorina at each other's throats. It may be the Law, but there was an inherent wrongness in this fight. Whatever happened, whoever died, the other would never be the same. The *victrix*, he knew, would lose part of herself when the other's soul fled the body. When one fell, part of the other would die with her.

'Does your owner mind you being away?' Doris interrupted his reverie, causing him to look up sharply. 'You seem to be out over-much for a slave, that's all.'

How very civilised, Catuvolcos thought bitterly. She was a prostitute, who made her living from the groaning pleasures of strange men, yet she saw fit to bring up the matter of his own bondage. His face darkened with anger for a moment, but Doris seemed to have no idea that she had said insulting words. In fact, the look on her pretty, painted face was almost one of concern. He took a deep breath and was about to reply but Doris spoke first.

'It's just that I know you like me for who I am, and...' she paused, 'not for what I do. I wouldn't want you to be out without permission and get into trouble over me.'

'I am allowed out,' he said, feeling somehow relieved at the reason for her question. 'My *lanista* is good like that. He treats us with respect even if we do belong to him. It is a better lot than many slaves have.'

'Well, I am glad he is good like that.' Smiling, she tucked her knees under her chin. 'I love it when you come to visit. I feel like you are rescuing me for a few hours. Silly, isn't it? Soon, the games will be over and you will be gone.'

'Yes, but my *ludus* is only a few days from here. I will come to see you as often as I can,' Catuvolcos said it in a rush and realised that he meant every word.

'I don't mind if you don't,' Doris said seriously. 'But do not promise me you will, if you don't mean to keep your word. I would hate that.'

'On my honour.' Catuvolcos put his hand on his heart. 'I swear that I will visit you as often as I can.'

'Catuvolcos,' Doris almost squeaked. 'That's... wonderful!' In a rush of silk and perfume, she was upon him, her arms about his neck. 'No one has ever treated me so well.'

The big man stroked her hair, wanting to kiss her but unsure if she would take his action as an affront. So much of their friend-ship was based on his restraint. He wanted more but would not take it. She had been through much, and he knew her well enough to realise that her sometimes brassy front was mere armour for a girl who lived a hard life in hard circumstances.

So when her lips sought his, it was a surprise.

Lysandra's heart was in her mouth as she watched, her knuckles bone-white on the bars.

The blades of Eirianwen and Sorina whirled in their deathly dance, meeting again and again, their song as discordant as it was violent. The length of the swords made the short thrust impos-sible, so the contest was fought in the truly barbarian style. Huge sweeping cuts and arcing blows were countered by blocks so solid they caused sparks to fly.

Eirianwen attacked in force suddenly, the sword cutting down-wards to Sorina's head, but the older woman met the assault and parried again as the Silurian's blade swung round, seeking to slice her head from her neck. Again, Eirianwen pressed in, a furious speed and intensity in her attacks. She slashed at the Clan Chief's head but Sorina ducked low, her sword licking out. The crowd gasped as Eirianwen's blood flew brightly and she stumbled back, reaching for the wound in her belly.

Sorina roared, battle rage clearly upon her, and charged in, battering Eirianwen back, using her sword as a bludgeon, knowing that with the blood loss, so the strength leeched from the body. Eirianwen was forced down to one knee and only barely managed to deflect a blow that would have opened her skull. For a moment, the two women's blades locked together, the Amazon seeking to drive her foe into the ground.

Lysandra screamed and it seemed to her that Eirianwen heard, for she surged upwards, forcing the older woman back and away her own sword hissed down diagonally, slicing across Sorina's chest. The cut was not deep enough to finish her, but it bled profusely, staining the Amazon's sweat-slick skin with blood. The crowd went into paroxysms of excitement as the two fighters, bloodied and hurt, closed in, their faces set in pale determination.

The contest continued at a furious pace, neither woman giving ground despite their wounds. They stood in full reach of each other's blades, trusting more on their skill than avoidance. Again, Sorina hit home, this time cutting across the heavy flesh of Eirianwen's left breast. The crowd hissed as blood sluiced from the wound, drenching her torso. She cried out in pain and Sorina struck out once more but her blow was parried. Eirianwen used her momentum to follow through, the pommel of her sword hilt smashing into Sorina's face.

The Amazon fell over backwards, hitting the sand heavily. But Eirianwen could not press her advantage. Her own wounds were taking their toll, and in a moment Sorina had recovered and rolled to her feet. Her nose was shattered, sheeting her mouth and chin in thick, purplish globules.

Slower now, they came together again. Stroke met counter-stroke, all thought of skill and technique fled. All that mattered was to beat the other into exhaustion. Time and time again their blades met flesh but both lacked the power to land a killing blow.

Lysandra could not bear to watch, but neither could she tear her eyes away from the awful scene as the two hacked at each other. Each time Sorina struck home, she felt the blow as keenly as did Eirianwen, each time the Amazon cried out in pain, the fierce exultation was her own.

Drunkenly, the tribeswomen tottered towards one another, barely distinguishable, so coated were they with blood and arena filth. As they came together, Sorina's sword dipped imperceptibly, her years seemingly catching up with her, and it was then Eirianwen struck. Her sword hammered down on the older woman's blade, knocking it from her hands. She lunged in, her weapon spearing straight for the Amazon's throat.

Sorina twisted aside, her arms clamping onto Eirianwen's wrists, and she spun about, now in control of the blade. For a moment, they struggled, then the Amazon stiffened and pushed with the last of her strength.

Eirianwen's cry was loud as her own blade was rammed into her stomach, exploding from her back in a bloody mist. Sorina stepped back, her face a hideous mask of horror as the Silurian lurched away, fingers scrabbling desperately to pull the cold metal from her body. Her mouth worked, but no sound came forth as her ruined innards forced bile into her throat. It dribbled obscenely down her face as she fell to her knees and rolled slowly onto her side.

She lifted her head in the direction of the Gate of Life, her hand reaching imploringly to Lysandra.

Lysandra wailed insanely and hurled herself at the gates, trying to smash the iron with her own body, desperate to be with Eirianwen. But through tear-blurred eyes, she saw Eirianwen's

256

arm fall and her head loll to one side, and knew that she was gone.

Howling with grief, Lysandra felt many hands upon her, pulling her back. Spittle slavered about her mouth as she struggled against them, screaming incoherently. Something heavy slammed into her head, but she did not relent, surging away from her captors as she crashed into the Gates once more.

Again, she was struck, and again, until finally the darkness took her.

Lucius Balbus hummed tunelessly as a slave went through the complex process of adjusting the *lanista's* toga. Despite the permanent loss of Eirianwen, the profit that he had made from her demise was enormous. Somewhat worrying was the current state of Sorina: the Amazon had sustained serious injury in the battle, and now lay close to death in the surgery.

But it was still worth the payoff. With the money from the games as a whole and his cut of the betting he could buy more quality slaves to replenish his stock. Experienced slaves at that. And of course, there was Lysandra: Stick had informed him that there had been some trouble with her when Eirianwen fell. Apparently, the two women were intimate and the Spartan had taken her death badly. That sort of thing was impossible to control, he mused, as the slave applied a sweet-smelling pomade to the sheer white cloth of the toga. It would not do to meet Frontinus smelling of the fuller's piss.

Deprived of the company of men, the women inevitably fell to relationships with their own sex. Other *lanista's* were much harsher on their stock, banning any kind of liaisons, but Balbus was prepared to endure the difficulties that a freer *ludus* gave rise to in return for the emotionally stable fighter. It was all about compromise in the business.

Lysandra was young and would get over Eirianwen's death – of that he was certain. And, with the right touch from Falco, she could be promoted to attain phenomenal adulation from the masses. With Frontinus's endorsement, the women's event was attracting more attention from the public, and that meant more money for hard-working *lanistas* like himself. The crowd, then, would need a heroine.

Lysandra, he decided, would be that heroine. All it would take would be a few more matches against quality opposition and she would gain some renown and critical experience. It was all he could do to refrain from dancing with glee all the way to his litter.

Catuvolcos stood over the still form of Sorina. The surgeon, a small, fussy-looking man who sported a fading black eye, was applying a stinking unguent to the grievous wounds the Amazon had sustained. Her face was pale, the lines about her eyes seeming more pronounced.

'Will she live?' Catuvolcos found his voice to be too loud in the stillness of the surgery.

The surgeon looked up from his work. 'I don't know,' he said. From his expression, Catuvolcos knew that he had bitten down a harsher response to the too often-asked question. 'She is not young,' the surgeon added, 'but she is strong and tough. None of these wounds are mortal by themselves... but you can see for yourself the state of her.'

Catuvolcos gazed at the near lifeless form of his friend, tears in his eyes. He prayed that she would live so that some sense, some meaning could come from her struggle with Eirianwen. The gods, he hoped, would not be so cruel as to take them both.

'I have work to do.' The surgeon's voice cut into his thoughts.

'If you want to wait, wait outside, but I won't know much till the morning. You should go to the banquet. Have a few drinks.'

It was good advice, Catuvolcos reasoned. There was nothing he could do here, and the oblivion of the beer cup was a better prospect than sitting around this place of blood and death. He nodded his thanks to the surgeon, and made his way back to the gaol.

The atmosphere in the compound was charged with relief. The games were over and those who remained basked in the knowledge that sweet life was theirs. As was the tradition, a revel had been arranged for those warriors who had survived. It would be held later that night on the very sands on which they had fought and always followed the usual stages of drunkenness. Celebration at life would be followed by melancholy for lost comrades, and all would finally be overtaken by unconsciousness. This was wise policy on the part of the *lanistas*: the day following the revel the fighters would be too ill to cause any trouble when they were loaded back into their carts for the journey home.

Catuvolcos wondered if Lysandra would be present. Stick had recounted to him how she had reacted to Eirianwen's death and that he had imprisoned her. There was an injustice in that, he thought. It was in no small part due to Lysandra's successes that Balbus and his troupe had gained a reputation in the games. To keep her under lock and key whilst all others were free – at least for the night – was unfair.

Though Stick had promised to check up on her and let her out when 'the serious drinking got underway', Catuvolcos resolved that he would undertake the task himself. For one thing, Stick's thirst for alcohol far outweighed his tolerance and he was likely to forget; for another, he wanted a chance to mend bridges with Lysandra. He had treated her harshly through no fault of her own and, whatever faults he had,

Catuvolcos prided himself on his honesty. He had been wrong, and he would tell her so.

Lysandra stared into the darkness of her cell, aware only of her pain. It went far beyond anything physical she had ever suffered; the agonising grief raked her soul, allowing no respite in its merciless torture. Never in her life, she now knew, had she cried until this day. Her throat was raw from sobbing, her cheeks brittle and taut with the salt of her tears. Visions of Eirianwen haunted her, tormenting her with images of her love. Forever frozen in her mind's eye was the sight of the beautiful Silurian reaching out for help in her last moment. And she could not save her.

Lysandra held her face in her hands, her chains clattering as her body shuddered with misery. It was not right: *she* should have faced Sorina, not Eirianwen. If *she* had fought, then no tie of kin or clan would have stayed her hand. Sorina would lie dead and all that she and Eirianwen hoped for would have come to pass.

Now, hope was dust. Her heart had been torn from her breast and there was no reason to carry on. Athene did not speak to her and Lysandra knew that she had angered the goddess with her love for a barbarian. There could be no other answer.

She tried to invoke the discipline that had been ingrained since childhood to stave off the dreadful emptiness that was within her, but she could not. There was nothing. Nothing besides the loss of Eirianwen.

Outside the cell, she could hear the gladiatrices laughing and chatting and, in that moment, she wanted to die. In death, the hurt would end; in death there would be no knowing. Love was too cruel, too much for anyone to bear if it went awry. She understood that now and the knowledge had changed her. How could life go on without love? There was no point. To honour Athene? To serve Balbus? It was all so utterly meaningless.

There had been a time, before the *ludus*, when everything had been so clear. Then, she had been made slave, but her Spartan superiority had allowed her to triumph and serve her goddess in even the most trying of circumstances. To meet Eirianwen in such a place had assured her that it must have been in Athene's plan. She had been happy: for the first time in her life, she had known the joy of true companionship.

And now it had been stripped cruelly away. It was not the Spartan credo to lament one's losses. Lysandra could hear her own voice mocking her, admonishing Danae that one should not weep for fallen comrades. Only now did she understand what it was to care.

She lifted her arm, examining the chain that secured her to the wall. It would be so easy to wrap it around her neck and let it squeeze till the pain went away. Let Hecate, goddess of suicides, embrace her and bear her to the kingdom of Hades. Far better that than facing life alone.

She thrust the chain away, bitter frustration welling up within her. That she chose to die was testament that she must live on. The Spartan way demanded such sacrifice.

XXXI

This, Balbus, decided, was the life.

Certainly, he himself lived in the manner of a cultured and wealthy man, but the opulence of Frontinus's house was exquisite; all was perfection. And that he, Lucius Balbus, sat at the governor's table was evidence of the New Man Made Good. In the modern world, hard work and diligence could bring a man to great heights.

Fat Aeschylus was there as well, basking in the success of the games that his money had paid for. Well, more power to him, Balbus thought. Should his campaign for election to *aedile* be successful, the Greek would not forget that it was Balbus who made his show a success. He raised his cup to the corpulent demagogue who responded in kind.

'Your troupe has gained renown, Lucius Balbus.' Aeschylus smiled at the *lanista*. 'A most impressive show. You have brought the women's game to new heights.'

Balbus nodded gracefully at the compliment and returned with one of his own. 'There would have been no stage for my gladiatrices had you not provided the arena, good Aeschylus.'

'So what now for you, *lanista*?' the Greek asked.

Balbus shrugged. 'The loss of Britannica is costly. She was a great favourite with the crowd. But my new girl, Achillia, is proving to be most popular.'

'Indeed, yes,' Frontinus broke in enthusiastically. 'An excellent fighter and she is delightful company.'

Balbus smiled in acquiescence. Evidently, Lysandra had made an impression on the governor. 'I hope to build on her popularity in the future. She is a rare find and I think she can surpass Sorina and Eirianwen in the esteem of the people. For one thing, she is *not* a barbarian.' This small comment produced a polite scattering of laughter from the notables.

'I agree.' Frontinus set his drink down. 'But I think that a better vehicle can be found for Achillia than the norm. Whist the one-to-one battles are entertaining, the mob is ever fickle. I think we – and I include the noble Aeschylus – can come up with a spectacle that they shall marvel at even in Rome. Thus, I have a proposition for you, Balbus.'

'Oh?' Balbus suddenly felt as though he were a mouse under the gaze of two hungry cobras. The problem with being entertained by the height of society, he thought to himself, meant that they could make demands that it would be impolitic to refuse.

'Thanks to your *ludus*,' Frontinus said, 'the women's game has enjoyed a surge in popularity. Your fighters have elevated these combats from mere sideshow to something worth getting excited about. But as I have said, the mob is capricious. It is my intention, therefore, to provide an event as yet unheard of.' He paused, the natural politician, allowing anticipation to build. 'A *gregatim* composed solely of women.'

Balbus was relieved. The *gregatim*, the combats involving teams of gladiators, were little different to the single combats, save for the mortality rate. However, with his recent windfall, this was something he could wear. 'In that, noble governor, I can facilitate you,' he glanced surreptitiously at Aeschylus, 'with no need for other contractors.' Truth be told, Balbus was still stung by the Greek's idea to use schools other than his own for the last spectacle. 'I do have over a hundred women, after all.'

Frontinus flicked a glance towards Aeschylus before continuing. 'I am talking on a grand scale, Balbus. A true battle, on such a scale that people will talk of it in the same breath as they speak of the *naumachia* of the Divine Claudius.'

Balbus nearly choked on his wine. 'But governor! Claudius's naval battle had over nineteen thousand convicts...' he trailed off, aware that governor and soon to be *aedile* were serious. He cleared his throat. 'Exactly what sort of numbers are we talking, Excellency?'

Frontinus gave a dismissive wave. 'Not *that* many, of course. But let me first tell you what I have in mind. Domitian will be visiting the province the year after next. This visit coincides with the fifth anniversary of his ascension to the purple... and his birthday. I have it on good authority that our Emperor too enjoys watching female combatants and I can see no better way of thanking him for the honour of his presence than by staging this grandest of events for his entertainment.' Frontinus leant forwards, evidently enthused. 'Your Achillia gave me this idea. You know the girl is well versed in military tactics, due to her youth in the Spartan *agoge*.'

Balbus nodded, silently thanking the priest Telemachus for enlightening him all those months ago.

'She is perfect to lead an army of female warriors, Balbus. My plan is to recreate the mythical battle between the Athenians and the Amazons. On the one side, Achillia with her Greeks, the other, a barbarian horde! Think of it, Balbus. We could take the games out of the arena, and make an arena of the landscape instead – just as old Claudius did.'

The idea had merit, Balbus conceded to himself, and it was not unprecedented. But the cost of such a venture was too prohibitive to be practical. He said as much to the governor. Frontinus was not to be dissuaded, however.

'Money is not an object to art,' he said. 'We, Aeschylus and I, can aid you in the purchasing and upkeep of the slaves. It will be up to you to ensure they are trained and ready to fight when the Emperor comes. It will make you the owner of the largest troupe in the Empire. At least for a time.'

Of course, Balbus thought. At the end of the slaughter, there would be few left alive. Leaving Balbus with a much expanded but empty *ludus*. 'I am honoured you think me capable of this task. If I may be so bold, I can see two problems. Firstly, Achillia must continue to fight. Her reputation must be such that the people will *want* to see her head such an army. In this there is risk – she may, after all, be killed. Secondly, and I dislike admitting it, but it is true: no one *ludus* could support so many slaves. Indeed, if we were to place two rival 'armies' in close proximity, the likelihood is that the war would begin not of our volition. And then we would have a problem.'

Frontinus nodded. 'If Achillia is killed, we shall continue regardless – the crowd loves blood. But you could be right on your second point. What would you suggest?'

Balbus gritted his teeth. 'I would suggest splitting the contract, Excellency. Another *ludus* could handle your 'Amazons', whilst I set about finding and training your Greeks.' It hurt to kiss half the deal away, but the overheads after the event could ruin him. 'What sort of numbers *are* we talking, governor?'

Frontinus's smile was wolfish. 'Five thousand. On each side.'

Balbus forced himself not to baulk. 'I can promise nothing at this stage, my Lord,' he said. 'I shall endeavour to find such a number, but the cost will be massive. And it is a matter of time, also. We have but two years to arrange such a thing – not long when we consider all that must be done. Also, I will not disgrace you, myself, or the Emperor by providing less than adequate stock for this spectacle.' He was a professional and he had standards. It would not do to send half-dead criminals from the mines – the cheapest source of flesh on the market – onto the sands of the arena; he had a reputation to uphold. 'Finding the right calibre of gladiatrix will not be quick, or easy. But I shall do my best.'

'I have every faith in you, good Balbus.' Though the governor smiled, the *lanista* realised that failure in this undertaking would not be acceptable.

Stick, Catuvolcos noted, was well past mellow as the evening wore on. Glancing ruefully at his beer, he realised that he was not far behind him. They staggered past the tables that had been arrayed for the surviving fighters, stopping to spread a few words here and there. Nastasen had declined to join them. The Nubian had met up with his coterie from the other *ludi* and they sat apart, filling their lungs with smoke from their cones of hemp.

Stick paused at the Greek women's table. 'Well done, you fierce bitches.' Despite the absence of Lysandra, they seemed to be in good spirits. He sat on the edge of the table and swilled his beer. 'I have to be honest,' he told them. 'I didn't think you sluts had it in you. But, you've made it through your first games – no small thanks to me.'

'We're so grateful, Stick,' Thebe said, the drunken grin on her face somewhat belying her mockery. 'What would we do without you?'

'You'd be dead,' Stick exclaimed. 'But you live! You are true warriors now.'

The women were silent at that. Stick was not given to making compliments, and to have gained his respect, however perverse it might be, meant something.

'How did you come to be here,' Thebe ventured after a moment.

'In Asia Minor?' Stick belched mightily. 'I was a soldier in the Parthian army. I trekked across the whole stinking Empire – wore out more boots than I can count. We marched all the way to Armenia, which you uneducated trollops will not know is the buffer between the Empire of the Romans and the Empire of Parthia. Well, I'd had enough of soldiering, taking the shit that the clueless officers dealt out to more capable men such as myself. So I skipped across the border, looking to make a new life, and...' he trailed off, his ugly face twisting in a self-mocking grin. 'I was captured as a Parthian spy and sold into slavery. I call that shit luck.'

The women fell about laughing at Stick's story. It was truly unfortunate, but the Parthian bore it with such a sense of irony, it could not fail to be humorous.

'Don't think because we're talking now that I'll go easy on you when we get back to the *ludus*,' Stick admonished, sliding onto the bench. 'But you're veterans now and you won't get the same treatment as the new girls. You've earned that much, at least.'

Catuvolcos also sat, enjoying the easy banter. As they poured more drinks for themselves he decided that he would visit Lysandra shortly.

After a cup or two.

Lysandra squinted at the torchlight, gritting her teeth against the high-pitched scream of the opening cell door. She found that she did not care if they had come to release her or not.

'Well, well, well.'

She stiffened at the sound of Nastasen's voice. The trainer entered the cell, flanked by three other men who were unfamiliar to her. The Nubian placed his torch in a holder on the wall as his men regarded her. The light from the naked flame shone weirdly on Nastasen's ebon skin, and, despite herself, Lysandra felt a twinge of fear in her gut. She swallowed. 'Have you come to release me?'

'Have we come to release you?' Nastasen mimicked, his voice a high falsetto. He kicked the door shut with his heel and his compatriots laughed.

Lysandra got to her feet and met his gaze levelly. 'If you have no purpose here, then leave me, Nastasen,' she said with a sternness she did not feel.

The trainer came close to her and she saw that his eyes were shining with a strange madness, the pupils impossibly large. His fist lashed out, crashing straight into the side of her head. Though she tried to raise an arm to block the blow, the chains she wore restrained her and the full power of the punch smashed her to the ground. The men were suddenly around her, kicking her savagely and repeatedly. She curled into a foetal position, trying to protect herself, but the blows were too many and too fast.

Dazed, blood pouring from her head, she was dragged to her feet. Lysandra opened her mouth to scream for help but Nastasen punched her hard in the stomach, knocking the wind from her. His rough hand gripped her tunic and tore it over her head and his friends laughed at her nakedness. Fear gave her strength and her foot lashed out, catching him in the midriff. Nastasen staggered back as one of his compatriots locked his arm around her neck, choking her.

'Turn her over.' Nastasen's voice was thick with lust and fury.

Lysandra struggled, but the strength of the men was too great. Annoyed at her actions, one of them cracked her head into the stone wall and stars swam sickeningly before her eyes. She felt fingers pulling at the flesh of her buttocks and between her legs, invading her cruelly. She screamed then, and the men laughed.

'Better shut her up,' one said.

'Use this.'

There was a moment of shuffling, then one of the men pinched her nose; after some time, forced to gasp for air, she opened her mouth, and the man shoved a cloth into it. It tasted foul with sweat.

'Look at that,' Nastasen crooned, spreading her buttocks wide. 'All nice and pink. And tight. Really tight.'

She felt him position himself behind her, steadying himself. Then came a wave of agony as he rammed himself into her. She screamed into the cloth, the cords of her neck standing out.

'How do you like that, you fucking bitch?' Nastasen bore her to the filthy floor, thrusting with all his weight. 'You've been asking for it,' he grunted, taking pleasure from her pain. 'You deserve it!'

Tears came to her eyes, hot and salty, as he continued and she screamed again, shaking her head, begging for the ordeal to be over.

'You deserve it!' Nastasen gasped again. 'You...' He trailed off, lost in his pleasure.

Lysandra felt him quicken his pace, his breathing becoming ragged before he collapsed on top of her, sated for now. Moments later, he pulled himself out, and climbed to his feet. She began to shake and he aimed a kick into her ribs. 'She *loved* it!' he chuckled. 'Who's next?'

'I'm next,' the one who had choked her said. 'But turn her round and lift her head up. I want her to see my face while I fuck her.'

Lysandra closed her eyes as she felt the next force his way into her flesh. She was lost in a sea of torment, her most intimate parts open for the abuse and pleasure of the Nubian and his gang. All manner of depravities were visited on her, acts that were designed to humiliate as well as cause pain, and all the while they mocked. When the three had at last spent their first issue they resumed beating her, letting their ardour rise again at the sight of her suffering.

Then it began again.

XXXII

'Wake up, Gaul!' Catuvolcos looked about blearily. Hildreth, was pulling him off the table where he had slumped. 'You can't pass out!' Hildreth herself was flushed red from excess, her breath reeking of beer and garlic. Catuvolcos recoiled, and was sick down himself.

'That's disgusting,' Hildreth observed.

'Lysandra,' Catuvolcos mumbled.

'She's locked up, idiot.'

'No, we must let her out,' Catuvolcos announced with all the conviction of the truly inebriated. 'It is not fair that we should enjoy ourselves whilst she is in chains.' He got to his feet, and over-balanced, falling onto his rear. He looked up, and began to laugh.

Hildreth shook her head, offering him a hand up. 'Come on, I will help you then. You won't get there on your own, I think.'

Supporting each other, the two weaved towards the catacombs, sniggering.

'Shussh…' Catuvolcos put a finger to his lips as they walked through the tunnels, their mirth echoing off the walls. Trying to cease their hilarity only made it worse and the two leant against the wall, shoulders shuddering with repressed mirth.

'No, stop.' Hildreth waved her hands, tears running down her face. 'It hurts.' She slid down the wall, clutching her stomach. 'Help!'

Catuvolcos doubled up at her antics. For a time the two were incapable of even moving, both close to hysterics. 'The thing is,' he gasped, 'I don't know what we are laughing at.'

'Your face,' Hildreth exclaimed. 'Shussh,' she imitated him. 'Was so funny.' She rolled to her knees, and climbed up, using the wall to support herself. The two staggered on, and made their way to Lysandra's cell. Grinning, Catuvolcos opened the door.

Lysandra lay naked on the ground, her body illuminated by the light of a dying torch. From head to foot, she was a mass of bruises and lacerations, blood oozing from a cut on her head.

'Gods!' Catuvolcos rushed to her side, knelt by her.

'Is she alive?' Hildreth was stunned by the sight.

He placed a hand to Lysandra's neck. 'Yes. But barely. Get help.' He fumbled with the locks on the Spartan's chains now cursing his drunkenness. He looked around, to see Hildreth still standing in the doorway, her expression horrified. 'Go!' he roared, but Hildreth was pointing at an area of the floor. Where Catuvolcos had moved Lysandra, the true extent of her injuries was apparent.

The floor beneath her lower body was stained with her blood.

'Don't tell me this!' Balbus put his face into his hands. Sunlight fell across his face and made him wince. The hour was early and he had over-indulged in the governor's hospitality. Stick and Catuvolcos looked like two corpses standing before himself and Titus. 'Who did it?' The *lanista* resisted the urge to curse.

'We don't know.' Stick shrugged. 'It could have been anyone. We were celebrating with the others.'

'You mean you were drunk,' Titus growled. The two trainers stared sheepishly at the floor.

'… And it couldn't have been just anyone, you imbecile!'

Balbus stood up, his stomach lurching. 'She was locked in a cell, you say. By your own hand! So whoever did it had to have a key.'

'Keys can be stolen,' Catuvolcos offered.

'And has anyone reported one missing?' Balbus shouted him down. When this rhetorical question was met with silence the *lanista* threw up his arms. 'I can't leave you two alone for one night!' he blustered. 'Every night is party night for Stick and Catuvolcos, but when Balbus takes one night off – *one* – what does he find? The place in disarray and his most promising gladiatrix raped, beaten and stabbed near to death. I'll bet you've not even begun to get the other women on to the carts, have you? No. And who'll have to foot the bill to the arena for the overstay? Lucius Balbus will!'

'Sorry, sir,' Catuvolcos mumbled.

Balbus glared at him. 'Sorry, are you? You'll be more sorry if I have you nailed to a board for your idiocy,' he waved a finger, 'and that includes you, Stick.' The two trainers said nothing, merely looked down at the ground, shifting uncomfortably from foot to foot. 'Damn the pair of you,' he added in a tired murmur.

A silence hung in the room for some time while Balbus pinched his nose between his thumb and forefinger, trying to let the anger drain out of him. This was just not fair: not when he was on the verge of the biggest deal of his life, the greatest purse that any *lanista* outside of Rome could hope to make and the fame that the proposed extravaganza would bring him. 'What did the surgeon say?' He decided to ask a practical question. Better to hear the worst, and get it over with.

'She's in a bad way,' Catuvolcos said at once. 'Balbus, terrible things have been done to her. The surgeon says…' He paused, and swallowed. 'The surgeon says it must have been a group that attacked her. It was – he said to me – not like she was just raped – they treated her in the vilest manner they could. There was hatred behind this attack.'

273

Something stirred in the back of Balbus's mind.

'Where's Nastasen?' Titus said beating him to the question.

'Still in his quarters, I suppose,' Stick said.

'Guards!' Balbus screamed. Presently, an arena watchman appeared in the doorway. 'Get me Nastasen here. You know who I mean, boy? The big Nubian trainer from my *ludus*?'

The lad nodded. 'Yes, sir.'

The four of them waited in silence for the guard to return from the arena. None were surprised to learn that Nastasen was nowhere to be found.

Sorina felt a sense of keen disappointment when she had opened her eyes. Her last thought before consciousness had fled in the arena was that the gods would take her. The sight of Eirianwen falling, her hand reaching out for her Spartan lover, and the blood – so much blood – haunted her. That her own wounds pained her was nothing compared to the emptiness she felt in her heart.

She could she realised – and perhaps should – have turned her head from Lysandra and Eirianwen. Hindsight was so easy, the closeness of death putting things into harsh perspective.

Clan Chief: the title mocked her now. Chief of what, she asked herself. Itinerant slaves from all over the world – where was the honour in that? Was honour worth the death of one whom she had come to regard as daughter? She tried to sit up in her cot, gritting her teeth as her wounds pulled.

'Lie back.' A man's voice broached no argument. Moments later, the surgeon was leaning over her. 'I spent a long time stitching you up, Sorina, and I don't want you splitting your wounds. You must lie still; I have others to attend to. Do you want some water?'

Sorina nodded, finding that her throat was too cracked and dry to speak. The surgeon tilted her head, and tipped some water onto her lips. The taste was heavenly and she tried to take more.

'Not too much,' the surgeon admonished. 'Just a sip. You can have more soon.' He laid her head back and moved on. Sorina followed him with her eyes and was stunned to see Lysandra in the cot next to hers. It was the long, raven-coloured hair by which the Amazon knew her for the Spartan was disfigured by so many bruises as to be near unrecognisable.

'What happened to her?' she croaked.

'Rest now.' The surgeon looked over his shoulder at her. 'Don't worry about her, concentrate on your own mending.'

'What happened?' Sorina injected as much force as she could into her voice.

The surgeon sighed. 'She was raped, beaten and stabbed – probably by your trainer, the Nubian. Does that knowledge make you feel any better, Amazon? Now, do as I say. Rest.'

Sorina laid her head wearily on the pillow. She found that there was still hatred in her heart for Lysandra. If not for the Greek, none of this would have come to pass. Yet she was still womankind and rape was the vilest act that could be committed upon her. It was an abomination against the goddess herself.

No one, not even the Spartan, deserved that.

Her eyes were drawn once again to her unmoving form. That Lysandra would be much changed by this, she knew well. On the steppes, she had seen women who had been taken and so abused. Some recovered, some broke – but none were ever the same after such an ordeal.

She and Lysandra could never be friends, that was certain; yet, even though she still despised her, Sorina decided there should be a mending between them. Eirianwen was gone, the cause of their dispute passed on. Life without her would be intolerable enough and abiding hostility between herself and the Spartan would be a constant reminder of Eirianwen's passing. But Lysandra would never make such a gesture, would not deign to lower herself to make peace with 'the barbarian'. It would be she, Sorina, who must make the first move.

That would hurt her pride sorely, but it was something that had to be done for the good of all concerned.

'*A ve*, gladiatrix.'

Lysandra opened her eyes, aware only of the pain that coursed through her body. Every nerve was alive, as if burnt raw with fires of agony. Though her vision swam, she could make out the surgeon. For a moment, confusion reigned, then the memories came crashing back.

The cell.

Nastasen.

What they had done to her.

She shuddered and shrank back on the bed, crying out suddenly at the pain of moving.

'It's all right,' the surgeon said gently. 'You are safe here. No one is going to hurt you, Achillia. Here, drink this.' He held up a small cup. 'It is an opiate,' he added. 'It will help… with everything.'

Lysandra allowed him to lift her head and tilt the bitter liquid down her throat. She almost gagged at the acrid taste but she managed to keep it down. No sooner had the vile stuff been emptied from the cup than the surgeon was giving her water to rinse her mouth. He let her head rest back on the hard pillow and she squeezed her eyes tight shut, but tears burned hot down her face.

She could see them, feel them, their hands all over her, inside her, their laughter, the stench of their sweat.

'Oh, Athene,' she whispered. 'Help me.'

'She will help you,' the surgeon said in Hellenic. 'The goddess does not forget her own.'

Lysandra could feel the opiate flowing through her veins. The pain of her body retreated and, though the memories remained, she found that it was as if she were looking upon them as a detached observer. The whole scene, the terrible ordeal, was played over and over again in her mind, tearing open a wound in her soul that was numbed by the drug in her system.

As the narcotic took hold of her, Lysandra found herself not knowing if she were asleep or awake; she floated in a nether-world of dreams, images from the past month ebbing and flowing before her. Penelope died again before her eyes, as did Eirianwen. She watched herself with indifference as she cut down her opponents, the fierce joy and triumph she had felt at her victories now fled. And again, the rape.

Her rape.

She could hear men's voices talking by her bedside, and though she tried to open her eyes, the lids would not respond. Cool hands touched her forehead, wiping away the sweat, and she found that she was not afraid.

As the voices became distant, some part of her realised that she would have to face up to the truth of what had happened when she was lucid.

But for now, she embraced Morpheus.

Nastasen moved as fast as he could through the crowded streets of Halicarnassus. At every second step he took, he found himself casting a glance over his shoulder. Every passer-by seemed to be staring at him, as if they knew he was on the run.

Sweat coursed over his gigantic frame, the heavy cowl he was wearing unbearably hot in the noonday sun. Yet it was necessary to bear the discomfort, for he could not risk being recognised. He needed to find a place to hide, to breathe the hemp and let the drug ease his mind. He felt queasy and sick, a gnawing need inside him to taste the peace-giving smoke. He knew that once he had taken the smoke, all would be well. He clutched his cloak closer to him, noting his blood-encrusted nails.

Lysandra's blood.

That the bitch had got what she deserved, and secretly wanted, was not at issue. But Nastasen was unsure whether the thrust from his knife had killed her. He cursed himself for a fool. He should have checked that she was dead, but he had been lost in the drug, lost in the pleasure. But if she were still alive, she would name him, and all would be out to hunt him down. Perhaps, even now, agents of Balbus were looking for him and there were always citizens out to make a fast sesterce by capturing an escaped slave.

Everyone was against him.

He glanced about furtively again, the need for the drug gnawing away at him, heightening his paranoia. His companions had agreed that it was best that they spilt up and take their own chances. Nastasen regretted that now, because if they were taken, they would name him.

He made his way to the lower town, the city's underbelly, inhabited by the dregs of Halicarnassus. Here, whores rubbed shoulders with thieves, murderers and indeed rapists. No questions were asked in this part of town; money ruled, and could buy discretion.

He found a grimy inn and, having paid the boil-faced keeper, retreated to his room. At once he cast his cloak onto the bed and fumbled for the twists of hemp in the satchel at his hip. He lit one of them with room's solitary dirty lamp, blew out the flame and watched it smoulder. At last, the room was full of the pungent aroma of the narcotic. Nastasen put his clay cylinder around it and allowed it to fill with smoke before inhaling deeply. He felt his heartbeat slow, his thoughts become less ragged.

What a fool he had been to fear, he realised. None of the city watch would be eager to track him, not a man of his known skill. He would kill anyone who came after him and he was wise enough to know that the local *urbanae* would not risk their lives for the pay they received. Especially over a slave, which, despite what she may think, Lysandra most assuredly was.

He grinned and sniffed his fingers, savouring the female fragrance mingled with fresh blood. She had loved it, he knew. Oh, certainly she had writhed and cried out but there were moments when he saw the wanton gleam in her eye as they degraded her – he was sure of it. She wanted more, the slut.

He grew hard at the thought of it.

A plan formulated in his mind. He would flee the city and buy passage on a ship to his homeland. Once there, he would be greeted as the returning hero, honoured by his tribe. Yes, he had been foolish to be fearful. Drawing the last of the smoke deep into his lungs, he lay back on the bed and began to stroke himself, imagining the sight of Lysandra's pale white skin and the sound of her cries loud in his ears.

XXXIV

It was hard for her to move, but Lysandra persevered. She was beaten to an extent that merely lying down caused her pain, and sitting brought its own agonies.

Yet she was could not simply lie there. She had been in the bed for over a week – an unbearable eternity of nightmare, misery and pain.

Sorina was convalescing too but the Amazon had made no effort to speak, for which Lysandra was profoundly grateful.

With painful slowness, she edged herself from the bed and tottered towards the doorway, and looked out at the now silent corridors. Tired suddenly, she leaned heavily on the wall, hating her weakness. She knew that the physical hurt would pass; but a rage burned inside her that Nastasen had escaped unpunished for his crime. The surgeon had told her that every effort was being made to track him down, but Lysandra reckoned that it was unlikely he would be found. Never in her life had she felt so powerless, so unable to meet life on terms that she dictated. Had she not risen above slavery, conquered her captors and the mob with her skill and genius? But this was something she could do nothing about. Nastasen and his friends would escape and live out their days knowing they had won, that they had taken their pleasure from her and that she was helpless to prevent it.

They had forced her to submit, and the shame of it burned within her like acid. What she would give to have Nastasen before her with a sword in his hand. She would cut the bastard to ribbons and bathe in his blood. That he still lived mocked her. She smacked her fist into the door, and regretted it instantly, for the action sent a wave of agony through her.

'Feeling better?' Sorina's voice sounded from the stillness of the room.

This was all she needed. They had not spoken in all the time they had been in surgery, and she could do without the old bitch's meaningless inanities. 'I shall be well,' she replied shortly, realising that to ignore her would be to sink to the level of the barbarian.

Sorina hoisted herself from her bed with difficulty, and Lysandra sneered at this open show of her discomfort. A Spartan may suffer pain like any other mortal but would not show it – especially to an enemy. She was certain that, even in her drugged stupor, she had not let herself down in such a manner.

'I am sorry for what happened to you,' Sorina said. 'It is a crime against all women that a man should do this.'

Lysandra recoiled. How dare she have the gall to offer her sympathy? It was insulting. 'Perhaps you should be more sorry for killing Eirianwen,' she snapped, feeling the cords that held her temper in place begin to fray.

'I am. Truly. I loved her as a daughter. But I could not have fought less than my best. To do so would be to dishonour Eirianwen.'

She was, Lysandra noted, making a good show of genuine regret, but it did not fool her; Sorina was trying to assuage her guilt by making amends. 'Spare me your platitudes,' she hissed. 'You, in the autumn of your worthless existence, destroyed someone who was only pure and good. Your vanity would not allow anything

282

less; you claim to have loved her as a daughter? Then you are the first 'mother' I have heard of that would put her own life before that of her child. You murdered her, Sorina, for I know she did not come at you with her best.'

'Lysandra, you don't understand the ways of the Tribes.' Sorina's voice was gentle, almost pleading.

'Do not speak of your barbarian nonsense to me. I will not be Ate to hear your confession,' Lysandra declared, naming the Goddess of Guilt. 'My body may be injured, but my mind is sound. And know this: you are marked, old woman. I *will* kill you for what you did.'

Sorina's hazel eyes flared with anger. 'You arrogant bitch,' she spat, struggling to her feet. 'I was trying to make a peace between us that Eirianwen might be at rest, but you throw it in my face. I have my pride, yes, but it is not the blind arrogance that taints *your* soul.'

'You have nothing to be proud of, *kinslayer*,' Lysandra said, hurling out the word Eirianwen herself had once used. 'I know that you are a spent force, and that you used Eirianwen's care of you to your advantage. Well, hear this: I challenge you. And I will not spare my hand, I swear by Athene. I will cut you down with impunity, and nothing will give me greater pleasure!'

'You don't have the skill.' Sorina took a tentative step forward. 'I beat you before when you crossed me at the *ludus* – if you were not too drunk to remember it! I will do so again. With a sword, or without it.'

'Come then!' Lysandra's temper snapped and she lunged forwards, blind to everything save the need to crush the life from the Amazon.

Just as she came within striking range of Sorina, strong arms gripped her from behind, and hoisted her away. Unable to turn and see who held her, she kicked and screamed furiously struggling to break the iron grip.

283

Alerted by her howls, the surgeon rushed into the treatment area, with Stick and Catuvolcos in tow. 'What in Hades name is going on here?' he demanded.

'I will kill her!' Lysandra screamed, as the surgeon and Catuvolcos rushed past to restrain Sorina who was now hobbling forwards, screeching obscenities. Lysandra lashed out to kick her, but Stick lunged and grabbed her flailing legs.

'Get her out of here!' the surgeon barked, and Lysandra was powerless to prevent herself from being borne away.

'We came to see how you were doing…' Stick grunted as she struggled to break free. 'Stop now, Lysandra!'

She glared at him, but was too weak to continue the fight. In silence, the two men bore down the corridor and to a cell; here, they let her to her feet.

'Fine way to act in front of your friend,' Stick glowered and jerked his chin at the man behind her before stalking off.

She turned, still furious, but stopped short.

'Hello, Lysandra,' Telemachus said, smiling at her. His grin faded suddenly. 'You're not going to strike *me*, are you?'

Lysandra drew herself up, fighting back her anger. 'Do not be absurd, Brother. Servants of the Goddess do not hit one another. I shall reserve my anger for the barbarian bitch you saw me with.'

'That's good. You should sit.' He indicated a bunk. 'You look as though you will fall down at any moment.'

'I shall stand,' Lysandra said defiantly. The fact was that Nastasen's atrocities had made it extremely painful for her to sit.

Telemachus, however, was insistent. 'Lie on your side then,' he said. Lysandra flushed with shame, that he offered this advice meant that he knew well what had been done to her, but, feeling her legs go weak, she complied, forcing her face to stony stoicism: it would not do to show that an action as simple as lying down caused her discomfort.

'What are you doing here?' Lysandra asked as soon as she had arranged herself into a position that was bearable.

'I came to visit you,' he replied. 'Balbus asked me, having told me what happened. He considers that we are friends. We are, aren't we?'

That they had met but once was of no matter, Lysandra supposed. They shared a common ancestry, and practised similar devotions. 'I suppose that we are.' She shrugged. 'I thank you, but I shall recover quite soon.'

'I'm sure.' Telemachus nodded. 'I have asked Balbus that you spend your recuperation with me.'

'Why?' Lysandra straightened. 'My place is at the *ludus* with the Hellene women. I am their leader, and they will not manage without me.'

'I'm sure they will survive. And I think that some time away from all of this will do you good.'

'I am quite well, and have no need of sympathy, Brother.'

'I'm not offering you sympathy. The fact is that I need your help. I'm well aware of what you have been through with your trainer – and the loss of your friend. Balbus has told me everything, so I feel somewhat guilty asking you at what must be a sad time for you.'

'What help?' Lysandra frowned. 'I am no good for anything at the moment. Though we Spartans bear pain with dignity, I am not so vain as to think that I am at my full powers.'

'This is so,' the Athenian agreed. 'You're no good for training at the *ludus* till you get your strength back. But I know that Sparta makes well-learned priestesses with sharp minds. That your body has suffered will not dull the keenness of your thoughts. If you were anything other than Spartan, I would not trouble you after what you have been through.'

Lysandra found herself smiling slightly. Truly, Telemachus was a good man and, as a Hellene and priest, had an innate understanding of the superiority of the Spartan race. 'You are correct. Great indignities have been visited upon my body and I am somewhat distraught at the loss of my love.' She felt no shame in pronouncing her devotion to Eirianwen. 'But if I can help a friend, of course I will.'

'It's a big task…' Telemachus hesitated. 'I need works from my library copied up: Hesiod, Thucydides, Plato… that sort of thing. Are you sure you are up to it?'

'Of course.' Lysandra answered levelly, betraying no sense of the relief she felt. It would be good to feel something other than utterly useless and abused. It would in no way assuage the helpless anger that she felt at Nastasen's deeds, but at least there was some practical thing to which she could divert her attentions. Obviously, Telemachus was guilt-ridden at asking her in her current state, but he evidently could find no one properly qualified in both religion and scripting to aid him. Certainly, their association was a good one; he had helped her in the past, and it pleased her to be able to help him. And, if she was honest with herself, such tasks might also keep her from thinking too much of Eirianwen and the pain those memories brought with them.

Aside from her personal needs, she also considered that her grasp of language and literature would be far better than Telemachus's. Doubtless she would produce work of better quality. 'Balbus has agreed to this?' she asked.

'Yes. He is pleased to know that a healer of skill will look after you, and that it is costing him nothing.'

'A healer?'

'I have no small expertise.' Telemachus did not waste time with false modesty, she noted.

'And, in such a way, I shall repay you for your skills with my work.' Lysandra smiled slightly, refusing to wince as her lip split.

'Precisely so.' He handed her a cloth. 'We have a deal?'

'Yes, we have a deal. When should we leave?'

'Right away.' Telemachus got to his feet and offered Lysandra his hand. She spurned the offer. 'Follow me,' he said, turning away.

His back to Lysandra, Telemachus smiled grimly, pleased with his success. When Balbus had come to him, he had realised at once that leaving her to her own thoughts would be damaging to her. The *lanista's* concern had been for his fighter, his stock, but Telemachus's anxiety was over the girl's health. In truth, he did not know her well, but then she was a priestess and it seemed to Telemachus that she had had more than her fair share of bad luck. He wanted to help her, both as priest and fellow Hellene. One thing he did realise was that keeping her mind active would help her with the trauma she had suffered. He had assured Balbus that a change of environment would be the best medicine for the girl's mind.

He offered a prayer to Athene and then to Nemesis that they would catch the pigs that had raped her – the goddess of justice that they would be found and the goddess of vengeance that they would suffer the torments that their evil deserved.

XXXV

Lysandra surveyed her new surroundings through bruised, puffy eyes. Extensive building work had recently been completed on the shrine, that much was obvious. She could tell that this had once been a fairly modest establishment, but now, whilst not opulent and grand, much space had been added to the rear of the temple proper. Evidently, Athene's shrine in Halicarnassus had prospered under the auspices of the Athenian priest.

Telemachus led her to a small anteroom, where he placed her bucket of books on a bunk. 'Well,' he said, 'this will be yours while you recover. I know it's not much, but then again...' he gestured and Lysandra rewarded him with a half smile.

'It is most pleasant, Brother,' she said, aware that he would know all about the austerity of both *agoge* and *ludus*. 'Though I should not wish to live in such luxury all the time, whilst I heal, this will be acceptable.' She saw him take a sidelong glance at her, unsure of whether or not she was being serious. She decided to leave him in the dark. 'When should I start my work?'

'Oh, there will be plenty of time for all that,' the priest replied. 'It's not at all pressing. But as I said, there is a lot of it and your help will be invaluable to me.'

Lysandra lowered herself gingerly onto the bunk and lay on her side.

'Let's take a look at you, then,' Telemachus said. 'I have some healing salves which I will apply for you. I shall bring them.' He turned and exited swiftly.

Lysandra suddenly felt very tired. Though she was loath to admit it, even the short wagon ride from the arena to the shrine had utterly exhausted her. However, she told herself that wallowing in self-indulgence was no way to get back to full health and so she sat up and began to struggle out of her tunic. It was slow, agonising work and she fought the urge to utter a curse. Nastasen had made even the simplest of tasks a Heraclean effort for her. Though the tunic caught over her head she struggled on gamely. There were footfalls and Telemachus was there: a sharp tearing sound and the garment fell away.

'You know, Lysandra,' he said, 'it does not always have to be the hard way.' He gestured with the knife he had used to cut away the cloth.

'It is what I am used to,' she responded. 'The acceptance of hardship is a virtue, Brother.'

Telemachus grunted, looking at her ravaged body. She could tell that his face was a carefully composed Stoic mask: she looked in bad shape, and well she knew it. 'It looks far worse than it feels,' she lied.

'Does it?' Telemachus did not seem at all convinced. 'I will apply the salve, if you have no objection.'

'Of course not.' Lysandra settled herself back. 'Though I am used to the wanton cries of lewd men, I hardly think that you will receive any gratification from the sight of me, Brother.'

'Just call me Telemachus,' he said, rubbing the unguent into her shoulders as gently as he could. Carefully, he covered her torso and back with the vile-smelling stuff, but advised her to deal with her personal areas herself. 'How's that?' he asked after a while.

'It feels strange, as though it is lifting the soreness from the bruises. Not that they were causing me overmuch discomfort,' she added hastily.

'Good. I want you to drink this now.' He handed her a cup. 'It's a healing draught. Unlike an opiate it won't turn you into a walking corpse. But it will help you to rest.'

'Thank you.' Lysandra took the cup and sipped the bitter liquid. 'It is utterly foul,' she told him after a moment.

Telemachus chuckled. 'Well, it must be if even a Spartan passes comment on its flavour. But is that not the way of the world, Lysandra? All things that are bad for you taste wonderful, all those that are not taste vile.'

'Only if one is used to the decadent lifestyle of Athens,' she said blithely.

'You're welcome.' Telemachus's expression turned sour, but there was kindness in his eyes. 'I have this.' He turned and produced a lengthy *chiton*. 'It ties at the front, so you won't have to struggle in and out of a tunic.'

'You are most considerate,' she told him as he helped her into the garment.

'I'm a priest. It's part of the job… as we are taught in Athens at least.'

'Perhaps…' she said, lying down once again, her voice floating, 'there is something to be said for that.'

Telemachus watched as Lysandra drifted into slumber. He waited till the rhythmic rise and fall of her chest told him she was deeply asleep before brushing the raven hair away from her face and leaving her to her rest.

There were tasks he had to attend to and the faithful would be gathering soon. His workload had increased threefold since the money he had received from Balbus had been ploughed into the shrine. With better facilities the congregation had increased a great deal, as had his standing in the expatriate community.

That the money had been gained by helping Lysandra the first time had not sat well with him initially. But on reflection, he had realised that things were in balance and he had acted properly. He had performed a service and all parties concerned had been better off because of it. Balbus had his gladiatrix back, Lysandra was prepared for her life in the arena, and the goddess had a more opulent place of worship.

This, however, was different. Balbus had rushed to him after the rape, knowing that a degree of trust must exist between Spartan priestess and Athenian priest. The *lanista* was not an evil, or even cruel man, and knew that the abiding horrors of Lysandra's ordeal could destroy her. He had offered Telemachus money to help the girl, but this time the Greek had refused payment.

His day's work done, Telemachus retreated to what he optimistically termed his library to find some texts for Lysandra to re-copy. The truth of the matter was that he had no such work for her and would have to make some. This took some time, as most of his collection was of the more popular works and he had decided that it would be unfair to engage Lysandra in useless tasks.

So occupied had he become in the task of seeking out older texts, he did not realise the hour had grown late. That his lamp was beginning to flicker told him he'd been searching for some hours now. He rubbed his eyes and glanced at the pile of scrolls he had amassed: certainly, it was enough for her to be getting on with.

He rose, his back clicking, and made his way to his room. In the silence of the shrine, the sound of Lysandra's voice was clear. She was calling out, desperate for help. Cursing, Telemachus rushed to her quarters, hoping that his lamp would last out.

Lysandra writhed and thrashed on her bunk, in the grip of a

terrible nightmare. It was all too obvious from her cries that she was re-living her ordeal at the hands of the Nubian. He rushed to her side.

'Lysandra!' He shook her gently, not wishing to hurt her, or snap her from her slumber too suddenly. Her lids flickered open, the ice-coloured eyes wide with fear and panic.

'Get away!' she screamed. 'Get away from me!'

'Lysandra, it is I…' the priest began to say, but the young Spartan merely screamed incoherently. She was, he realised, still in the grip of her dream and the presence of a man in her room in the dark could not help her. Defeated and helpless, he retreated, listening as the cries began to abate. Telemachus sighed and sat on the floor outside her room, his back leaning on the wall. It was going to be a long, uncomfortable night. But he did not wish to leave her alone.

XXXVI

It took some days for Sorina's fury to abate.

The hated Spartan's face swam before her eyes, the grating voice, the strange eyes and, most of all, the arrogant demeanour. It was obvious now that what Eirianwen had said was true. The Morrigan had marked all three of them, intertwining their destinies. Clearly, the Goddess of Dark Fate had a competition in mind, where only one would be left alive. Eirianwen was dead by Sorina's own hand, and the Spartan had challenged her in turn.

Soon there would be only Sorina, as it was in the beginning. She knew that she had the beating of Lysandra, and she prayed furiously that the Spartan recover soon in order that the matter between them might be settled. The Greek's overweening conceit grated but, worse, the bitch had thrown the Friendship Gift back in her face. She was sick with anger at Lysandra's mistreatment of her honour. It had taken a great deal for her, as Clan Chief, to make the first words, yet the ingrate had used this merely as an opportunity to insult her. Well, the challenge was laid at her feet and Sorina had never shirked a foe in her life. In normal circumstances she took life with regret, but in her heart she knew that she would enjoy killing Lysandra. To ram three feet of iron into her belly and watch those ice blue eyes widen in pain and surprise would give her great pleasure. More, to send the Greek to Helle knowing that a 'barbarian' had bested her would be revenge of the sweetest kind.

Sorina's rage gave her strength and helped score out the grief she felt at her slaying of Eirianwen. There was guilt still, but she would wash it away in Spartan blood. If not for Lysandra, none of this would have come to pass. She had come into the world of the *ludus* seeking to take it over and make it her own. She sought to corrupt the best and bravest of the Tribe, mocking them with her seduction of Eirianwen. There had been times when Sorina had doubted in her conviction of this, but now she knew that she was looking for good where there had been none.

Lysandra was evil. That she had been raped was a sign from the gods that she curb her arrogant ways but the 'priestess' had ignored it. Sorina knew that this discounting would cost her her life.

This hatred of Lysandra was a contentious issue between her and Lucius Balbus. The *lanista* visited her often as she recuperated – more, she knew, to keep an eye on his best remaining asset than over any real concern for her health. Balbus needed his best fighters training and earning, not laid up in expensive arena surgeries. The Roman had quizzed her ruthlessly over the cause of her spat with Lysandra but Sorina had remained tight-lipped.

'It is something between us, *lanista*,' she said.

'Well,' Balbus stabbed a finger, 'I don't want any more of it. Lysandra is here to stay so get used to it.'

Sorina grunted. 'Have it your way, Balbus, but I will not stand to be upbraided or attacked by that little slut.'

'I'll see to it that she is kept busy, and far away from you.' Balbus smiled at her, and changed the subject. 'How are you doing?'

'Stiff and sore, but the surgeon tells me that I am healing well and will be able to return to the *ludus* soon. Although by wagon. I am not ready to ride just yet.'

'Well, that's no problem.' He patted her hand. 'Just as long as my best fighter is back up to speed soon, that's the main thing.'

'You're in very good spirits, *lanista*,' Sorina said, eyeing him archly. 'Why are you still in the city, anyway? Shouldn't you be back at the *ludus*?'

'Business,' Balbus replied glibly. 'The gladiatrix has only to concern herself with the next bout, but the *lanista* must arrange those bouts. Also, I'm looking at expanding,' he added. Sorina could see that he was having difficulty in expressing his obvious delight at making a fortune and tempering it with a suitably solemn demeanour. After all, the fortune was earned with the blood of his slaves.

'You are buying more slaves, then?'

'Well, yes.' Balbus cleared his throat. 'And meeting with building contractors to increase the capacity of the school itself.'

'We have enough room at the *ludus* for more than twice the number it now holds,' Sorina pressed him. 'Just how big are you going, Balbus?'

'Very.' He smiled, somewhat uncomfortably. 'But don't you worry about that now. Just get yourself well. I'll have you taken to the *ludus* as soon as you are ready to travel.'

Sorina was about to speak again, but Balbus got to his feet, indicating that their conversation was at an end, so she dismissed the matter. She would see what his plans were soon enough.

Lysandra tried to immerse herself in the tasks that Telemachus had set her, hoping it would be a diversion from her thoughts and the recurring memory of Nastasen. But she could not escape her mind, filled as it was with visions of the rape. Worse, when the sun played across the pages, she was reminded of Eirianwen, and the light she had brought to her life. If the days were bad, she feared the night. Sleep, if it came, was a constant torment: Nyx, the Goddess of Nightmares, denied her the embrace of Morpheus with savage malice. When she was not forced to relive the horror of the cell, Eirianwen's death was played out for her in bloody detail.

The lack of sleep began to fray her already taut nerves and, one afternoon as she pored over a scroll, she finally broke down. Tears flooded in her eyes, her throat filled with shards of glass. Telemachus had heard her, and rushed to the small area in which she worked. She looked up at him, her face red and stained. 'There now,' the priest said, sitting opposite her. 'What's amiss?'

Lysandra shook her head mutely, her tears splashing on the parchment, spoiling the ink. 'I miss her so much,' she said after some time. 'I just cannot bear it.'

Telemachus sighed, his mouth setting a grim slash in his beard. 'To lose a loved one is the worst pain of all, Lysandra. I know this. But I know also that no one in the world has ever suffered as badly as you.'

Lysandra sniffed. 'Of course they have.' She was about to speak again but fresh spasms of grief welled up in her. She felt the priest's hand on her shoulder and she jolted at the male touch. But it was brief and he was already past her, returning momentarily with a *krater* of wine.

'What I mean is,' he said as he poured, 'our own suffering is always the worst. Logically, we know that others feel pain too – but logic has no place in the heart, Lysandra.'

'I am ashamed of my weakness,' she said. 'This is not the Spartan way.' She wanted to claw at her face, so strong was the pain that wracked her chest.

'You have nothing to be ashamed of,' Telemachus told her. 'These wounds you bear have cut you worse than any sword can. A lesser woman would have died, but you…' he trailed off for a moment. 'You have more strength than you know. It may not seem so at the moment, but you do.'

'I feel that I have not the will to live.' She shuddered and reached for the wine cup. Telemachus did not comment as she drained it. 'What Nastasen did to me, I could bear if only Eirianwen were here to hold me. But I am alone, Telemachus. In here.' She tapped her chest.

He shook his head. 'You are not alone, dear Lysandra. In times of grief, to share it with one's friends is the best thing. And I am a friend to you, Spartan. Any hurt takes time to heal and you are welcome here for as long as you wish it.'

'But I must return to the *ludus* as soon as I am able to fight,' she said earnestly.

'Yes, but you are not able to fight yet.' The priest poured her a stiffer measure of wine and she took it, knowing that to walk with Dionysus was to keep Nyx at bay.

Telemachus watched as Lysandra threw back the un-mixed wine. There was a chilling eagerness in her voice when she expressed her desire to return to the *ludus*, but to send her back to the sands before her mental scars had healed would be tantamount to assisting her suicide. He did not see fit to bring this up with her, as she would only deny it. 'Have another drink,' he offered. 'It is not always the answer, but sometimes it helps.'

Lysandra did as she was bidden and in time she became drunk, and erupted once more into floods of tears, rambling about Eirianwen and the attack in the cell. It was all Telemachus could do to keep a tear from his own eye at her plight. He was, by nature, a cynical man, but he could not fail to be moved by the desperation in the girl's voice when she spoke of the Silurian gladiatrix. As for the terror she had suffered at the hands of Nastasen, Telemachus prayed that the giant would be brought to justice and suffer such an end that would even turn the stomachs of the hardened Carian mob.

Eventually, Lysandra became incoherent, her head falling forwards onto her chest. When he was sure she had passed out, Telemachus carried her to her room and laid her gently on her bunk. This done, he made to prepare a healing draught, as he knew well that she would be sorely ill when she awoke.

The first month of her stay with Telemachus passed slowly for Lysandra. The nightmares were a constant plague to her, but Telemachus was always there, shaking her awake, saving her from reliving the pain of the past. The presence of a man in the dark had panicked her at first, but once she became sufficiently accustomed to him to realise that she was not in danger, Lysandra was truly touched. She did not mention this to him as she felt it would shame them both.

True to his word, Telemachus was a healer of some accomplishment. His potions and salves quickly restored her physical health, so that she was able to move about unassisted in short order. More, the unguents had prevented any scarring to her face: whilst it was not the Spartan way to be vain, Lysandra had secretly feared that she would be disfigured by the beating she had received. Thankfully, this was not so.

'How would you like to help me today?' Lysandra looked up from her work, a passage from Thucydides, as Telemachus entered her room.

'I am almost complete with '*The History of the Peloponnesian War*' she said. 'I have made no amendments though Thucydides is, frankly, biased.'

'That's not what I meant.' He sat on her bunk. 'I meant in the shrine.'

She put her stylus down carefully. 'In what capacity, Telemachus? I am a priestess no longer.'

'I don't know about that,' he responded.

'I have been known by a man,' she swallowed. 'This is forbidden.'

'In Sparta, perhaps,' Telemachus said, making a dismissive gesture. 'It would do you good, I think, to help others commune with Athene. Truth be known, Lysandra, it is not for the Orders of Men or Women to cast out a priestess. This is vanity, I think. Athene will look after her own.'

Lysandra's heart beat a little faster. True, she knew she could not return to the life of priestess; yet to help, to enjoy the rituals once more, to hear the goddess speak to her in the sanctity of a temple; it was something she had thought denied her forever. 'I would be honoured to assist you,' she said finally.

'Excellent. I thought you would. To that end, I have a gift for you.' He handed her a small package.

'Oh!' Lysandra felt herself blush, which was rather unseemly, but the suddenness of the priest's gesture had caught her unawares. Carefully, she unwrapped the cloth bundle and drew forth a brand new *chiton*. It was long, and dyed in scarlet.

'Is it the right shade?' Telemachus asked, grinning. 'There's a fellow who works in the market who claims to have spent time in Sparta. He swears that this is the colour of your Order.'

'It is so.' Lysandra beamed with delight. 'This is so that the enemies of Sparta will never see the colour of our blood.'

'Well, I don't imagine there will be any enemies around here, but I am glad it meets with your approval.'

'Oh, it does, Telemachus, it is a most lavish gift!'

'Hardly. But I am pleased that you are pleased.' He got to his feet. 'Well, get changed, then. I shall see you in the shrine. It will be good for me to put my feet up for once and simply watch.'

Telemachus was well pleased with Lysandra's progress. With help and care she was coming to terms with her grief; she spoke of Eirianwen often, but the bitterness in her voice was slowly replaced with a yearning sadness. Of Nastasen she said nothing, but he knew that the Nubian still haunted her dreams. He frequently

299

asked the soldiers assigned to town watch if there were any news of the trainer but they had found nothing. He did not mention this to Lysandra, lest he distress her, but that she had agreed to conduct the ceremony showed a marked improvement. There was, he admitted to himself, something to be said for Spartan stoicism.

Telemachus waited at the entrance to the shrine, greeting the worshippers as they filed in. If some thought it was a little odd that he was not already in his place to begin the ceremonies, none mentioned it. Soon, the building became full and he closed the doors, marking the sign to inform others that no more would be admitted for this service.

Incense hung thickly in the air. He grinned to himself. Spartans might be austere but it seemed that Lysandra had been heavy handed with burners. Still, it all made for good theatre.

From behind the statue of the goddess, Lysandra emerged, carrying the Ritual Spear in her hand. There was a muted gasp from the gathering. Her wounds healed, Telemachus realised that she was truly beautiful. In the dim, half-light of the shrine, her form obscured by the smoke, it appeared as though Athene herself had come from Olympus to grace his small place of worship. Lysandra's voice resonated strongly through the small shrine, lifted in hymn to the goddess:

> *I start to sing of Pallas Athena, City Guard,*
> *The fearsome, who with Ares cares for warlike deeds,*
> *The sack of cities and the battle-cry of war;*
> *She saves the soldiers as they come and go away.*
> *Be welcome, goddess, give me fortune and good cheer.*

Lysandra continued in a typically Spartan manner, exhorting the people to bear hardship with fortitude, speaking on the evils of excess and extravagant living. Telemachus realised that the address was well rehearsed and often spoken. The girl's rhetoric was flawless, even if it was delivered in the rustic Laconian accent.

He did wonder, however, whether the words would have much bearing outside of her strange little *polis*. Modern folk did not want to be told of sacrifice, duty and moral obligation: the world had changed and the old-fashioned values adhered to by the Spartans were so outmoded as to be almost quaint.

Lysandra finished her lesson, her ice-coloured eyes sweeping over the people for a moment. There was a pause – then a youth at the front began to applaud. The others took up his motion and soon the shrine echoed to appreciative shouts and cheers, hailing the priestess's words. Telemachus was taken aback. He had certainly had not expected the dour service to be received so enthusiastically. He clapped politely himself, feeling a little self-conscious.

'Is there anything specific a worshipper wishes to ask of the goddess or her priestess?' Lysandra said when the cheering died down. The youth raised his hand, and she gestured to him.

The lad stood, looking this way and that, urged on by several of his fellows who flanked him. 'I wanted to ask,' he cleared his throat, 'if you were... I mean... are you Achillia?'

Telemachus put his hand to his forehead. He had been an idiot. Of course the crowd had not been enamoured of Lysandra's speech. They were enamoured of *her*, the gladiatrix. He knew the girl and was not blinded by her recently acquired fame; he had all but forgotten that the public would be unfamiliar with Lysandra as a person. All they knew was that the heroine of Aeschylus' games, a Hellene heroine at that, had come to lead them in prayer.

He saw Lysandra's nostrils flare, and she drew herself up. 'I am she.'

'I think you're brilliant.' Telemachus could almost see the boy's cheeks burning through the incense smoke.

'That is as maybe, young *ephebe*,' came the Spartan's response. Though it was stern, the priest could see that Lysandra was fighting the urge to grin at the recognition. 'But,' she went on, 'that is not relevant to this time or place. Do you have a question?' The boy hesitated, and then sat down, being nudged mercilessly by his compatriots until a glare from Lysandra quietened them.

There were several supercilious queries from the older members of the gathering, which were answered laconically by the Spartan ('How can I raise my sons to be good men?' – 'Discipline breeds goodliness') but most now seemed anxious to get the service over with because, Telemachus realised, they could then meet and talk with the priestess. Lysandra bade the people make their offerings to Athene and this done, the ceremony would be over.

No sooner had Lysandra closed the ritual than the doors were flung open and people spilled into the street, awaiting 'Achillia'. Telemachus noted too that some of the gathering had already begun to spread the news to passers-by that the gladiatrix was in the shrine.

'Are you sure about this?' he said to Lysandra as she moved to the door.

'Of course,' she said. 'Have you seen the offerings?'

Telemachus rushed to the altar, to see the bowl overflowing with coin. Normally, a mere few sesterces rattled about at the bottom of the pot but, this day, people had been more than generous. He gathered the fame-garnered loot quickly and glanced up at the statue of Athene. He could swear that the cold marble lips were curled in a half-smile.

'The goddess looks after her own,' he muttered. The irony was not lost to him. His efforts to help Lysandra were totally selfless, made out of a desire to somehow retain a balance between the good and ill in her life. But her mere presence in the shrine this single day had paid more in offerings than Telemachus was used to seeing in an entire week. And each day she was with him the coffers would grow.

Outside, the people had begun to chant 'Achillia, Achillia,' over and over again. The priest chuckled. 'Why not,' he said aloud. He could understand why they were cheering: the Hellenes were a proud race, yet in the Empire they were not regarded as true equals. More, the sands of the arena were usually the dominion of barbarian champions. That Lysandra was Hellene gave them someone to cheer for, someone who carried their pride like a badge of honour.

He moved outside to see Lysandra being swamped by many admirers. Pieces of parchment were being thrust into her hand in order that she make her mark as a souvenir. Others just wanted to touch her dress for luck. The priest was taken aback when he looked upon her. The girl was basking in the adulation; beneath her severe façade, it was evident that she was revelling in the attention. She seemed to grow in stature, feeding off the energy of the crowd. Telemachus was buffeted about in the rush to be close to Lysandra and momentarily feared for her safety. Yet, she seemed to know instinctively how to handle the mob of people, easing them back, so that she could greet them in an orderly fashion.

He stepped back, ignored by the well-wishers, into the quiet of the shrine and leant against the wall. That Lysandra was scarred by the loss of her lover and her ordeal was undeniable. Yet Telemachus perceived that in the adoration of the mob she had found her own salve. It healed her in a way that handholding and quiet words never could, burying her hurt beneath an avalanche of self-indulgence.

Being Spartan, she would never see it that way, of course. Self-indulgence was anathema to the harsh Lakedaimonian code. But he could see in Lysandra a recovering of egocentricity. Perhaps, he thought, that was not as great an evil as self-neglect; yet, if not tempered, this confidence, this love of popularity could turn quickly to conceit.

The mob was fickle. They would love Lysandra as Hellene and *their* champion. Yet, if she were to falter on the sands, they could turn against her. How then would she react, if the cheers turned to catcalls, the adulation to scorn?

But that was another matter, he thought. For now, if they could help her heal, then he was content to let it pass.

XXXVII

Lysandra was grateful to Telemachus for allowing her to lead the afternoon rituals. This, coupled with her work on translation and copy, kept her mind fully engaged and she understood that this was his intention. It was, she considered, part of the strange destiny the goddess had marked for her. It seemed her life was to be spent in service to the public – first, her Mission, then the arena, now again the Mission and soon to return to the sands.

But for now, it was good that she had a chance to deliver some proper Spartan teaching to the local Hellenes – they certainly needed to hear them. She had heard Telemachus's rituals during her stay in the shrine and he preached the misguided and liberal values of the Athenians, which verged on the immoral. Yet, for all this, she realised that he was a good man who had her best interests at heart.

Her fame had undeniably increased his congregation: once word had got around the Hellene community that 'Achillia' was serving for a brief period in the shrine, the building was packed to the pillars each day. This was right and proper, as Lysandra fought to honour Athene and this was Her shrine. Her fame was a by-product of this worshipful combat and there was no shame in it.

The expatriate community had come to regard her as their heroine; this was unsurprising, as there was not a Spartan amongst them, and she knew that other Hellenes held her *polis* in such respect that it bordered on reverential awe. To have a Priestess of Athene amongst them, and she a famous gladiatrix to boot, was a great honour to them and they responded with enthusiasm.

As the weeks passed, Lysandra found that she could now think of Eirianwen without tears though the loss still pained her. The memories were hers forever she realised, and they could not be taken from her. But she knew she must also harden her heart. She could not afford to allow herself such intensity of feeling again, the pain of loss was too great. Love was a madness that none could fight against. The best cure for this ailment was avoidance and Lysandra vowed that this was the path she would tread.

Sleep was also coming to her more regularly: though her nights were never uninterrupted, she had at least some small peace. The night of terror at Nastasen's hands was still vivid, as was the feeling of helpless anger at being powerless to stop him. She told herself that, though fear was an alien concept to her race, there must have been some lingering trauma of the attack that was causing her nightmares. However, she was convinced it was evidence of the superior Spartan *psyche* that she had gone some way to overcoming this. She only prayed that one day she could repay the Nubian for his assault.

Lysandra found that her experiences helped her deliver more accessible truths to Telemachus's congregation. Having gone through more than any of these suburbanites would experience in a lifetime, she was sure that her example would be an inspiration to all those that cared to listen. That her fame and obvious natural charisma *made* the people pay attention to her words was so much the better.

She refused to allow herself to drift back into the mindset of being a priestess proper. She was a gladiatrix now. That was her path and it would be folly to think otherwise. She confided this to Telemachus as they shared their evening meal.

'It does not have to be so,' he said after some thought. 'You could run from this place, and disappear. Return to Sparta or make a life elsewhere.'

Lysandra was taken aback. 'That would be a dereliction of duty,' she retorted.

'A duty to whom, Lysandra? To Balbus, your owner?'

'To those people out there.' She gestured towards the doorway. 'The people who come here to hear me. The people that take pride in what I do in the arena. And to Athene herself. Did you not say that to fight for the goddess was my true path?'

Telemachus flushed. 'Yes, but that was before I had come to know you. Then, you were just another arena slave to me and Balbus paid me well to speak to you, to encourage you in your hour of need.'

Lysandra was silent for a moment. 'I did not know that you had been paid to be my friend,' she said, unsure of how she felt about it.

'I was not paid to be your friend, money cannot buy that,' he said at once and in her heart Lysandra was relieved. She would have felt a terrible sense of betrayal if one of the few people she felt she could trust had been revealed as false. 'Balbus is not a cruel man, Lysandra, but he trades in people's lives,' the priest continued. 'There is an ambiguity in all of us when it comes to slaves. There must be slavery, after all, yet it is difficult to look at you as a slave now that we have spent time together and become friends.' He sighed. 'I would not wish to see you die in the arena.'

'Have no fear,' Lysandra said. 'There is little possibility of that happening. I am extremely skilled and, though your first words to me may have been bought, they rang true for me. You were right in many things,' she hesitated, 'and as such, I do not judge you harshly. Furthermore, I am slave only in legal terms. When thousands of people scream your name, it is difficult to perceive oneself as subservient.'

Telemachus smiled at her, a little sadly, she thought. 'Balbus has been writing to me, enquiring as to your health and state of mind,' he said. 'Till now, I have put him off, yet I can see that you are healed in body and spirit.'

'That is so, Telemachus.' Lysandra nodded. 'I would return to my rightful place.'

'I will miss you.'

He was being honest and this pleased her. 'You make it sound as if you will not see me again,' she responded brusquely. 'I am not a prisoner in the *ludus*, Telemachus, and you may visit me when it suits you. It may be that I will be allowed out alone as I have shown myself trustworthy in your care.' She grinned at him. 'In that I did *not* flee and start a new life for myself.'

'You will stay till he responds to me?'

'Of course. The people must know that I am to depart. I would feel as though I had betrayed them if I just upped and left.'

'You're most considerate,' he mocked gently.

'And you are most disappointed,' she countered. 'Your coffers will no longer be as full after my departure. Evidence, if it was ever needed, of the superiority of Spartan religious doctrine.'

'We all enjoy an oration on self-sacrifice and discipline, Priestess,' Telemachus said, his face solemn. 'I prefer some largesse in my themes, however. Perhaps, outside of Sparta, your thematic content might be considered dull, boring, and perhaps even pompous.'

Lysandra sat upright, her eyes dancing with mirth. 'Pompous! I? Do not be absurd, Athenian. Pomposity is not the province of Spartans; it is rather an art form perfected by the effete democracy of Athens.'

Telemachus laughed then, and she joined him. It was some

time since she had indulged herself thus and she enjoyed the moment's lack of decorum. 'Come.' The priest stood. 'We should share a few drinks in the town tonight.'

'Yes,' Lysandra agreed. 'That would be most pleasant.'

XXXVIII

It was Catuvolcos who came for her. She could tell he was nervous, shifting from foot to foot, unwilling to meet her gaze. And well he might feel uncomfortable, Lysandra decided. He had acted abominably towards her and that he felt guilty at her suffering was just reward.

She was inwardly delighted at the turnout for her departure. The expatriate community had gathered in force, wishing her well and bringing many gifts for her to take back to the *ludus*. Some were practical, others not so but she received all the offerings with good grace and had Catuvolcos load them onto the low-backed wagon in which they were to travel.

Telemachus was somewhat misty-eyed at their parting, embracing her warmly and promising that he would visit her soon. She hoped he would. In truth, she was most grateful to the priest for his help and his friendship. It had been twice now that the man had aided her: admittedly the first time for pay, but the second was out of genuine concern for her welfare. Whilst she could not look upon him as any sort of father figure, she did feel as though she had an older brother living in Halicarnassus.

The farewells said, and to the sound of her name being hailed loudly by the Hellenes, the wagon began to wind its way through the city's narrow streets. Catuvolcos looked uncomfortable in the extreme and Lysandra found herself taking a vindictive pleasure in this. Certainly, she made no effort to speak to him, apart from perfunctory necessities. This was of no concern to her. She knew she could be loquacious if the occasion demanded it, but Spartans were famed for the sparse use of words. Besides which, she doubted if Catuvolcos could give her anything in the way of intelligent conversation.

She was sure her time in the company of her fellow Hellenes may have spoiled her somewhat. Even if Telemachus was an Athenian, her discourse with him had been much more interesting than the banter of the *ludus*.

Some hours into their journey, with Halicarnassus retreating into the distance, Catuvolcos broke the stony silence.

'I wanted to apologise,' he said. 'I was wrong.'

Lysandra turned to face him. 'Yes,' she said at length. 'You were.' There was no point in being magnanimous. Catuvolcos deserved to squirm. She remained silent, fixing him with a cold eye.

The trainer cleared his throat. 'I shouldn't have acted towards you in such a way after our... talk. I should have taken what you said at your word. But I was hurt by your refusal, though I can see now that you were right in what you said.'

'Better if you had listened to me in the first place,' Lysandra agreed. 'I did not intend to hurt your feelings, of course.'

'I know that now.' He shrugged. 'I was not thinking clearly at the time.'

'Obviously,' Lysandra saw him flush and decided to relent, perhaps a little earlier than she had originally intended. 'But it is past. I hope we can put the incident behind us.'

Catuvolcos looked somewhat relieved and smiled at her, if somewhat tentatively. 'How have you been after... after what happened?'

Lysandra looked away, her eyes on the arid landscape. 'Angry,' she said after some thought. 'I continue to feel a sense of helplessness that is foreign to me: that I was powerless to prevent them from doing what they did. They have not been caught, then?' She looked back at him.

'No. Though every effort was made.'

'I'm sure,' Lysandra snorted. Catuvolcos seemed that he was about to protest, and she waved this away. 'It does not matter. Again, this is past, and the goddess will decide whether I am to be vindicated. How are things at the *ludus*?' she asked, changing the subject abruptly, not wishing to dwell on her lack of ability to deal with Nastasen.

'The same, but different. Your friends have been moved to the bigger houses now, as Balbus promised. Of course, he takes a maintenance cut from their profits, but they earn more from each bout as their ranking has increased. They seem happy enough.'

'And Sorina?' Lysandra arched a quizzical eyebrow.

'She trains harder than ever,' Catuvolcos said. 'I have heard about your challenge.'

'Typical of Sorina to publicise it.' Lysandra said derisively.

'She has told no one but me. She knows that if word of this gets to Balbus, he will put paid to it. That he let her fight Eirianwen was one thing but he will not permit a contest between the two of you. You are his rising star; she a tried and tested champion. He will not risk you both in a match so soon after Eirianwen's death and well Sorina knows it. She will keep her mouth shut.'

Lysandra flinched at the mention of Eirianwen. It was not that Catuvolcos was being cold but that there was an awful finality in what he said. She pushed sadness from her mind and considered his words for a moment. The thought was bitter, but she decided that Sorina had the rights of the situation. 'She can train as much as she likes,' she muttered. 'Your friend she may be, Catuvolcos, but she has little time left. You can tell her I said so.'

'I'll do no such thing! I've had my fill of these little wars between you. I like you both and wish there was an end to it.'

'You can blame her for all of this.' Lysandra did not raise her voice, but merely thinking of Sorina brought her to anger. 'If she had held her peace in the first place, none of this would have happened. Her blind prejudice is the cause of the trouble. Her hatred of me sent Eirianwen to an early death, and Sorina must pay in full for her crime.'

Catuvolcos raised his hands. 'As I say, I wish there was an end to it. But you are both set on your course, it seems.'

'Quite correct.' Lysandra wanted to say more but knew it would be superfluous. Catuvolcos had made an effort, and apologised to her as was right and proper. But Sorina *was* his friend, however misguided he may be in that choice and she saw little point in aggravating what must be a difficult situation for him. That would be beneath her. She scrambled into the back of the cart to retrieve one of the new books she had taken from the shrine, indicating that the conversation was over.

It took several days to travel to the *ludus*, and the journey had been for the most part pleasant enough. They had skirted the issues of Sorina and Nastasen, confining their conversations to the mundane. Lysandra considered that, if not completely repaired, their friendship was patched up somewhat.

Catuvolcos, of course, did most of the talking, extolling the virtues of his new lady friend. That someone else had caught his eye caused Lysandra to feel a stab of jealousy. Intelligence told her that this was unwarranted and indeed unfair, as she had no interest in him whatsoever. However, inexplicable as it was, she was slightly put out that another now ruled his affections. She masked her initial fit of pique well and soon, the feeling passed. Indeed, she found Catuvolcos's inept attempts at using poetic terminology to describe his cheap little tart amusing.

'It's not the most glamorous of professions of course,' he said, as though trying to defend whoring as an acceptable career choice 'but it's an honest one. She's no beggar, I can tell you that.'

'Certainly not,' she said levelly. Inwardly, she seethed with the desire to take the rise out of him, but decided that it would be unfair to do so. Catuvolcos was probably trying to be delicate as he knew that she was a former-priestess of a virgin goddess. The fact that his woman made her living on her back evidently did not bother him in the slightest.

'You'd like her, Lysandra, I'm sure,' he went on. 'She's Greek, like you, and very intelligent as well.'

Lysandra could well imagine what sort of intellect Catuvolcos's paramour was versed in. Her lip curled in contempt but she saw the Gaul waiting for a response so she turned it into a half-smile, remaining silent till the wagon passed through the gates of the school.

'Well, here we are then,' he said.

Lysandra climbed down from the wagon and looked about, drinking in the familiar surroundings. The clatter of the practice swords, the grunts of exertion, the shouts of the trainers that made the music of the *ludus* were sweet to her ears. It was, she decided, good to be home.

'Lysandra!'

She turned to see Varia running towards her, arms outstretched. Before she could protest, the little slave girl had embraced her enthusiastically, the dark curls buried in her chest. Somewhat awkwardly, Lysandra patted the girl's scrawny shoulders.

'It is good to see you!' Varia exclaimed.

Lysandra's smile was somewhat forced; such a display of emotion in public was unseemly and there was indeed quite a gathering to watch the reunion in progress. 'Yes, well, quite,' she said, disengaging herself. 'It is good to see you as well, Varia.'

314

'Let me show you your new quarters.' Varia took her by the hand. Feeling somewhat helpless, Lysandra could only follow.

She was impressed.

Certainly, her new domicile was far superior to the tiny cell she lived in before the Games of Aeschylus. Varia had also given the place a homely feel, adding flowers, whatever furniture she could scavenge and some dubious artwork, painted by her own hand.

Lysandra decided that it would be hurtful to the child to throw the hideous stuff away. Overall though, there was little in the way of luxury and this was in keeping with the Spartan way.

'I hope you like what I have done,' Varia said, interrupting Lysandra's train of thought. 'All of this,' she indicated the furniture, 'is from Eirianwen's place. I know she was your friend and thought you would want her things. Sorina tried to stop me but I managed to get this much away first.'

Lysandra sighed, fighting back her emotions – the wound she had thought nearly healed was still raw. She picked a blanket from one of the couches and held it to her face, breathing in the scent. She imagined she could still taste Eirianwen. 'That was very considerate, Varia. My thanks.' The child positively glowed under her praise.

There was no time for more discussion, as the Hellene women appeared, wanting to greet Lysandra themselves. They were enthusiastic, but she noted they were not the same women who had departed with her to Halicarnassus. There was a hard look behind their eyes, a look that had been won in the arena. They were the better for it, no longer slaves but warriors. Though they would never be able to match her in skill and natural ability, Lysandra recognised the change in them. Tempered by blood, they could at least be worthy companions.

It was a pleasing thought.

XXXIX

Lysandra trained lightly in her first days back at the *ludus*. Her body was not used to strenuous exercise and to push too hard, too soon would only result in injury and another lay off.

She was content to let the Hellene women exercise in their accustomed manner for the time being. Though Balbus had given her the right to train them, she would not have felt comfortable giving instruction if she could not match and indeed exceed her students. Instead, she concentrated on her own fitness, running and strength-building routines designed to bring her to full vigour in as short a time as possible.

As she worked on herself, she found her eyes wandering to what had become the barbarian section of the training ground. The Tribeswomen had grown increasingly insular since returning from Aeschylus's games, mixing less and less with the other women. The effect on the *ludus* was palpable as each gladiatrix, whether novice or veteran, began to keep to her own ethnic group. Lysandra saw this more keenly than most; Eirianwen was lost to them now and much of the connection she had with the tribal peoples was severed. Of course, there was still Catuvolcos, and even Hildreth, who was in her opinion a decent sort.

Sorina, Lysandra noted, was indeed pushing herself hard. The older woman was first to the grounds in the morning and last to leave when the trainers called for the evening rest. However, as she had told Catuvolcos, let the barbarian train all that she wished; the result of their fight would not be in doubt. Sorina was old: she herself was young – and such was life.

It took some weeks for Lysandra to regain her fitness, her speed and her sharpness. She began to exercise with the Hellene women, offering pointers and help, but still not leading them in their sessions. She felt that she must regain their utter confidence in her superiority before she took over in a formal manner. Respect had to be earned and the Hellenes were no longer green novices.

However, as time progressed, her position as foremost amongst them became clear. Indeed, she felt that they welcomed her return to form as in her absence they had lacked any real leadership. As she began to train them in earnest, many of the other civilised women in the *ludus* made it clear that they wished to be part of her coterie. This was unsurprising, of course. Whilst Stick, Catuvolcos and especially Titus's training methods were good, they were not conceived in Sparta, and naturally were inferior to her own regimen. That Balbus allowed this split to happen was, in Lysandra's view, extremely astute. The *lanista* was in no doubt that her charges were becoming the fittest and most deadly of his stable.

'Remember,' she told them after a particularly gruelling session, 'discipline is the key to victory. Any fool can wave a sword about and batter an opponent into submission with no thought of tactics and strategy.' She jerked her head disdainfully at the barbarian quarter of the grounds where the fighters there went about their work with the usual unordered gusto. 'Discipline and fitness are your first weapons. How many times have you seen fighters falter when tiredness sets in? Next time you think I am pushing you

317

too hard think about a sword in your guts. Remember that if you are fitter, more prepared, you will survive. We have all seen our friends die in the arena, choking on their own blood. That could be you. You can never have too much stamina. To go the extra lap is everything in life, not only in the arena. Push yourselves.'

The women cheered at this and Lysandra allowed herself to smile.

It turned Sorina's stomach to have to share her meal times with the hated Greeks. Though both sets of women stuck to their own sides of the dining area, the fact that she had be so close to Lysandra's sycophants, Greek and Roman both, was almost too much to bear.

The Amazon knew that she was being mocked in the sibilant Greek tongue, as often they would turn and look at the Tribeswomen, before erupting in laughter. She thought of speaking to Balbus about staggering the evening meals but decided against it. She could not let the *lanista* realise that the tension between the two camps was so great. She could not afford to let anything stand in the way of her killing Lysandra.

And she wanted to kill her so much she could taste it.

'Are you all right?' Teuta's voice brought Sorina's attention away from her fantasy of impaling the Spartan on her blade.

'Look at them.' The Clan Chief shook her head as the Greeks spoke amongst themselves. 'Rhetoric, no doubt,' she sneered. 'They make me sick.'

Teuta grunted. 'So ignore them.'

'Get away, girl.' Sorina pushed at the slave, Varia, as she offered her more wine. Varia stumbled back, dropping the *krater* on the ground. She felt guilty at the action: despite the fact that the child was the spawn of Italy she was harmless enough.

She was just about to help the girl to her feet, when she noticed that the dining area had fallen silent. One of the Greeks,

318

an Athenian she knew to be called Danae, had broached the border between the two camps.

'There's no need for that, barbarian,' Danae helped Varia up. 'The girl was just doing her job.'

'Don't call me barbarian,' Sorina spat.

Danae arched an eyebrow – a gesture so reminiscent of Lysandra it infuriated Sorina. 'It is an act of barbarity to bully a child,' she said shortly.

Rage coursed through Sorina. Her body acted of its own volition and she was on her feet, wine cup in her hand. There was a crunching sound and a scream. Danae was falling, her face a ruined mass of blood. In her hand, Sorina felt the broken crockery of the wine cup.

As one, the Greeks and Romans across the dining area rose to their feet, and began to move across to the Tribeswomen's section. They were, Sorina thought, so passionless. Here, she had insulted and physically abused one of their number but there was no battle rage about them. That they came to settle the matter in blood was one thing; that they approached as would a colony of ants was an abomination to the War Goddess.

Her own kind were on their feet, knowing that combat was come upon them, and with a scream they lunged towards the hated women of the middle-sea, intent on hammering the arrogance out of them. Chaos reigned then, as the gladiatrices hurled themselves at one another. With no weapons to speak of it was a clash of flesh against flesh, strength against strength.

It was the element of the Tribal warrior. Sorina felt a power unknown surge through her as she dived into the fray, punching and kicking, her blows pulping flesh and breaking bone.

Above the milling heads she could see the tall form of Lysandra pushing her way towards her. She grinned savagely, her hands forming claws. Now she would have her reckoning.

*   *   *

319

'*Lanista!*'

Balbus looked up from his work to see Stick careering into his office. The Parthian was in a state of panic. 'What is it, Stick?' he said, becoming alarmed. Stick was unflappable for the most part.

'Riot!' the trainer screeched.

'Call the guards!' Balbus propelled himself up and out of his chair as fast as his chunky body would allow.

'I have.' Stick began to run back towards the training ground. 'Titus is out there now, leading them in.'

The *lanista* chased him outside and wrung his hands at the scene before him. His guards – all of them – had waded into a brawl, desperate to separate the two camps that had formed in the *ludus*. On the one side were Lysandra and the women of the middle sea; on the other, Sorina and her barbarians. The women were tearing into each other with fury, screaming and shouting as they rained blows upon each other. Hildreth, he noted, was shoving her German women back, seemingly unwilling to become involved.

Balbus winced as she saw one of the Roman women dragged from her feet and slammed into a table by two barbarians and he cried aloud as they tipped the table over, crushing her beneath.

'Stop them!' he screamed, rushing forward. Stick grabbed him about the waist, and dragged him back.

'Are you mad?' the Parthian shouted. 'You'll be killed. Let the guards handle it.'

Protected by armour and shields, the hired men were having some success in forging a path between the two embattled antagonists; their attentions were none too gentle and batons rose and fell with alarming force. Balbus could see a fortune being wasted in broken bones and incapacitated fighters; nevertheless, he silently admitted to himself that this was partially his fault. But Lysandra's Greeks were winning – fighting together, and winning. Balbus considered that a sign from Fortuna.

*   *   *

320

The tide swept Lysandra from her path. Sorina screamed in rage and frustration, trying to claw her way through the throng to reach her. But each step she took, she realised that there was another Greek, another Roman to deal with. Even with the battle rage coursing through her she realised that, though fewer in number, Lysandra's women were gaining the upper hand in the brawl. They had formed a line across the dining area and, where one fell so another moved forward to take her place, hammering the tired Tribeswomen from their feet.

She must call her people back, so that they might gather for a charge that would snap the spine of Lysandra's women. But as she looked about, she felt a sharp blow to her head from behind. Turning, she struck out furiously, only to encounter the unyielding wood of a guard's shield. He hit her again, and twice more before she felt her legs go beneath her and the darkness closed in.

'I've had everyone locked down.' Titus's voice was tired. He ran a hand across his sweating forehead. 'No one gave much trouble,' he went on. 'The fight has been knocked out of them.'

'Good, good.' Balbus nodded. 'What's the damage?'

The older Roman sighed. 'Three dead, sixteen in the infirmary with Quintus. A healthy brawl indeed, *lanista*.'

'But it could have been much worse.' Lucius Balbus was feeling much more himself after the initial shock of the riot had worn off. 'The ringleaders?'

'Lysandra and Sorina.' Titus sat down. 'Who else?' The question was rhetorical. The trainer paused, and Balbus could tell he was about to receive some advice from the veteran. '*Lanista*,' Titus said at length. 'I've noticed that the women have become separate from each other in a way that I've never seen before.'

'Yes.' Balbus decided to share his plans with him. 'I know. I've allowed this to happen – in fact I positively encourage it to continue.' He could tell that he had shocked Titus and took a moment to savour the reaction. Titus was a good man, but his self-perceived older and wiser head sometimes made him forget just who knew best. An excellent trainer he may be, but Lucius Balbus was *lanista*.

Titus cleared his throat. 'Are you sure that's wise? The situation can only worsen.'

Eros arrived with wine for the two men, and winked at Titus suggestively; Balbus had to suppress a grin. He knew that the trainer loathed the boy, whom he referred to as 'that mincing catamite.' He dismissed the slave, however, as he wanted Titus's full attention. 'Things are going to change around here,' he said. 'If we play this right, we could be stinking rich. All of us,' he added meaningfully. 'I've been approached by the governor to organise a spectacle. A spectacle the like of which has never been seen outside of Rome.'

'I've heard that sort of claim before,' Titus said, the jaded 'voice of experience' grating with Balbus somewhat.

'Not like this.' Balbus allowed himself to be smug. He went on to relate the details of his conversation with Frontinus and Aeschylus regarding the grand battle they had envisaged for Domitian's birthday. When he was finished, he could see that Titus was suitably impressed. 'This is why I have allowed the Greek and Roman women to form their faction around Lysandra. If she is to lead them in battle, it is good that they are gravitating towards her.'

'But you've not told her of your plans yet?' Titus grunted.

'Not yet, but today's little spat means I will have to hurry matters along. You all know that we're expanding the *ludus*. My plan is to move the Greeks and the others to the new wing and let them train as one group there. I'll be importing as many slaves as I can get my hands on – and that Frontinus's money can buy – as quickly as I can.'

'Makes sense,' Titus agreed. 'Who will be training this 'army' of Lysandra's?'

Balbus grinned. 'She will. But I'd imagine she'll need some help, Titus. You're the man they call the Centurion after all. Look…' He leaned forward. 'You can help her… and by helping her, you'll be helping me. When all this is over, you'll have a huge reputation and you'll be as rich as Croesus – the world will be at your feet. Everybody wins.'

'Not everybody,' Titus said. 'There will be many dead after this, Balbus.'

Balbus thought that the sentiment had merit. But money bought toughness. In the end, arena fighters got killed, a fact he elucidated to the trainer. 'That, Titus, is the name of the game.'

'And in the meantime?'

'In the meantime, it's business as usual. I want Lysandra out there and fighting. I want maximum public exposure. Falco will have to work his balls off for the next two years.' Balbus considered that the promoter would relish the prospect. 'Keep the women segregated as much as possible, till I can move the Greeks to the new wing. Once they are out of here, things will return to normal.'

'I'll drink to that.' Titus raised his cup.

XL

Lysandra's respect for Lucius Balbus's judgement increased when he told her of his plans. The *lanista* was correct in his assessment that she was the ideal person to lead and train an army. Now, she knew, Athene's plan for her was revealed. All her training, her excellence in combat and her understanding of matters military had led her to this task.

Though excited, she had relayed the news calmly to her women and they had received it with an equanimity that was worthy of their association with her. Even Danae, who once had quailed at the prospect of blood, seemed inspired. The Athenian bore a livid scar from her encounter with Sorina and she burned for revenge.

'Any chance to rid the earth of their filth is to be welcomed,' she told Lysandra. 'These barbarians grow arrogant in their success on the sands. It is for us to cull their number.'

Lysandra started at the comment. Before Eirianwen, she would have fully endorsed such a statement, yet now she could not bring herself to hate the barbarians merely because of their unfortunate birth. Perhaps Eirianwen was rare and special: she was spawned of the most savage of tribes and yet there had been much beauty in her soul as well as in her body. But, she knew that to mention it would be bad for morale, and her duty to the women came before her personal considerations.

'It is good that you are keen for the fight, Danae,' she acknowledged with what she felt was convincing enthusiasm.

It was not only Danae who displayed an extra degree of confidence in her own abilities. After the confrontation in the dining area, the Hellene and Roman women were buoyed as a whole. They assumed themselves correctly to be victors of the confrontation, despite barbarian claims to the contrary. The fact that Balbus had let it be known that Lysandra's women, as they had now come to be known, were to be moved to the new wing re-enforced that view.

Yet, now that she was to command the women as an army, Lysandra kept a tight rein over them. She forbade conflict with the barbarians, ordering her women to stay well away from them. They had proven themselves once and that was, in her view, enough. There was little to be gained by constant brawling and squabbling. She knew well that aside from the military training to come, each of her charges had to maintain their gladiatorial skills as there would be many returns to the arena before Balbus's great spectacle.

As soon as the *lanista* had revealed his designs, Lysandra's mind had begun to work. Though he probably did not realise it, Balbus was, in fact, emulating Gaius Marius. Marius had revitalised the Roman army, turning it into a motivated professional force. To train his men in close combat, the politician-general had recruited trainers from gladiatorial schools.

Lysandra considered that if she could train the current group of Hellene and Roman women to proficiency in marching, drill and tactics, they, in their turn, could pass this on to the untried slaves that Balbus would be drafting in ever increasing numbers.

As things stood, the combat skills of her core women were adequate, if nowhere near her own standard, but she was confident that this would be more than enough to turn her recruits into fearsome fighters.

She had to impress on them a sense of leadership, discipline and a degree tactical acumen. This was something of a challenge since, because of their inferior heritage, so few of the women could read. As it was, Lysandra was forced to request trained slaves from Balbus to assist her in teaching the less educated. Nevertheless, these women were Hellene or Roman, and most had an aptitude and even enthusiasm for learning. Such things had been denied many of them and the possession of letters was a treasure beyond value to all.

Though the barbarians viewed these activities with increasing scorn Lysandra encouraged her women to rise above the jeers and insults. The barbarians, she told her fellows, did not know the value of such learning. It was not their way.

Lysandra did her best to foster a spirit of togetherness amongst her companions. They were slaves in name only: they felt free; *were* free in their hearts. With sweat and toil, they were forming a bond, not only as gladiatrices now but also as soldiers. This was akin to the sisterhood of the temple and Lysandra knew well that such ties were hard to break.

They were special now; they were the elite, and they knew it.

'I will need some dispensation for the women,' Lysandra advised Balbus and Titus as they lounged in his *triclinium*.

The *lanista* eyed her. 'What do you mean?'

'These women cannot be treated as prisoners, Balbus. The whole project will fail if this is so.' She turned her attention to the older man. 'Titus, you were a soldier, were you not?'

Titus grunted an affirmative.

'Well, then you must know the importance of morale, of spirit. We cannot be cooped up in here at all times. We must be allowed to make route marches and, as our forces grow, to operate on open ground.'

Titus nodded. 'She has a point, Balbus. But we must have your word there will be no escape attempt. This is on your honour, Lysandra.'

'By Athene, I swear it. We want this, Titus,' she said meaningfully, her eyes alight. 'This makes us more than mere arena fighters. This has never been done before, we are the first.'

'What is the world coming to?' He grinned. 'Armies of women – like the Amazons.'

Lysandra snorted. 'Sorina is an Amazon. Savage and undisciplined. Even if they set ten to one odds against us, we will win on the day. Before your Emperor, we will crush our enemies and see them driven before us.'

'Well, don't carried away,' Balbus admonished. 'All this marching and drilling is well and good but there are bills to be paid and you'll all be fighting regularly. More than regularly, in fact.'

'We are well aware of that,' Lysandra replied loftily.

'Good, because I have an engagement booked.'

Lysandra inclined her head. 'That,' she said, 'is good training.'

Sorina clenched her toes on the sand, feeling the grains flood over her feet. The leather sword hilt felt familiar and safe in her hands, the sun warm on her skin. Though it was a minor festival, the arena was still packed to bursting point, the mob still insatiable in their desire for spectacle.

Since her combat with Eirianwen, there had been demands to see more of the tribal fighting style so she was armed once again with the long sword. This time, however, there was no blood feud, and she wore her armour. Her opponent was a Gaul who fought under the name of Epona. It mattered little what she called herself. Soon, the she would be dead, and all would see that Sorina was still Queen of the Sands.

Epona was tall, her blonde hair cropped short. This, coupled with her ruddy, pig-like face served to give her a brutish appearance. Her body was heavily decorated with woad: bright blue on her white skin. She gave Sorina a broken-toothed smile and advanced, hefting the heavy iron blade as if she intended to use it as a club.

Sorina returned the smile coldly, her eyes flat. She set her stance, ready to react to her opponent's movements. For a moment, the two women shuffled about, measuring the other's speed and balance. Then, with a shout, Sorina leapt in, her sword arcing towards the other's neck.

Epona barely got her blade up in time to deflect the blow, but this accomplished, there was little respite for her. Sorina fought like a woman possessed, sweat standing out on her tanned skin as she forced the issue with the bigger woman.

There were no exchanges, no counter blows. After only a few moments fighting it became obvious that the Gaul was hopelessly outclassed. The crowd began to clap their hands slowly, showing their derision at the mismatch.

Sorina heard them, and slowed her assault. It would not do to disappoint the mob by ending the battle too quickly. She realised that she herself was on edge, almost desperate to prove that the gruelling bout with Eirianwen had not robbed her of her sharpness.

But Epona's heart was no longer in the fight; Sorina could see it in her eyes. The early battering had convinced the big woman that there was no hope for her.

'Come at me,' Sorina hissed in Latin. 'You cannot win this fight, but at least you can try for the *missio*.' She said it not from compassion, but rather because Epona was making her own performance look awkward.

It was to no avail. Epona tried gamely to attack but her

movements were slow and clumsy. She wielded the sword like an axe, hacking more at Sorina's blade than making any real effort to hit her. In disgust, Sorina twisted her own weapon and sent the Gaul's sword flying from her grip. Even as the iron went skywards she spun about, smashing her elbow in the big blonde's face, sending her crashing to the sand in a spray of blood.

She stood over the prone form, her eyes flicking to the governor's box. Frontinus's response was instant and a short thrust sent Epona into her death spasm.

Boos and catcalls erupted from the watching crowd. Usually, Sorina would have expected to soak up applause. She had never suffered a reaction like this before and she moved quickly to the Gate of Life, insults ringing in her ears.

'Call that a fight?' one outraged spectator screamed. 'It was a joke. Why don't you fight someone who can defend herself?'

'She ain't got it no more,' came another shout. 'She's too old.'

'They're giving her easy matches. Achillia would take the Amazon, I reckon.'

Sorina stopped, her brown eyes sweeping the crowd, searching for her accuser. She spotted him, a skinny, unwashed fellow sporting a yellow tunic. She growled and leapt towards the stalls, bashing her sword on the bars that separated fighter from audience. Many spectators yelped and leapt away, falling over themselves at this sudden, violent reaction.

'Get yourself in here, you little bastard,' Sorina screamed. 'Achillia is nothing! Do you hear me? Nothing!' She was going to say more, but the arena attendants rushed over and tackled her, bearing her to the sand. She did not struggle as they disarmed her and dragged her to the tunnel.

The jeers rang loud and long.

Balbus blanched at the crowd's reaction. After such a spectacular showing in Aeschylus's games he had wanted to prove that this was merely the beginning. But the truth was inescapable: the other *lanista's* could not provide women of quality to match his own or else were reluctant to send their best fighters against his. Gladiatrices cost money, and there seemed to be a widespread belief that to face a woman from Balbus's *ludus* was to invite death – hardly a sensible proposition for any man of business.

That Sorina's popularity appeared to be on the wane was only of slight concern to him. She had served him well but her time was coming to an end. She was getting old and he now had Lysandra. Fortuna had indeed smiled on him when the arrogant young Spartan had come his way. For a long time, he had viewed Eirianwen as the natural successor to the old lioness. But it was Lysandra now who carried all his hopes.

Sorina was, he decided, becoming a spent force. Not her fault that the opposition had been poor; not her fault that the crowd reacted badly. But he had a reputation to think of and it was a problem that he would have to address.

More pressing, however, was the fact that Lysandra was due to fight a woman from the same *ludus* that had produced Sorina's opponent. Given that the Spartan's reputation was growing, it was apparent to Balbus that the *lanista* would not send out one of his best to probable death at the hands of the rising star of Halicarnassus. He called Stick to him and bade the Parthian contact the opposition school's owner. He had a plan. Of course he did. That was why he was successful. He rubbed his hands together gleefully, pleased with his own invention.

'No problem.' Danae flexed her neck as she returned from the arena. After Sorina's bout, the Athenian had put on a good display against her own opponent. With the previous fight in mind, she had gauged her opposition well and not gone all out to finish her. Rather, she eked out the battle, allowing the other woman a sniff at victory before sending her to Hades with a blow to the head.

'You fought well,' Lysandra acknowledged, unlacing her *manica*.

'Too easy,' Danae said. 'I had to carry the bitch.'

'True enough,' Thebe broke in. She had not fought yet that day and was in good spirits. Their opposition looked easy and that meant in all probability that they would come out of the spectacle alive.

'That is the result of your training,' Lysandra reminded them. 'You are learning the Spartan ways and this is an improvement over anything you have been taught thus far.'

Danae refrained from comment but Thebe winked at her when Lysandra was not looking.

'How are you feeling?' Stick sauntered into the Hellene women's cell.

'I am quite well, and ready for my bout,' Lysandra informed him, tossing Danae's *manica* at him.

'Not you.' Stick snagged the piece from the air, and tossed it back immediately. 'Danae.'

'I'm fine, Stick,' she replied. 'The bout was easy.'

'Good.' Stick gave her his buck-toothed grin. 'You are fighting again.'

Danae was taken aback. 'Why?' she said. Though her bout had gone smoothly no one wished to risk her life twice in the same day.

'The crowd is getting restless. This other *ludus* is in the shit because they've brought novices and thrown them in against you lot. Anyone with an eye for the fight could see that you carried that useless trollop all the way through. It wasn't as bad as Sorina's showing, but...' he trailed off.

'When?' This from Lysandra.

'Later,' Stick said. 'There's no easy way to tell you this, so I'm just going to come out with it. Frontinus has decreed that the

331

other school is voided from the games. That means it's just our *ludus* providing the fighters from now on.'

There was a collective gasp from the Hellene women. Almost instinctively, Danae took a step away from Lysandra. They all knew what this meant. If the lots came out badly, the two could end up facing each other.

'The governor has rescinded some pardons due to be given to the local criminals,' Stick went on. 'He's having them fight each other now, by way of an apology to the spectators for the shit they've seen so far. This is while we work out the new schedule.'

The women looked helplessly at each other, even Lysandra seemed taken aback.

'These things happen,' Stick said shortly. 'I expect you to be professional about it.'

'But, Stick…' Thebe broke in.

'No buts. There's nothing we can do.' He hesitated for a moment. 'I'm sorry.' The shock was that the women could see he meant it. He said no more – just turned on his heel and left.

The silence was heavy in his wake.

XLI

'An excellent solution,' Frontinus said, saluting Balbus with his wine goblet.

Balbus inclined his head in acknowledgement. 'I thank you, Your Excellence. Business partners they may be, but the *lanista* knew that he could not overstep the boundaries between them.

'The other *lanista* was not put out by your suggestion?'

'No, sir, he was not.' Balbus smiled. 'Positively enthusiastic in fact. Yes, I gain his purse for this spectacle, but he stood to lose much more in facing my troupe. It would have been a fiasco.'

'But you also stand to lose out, is that not so? If your best are killed by each other?' Frontinus's gaze was hard.

'That is true,' Balbus acquiesced. 'But it is my hope that they will fight well enough to gain the *missio* from you.'

The governor fixed him with a withering stare. 'I hope you are not suggesting that our plans for the future will influence my vote in this matter.'

Balbus flushed. This had been precisely his hope. However, he cleared his throat and steeled himself. 'All business is risk,' he said. 'I have a reputation to maintain and cannot deprive the loyal

333

spectators, and yourself, of the entertainment they desire. There are many good fighters in my school, sir. If I lose some, it is the will of the gods. I am shocked that you think I'd expect you to be anything other than honest in your voting,' he added.

This seemed to placate the governor. 'I should hope not. Who is Lysandra to fight?'

Balbus spread his hands. 'I don't know,' he answered truthfully. 'I am an honest man, my lord. The lots will be drawn and she will fight whom the gods decree.'

'She will win,' Frontinus declared confidently. 'How does her 'army' progress?'

'Well, sir. She is training her coterie at the moment, and I am having the *ludus* expanded to house our new 'recruits'. Once her own women are sufficiently trained, she will have a chain of command, as she calls it. Her women will pass the skills on to our new slaves.'

'Just like a real army.' Frontinus beamed.

'She is taking it all very seriously,' Balbus said. 'There is good news on the market, too. Falco, my promoter, has been working hard. Many *lanista's* have bought into your excellent idea, so there will be no shortage of women for the grand battle.'

'A bloodbath.' Frontinus nodded. 'The Emperor will love it.'

'As will the populace. I salute *you*, sir. The idea was genius.'

'My thanks, *lanista*. I hope you will stay with me for the entertainments.'

'I would be honoured.' Balbus smiled, silently praying that all would go well that afternoon. The spectre of Lysandra lying dead on the sand haunted him.

No one had spoken since Stick's announcement. The Hellene women kept their gazes fixed to the floor. Thebe had helped prepare Lysandra; she was to fight again as the *Thraex* – the Thracian – nude save for her loincloth. Every effort was going into placating the crowd and, though she had been scheduled to fight in heavy armour, it was decided that the sight of her naked flesh would salve the rancour of the mob. Thebe, they learned, was to fight as the *retiaria*, again unclothed bar the *subligaculum*.

They oiled one another in silence, each avoiding the gaze of the other. This task complete, there was little to do but sit and wait. They could hear above that the crowd had quietened down, meaning that the criminal bouts had come to an end. It would be their turn soon.

Lysandra had been shocked initially. The thought of turning her blade on her friends was anathema to her. It was not the Spartan way to slay one's allies. But it was not the Spartan way to lose a battle, either. She could not, she knew, stay her hand or hold back. She was sure this had occurred to the other women, but just as quickly would have been dismissed. Lysandra pressed her lips into a thin line, recalling her admonishment to Eirianwen not to stay her hand before the bout with Sorina. She cursed herself silently; it would not do to think of her now, lest she wished to join her in Hades. Part of her may have once wanted to do so, but to go willingly to her death would cheapen her in Eirianwen's eyes if they were to meet on the other side of the Styx.

She glanced around at the others. Despite their growing closeness, the camaraderie gained both in the *ludus* and in their military training they were going through, each of them wanted to live. And the only way to ensure survival was to see your opponent dead.

Your *enemy*, Lysandra corrected herself. The woman she faced on the sands would be her enemy. Enemies could expect no mercy, no quarter. If she must cut Danae down, or kill Thebe, then she would do it.

'Lysandra!'

She looked up to see the large form of Catuvolcos framed in

the doorway. His face was grim as he looked at her. She got to her feet swiftly. The *psyche* was a weapon also. If she were to fight another Hellene woman, they would see that she was prepared. To hesitate might show her to be unwilling. The first battle was already won, she told herself. But in this victory, she could not help but feel cheapened despite herself.

Lysandra bade Catuvolcos leave her when she exited the cell. She wanted to take the long walk to the Gates alone. She did not wish to know whom she faced, and feared that the Gaul would call another woman from the Hellene cell. She could not afford to think of her foe as anything but that. To name her would be to make her human.

The bustle of the arena workers seemed to fade as she walked, trying to calm her mind, to stay focused. She must win, she told herself. So much rested with her. The army, the Hellene women, would be lost without her. She prayed that it would be Sorina she had drawn, that she might unleash her hatred on her enemy.

Lysandra stopped by the Gates, and closed her eyes. She breathed out through her nose and stepped onto the sands, raising her arms as Achillia once more – prepared to fight.

The crowd roared in acknowledgement of her salute and began to chant her name. They knew that Achillia would not fail them, that she would elevate the spectacle to something magnificent.

Lysandra stopped in the middle of the arena. The Gates opposite clanked open and her opponent stepped out onto the sands. At the sight of her, the crowd went berserk. They knew that this would be a battle of equals from which only one would walk away.

Sorina was furious. Furious with the mob, furious with herself for not thinking as she fought. Even the Greek, Danae, had known to carry her weaker opponent, whereas she, Sorina, the famous Amazona, had rushed in to deny the crowd their entertainment.

But most of all, she was furious with Lysandra. Her hatred for the Greek seethed in her heart, burning hot. The words of the yellow-clad man in the crowd haunted her. The Spartan had replaced her in the hearts of the populace and, though she despised the mob, this hurt. It was a blow to her honour, her esteem. Lysandra was nothing. An arrogant girl-child with well-learned tricks. Not a true warrior.

When she learned that the agenda for the spectacle had changed, her heart leapt. It was as if the gods were smiling on her at last. Here was a chance to fight the Greek bitch, offered to her so soon. She had gone to her cell and prayed, prayed with all her heart that her name was drawn with Lysandra's.

Her mind swam with images of her enemy's death at her blade, so strong that she felt a flood of heat in her loins. She could see herself, drenched in Spartan blood, hacking the pale body to pieces as the crowd screamed her on. Lysandra's eyes alight with fear and pain, pissing herself in her death throes. Her own body shuddering in ecstasy as her iron blade drove deep into her hated foe.

She wanted her death so much, it had become an insatiable hunger. Never in all her life had she felt such hatred. Not even towards the Romans who had taken her freedom, and spilled much Dacian blood. *Just one chance*, she begged silently. *Please, gods, just one chance to face her.* She'd gladly die to send Lysandra to Helle first, safe in the knowledge that the arrogant bitch knew that she was the better woman.

The door to her cell opened.

'Sorina.' Stick's ugly face was grim. 'You had better start getting ready.'

She looked up at him, her eyes glazed and pleading. 'Who am I to fight?'

The mob had begun to stamp its feet in appreciation of the match. Here was something worth cheering about. Frontinus tried to appear aloof and disinterested, but could not resist shifting on his couch as Lysandra's opponent strode towards her. It was a match that promised everything. The other held the great *scutum* of the *murmillo*, her arms and shoulders heavily armoured with *manica* and plate. Aside from this, she wore only a short leather kilt, and the crowd screamed their appreciation. They were both magnificent specimens of womanhood, tall and beautiful, their charms exposed to the slavering spectators. Sex and death – there was no greater narcotic to sate them. And Frontinus was providing both in abundance.

Lysandra narrowed her eyes as her opponent stepped up.

'Hello, Lysandra, how are you today?' Hildreth's smile was cold.

'I am well, Hildreth,' she responded to their once friendly ritual. 'How are you?'

'I am well,' the German said. 'I am sorry that you will die. I like you.'

Lysandra hesitated, memories flooding back to her. She recalled her first journey to the *ludus*: Hildreth's kindness as she had shared her bread; the German girl's laughter as she had shouted out the unfamiliar Latin words Lysandra had taught her; her own amusement at the German's hairy body before she had been shorn like a civilised woman.

And their fight.

The speed and strength of the tribeswoman, the ease with which she had defeated her. For a moment, Lysandra felt her mouth go dry and her stomach knot. Hildreth nodded, reading the look in her eyes, and her smile turned to a sneer.

It was akin to a slap around the face. Lysandra blinked, and straightened her back. Distantly, she heard an arena attendant shout '*Pugnate!*' the order to fight. At once the German dropped into a fighting crouch, but Lysandra remained erect. She stretched her neck from side to side and spun her sword twice, this piece of show fast becoming her signature and the crowd hooted in appreciation. But more, she had shown Hildreth that she did not fear her.

Hildreth snarled, but Lysandra's casual disdain had not proven enough to make her rush in. Whilst Hildreth believed herself to be the superior fighter, she was not so foolish as to think her task would be an easy one.

Hildreth raised her sword, pointing it over the top of the *scutum* at Lysandra, who responded by finally assuming a fighting stance, her own small buckler angled to deflect a thrust from the German. The redhead scuttled to one side, trying to create an angle of attack, but Lysandra matched her movement to cut off this avenue.

Though the crowd had been derisive of such posturing in the earlier bouts, they now watched with rapt attention. Both fighters were known to them, both rising to the top of their game, and the winner of this bout would be on the path to greatness. Connoisseurs and casual observers alike realised that when the battle was finally joined, it promised to be spectacular.

Then Lysandra attacked and they roared for her.

Her blade lashed out and was greeted by Hildreth's own iron, the retort loud and clear. Hildreth struck back at once, not allowing Lysandra to take the initiative, but her own strike was deflected on the Thracian shield. Lysandra danced away, making Hildreth come on to her. The German had the protective advantage of armour, but this and the heavy *scutum* would weigh a fighter down. This was the fascination, the contrast that the mob craved.

Hildreth was strong. She waded in, her sword arm lashing out, seeking to bludgeon her way through Lysandra's guard. Lysandra parried and hit back but the *scutum* was a formidable obstacle, time and again slamming her short sword aside. Hildreth stepped in and there was a furious exchange of blows, iron meeting iron with disjointed rapidity. The German rammed out her shield, turning it from a defence into a weapon of attack. It crashed into

Lysandra's chest, knocking the breath from her and smashing her to the ground.

The crowd screamed as Lysandra fell back, rising as one to their feet.

Hildreth rushed in, hoping to finish the fight quickly, but Lysandra rolled onto one knee, bringing her buckler to bear just as the redhead's sword sought her neck. Again, Hildreth punched forward with the shield, seeking to force her to the ground once again. Lysandra lunged forwards, shoving Hildreth away, confounding her with the sudden movement.

Hildreth stumbled and the slight respite allowed Lysandra to surge upwards and launch an assault of her own. The tribeswoman was off-balance but she weaved away from the onslaught, wielding the shield with efficiency. Lysandra pressed in and a looping, over-hand lunge got past the German's guard, crunching into her armoured shoulder. Though the tough leather afforded some protection, it could stop a direct thrust, and Hildreth cried out as blood burst from the wound.

Enraged, she struck back furiously, but the two women were now locked together and the German was unable to get sufficient leverage to strike with her long blade. Thinking quickly, she smashed Lysandra on the side of the head with the pommel of the weapon, stunning her.

Freed from the clinch as Lysandra spun away, Hildreth swung out, the tip of her sword slicing a bloody cut down her opponent's back. The crowd roared in delight as the scarlet fluid sprayed up, catching the sunlight in glistening droplets.

Lysandra shouted out, more from frustration than pain, as she twisted back to face Hildreth. The German girl's face was flushed; her blood up, her face twisted into a snarl. The wound she had inflicted acted as a spur and she attacked with a maniacal fury.

Lysandra kept her at bay, using blade and shield to defend

herself against the onslaught; but now she could see that the German's breasts, slicked with sweat, begin to heave with exertion. Soon, she told herself, *soon*.

She led her on, trying to coax a mistake, leaving her own parries desperately late. A dangerous game, but she prayed that the tribeswoman would not see her ruse through her battle fury. If Hildreth thought *she* were tiring, she would redouble her efforts to finish her. Again and again, their blades met; Lysandra mistimed a parry, and this time Hildreth's weapon struck true, cutting deep into her side. Lysandra gasped as she felt cold iron grate sickeningly against her ribs, and flailed wildly with her sword to keep Hildreth at bay.

Hildreth leapt back, content to allow the respite; her eyes flicked to the gash in Lysandra's side. Blood coursed from the cut, dribbling wetly down her thigh. Such a wound was a slow kill. In time, the blood would drain away, and with it her strength. Exhaustion would follow, making the finish that much easier.

Lysandra bit her lip. Hildreth had beaten her before and was winning again. The tribeswoman's war experience was telling; she seemed to read her strategies with ease. True, she was bleeding and tiring herself, but her wound was nothing compared to that which she herself bore. She straightened up and stretched her neck from side to side, spinning her blade twice. The crowd their approval roared at her flamboyant defiance; Hildreth's eyes, she noted, widened in surprise.

Lysandra knew that it would take more than bravado to carry her through. She saw Hildreth square her shoulders and advance, her defence high. Yet she noted that the *scutum* trembled in the German's grip as if it were gaining weight as the fight wore on. She waited, gauging the distance between them.

Then, as Hildreth stepped to close the gap, Lysandra herself skipped forward, her foot lashing out in a classic *pankration* kick, hammering into the wall of the tribeswoman's shield. Hildreth screamed in agony, the *scutum* falling from nerveless fingers. Lysandra stopped short, wondering what the cause of her opponent's distress was. Hildreth back-pedalled and, as she did so, Lysandra could see her shoulder bone horribly distended. The kick had dislocated it, rendering her arm useless.

Their eyes met, and Lysandra could read the pain and frustration there. Hildreth was finished. Lysandra shook her head. This was not the way.

She tossed her own shield aside, sending it skittering across the sand and moved slowly away. The mob howled their approval, stamping their feet rhythmically in appreciation at this sporting act.

Hildreth tottered to the wall of the arena, oblivious to the enthusiastic spectators reaching down to try to touch her. Lysandra watched her grit her teeth, and then slam herself into the unyielding stone. She fancied that she could hear the grind of cartilage as Hildreth popped her joint back into place and winced involuntarily.

The tribeswoman collapsed, sobbing as waves of agony flared through her; Lysandra kept away, pressing her hand into the wound at her side, trying to stem the flow of blood. She felt light-headed and crouched down on the sand, her breath coming in short gasps. Time seemed to slow down then. She could hear her heartbeat, pounding as if in time to the feet of the stamping mob.

The sky darkened for a moment and she looked up; it was Hildreth's shadow falling across her. The German's face was pale and pinched with pain, her eyes glazed with exhaustion. Her arm, though back in place, still hung at her side. The agony had to be almost unbearable. Lysandra set her jaw and stood.

Hildreth nodded. No words were needed between them.

Both women raised their blades, coming at each other right

side on. Lysandra knew that she must strike now, for she felt herself close to fainting. Hildreth must have sensed her weakness; with a shout, she attacked. Frantically, Lysandra lifted her blade and parried; she hit back, but in turn her sword was battered away. They fought mechanically now: each cut met by a parry; each thrust turned aside.

Lysandra was becoming desperate; she was spent and she knew it. Hildreth was like a rock before her, refusing to give way. There was time neither for thought nor tactics; it was simply a question of who was the stronger. She surged towards the German, cutting with the last of her strength. Their blades met again and again, the exchange seemed faster than any before.

Lysandra struck low, and encountered only soft resistance.

Hildreth gagged and both women looked down to see the blade embedded in her stomach to the hilt, her blood coursing out over Lysandra's hand and wrist. The German staggered against Lysandra and her weight bore them both to the sand.

'Hildreth!' Lysandra gasped as the German rolled on to her back, her blue eyes looking skyward. She held the tribeswoman's hand, tightly, as if by her own strength she could keep her from Hades' grip. 'Hildreth, I am sorry.' Her voice cracked and tears sprung to her eyes. 'I meant only to wound.' Despite her earlier thoughts, it was only at that moment she realised that she spoke the truth. She trailed off as Hildreth's eyes focused up on her.

'You didn't fight shit,' she said, coughing blood as she spoke. She tried to smile, the gesture made obscene by the blood that stained her teeth. Her body spasmed, and she cried out in pain. For a moment Hildreth struggled, but then she became still, her hand suddenly relaxing in Lysandra's grip. The warrior woman's brave soul had fled.

Lysandra staggered to her feet, pressing her hand to her side to staunch the flow of blood. The noise from the stands was deafening, the crowd screaming her name, chanting it as if in prayer. She raised a fist in salute and, on unsteady legs, made her way to the Gate of Life.

XLII

Danae, kitted and ready for her second bout of the day, nodded to Lysandra as she came through the Gate. 'You're all right?'

Lysandra mumbled something in response but Danae did not really hear her; her mind was fixed on her bout, and she scarcely noticed the Spartan stumble down the tunnel towards the surgeon.

She swallowed, forcing her breathing to slow. Like many of the other girls, she had compelled herself to become hardened to the arena. Long gone was the young wife from Athens; she was a killer now.

Steeling herself, she stepped on to the sands, hearing the Gate of Life slam shut behind her. The crowd were still buoyant after Lysandra and Hildreth's brutal display and were delighted that another combat followed so quickly. Any misgivings they might have had about the earlier mismatch seemed to have been forgotten and they cheered Danae enthusiastically.

An arena attendant walked up to her and handed her a gladius, which she raised in salute to Frontinus and then to the crowd. The largely expatriate Hellene audience stamped when they

345

heard her announced as 'Theseis' – like 'Achillia', she was one of their own.

'And her opponent,' the announcer screamed, trying to make himself heard over the din, 'the fearsome warrior from the savage steppes of the north…'

Danae's heart beat faster.

'She has fought once today, but did not impress. Now, she will redeem her honour, proving her status on the body of this woman. Citizens, I give you Amazona!'

The Gate opposite Danae's own clanked open with menacing slowness, revealing the lithe form of the Dacian. She too was clad as the *secutorix*, and the crowd gave voice to their enthusiasm at this favourite of bouts; two heavily armed opponents were liable to engage in a bloody slogging match.

Danae set her teeth, fighting down a roiling fury within. She had once been a beauty, but the Amazon had taken that away from her, casually, carelessly even, in a brawl.

Now she had a chance to even the score.

She had seen Sorina fight and knew she could match her. In addition, the Amazon was older than she and, weighed down by the heavy panoply, Danae reasoned that she could wear her out.

Gripping the gladius tightly in her fist, she advanced on Sorina, her face beneath the helmet drawn tight in a battle grimace.

Sorina matched her stride for stride and the two women met dead centre of the arena, each raining a hail of blows upon the other. Shield met sword and sword hammered off lacquered wood with furious swiftness. There was no taking the measure here. Each woman was determined to kill the other in the short order.

Their shields crunched together as both combatants punched forward at the same time. Locked together they spiralled in a circle, each trying to thrust over the other's protective barrier.

346

Danae grunted with the effort of holding the Amazon at bay, sweat bursting out on her back. Snarling, she shoved as hard as she could and forced the older woman back. Sorina stumbled and Danae swung out, her blade clanging from the Dacian's helmet.

She heard Sorina curse and felt a burning surge of elation. Thus encouraged she ploughed in, her sword raised. But the Amazon moved swiftly, changing her angle, her own blade flicking out like a viper's tongue. She caught Danae on the thigh with a low thrust, the sword raking up flesh towards her hip. Danae gasped and struck back, but her blade merely met the wood of Sorina's shield.

Even as she tried to break away, the Amazon's blade stuck her again, this time in the side and blood oozed from her bare torso. The crowd booed and hissed: they wanted the Hellene to win but 'Amazona' seemed to have the upper hand.

Buoyed by the encouragement of the mob, Danae ignored the pain and moved forward once more, determined to cut the elusive Sorina down. As she lunged with the gladius, the Amazon spun away, her own weapon arcing out. Danae cried out as she felt the iron bite into the back of her shoulder as Sorina moved past her. She whirled about and only raised her shield at the last moment to deflect what would have been the killing blow.

It was becoming intolerably hot in the heavy helmet and Danae wished she had a respite to tear the thing off, but Sorina pressed her hard now and she back-stepped, taking blow after blow on her *scutum*. She realised with despair that she had not yet struck home herself. She *must* counter. Hurling herself forward, she attacked, but again the Amazon's shield was there and, too slow, Danae tried to withdraw her arm.

The pain of the cut to her forearm burnt through her, and she heard Sorina's laughter, muffled by the helm she wore.

Lysandra slid off the surgeon's bench, somewhat gingerly.

'You'll be all right,' the man told her. 'I've added honey to the bindings to hold back infection. Just...'

'Make sure the bindings are changed regularly and the honey is fresh,' Lysandra cut him off.

'Yes,' the surgeon said; if he was offended by her abrupt manner he did not show it. 'Your tunic.' He passed her garment and then assisted her into it.

'My thanks.' Lysandra nodded briefly and made her way into the catacombs, towards the Gate of Life. The crowd was somewhat muted, but isolated shouts told her that Danae's combat was still in progress. She shoved her way to the front of the usual gaggle of warriors, eager to see Danae at work. But her eyes widened in horror at the sight she beheld.

The Athenian was bleeding from a dozen wounds, stumbling about the sands as if drunk. Lysandra at once recognised the hated form of Sorina as Danae's tormentor.

The Dacian banged Danae's sword contemptuously aside and cut her again. The crowd hissed, half enjoying this prolonged display, yet disappointed the Hellene girl was on the receiving end.

Danae's body was a mass of gore. Though bleeding profusely she seemed game to fight back: driven on, Lysandra assumed, by her hatred of the woman who had scarred her.

'Fall!' Lysandra shouted, willing her friend to drop so that she might receive the *missio*. But it was as if Sorina had heard her cry. The Amazon turned towards the Gate of Life and cast her helmet to one side.

Her eyes met those of Lysandra's. The Amazon smiled and gave a slight, mocking half-shrug. Then she turned back to Danae and beckoned her on. Danae struggled forward, at last discarding her shield, determined to win or die.

Sorina parried the attack with ease and dropped low, plunging her sword into Danae's belly. The Athenian stiffened as the weapon sliced into her vitals, blood and viscera bursting from her gut, spattering the howling barbarian. Sorina dragged her blade free, leaving Danae to topple forward, to twitch helplessly on the sands as her lifeblood spread out beneath her.

As the crowd applauded politely at the artful kill, Sorina raised her sword, and then pointed the dripping weapon at Lysandra in a mockery of the Spartan's own salute to her goddess. Laughing, she acknowledged Frontinus and took time to spit on the still form of Danae, before turning on her heel and exiting the arena.

Furious, Lysandra slammed her palms into the iron gate. Rage all but consumed her and it took all the self-control she could muster not to rush into the arena and attack Sorina. Hatred boiled in her blood. First her love, now her friend.

Sorina would die. Not in some illegal tussle at the *ludus*. No, she would send her to her gods a ruined piece of flesh under the eyes of the screaming mob.

'Wonderful, wonderful!' Frontinus had heartily enjoyed the bout. Balbus smiled through his disappointment – another trained fighter was down and the cost was mounting.

'Tell me, *lanista*,' Frontinus asked. 'Who did Amazona challenge at the end of the bout? She seemed to point at the Gate of Life.'

Balbus considered lying as he had once before but again decided against it. It was just not worth being found out. 'Lysandra,' he said miserably. 'They hate each other. Theseis – the woman who fell just now – was one of Lysandra's friends and confidants. As you know, Amazona killed Britannica. There was some talk that she was Lysandra's lover. There is much bad blood between them.'

'An opportunity for us, no?' Frontinus grinned wolfishly.

'I think not, Excellency,' Balbus hedged. Lysandra was good but still inexperienced. Though she waxed and Sorina waned, there was a conflict and rivalry that he wished to nurture. Only when she was in her prime did he want her to face the Dacian.

'I don't think Lysandra could win against Amazona,' he said. 'All our efforts towards the grand battle would be for nought.'

Frontinus considered that. 'Perhaps you are right. But I am not convinced. I think Lysandra would beat her, this...' he paused and grinned, 'this *nemesis* of hers. But, you are the expert.'

Balbus shook his head. 'No, my lord, your eye is as keen as mine,' he said, not above a little flattery to smooth ruffled feathers. Frontinus's glance however, told him that the governor knew he was being sycophantic. Well, Balbus thought, what did he expect? With patricians, one could never win. 'But, perhaps because I spend more time with both women than you...' he added. 'And can see their development continually... Performances in the arena are never as telling as the day-to-day training. Anyone can have an off-day, as you saw with Amazona earlier. Though she won, her performance was poor. No entertainment.' He summed up with distaste.

'True,' Frontinus agreed. 'But she did redeem herself just now. Consummate skill.' He nodded appreciatively. 'She took Theseis apart with ease yet strung it out so that the mob could have their fill of blood. A true professional in the end, Balbus.'

'One tries to endow them with virtue,' the *lanista* said modestly and trying to smother any hint of irony.

'Very well,' Frontinus said. 'We shall keep them apart. For now.'

Balbus inclined his head, hiding his expression; inside he was somewhat perturbed. Frontinus, and indeed Aeschylus, had pumped money into the *ludus* but he was already discovering that it came at a high rate of interest. Balbus was used to making his own decisions about who fought whom and when. The same rules applied here as anywhere, he thought bitterly. Money bought influence, and Frontinus now had influence in the decisions of the school. The thought made the wine taste sour on his tongue.

XLIII

The games went on. Because of her wound, Lysandra could not participate but she watched with growing concern over her women. She found herself analysing their performances more and more and had taken to noting down strengths and weaknesses that these might be corrected on return to the *ludus*.

It was, she knew, an effort to keep her own mind busy. The loss of Danae had hit her harder than she cared to admit and certainly she could not share her feelings with the others. She must remain implacable at all times, an example of Spartan fortitude and strong-mindedness.

But, in her quiet moments, Danae's death somehow compounded that of Eirianwen's. She thought she had buried her feelings deep, but Sorina had re-opened the wound. Always, it was Sorina. Her dreams were once again haunted by Eirianwen's last agonising moment, and now this image was joined with that of Danae, caring Danae, cut to bloody ribbons by the barbarian. With the return of Eirianwen to the night, so came Nastasen. The death of her love and the rape of her own body could not be divorced in her mind and once again she knew fear in the darkness.

There had to be a reckoning, and soon. Perhaps killing Sorina would serve to exorcise her of the nightly torments. If she could not revenge herself on Nastasen then at least she could kill Eirianwen's murderer. Yet, Lysandra knew that she would have to be at her best to match the Dacian. Spartan bravery and courage was one thing but, injured as she was, she would be easy prey for Sorina. She kept well away from her and her coterie, salving her conscience with the knowledge that this was not cowardice, but prudence. It was, she considered, the barbarian way to charge off into a fight with little or no forethought and thus fall to easy defeat.

Catuvolcos spoke to her often, seeming to sense the darkness of her mood. He did his best to seal their renewed friendship in this time, even inviting her to the city one evening to meet his paramour, Doris. He had at least the good taste not to bring her to the brothel. Lysandra had sent word to Telemachus that she would be abroad, and she was pleased when he agreed to meet them. The four had an entertaining evening, despite the constant interruptions from Lysandra's admirers.

She herself found it a welcome diversion from the black thoughts that never left her mind. Revenge was an all-consuming force, she decided.

The gladiatrices returned to the *ludus* under heavy guard. Balbus was at pains to keep the various factions separated, as tensions were running higher than ever.

To her credit, Lysandra kept her women under close control, marching them out of the *ludus* each day to train on the arid landscape. Though this rankled with the barbarians it could not be helped. But disgruntled was one thing, violent another so, to placate them, Balbus increased their beer rations so that most evenings were clouded with alcohol. The *lanista* knew that everyone had a price and buying the tribeswomen off with liquor seemed the best solution.

One morning, he decided to take a look at how 'the troops,' as he had come to call them, were progressing. Flanked by Titus and Stick, he rode out to watch the proceedings.

'It follows the same format every day,' Titus told him, 'so you will get a good picture from this.'

The early part of the day was taken up with physical training, each woman carrying a round *hoplon* shield and eight-foot spear. Their armour was the cheap, army surplus chain mail that Balbus had procured at Lysandra's request: made of tiny iron rings linked to form a mesh, it provided lightweight, flexible protection. However, in a nod to the historical theme of the battle, the women were equipped otherwise as Greek hoplite warriors, the great crested Corinthian helms nodding as they were put through their paces.

'It looks very impressive,' he observed.

'She has got them up to speed in a remarkably short time,' Titus admitted.

After the running and exercise in the armour, came drill, and this was truly the mark of Lysandra's success so far. At barked orders from the Spartan and some embarrassingly poor blasts from Thebe on the rusted *buccinae* – their signalling trumpet – the women formed into the ranks and files with effortless ease. They set off at a march and, at specific refrains from the trumpet, they performed a variety of different manoeuvres to Balbus's delight.

'They look so *authentic!*' he enthused to Stick. 'Just as I would imagine a hoplite army to look like from the histories. Truly, I had heard that her warrior order in Sparta was the only place in the world one could see a force such as this. But now, we have one of our own.'

Stick grunted for want of something to say. To him, it was all a silly game.

The drilling went on for some time, the manoeuvres becoming more complex. Any infractions in the ranks were punished harshly by Lysandra and her seconds in the form of what Titus told the *lanista* was called 'beasting' – extra physical duties. Balbus noted that she had not resorted to the whip that had evidently been used on her in Sparta.

'They will soon rest and go on to the usual gladiatorial training,' the veteran trainer advised Balbus.

'I've seen enough,' Balbus responded, and rubbed his hands together before turning his horse about. Just as he was about to nudge the beast away, a sweating Lysandra called after him. Balbus pulled his mount to, thinking that she looked very military, with her helm tucked under her arm and her greaves all dusty. Still, he had noted that she had not taken part in the training, evidently nursing her wound. She had such good sense, he thought to himself.

'I am very impressed,' he said before she had spoken.

'Good,' she responded shortly. 'But it is not enough, Balbus.'

'What do you mean?' He regarded her carefully.

'This is heavy infantry. I need other types of troops if I am to succeed. The barbarians will use hit and run tactics, I think, if the legends of the Amazon wars are anything to go by. I will need to train some of your new… slaves… as light troops – archers and slingers, and…' She trailed off.

'And?' Balbus thought the demand reasonable. After all, he did not care how Lysandra trained the women, only that they performed on the day, and she was proving her mettle as a gifted 'commander'.

'Cavalry,' she said quickly. 'Heavy and light.'

'Cavalry?' the *lanista* sputtered. 'Horses! But the cost… No, Lysandra, it could ruin me!'

'*Lanista*, I have seen a squadron of Thessalian women that are used in the execution of criminals at the Games of Aeschylus. And I have heard of an Egyptian troupe that wear heavy armour and perform 'tricks'. I am sure that more such women could be found. If you want things to be authentic – and you want us to win – I must have this support.'

Balbus decided to be reasonable. 'Lysandra,' he said, 'I appreciate that you are trying to make things true to the myth and you should be commended for your thoroughness, but ...'

'Spartans are always through, *lanista*,' she interrupted. 'I must have these horses.'

Balbus pursed his lips at her impertinence but realised that such a change in attitude was inevitable given the freedoms he had invested upon Lysandra. On the other hand, he knew that she was the only woman in his entire *ludus* that could be trusted to maintain discipline given such latitude, so he tolerated it. 'The cost of keeping horses is too prohibitive, Spartan,' he said, knowing that referring to her in such a manner would be flattering. 'I am already constructing a new wing at the *ludus* and purchasing a huge amount of... troops for your army.'

Lysandra pressed her lips into a thin line. 'You are but one man, Lucius Balbus. The forces arrayed against us are the product of many schools banding together. On aggregate, they can raise more cash than you, and as such they can buy horsewomen. The barbarians you say will comprise the enemy are famed for their skill *on horseback*, even their women. If we face such on the field of battle without adequate support we will be cut to pieces. There will be no way that I can make use of the terrain – we are to fight on an open field, I presume.'

'Well, that is so,' Balbus was forced to admit. 'What would be the point otherwise? People will need to see what's going on, and we cannot transport the whole mob to a battleground of your choosing, Lysandra.'

'Precisely, *lanista*. If I were to choose a battle ground for an infantry against cavalry action, I would ensure that I had higher ground at least, and my flanks unassailable at best. In our scenario, this will not be the case. I do not know the disposition of the

355

enemy, and if they *are* heavy in their use of horse soldiers, I could be out-flanked by these faster-moving troops. I cannot predict how the enemy will array herself, so I will have to array myself in accordance to correct military practice. This could result in a defensive action, or worse, a complete exposure of my force if the enemy arrays non-conventionally. For instance, a refusal of flank could be disastrous unless I have my own fast-moving troops to engage theirs. After that the phalanx can do its work. But the phalanx can be exposed…'

Balbus held up his hand; it was getting far too technical for him. He glanced at Titus and could tell by his expression that Lysandra evidently knew what she was talking about. He sighed. 'This is dependent on the 'enemy' having horses.'

Lysandra nodded.

'I will make an investigation. If I find that the other schools are preparing cavalry, I will seek extra funding and you will have your horses. If they are not, then there is no need for any of this.'

'Thank you.' Balbus thought that she was about to salute him, but evidently she thought better of it and turned away without another word.

'This could ruin me,' he said again, this time to Titus.

'Aye, it could.' The grizzled trainer laughed. 'But it would be a show like no other before it, Balbus. You have to admire her spirit.'

Balbus's answering grin was a little forced but he concurred with the trainer. 'I'll get Falco to look into it,' he said. 'Whatever happens, Titus, with this much investment going into this spectacle, I want very much to win.'

'I was a soldier before I came to this,' Titus said, and Balbus braced himself for a lengthy anecdotal story from an old legionary sweat. 'She will win, *lanista*, I can guarantee it. If she is given the materiel she needs. She reminds me of a young tribune I knew when I was serving in Germania…'

'I will have Falco look into it,' Balbus cut in quickly.

Titus looked crestfallen and turned his attention back to the training.

XLIV

'He's coming? Here?' Sextus Julius Frontinus was as close as he ever got to panic.

'Yes, my lord.' Diocles, a Greek freedman, regarded his former owner calmly.

'When?' Frontinus clambered from his couch.

'Perhaps three months.' Diocles ran a hand through his thinning hair. 'Perhaps sooner. The letter is dated July and we are close to September now.'

Frontinus began to pace. 'But this is unscheduled,' he accused, as if there were something the secretary could do to alter the matter.

'Rome feels no need to observe protocol, Governor,' the slender freedman commented, slightly disdainful. 'She *makes* protocol.'

Frontinus glowered at him. 'Shall I tell you what this is, Diocles?'

Diocles nodded, a man who had no choice in the answer to the question.

'This is a spying mission. There's no other explanation. He's coming here to make sure I don't botch the preparations for Domitian's birthday celebration. These new men think we of the old guard can't take a shit without their help.'

'Yes, my lord.' Diocles said, keeping his expression neutral.

'Well, I'll show this Trajanus how we do things in Halicarnassus. Not by half measures, eh, Diocles?'

'No, my lord.'

'Three months, Diocles. Not long to put an extravaganza together for his elucidation. But, this is something we must do. Can't have Rome saying my province wasn't up to scratch!'

'My thoughts exactly, sir.' Diocles injected enough boredom into his voice to let Frontinus know that he was rambling and that decisions should be made – and quickly at that.

The governor bristled for a moment and then laughed. 'Well, no sense in panicking over something we can't change.'

'No, my lord.'

'Well, let's start to call in the debts and the favours, my boy. Get me Balbus. Get me that Syrian whoremaster – you know the one. Get me…'

'I am sure that I can find what you are looking for. Catering, entertainments, both visual and sensual – and, of course, a games. Accommodation for him and his retinue – *et cetera, et cetera.*'

'Yes, Diocles, that's it.' Frontinus sat back on the couch and mopped his brow. 'The buggers thought they had the General outflanked! Well, not this old soldier.'

'Of course, my lord. I shall make sure all is in order.' Diocles smiled slightly, inclining his head, and turned away. There was much work to be done.

'It's going to be huge,' Balbus told his retinue of trainers. 'Bigger even than the Games of Aeschylus. In fact, the perfect prelude to the grand battle we plan next year. I want the women in top shape,' he added, stabbing a finger.

Stick lounged on a couch. 'What about the growing army?' he said. '*General* Lysandra will be most displeased if her training regimen is interrupted.'

'I think all will be well with that,' Titus broke in. 'She has her daily routine off to a fine art.' He turned his attention to Balbus. 'Did Falco get back to you with reports on the acquisition of mounts for the other schools?'

Balbus did not want to let the conversation gravitate to matters totally concerned with Lysandra but he realised the veteran very much saw this as his own project. 'Yes, and Lysandra was right, an annoying habit of hers. Word is that the other *lanistas* are playing to their strengths, and are investing heavily in their women's natural skills in horse riding. So, our Spartan shall have her way. Frontinus, however, is being tight with the purse strings, now that we have our visitor from Rome to contend with. But I am sure the proceeds from this next game will more than cover our expenses.'

'*We're* putting the money up for the horsewomen?' Stick was incredulous.

Balbus made an expansive gesture. 'Speculate. Accumulate. If Lysandra loses, we'll be ruined. If she wins, we'll all be rich beyond the dreams of avarice, with fame to match. But moving on to more immediate matters…' Balbus determined to get the discussion back on track. He prided himself on his man-management skills. 'There can be no mistakes, men,' he said, feeling rather like a general himself. 'Our women must perform to their best in front of this advisor of Domitian's. Rome must hear of our work and, perhaps…' He trailed off, his eyes swimming with visions of the capital and the adoring Roman populace. He brought himself back to the present. 'Our reputation will stand on these… *Games of Trajan*, as they are coming to be known. This means that we cannot afford internal strife. Let the women know that Romans are enthusiastic with their granting of freedom in such events. Let them know that any infractions between them will result in not only severe punishment, but also they will be denied the chance to appear at the games.'

360

'And so deny them a chance at freedom.' Titus looked satisfied with that. 'A worthy solution, Balbus.'

'I thought so,' the *lanista* agreed smugly.

New slaves began to arrive in increasing numbers, wide-eyed and frightened at their unfamiliar surroundings. Lysandra realised that Balbus was doing his best not to scrape the bottom of the barrel and was grateful: the newcomers were of sturdy Hellenic stock for the most part, hands worn from the loom and the washing stone.

These recruits would form the main part of her army. Though she was well pleased with the women she had trained in the hoplite fashion, she knew that her force must be more flexible than the outmoded formations of centuries ago. Given the historical theme of the spectacle, she could not equip her women in the modern style but she felt that arming the main part of her troops after the Macedonian fashion would not be stretching the rules too much.

Thus, the bulk of the army now found themselves wielding the huge *sarissa*, the eighteen-foot pike used by both Phillip's and Alexander's soldiers with such deadly efficiency. When formed correctly, the phalanx presented an impenetrable wall of spears. On this wall she would impale the enemy and hold her fast whilst her elite troops finished the task.

Lysandra was keen to root out the Rhodians and Cretans amongst her women. The majority of the former were shepherd-girls, well skilled with the use of the sling; an ancient weapon long used to keep wolves and other predators away from the flocks though, its use in war was undeniably effective. The Cretans used the bow for much the same purpose and Lysandra knew that, by combining the ranges of these two weapons, she could rain down a withering hail of missiles on the horsewomen she would face. To supplement these troops, Lysandra also began to

361

form a detachment of lightly armed women: *peltasts*, would act in concert with the islanders as skirmishers to break up and disrupt enemy formations.

As before, she trained a core herself, and then allowed the natural leaders that emerged to train the newcomers: it was proving a most effective form of administration and a necessary one. Though much of her focus was on the training, she could not ignore the fact that a lavish spectacle was planned in the near future, and she could not afford to ignore her own preparations. But now that she had a command structure in place, the army was largely running itself.

'Hard to tear yourself away from the soldiers, *General*,' Thebe mocked gently after they had sparred one afternoon.

'Indeed,' she said, sitting, mopping her brow. 'There is a sense of satisfaction to be had when one sees one's genius come to fruition.'

'Of course.' Thebe grinned. 'Only you could have achieved such a feat, great one.'

Lysandra mulled that over for a moment. 'Perhaps you are right,' she agreed. 'Though any priestess of Sparta may have my skills, I feel that it is my natural flair and charisma for leadership that has been effective thus far.'

Thebe grimaced; Lysandra was *so* arrogant it was almost endearing. 'Alexander himself would be envious,' she said, and was rewarded with a self-depreciating smile from her friend. If anything had come from the tragic death of Danae and the barbarian Eirianwen, it was a slight softening in the Spartan's attitude. Certainly, she was still stiff-necked and haughty, but Thebe had seen her 'discipline' some of her recruits of late and there was no evidence of the horrific beatings and tortures that Lysandra advocated as 'the Spartan way'.

But it seemed to her that the twin deaths had caused her to

lose something of herself. She had become driven to the point of obsession, her only focus her troops and her training. She spoke of nothing else but tactics, weapons, and killing. It was as if she had armoured herself against all feeling, wearing the façade that was 'Achillia' to protect herself from further pain. The priestess was all but gone and Thebe found herself looking at the gladiatrix who had become a stranger.

'Are you mocking me, Thebe?' Lysandra broke her from her reverie.

'I?' she took on a scandalised expression. 'How could one such as I mock the great General Lysandra?' She would try to treat Lysandra in her normal manner and hoped that she came back to herself.

'These next games are being highly publicised,' Lysandra said, changing the subject.

'That's the truth. I heard that a Roman senator was coming to watch. That's what all the fuss is about. It will be the biggest spectacle this province has ever seen, that's for sure. Four months of games.' She shook her head. '*Four months!*'

Lysandra glanced in the direction of the plains where the women trained. 'I must see if I can be given dispensation to leave the arena after my bouts and return to the *ludus* to oversee the troops.'

'They'll wear that all right,' Thebe agreed. 'This whole 'battle' venture must be costing Balbus a fortune. He'll want to ensure that all goes well. And, with no joke, you are the best person to oversee that.'

'Naturally.' Lysandra got to her feet. 'Let us continue.'

Thebe shook her head as she rose. There was no doubt that the arrogance *was* still there.

XLV

The *ludus* was alive with a frenzy of preparation. The trainers drilled the gladiatrices ruthlessly, ensuring that each woman would be at her peak when her time came to step onto the sands.

With her time split between her own preparations and overseeing her growing army, Lysandra found herself pushed to the limits of her endurance. After a sparring match with one of the German girls that resulted in a near defeat for her, Stick took her to one side.

'You have to slow down,' he admonished her.

'I am perfectly aware of my limitations,' Lysandra snapped. She had her hands on her thighs, waist bent and chest heaving from exertion.

'No. You aren't.' He held up a hand, cutting off her protest. 'You must slow down, or you will be spent when the time comes to fight. Look at you now. You struggled against that girl when you should have put her on her arse in a moment.'

'Listen, Stick. I am not a child to be ordered about. I know what I am doing!'

'No, *you* listen!' The Parthian was genuinely angered and

Lysandra stiffened involuntarily. Stick glanced about and then stepped close to her, dropping his voice to a whisper. 'You think I'm deaf, girl? I walk past your villa on my rounds in the night, and I can hear your screams from outside. Your dreams are bad, aren't they?' Stick did not see fit to mention it but it was patently clear that he knew who inhabited Lysandra's nightmares 'Now, you'll rest or I'll have you beaten so as you can't train.'

'Balbus would never allow it.'

'Balbus isn't here.' Stick drew the vine staff. 'Get away with you, and take a bath. No more training. Not army. Not this.' He gestured expansively. 'You'll rest and that's that. Do some writing, pray to your Athene – or whatever you do to relax. I don't care. You've become very expensive, Spartan, and I won't have you spilling your guts all over the sand because you were too tired to fight. You must get proper sleep. Clear?'

'Clear, Stick.' Lysandra pressed her lips into a thin line. 'But you *are* mistaken in this.'

'I don't give a shit. Now fuck off, and take it easy! Gods, Lysandra, anyone else would be happy to be given time off.'

'You may have noticed, Stick, that I am unlike these others,' Lysandra retorted and stalked away.

He would not, Frontinus determined, be seen as parochial. He was a Roman, and would prove to this Trajanus that he knew how to entertain in the Roman style. Especially as it had come to his attention that Trajanus was of Iberian stock – a Spaniard, no less. Thus, no expense had been spared and not a moment wasted in preparation for the arrival of Domitian's confidant; Frontinus was eager to show the emissary that he could be as lavish as the best of them.

In addition to the more cosmetic nuances, Frontinus, with the help of the indefatigable Diocles, ensured that the local garrisons were well drilled, their *lorica* gleaming and their leathers well oiled and tanned. Nothing was left to chance; Frontinus feared that anything he overlooked was bound to come to the attention of the Iberian upstart and his reputation would be damaged.

Each day was taken up with duties and petitions from interested parties who wanted to cash in on the arrival from Rome. Frontinus was hard pressed to keep up with it all but, with the aid of Diocles, he managed to stay afloat.

At least Lucius Balbus was no cause of concern. The *lanista* had assured him that the preparations for the games were going exceedingly well. Balbus's associate, Septimus Falco, had been promoting the event since the news of Trajanus's visit had broken and people from all over Asia Minor and even Greece itself were flocking to the city. It all added to his prestige: that he, Sextus Julius Frontinus, could put on a spectacle so lavish that people would travel from far and wide to attend was good political capital.

On the appointed day of Trajanus's arrival however, Frontinus found he was somewhat nervous, despite himself. And when word reached him that the senator and his retinue were on their way to his home he was became positively rancorous.

'Peace, my lord,' Diocles soothed. 'Have some wine and relax. All is in order.'

Frontinus glared at the secretary but eased himself back on his couch; it simply would not do to be ill at ease when the Spaniard arrived. 'Yes, of course,' he said, then gestured for the wine cup and sipped its heavily watered contents.

Time passed slowly and Frontinus drifted into a light slumber, rudely shattered by several loud blasts of brazen *buccinae*. Fortunately, Diocles had taken the wine from him, and thus avoided any spillage on his pristine toga. He gathered himself and, straightening its folds, got to his feet.

The doors to the great *tablinium* opened and Frontinus's men snapped to attention as the Roman retinue entered. At their head was a tall, blond man in his early thirties. He was well built and clad in military attire, all buckles and bronze. He approached Frontinus and stood before him for a moment before throwing out a salute.

'Hail, Sextus Julius Frontinus,' he barked, his accent noticeable.

'Hail, Marcus Ulpinus Trajanus,' Frontinus responded, taking the measure of the man before him. He was impressed: Trajanus's military bearing was no mere affectation. Frontinus could see the criss-cross scars on his right forearm. No dandy whose military achievements had been won for him, this was a man – a soldier's soldier. And, Frontinus knew that, even as he assessed, he too was being scrutinised. He offered Trajanus his arm and the other's grip was firm. To his surpise, he found himself liking the man on first impression. 'Welcome to my home.'

'It is my honour, sir,' Trajanus said, inclining his head.

'Come.' Frontinus led the Spaniard through the avenue of soldiers. 'We shall bathe and you will tell me of your journey here, and,' he glanced at the younger man, 'your purpose.'

Trajanus chuckled. 'A frontal assault, General?'

Frontinus shrugged. 'We are soldiers born, Trajanus, and politicians by mere circumstance.' Trajanus swelled at the compliment – as well he might, Frontinus thought. His own military prowess was well regarded; he had been fighting battles when this young pup had been at his mother's teat. To acknowledge him as equal was an honour indeed 'There is little need for rhetoric amongst straight-talking men,' he added.

'Truth,' Trajanus said. 'We shall bathe and talk, then.'

The two men luxuriated in the opulent baths. Expensive Egyptian incense and steam wafted towards the ceiling, enshrouding them in an aromatic mist. Awaiting them at the poolside were several slaves, both male and female, chosen for their beauty and ethnic diversity; the governor wanted to ensure that any and all of Trajanus's needs were catered for.

At first, they spoke of matters concerning Rome and politics, and Frontinus was also eager to hear news of Trajanus's campaign against the rebel general, Lucius Antonius Saturnius and his Germanic allies.

'Indeed,' Frontinus said, 'I have seen one of these Germans in a recent games. A female, no less.'

'I am not surprised.' Trajanus lolled in the water. 'They fight alongside their men, and in some cases better than their men. Many tribes have the ridiculous belief that women are not inferior to the male. They hold them in some reverence, in fact.'

'Utterly absurd,' Frontinus responded, 'in *war*. But in the entertainments I find the combat of women gratifying on several levels. There is something exciting about it, do you not think?'

'I?' Trajanus arched an eyebrow. 'Until recently, I had never seen such a thing. But the Divine Domitian, is an advocate of the female combats. One of these Germanians – Aurinia they call her – has taken his fancy. Now in Rome, female matches are billed alongside those of the men's – equally, by torchlight.'

This last was said with distaste, leaving Frontinus in little doubt that the Spaniard himself held the women's games in low esteem. That he had mentioned the torchlight status of the matches meant that in Rome the female combats were being held at night, at top billing – unheard of till now. Then again, Frontinus mused, it was a modern age.

'It is said in Rome,' Trajanus went on, 'that Asia Minor is host to the finest of these… events.'

Frontinus paused before answering. He would have to tread carefully here and well he knew it. 'That is not so,' he said. 'Whilst we do our best, we are but a province. I am sure anything sponsored by the Emperor would make our poor events pale into insignificance.'

Trajanus laughed, his throaty chuckle echoing from the walls in the bathhouse. 'Come, Governor,' he said. 'You said yourself, we are soldiers born, not politicians?' He turned and fixed Frontinus with his gaze. 'You fear to say what is the truth. You fear to say it, because you fear that I will return to Domitian and report that you believe your shows are better than his own.' He lifted himself from the water, and stood by the edge of the pool, beckoning for a slave to dry him.

Frontinus found himself momentarily envious of the man's well-muscled, youthful body, scarred yet unhampered by the chains of old age. Gingerly, he hauled himself out of the warmth and shivered.

'*I* will say it, then.' Trajanus lifted his arms as a pretty Carian slave girl patted him dry. 'Word has reached Rome of the recent Games of Aeschylus. That you, and you alone, are responsible for elevating the female combats from mere sideshow to main event. That the quality of these... gladiatrices... is superior to anything we have in Rome. Your women, it is said, are superbly trained, that their combats are epic. That though we have good fighters in the capital, most of them are as nothing compared to the women of Asia Minor. He paused. 'Are the stories are to be believed.'

Frontinus gestured dismissively. 'I would be lying if I said that we haven't accomplished great things with the women's combats. But,' he added carefully, 'that is a niche entertainment. Perhaps the novelty will wear off.'

Trajanus laughed again, and the two men made their way to be dressed. Soon after, they reclined on couches in Frontinus's study, nibbling on grapes and olives.

'I am here, as you no doubt know, to ensure that your preparations for the Emperor's birthday celebrations are going in accordance to his preferences,' Trajanus took up the conversation once again. 'There's nothing worse than a disgruntled Emperor, Frontinus.'

The governor coughed. 'That's true,' he admitted.

'It is well known to me that you have been frantically preparing a spectacle for me.' Trajanus looked somewhat smug at Frontinus's startled expression. 'You must realise that espionage is a necessity in this day and age.'

'I wouldn't say *frantically*, young man,' Frontinus blustered. 'Your arrival was not scheduled. But, here in Asia Minor, I like to maintain that Roman skill of reacting to a situation and bringing it under one's control.' Like the boy or not, Frontinus was not going to be ridden roughshod by him – even if his observation was accurate.

Trajanus did not look in the least chagrined, but he did incline his head. 'A bad choice of words, *sir*.' The addition to the sentence was enough of an apology for both men. 'But in any event, I am here to see if the rumours are true. If your games are worthy of our divine Caesar.'

Frontinus smiled. 'Oh, I think you will find your stay here most entertaining, Trajanus.' The governor raised his cup, his mind racing. The young senator was demanding something special, that much was obvious. Frontinus decided that he would have it.

XLVI

albus had assigned the biggest six guards in his employ to stand in his study. Flat-eyed and brutal, the men held their batons loosely in their hands, ready for trouble. The *lanista* had decided he would take no chances with this meeting.

He saw the large form of Catuvolcos approaching, flanked by his charges. The Gaul had taken the precaution of having the two women chained, ankles and wrists, and Balbus winced. The pair of them would doubtless be furious at this indignity. It was like dealing with the worst kind of children, he thought sourly. Deadly children, though, he reminded himself. He forced a smile.

'Greetings, ladies,' he said, not wishing to acknowledge one before the other. They glared at him and he knew his assumption had been right. Balbus clasped his hands on the desk before him. 'I have summoned you *both* here as I have a gift for the two of you. Something you want very much.' He lifted a parchment from the desktop. 'This,' he said, 'is a communication from Sextus Julius Frontinus. Shall I read it to you?' Always keep the crowd hanging on, Balbus thought to himself – ever the showman.

'You should,' Lysandra said. 'The idiot barbarian has no letters.'

Sorina growled, lunging at Lysandra, but was intercepted by

Catuvolcos. He pushed her back into the arms of two waiting guards. Lysandra sneered at her.

'There's no need for that,' Balbus sighed, thankful for the precautions that had been taken. 'As you both know, Frontinus has organised a spectacle for a high-ranking member of the Senate in Rome. It is a huge endeavour, the biggest this province has seen thus far.' He paused for effect. 'You two will not fight in the usual supporting bouts; it has been decided that you will top the card. Above the men. You will fight a death match at the end of the games.'

Sorina's smile was feral. 'Why, Balbus, surely this senator wants a *match*. This girl-child will fall too quickly under my blade. Like her friend. And her lover.'

Lysandra's face reddened and Balbus saw her eyes narrow almost imperceptibly; he was grateful for the Spartan discipline that the former priestess cherished. He knew that had the barb been fired the other way, Sorina would be at Lysandra's throat. He was startled at the measure of hate in the Amazon's words. Sorina had loved Eirianwen too, and to use her death as weapon to wound Lysandra spoke volumes as to the depth of their enmity.

'Now you two listen.' He pointed a finger. 'You've got your wish. You can cut lumps out of each other on the day. But not before,' he added meaningfully. 'You have your own gaggles of friends and followers; you are both leaders. I expect you to stay apart and encourage your women to do the same. If there are any disturbances before or during the games, *any at all*, I'll hold you two responsible. Your eyes will be put out and I'll sell you to the mines. Don't think that I won't carry out *this* threat. My life is on the line if this goes awry, and I'll revenge myself on you both before anything happens to me.'

He was sure even Lysandra baulked at that. Pointless, he realised to threaten a gladiatrix with death, but maiming was something else entirely. 'I hope we understand each other.'

Neither woman spoke, but the hatred in the air was palpable. Balbus dismissed them, reminding himself to ensure that Falco played up the rivalry between them in the promotions. He was not pleased that Frontinus had forced his hand in this matter after their discussion, but he was a businessman. He would, he decided, maximise any profit to be made from the death of one of his best.

The two women, separated by guards, did not speak as they were escorted from Balbus's villa. Only when they had reached the training area did Sorina break the stony silence.

'I *will* kill you.'

The ice coloured gaze of her hated foe fell upon her, the arrogant lip curled. But Sorina saw nothing in Lysandra's eyes, no fire of anger, neither passion nor hatred. They were blank, the fixed stare of a marble statue. 'I think not,' was all she said. Catuvolcos released her from her chains and she strode away without further comment. Sorina watched her back retreating into the crowds, shaken by the exchange despite herself.

She shook off the feeling. That Lysandra had shown no battle joy was testament that she lacked the stomach for the fight. She feared her, and had been at pains to cover it with the gambler's straight face. Sorina's grin was fierce as Catuvolcos undid her chains. 'The gods have smiled upon me,' she said to him.

'I think the gods laugh *at* us, Sorina.'

She sniffed. 'She will be dead soon; her blight will be cut from the earth, and then perhaps you will get your head straight. There can be no friendship between us and the likes of her.'

Catuvolcos shrugged. 'Perhaps it will be as you say,' he said and moved away. The Amazon knew that he lied but did not care. Joy coursed through her as the reality became apparent.

Lysandra would face her in the arena.

And Lysandra would die.

*　　　*　　　*

Lysandra did not look back. She was pleased that she had buried her elation deep within; she had revealed nothing to Sorina and this lack of emotion would infuriate and confound her.

Whether the Amazon realised it or not, the fight had already begun, but Lysandra suspected that the barbarian would be in blissful ignorance of the fact. The key to victory would be in preparedness, in beating the old woman before they had set foot in the arena. The mind was the most effective weapon and one that barbarians overlooked. Perhaps, Lysandra thought, it was because most of them simply lacked the capability for higher levels of comprehension.

One thing she promised herself was that her victory would not be a quick one. No thrusts to the throat to end the old crone's life quickly. She would draw the bout out, make Sorina suffer as Danae had suffered.

As Eirianwen had suffered.

As she herself had suffered.

Sorina would go to her barbarian gods torn and broken, cut to bloody pieces. Lysandra regarded the statue of Roman-Athene that was at the far side of the training area. She raised both her hands and made a vow of her thoughts.

XLVII

Halicarnassus was alive with anticipation. The streets, usually crowded, were packed to overflowing. Every wall was adorned with parchments advertising the forthcoming Games of Trajan, the events the only topic of conversation in the city's many taverns. Betting amongst the professional gamblers had reached a fever pitch, vast wagers being placed on every bout; some would become rich from the event, but more would find themselves destitute. The betting fraternity aside, it seemed that every inhabitant of the city had staked money on the event.

When the inns became full, a metropolis of tents sprang up around the Carian capital. Industry boomed as taxable goods flooded into the city and so enriched the treasury. All manner of entrepreneurs flocked to Halicarnassus: slavers and food sellers; fine goods merchants and whoremasters with their retinues. It was as if everyone in the province and beyond wanted a piece of the profits generated by the enterprise.

Frontinus himself could scarcely believe the figures Diocles had shown him.

'A huge increase, my lord,' the deadpan secretary assured him.

'Despite your recent investment in next year's events, the treasury is much recovered. Actually, it is the healthiest it has been in years.'

Frontinus beamed at the freedman. 'Excellent,' he said. 'You know, Diocles, I had misgivings about Trajanus, but I have to admit that his unscheduled arrival really has brought out the best in me.'

'Of course,' Diocles agreed. 'Speaking of which, you must ready yourself. It would be unseemly to miss the opening ceremony of such an extravaganza – especially as you are its architect.'

'Quite right, Diocles, quite right.' Frontinus set his half-finished wine cup aside. 'Military attire or toga, do you think?'

The freedman stepped back and folded his arms, looking at him thoughtfully. 'Toga, I think, my lord. It will be hot, and you want to enjoy your spectacle, not cook in a set of armour.'

'Yes, but what if Trajanus wears *his* armour? I don't want him thinking that I can't take a bit of hardship.'

'Then Trajanus is a very silly boy, Lord. He will faint by midday.'

Frontinus grunted. 'That would be worth seeing. I like the lad, but he's a little too ambitious, I think.'

'You are an astute judge of character, Governor. Shall I summon the dress slaves?'

'Eh?' Frontinus asked. 'Oh yes, the toga. See to it, Diocles.' He reached out for his wine cup but the freedman deftly swiped it away. 'My wine!'

'It has become stale, my lord,' Diocles said primly. 'I shall have more brought.' He bowed and retreated, both men knowing that no more wine would be forthcoming.

Diocles could be such a curmudgeon, Frontinus thought sourly.

The parade was Dionysian in its frenzy. Lysandra had seen the crowd driven mad by blood and lust before but this was startling, even to her. Clad in her scarlet tunic, she marched at the head of the procession with Sorina by her side, stunned at the multitudes that packed the streets. The screaming was deafening, a roaring tumult that crashed about the marching gladiatrices.

Lysandra was reminded of her first time in the arena, but whereas then she had been overawed, she now welcomed the fury and the passion. She heard her name called out many times by the onlookers and she could not suppress a slight smile.

'They call for me now, Sorina,' she said from the side of her mouth. 'Where are *your* admirers?'

'They'll be singing a different tune come four moons, Spartan.' Sorina's grin was savage. 'Enjoy these days, for they are your last.'

'If the gods will it.' Lysandra said evenly. 'But, still – I think the people are bored with you.'

'Think what you like!' Sorina snapped, and Lysandra was gratified to see a vein pulse in her forehead.

She refrained from further comment. Turning to the crowd she acknowledged them with a wave and they roared their enthusiasm in return.

It was not the same in the gaol complex.

Lysandra was offered a room to herself, away from the other Hellene women, which she accepted. She realised that the public, the sponsors and indeed her own women acknowledged that there was a widening gulf between them now. There were many reasons for this, not least of all her upbringing. There was the matter of the army: a leader should be held in respect by her troops. She would act as Alexander had, sharing their trials with them, but always remaining a step above.

They still needed her influence, after all. Thebe was becoming a leader in her own right, but Lysandra was all too aware of the Corinthian's limitations. She had learned much in her time as

377

gladiatrix and benefited from the military training, but she could not hope to compare with the lifetime of learning she herself had garnered.

'You will defeat her,' Thebe told her at the feast that evening.

'Of course,' Lysandra responded. 'Look at her,' she jerked her head disdainfully at the barbarian coterie. 'Drunk, as usual.'

'Well, I might follow her example. I don't fight for some days,' Thebe said, eying the wine jug.

Lysandra was about to upbraid her, as she disapproved of drunkenness, but the retort died on her tongue. The eyes of the women were upon her. She forced a smile to her lips. 'That is so, Thebe. It should be that you celebrate with our friends,' her gaze swept the table, 'new and old.' Indeed, there were new faces amongst them, replacements for the fallen.

'You'll join us, Lysandra? A drink for the General?' one of the new girls, a pretty Argive called Helena shouted out.

Lysandra narrowed her eyes as she tried to place her. Helena was one of the phalangites, a ranker of good reputation as far as Thebe reported it. 'I will join you in a cup or two,' she responded. 'But any of you new girls that fight tomorrow will stay sober, and remain focused. Pass the word,' she added.

Helena got to her feet enthusiastically, bounding down the lines of tables, informing the Hellene women of Lysandra's orders. There were a few disgruntled expressions but, in the main, the new girls looked afraid and out of sorts. Even with the training, the knowledge that soon one would have to fight or die for the pleasure of the mob was unsettling for them. She recalled Danae as she had once been and the memory saddened her.

'You're all right?' Thebe asked, evidently noting her change in expression.

'I was thinking of Danae,' Lysandra responded. 'When she was like those others.' She jerked her head at the new girls.

'We were all like that once,' Thebe commented, draining her cup. 'Well, most of us, anyway,' she amended.

Lysandra allowed her this slip. 'Helena seems not to be affected overmuch.'

'Helena is a good girl,' Thebe nodded. 'Tough as old boots, as the saying goes. Knows her place in line, does as she's told when she's told. Titus marked her out early for the arena. She has potential, whereas many of the other girls are good for soldiering in the battle, but not for this,' she gestured, encompassing the arena.

'Truth,' Lysandra concurred. 'There is a difference in training the soldier and the gladiatrix. So few of us are gifted enough to do both.'

Thebe's expression darkened for a moment. 'We can't all be like you, Lysandra.'

'No,' Lysandra agreed. 'But I did not mean only myself, Thebe. You are a good leader for those women in your charge. And you fight well alone. Extremely well.'

'Really?' Thebe almost gagged on her wine.

'Yes. I would not train with you, nor work with you if this were not so.'

'I...' Thebe trailed off. 'Thank you, Lysandra.'

Lysandra got to her feet, and placed her wine cup on the table. 'Enjoy yourself,' she said, and moved away. It was, she thought, a good thing to praise at times. It inspired confidence, not only in her charges, but also in her leadership. Feeling rather pleased with herself, she made her way to her cell.

She was unfamiliar with the new route through the gaol, and made several wrong turns, almost losing herself entirely. Irritated, she trudged through the darkened tunnels, trying to retrace her steps.

A foul stench reached her nostrils and she realised that she had stumbled upon the condemned prisoners' section. These malcontents were kept in appalling conditions, living in their own filth, fed the slops and leftovers from the meals of their betters as they waited for certain death. And rightly so, for they were the dregs of humanity. Laws existed for a reason and should not be broken. Despite herself, she paused to look into one of the barred cells and her heart flew to her throat.

There, asleep in a corner, was the unmistakeable bulk of Nastasen.

XLVII

'You are sure it was him?' Balbus was not at his best. His secretary, Nikos, had woken him too early, advising him that Lysandra was demanding to see him. Irritated, he had thrown on a tunic, muttering about fighters getting above themselves. It was not as if she owned him, it was the other way around. But, when Lysandra told him of her discovery, he was astounded.

'Of course I am sure,' she snapped.

'Well,' Balbus pinched his nose between thumb and forefinger, 'he is in there with the condemned. I can arrange that he dies today, if you like. I assume you'll want to see it?'

The Spartan's ice-coloured eyes bored into his own. 'I want to kill him myself,' she said.

Balbus grunted. 'Yes, I can understand that,' he said. 'No problem, I'll see to it. Actually,' he added, 'the spectators will love it. The attacker trussed and helpless before the victim who takes her revenge will appeal to them.'

'I'm not sure you understand me, Balbus. I want to fight him, not murder him.'

Balbus was taken aback, but could see that Lysandra was deadly earnest. 'That's absurd,' he said after a moment. 'Lysandra, you are

381

a very good fighter, but you're only a woman. Nastasen, even if he is in bad shape, would eat you alive.'

Lysandra cocked an eyebrow. 'I think you are mistaken. And I *must* fight him.'

'Lysandra,' Balbus sighed. 'I have too much riding on this – on you – to let you fight a man. You are topping the bill with Sorina; if you were killed...' he spread his hands.

'I must fight him!' Lysandra slammed the palms of her hands down on Balbus's desk. He jumped at the sudden action, feeling the beginnings of anger at her presumption. But the emotion died in him as he looked at her face. The pale skin had reddened, but not through irritation. Tears brimmed in her eyes and began to spill down her cheeks.

'You cannot understand,' she said. 'The humiliation, the pain, the rage I feel. I live it again every night. The cell... those men all over me. What they did. Balbus, you cannot know my torment...'

'Lysandra...' Balbus thought to get up from behind the desk and comfort the girl, but decided against it. 'It must have been a terrible thing.'

'I *must* fight him,' she said again. 'I cannot carry this inside me, Balbus. Not now that I have seen him again. I see his face in my mind... I can feel him on me...' She hesitated, angrily wiping tears from her face. 'I can feel him *in* me. His stinking breath, the abuse...' she trailed off, gathering herself. 'I must make him feel what I have felt. He must suffer as I have suffered. I must beat him. To be free.'

Think of the money, Balbus told himself. *Don't think with your heart – think of the investment. Lysandra cannot beat Nastasen.* 'I understand how you feel, but no woman has ever fought a man in the arena, Lysandra. It's... well... indecent.'

'Indecent!' she screamed at him. 'And his rape and buggery of me was not?'

382

Balbus blanched at the blunt terminology. 'Well, of course. But consider this – what if I allow this, and you lose. Your last sight will be of your rapist taking your life.'

'That is my choice. Balbus, please.'

Please. Balbus almost fell from his chair, so much did the word take him aback. He realised that he had never heard her say it to him. Always it was Spartan pride, demands, threats and tantrums. But never *please*. He shook his head, looking at her through eyes that he often felt were jaded and dimmed. She was not Lysandra of Sparta to him; she was just a commodity, a piece of meat for the abattoir of the arena – mere merchandise. Wasn't she?

Ah, but he was getting too long in the tooth for this game. He had become involved with his stock, and could no longer look at her as simply a slave. He had gone soft, he thought ruefully. Recently, he had given in to demands from Sorina, beautiful Eirianwen and Lysandra herself. Years ago, they would have gone to the blocks for their antics. Years ago, he would have felt no compunction. But now? He hated himself for admitting that it pained him to see one so proud so distraught. Lysandra reduced to tears. He closed his eyes. Who would have thought it? But it was insane. That she risked her life for his profit in the arena was one thing but he had no wish to send her to certain death at the hands of Nastasen.

'It has never been done,' he said at length. 'The public will never accept it.'

'They *will*,' she said firmly. 'Balbus, they accept women at the top of the billing. Why not this?'

'It's simply not done,' he argued. 'Women and men are separate – and that's how it should be.'

'Think of the money,' she said suddenly.

'What money?' Balbus was not going to allow Lysandra to manipulate him as Sorina had done.

'The betting would be huge, and all against me. I will defeat him and make you a fortune. Think how it could be promoted. The virgin warrior priestess has a chance for vengeance on the man who raped her.'

Balbus felt his conviction waver. She was right. 'You want your rape advertised all over the city?' he said. 'Is revenge worth all that?'

'I do not care how lurid your promoter makes it out to be. Lysandra drew herself up, the cold mask falling over her face once again. 'You have never fought out there, Balbus, but you have been in the crowd. You know that lust drives the games and nothing more. It is base but that is the truth of it. You think that I cannot hear the shouts from the mob? The things that men scream out to me? Gods!' She threw up her hands. 'You have us fight naked more than not. And why? For speed?' Her smile was cruel. 'Or perhaps to give people a glimpse of that which is pink when we fight for our lives? To watch our faces as we win or die – agony and ecstasy – like copulation?'

And there she had it. Lysandra, in her infuriating way, saw straight to the heart of the matter. How many fortunes had rich men who desired to sleep with a gladiatrix offered him? How many fortunes had he thrown away, because, at the end of it all he could not see himself as merely a whoremaster? He had given in once: to Frontinus when the governor had asked for Lysandra and, though the old man had had no designs on her, the fact that he himself had thought so shamed him. In that moment, he came to his decision.

'I will allow it, Lysandra.' He watched the tension drain from her, a fierce elation in her eyes. 'But I want you to know that there will be no betting from me.'

'Why?'

'Because…' He trailed off. 'Because you are doing what is right. I cannot profit from your rape. There was a time when I

384

would have, but no longer. You know,' he smiled at himself, 'if you lose, I will be ruined.'

Lysandra lifted her chin. 'But I will not lose, Lucius Balbus.'

'There is nothing that bitch will not do to whore herself to the crowds!' Sorina was furious. The news of the bout between Lysandra and Nastasen had spread through the gaol like the worst sort of plague. It was all anyone could speak of. Sorina raged impotently in her cell, pacing like a caged tigress.

'Would you have done anything different if the opportunity had been presented to you?' Teuta, as always, tried to remain the voice of reason but Sorina had no wish to hear it.

'I would have never been in the situation to be raped by him.' Sorina whirled on her. 'She brought it on herself – I think she secretly wanted it and taunted him with her body.'

'Sorina...'

'No! She has done this to get at me, that is all. She will rob me of our contest and yet she will die with all honours at the hands of a man. The mob will remember her bravery and I will be denied my chance at vengeance!'

Teuta stood and put a placating hand on Sorina's shoulder. 'She may win. Have you yourself not killed many men?'

Sorina jerked away from her touch. 'That was different. That was in the heat of battle, where all is chaos. But this,' she gestured in the direction of the arena above. 'There is no way she can beat him. You've seen him, Teuta. How strong he is. She does this to go to her death and cheat me of my chance.'

There was a tapping, and the cell door opened. Varia was there, bearing a tray with wine and sweetmeats upon it. 'I have brought you some refreshment,' the child announced.

'Get out! Get out!' Sorina screamed at her, finding another vent for her rage.

'But I was told to bring...'

Sorina raised her hand but Teuta stepped between the two, deftly lifting the tray from the girl's hands. 'Go,' she said. Varia took to her heels and Teuta put the tray down. 'There's no need to take it out on her, Sorina. Just be calm. There is nothing to be done about it.' She took a swig from the wine jug and smacked her lips. 'Balbus has given us the good stuff,' she said. 'Have some.' She patted the bunk, indicating that Sorina join her.

Still angered she sat, trembling with suppressed rage. She snatched the jug, and drank deeply, the red liquid sliding from the lip of the jug down her cheeks.

Teuta's eyes did not leave her as she drank her fill. 'There,' she said as Sorina wiped her mouth. 'Better?'

'If not for her, Eirianwen would still be alive. I hate her so much.'

'I know you do,' Teuta sighed. 'But don't let it destroy you inside, Sorina. When it comes down to it, Lysandra will die and you will see her corpse. The gods will accept the sacrifice in whatever form it comes.' She reached out tentatively and put her hand on Sorina's thigh. 'Let us not think of Lysandra now.'

Sorina eased back on the bunk, opening her legs. Teuta knelt between them, her tongue gentle and probing. Sorina grasped her hair, dragging her in roughly. 'It is not loving I want,' she hissed. 'Give me release!'

Varia weaved her way through the crowded corridors of the gaol, avoiding the gladiatrices who milled about. She was the happiest she could remember being. This was her first time at the games; the first time she could remember being away from the *ludus*. And what was more, she was allowed to serve Lysandra and the other Hellene women.

Lysandra was not in her cell nor was she with the other women. Varia found her in the training ground, duelling with Catuvolcos. She knew better than to interrupt her, so she prepared a jug of water for her Mistress – the word sounded grand even in her mind – and sat down to wait.

Lysandra's movements were as quick as snake's and Varia marvelled at her speed and power. She knew that no one, not even Nastasen, could defeat her. Catuvolcos wielded a long stave, the length cut to that of a barbarian sword, whereas Lysandra held two wooden training swords; she would fight as the *dimachaera*, the two-knife girl.

'He's bigger and stronger,' Catuvolcos said, his breathing laboured. 'So you must be fast. Faster than you have ever been.'

Lysandra nodded, her eyes flat and focused only on her opponent. He yelled and attacked furiously, the stave blurring and hissing as he swung it at the lithe Spartan. Lysandra moved back and away but Catuvolcos pressed in and the hiss of the wood was interrupted by the staccato clack of wood on wood as Lysandra parried.

'No!' Catuvolcos shouted at her. 'You must evade!'

'I cannot run from him forever,' Lysandra snapped. 'I must engage him at some stage.'

Catuvolcos cast the stave aside. 'Only when he is worn down and exhausted. You don't stand a chance against him when he is fresh. He will overpower you in moments.'

'I am tired of hearing that! You have said little else all day.'

'Because it's true!' Catuvolcos exploded. 'If you are set on this insane course, you must at least try to survive. And to survive you must stay away and pick him apart.'

'Insane?' Lysandra arched an eyebrow. 'It is insane to seek vengeance?'

'No, it is not insane to seek vengeance,' he muttered, hating that she was using her small knowledge of Clan lore against him: vengeance was a holy thing. 'But there are other ways. We can arrange…'

'No,' she cut him off. 'He must die before the crowd. At my hand. He must go to his death knowing humiliation.'

He sighed and retrieved his weapon. 'Well, then,' he said. 'Let's go again.'

Lysandra's smile was fierce.

The routine was punishing but Lysandra pushed herself to her limit. Catuvolcos was extremely skilled and she was at her best to match him. Time and time again when she tried to push an advantage he ploughed into her, using his great strength to bowl her from her feet. It was frustrating and infuriating but she knew it was the correct manner in which to train for Nastasen.

Lysandra was surprised at how the old feelings of fear as well as the more sickening ones of inadequacy and shame had been awakened at the sight of the Nubian. She knew logically that she had nothing of which to be ashamed. She had done nothing wrong, yet she felt a terrible sense of guilt, the reason for which she could not explain. Each night since she had seen him in the cell, the nightmares were more intense, dreams of the trainer and his men and the violation they had committed to her person.

Outwardly, she maintained a façade of confidence, but inside she was gripped with fear – not for her life, but of failure. To face his great strength and skill might be foolhardy but how else could her guilt be assuaged? How else could she lay the fear to rest? She had to meet him on his own ground, match him and defeat him.

Catuvolcos, at least, was doing his best to help and, on her part, she threw her all into the training. She was bruised and battered but she had learned much. After some hours he called a halt, himself hurt and exhausted.

'Again, tomorrow?' she queried.

Catuvolcos was bent, resting his hands on his thighs, gasping for air. 'Aye,' he said. 'We'll see how you've progressed.'

Lysandra nodded and walked away. Varia, the slave girl trotted towards her, bearing the water jug.

'I got this for you!' she announced. 'You fought well,' she added as Lysandra drank deeply.

'Not well enough yet. You did as I instructed?'

'Oh yes.' Varia nodded enthusiastically. 'She was very angry, shouting about how you were only fighting Nastasen so he would kill you and she wouldn't have her revenge on you!'

'Not quite the correct assessment on her part,' Lysandra said wryly. 'She took the wine?'

'I don't know. I fled before she could hit me.'

Lysandra smiled slightly. 'If she was angry enough to try to hit you and yet she took it... Good. I would see her in her cups as often as possible. Her hatred of me will grow and she will lose her focus.' Focus was something she herself would have to be aware of, she thought. Nastasen first, Sorina second. Then the ghosts would all be gone. 'You have done very well, Varia,' she nodded. 'I am pleased with you.'

Varia blushed. 'Mistress?' she said hesitantly.

Lysandra was already moving away, but halted. 'Yes,' she turned. 'What is it?'

The girl seemed to gather herself for a moment. 'I want to be a gladiatrix like you. To be a heroine like you. You could teach me to be the best, couldn't you? Then I wouldn't have to fetch and carry like I do now – not that I mind serving *you* because that's an honour but I don't want to go back to just being a slave.' It came out in a huge rush, and Lysandra had to force herself to concentrate on the tirade.

'Balbus has no plans to make you into a fighter,' she said shortly, and the girl's face fell. Lysandra frowned; she did not need juvenile peevishness now. 'I cannot train you,' she went on firmly. 'It is forbidden for me to do so.' She did not know if that were the case, but it seemed expedient so say so. Varia was useful in so far as her insignificance made her the perfect tool for gathering information on Sorina's state of mind. No one took any notice of the girl.

Varia looked as though she would burst into tears and, though Lysandra was about to admonish her, the words died on her tongue. She could not now risk her 'spy' turning against her. Guiltily, she realised that she also did not want to hurt the girl's feelings overmuch. In her early days at the *ludus*, they had come to be friends. Moreover Varia had remained loyal to her, and that was a trait to be admired.

'But then again,' she said, 'Balbus doesn't have to know everything, does he?'

'No.' Varia toed the sand, looking down.

Lysandra nodded. 'Very well. I will train you.' Varia looked as though she would cheer. '*After* my bouts with Nastasen and Sorina,' she said quickly. 'And not before. You must understand, Varia, that I risk my life each time I step out there.'

'But you are the best, you will win.'

'That is true,' Lysandra agreed. 'But the superior warrior never underestimates her opponent.' She paused. 'Your first lesson for free. Never take *Nike* – Victory – for granted for that is the surest way to send her favour from you.'

'Yes.' Varia nodded, her face full of studious intent. 'Can I watch you as you train? To learn?'

'Of course. You do, anyway, do you not? I will tell the other women that you are now my personal slave and not subject to their orders. Is that fair?'

'Oh yes, Mistress!' Varia beamed. 'I will do everything you say.'

The girl's friendship was, as always, earnest and Lysandra could not help but smile at her enthusiasm. 'Very well then,' she said. 'Follow me.'

It was only as they walked away that Lysandra realised that she had referred to Varia as *her slave*. The realisation that she had done so was shocking but she could not bring herself to retract the comment; it would have shown weakness. She decided she would think of Varia as her *helot*; not only did this suit the girl's purpose, it also reminded her of her Spartan heritage.

It was, she decided, an agreeable solution.

XLIX

Nastasen flexed his fist, feeling the muscles in his forearm bunch. He had lost some weight during his incarceration but he could still feel the power latent in his flesh. It had not been long since they had taken him – not for his rape of Lysandra, but for petty thievery and murder. He had spent his money on hemp and thus was unable to book passage on a ship. He had headed for the countryside, intent on pushing hard to the east, but his habit had drawn him back to the drug dens of the city, forcing him to rob and steal. One of victims had put up too much of a fight and he had killed the man. It was an accident but it made no difference. The *urbanae* captured him and the magistrates marked him for execution in the great Games of Trajan.

It was, he thought, ironic, that he who had once been the trainer of those about to die on the sands would go to his own death in the arena – and with no sword in hand. It was a cruel way for a man to die, not in honour, but in shame.

The first days in the cells had been hellish: deprived of the drugs that sustained him, he had moaned and raved maniacally, lost in delirium as the need for them coursed through his very soul. The other prisoners had stayed well clear of him, for all knew that lunatics were dangerous in the extreme. Yet, like all things, the pain had passed and, for the first time in years, the Nubian saw the world through eyes that were unclouded. It was a pity, he thought, that his last clear look at the world should be in such a place.

A shadow fell across him and he looked up, squinting into the light of a torch. Slowly, the bearer came into focus. 'Catuvolcos?'

'Aye.' The Gaul's voice was cold. Several burly slaves flanked him, each holding a cudgel. The trainer himself bore a set of manacles, which he dropped through the bars of the cage. 'Put them on,' he ordered.

Nastasen complied, his heart pounding. 'Am I to be released?' he asked, not daring to hope.

Catuvolcos grimaced. 'No. You are to fight, though.'

'Until I am killed.' He put the bindings on and jerked his arms apart, showing his captors that they were secure.

'I don't know,' Catuvolcos growled as he unlocked the cage. He glared at Nastasen, his eyes black in the torchlight. 'But I hope so. If it were up to me, I would kill you myself.'

'Jealous, Gaul? You've not fucked her then? Maybe after me, she wants no other man. I know she loved the feel of my prick up…'

Catuvolcos leapt upon him, raining blows into his face and body. Bound as he was the Nubian was unable to defend himself and collapsed to the ground. The Gaul came in with the boot before being dragged off by the guards. Nastasen struggled to a sitting position and spat out a glob of blood. 'Maybe she'll come and visit me one last time,' he leered. As he struggled to his feet he savoured the look of impotent hatred on Catuvolcos's face. 'And I'll have that sweet piece that you are so desperate to enjoy.'

'Get moving.' One of the guards shoved him away, putting himself between them.

Nastasen could scarcely believe that he had been delivered; yet, as the guards led him from the stinking cell and through the tunnels, he began to hope. They would not allow Catuvolcos to harm him. Not if he were to fight. And if he were allowed to fight, he could win free.

There was justice after all.

'He's been moved,' Catuvolcos advised Lysandra the following day. 'He's segregated, but he's allowed to train as well. It can't look as though we serve him up to you half dead from gaol, though I'd prefer it that he had no preparation. Do you want to watch him?'

Lysandra paused in her callisthenics. 'You are joking,' she snapped. 'I have no wish to see him until I have to kill him.'

'You could learn something from watching him, Lysa.' She did not think he even noticed that his sobriquet for her had slipped out, but she let it pass. 'You'll need all the advantages.' He paused, his gaze seeking her own. 'And, it might be a shock for you to see him in the open for the first time. After what happened. It would be better to be re-accustomed to the sight of him – I know that it can't be easy…'

'There is wisdom in what you say,' Lysandra interrupted 'I will not be shocked. What has happened I have dealt with.' She realised that she might be exaggerating slightly but there was no need to enlighten Catuvolcos as to the fact. 'We shall watch him then. After I have finished with you.' She stooped and grasped the two wooden swords.

Sorina turned away. She had spent hours watching the Spartan at her training and it disturbed her. Though publicly she was dismissive of Lysandra's chances against her, she was beginning to think that she would be hard pushed to defeat the young Greek. As each day passed, Lysandra seemed to be growing stronger and more focused.

At first, she had believed that the re-emergence of Nastasen would work against Lysandra, wearing her down mentally. Now she realised that her enemy was using the rapist as a catalyst. Despite her hatred, she was moved to admiration at Lysandra's training methods. The former priestess pushed Catuvolcos hard, moving with speed and efficiency, striking her stronger opponent almost at will.

Lysandra, she surmised, was facing her fears in the only way she could: by confronting the man who had raped and tortured her in his own arena. Indeed, she realised that, if she survived, she would emerge from the combat even more powerful, and it was beginning to look by all the gods that she could beat the black warrior.

With Catuvolcos's aid, her fighting repertoire had certainly increased. He not only gave her experience in fighting a larger, heavier opponent, but also had her performing a punishing callisthenic regime that included lifting heavy weights and other rigorous strength-building exercises, all of which she bore without complaint. Even now, after a gruelling bout with her trainer, Lysandra sprang straight to the heavy iron bars. Red-faced and teeth gritted, she began to lift the weights over her head as Catuvolcos counted out the repetitions.

Sorina looked down at her hand and clenched her fist, as if by such action she could permanently erase the etching on her knuckles that marked the passage of the years. She shook her head; she knew there was no way to tip back the sands of time. Yet, she thought grimly, there was enough left in her to defeat Lysandra.

She was well aware that Lysandra had tried to play mind games with her in an attempt to unsettle her, but Sorina was too long in the tooth to fall for such obvious ploys. The gamesmanship had stopped however, as soon as Nastasen had been discovered in their midst. It was as if Lysandra had put their own bout out of her mind, concentrating only on the Nubian and her battle for vindication. It was time, Sorina thought, to turn the tables on her enemy. To resort to such mental warfare was not honourable and certainly beneath her. Yet she now realised that she must have all the advantages when the day came to face Lysandra. She would not be robbed of her revenge.

She turned away from the Spartan, her mind set.

Nubian and Amazon regarded each other.

'Why would you offer to help me, Sorina?' the black giant asked, squinting at her in the sun. He was clad in only a *subligaculum*, his ebon body glowing with a sheen of sweat. 'We have never been friends.'

'True.' Sorina met his gaze evenly. 'But I have my reasons. What you did...' She paused, measuring her tone. Nastasen's crime was abhorrent to all women, yet now she deemed it a fitting punishment for the arrogant Spartan. The thought surprised her; that her hatred for the raven-haired Greek had reached such intensity. 'What you did was wrong,' she said at length. 'Yet I cannot help but feel that Lysandra brought it on herself. She acts in an austere way, yet I know well she is aware of her own beauty. She seduced Eirianwen, and because of that my sister-daughter lies dead. I know Lysandra taunted you in ways only a woman can. It is no wonder that, after the hemp, you lost control.'

'Yes, the hemp.' Nastasen's voice became wistful for just a moment. 'Though I am free of its grip, I can find no regret in my heart for taking her.' He smiled, showing his teeth. 'I was her first.'

Sorina forced herself to grin in response. 'There is justice in that,' she murmured. 'But what do you think?'

'I think that you will be cheated of your chance, Amazon. I will not stay my hand when I face her.'

'You take her too lightly, Nastasen. I *can* help you. Like her, I am lighter and quicker than you. And,' she added, 'no less skilled than she. We women fight another way to a man. The mind,' she tapped her head, 'works differently.'

'You still haven't told me why you want to help. Surely you want the chance to kill her yourself?'

Sorina shrugged. 'Dead is dead is dead, Nastasen. Though I burn to transfix her with my blade, I somehow see the beauty of her being impaled on your sword.' She nearly grimaced at the play on words, but it was not lost to Nastasen who laughed. 'And besides,' she went on, 'there is no queue of people lining up to train with you.'

'That's true.' The giant glanced about. He placed his hands on his hips, as though he were sizing her up. 'Yes,' he nodded. 'Yes. I think we can help each other.'

Sorina grinned ferociously. 'Yes,' she agreed. 'I think we can.'

It took only a single glance for the activities to cause Lysandra's bile to rise. At Catuvolcos's insistence, they had crossed the arena's training compound to watch Nastasen at his work. In truth, she was more alarmed by the prospect of seeing the Nubian warrior again than she liked to admit, even to herself. As they walked, she found her stomach knotting up, her heart beating hard in her chest. She told herself she was being absurd, yet the panicked feeling would not subside.

Not, that was, till she saw Sorina duelling with him. That she had offered herself as training partner to Nastasen was akin to spitting in Lysandra's face. More than that, she was playing up to him, sharing the odd laugh and joke as they sparred. Lysandra sat down heavily on a bench, her chin in her hands, refusing to simply turn tail and walk away. That would have been beneath her.

'I don't believe it,' Catuvolcos murmured.

'Do you not?' Lysandra scowled at him, her ire coming to the fore. 'She does this to insult me, that is all. There is no limit to the woman's ignominy, Catuvolcos. She speaks of honour.' She shook her head. 'Where then is the honour of helping *him*? Does it honour Eirianwen that she trains with the man that raped me? No,' she answered herself. 'Of course it does not. She is a foolish woman if she thinks this will have some sort of adverse effect on me. Nastasen is merely a stepping-stone to *her*, Catuvolcos, that is all. A training tool on which I shall hone myself, ready for when I face that old whore in the arena. Besides,' Lysandra sniffed. 'It is not as if training against a man is even *her* idea. We thought of it.'

'Then don't let it bother you,' Catuvolcos offered. 'Instead, watch him for weaknesses that you can exploit.'

It was as if Nastasen had heard Catuvolcos speak, for at that moment, he launched an attack on Sorina that was as furious as it was efficient. Using his bulk and strength to maximum effect, he disarmed her and slammed his wooden sword into her gut, sending her to her knees.

'That man is strong.' Catuvolcos had not realised he had spoken the thought aloud until Lysandra glared at him. 'Well,' he said a little defensively, 'he *is*.'

'That is as maybe,' she snapped. 'But you are strong enough yourself to be useful in preparing for him.'

'I'm honoured you think so.'

'I have seen enough,' she said shortly and rose to her feet, daring Catuvolcos to protest. He did not, and she stalked away.

He watched the lithe figure storm off and sighed. He realised that the rivalry between Lysandra and Sorina had changed them both. As he turned his eyes back to the training area, he considered that it was the older woman who had let her ambition overtake all reason. That the two were trying to get the upper hand mentally *before* their bout was a power play so obvious that it was almost laughable. Yet, for Sorina to train with Nastasen was low. It was beneath the Clan Chief, and Catuvolcos decided that he would speak to her about it.

Lysandra fumed all the way to the arena's small bathing facility. Varia had spotted her striding to the squat building and had come along in tow.

'Get a massage table ready,' Lysandra barked at her. She tossed her soiled tunic at the girl before plunging into the heated pool. She swam with strong strokes, slicing through the water as if this exercise would somehow purge her of the anger she felt. She was being ridiculous, she told herself. Despite her claim to Catuvolcos, the sight of Sorina and Nastasen *had* unsettled her. They were, she realised, her *nemeses* made flesh: one black, the other white; one male, one female; one the taker of her virginity the other the taker of her love.

She climbed out of the pool, lifting her hands above her head so that Varia could dry her off. It was almost inevitable that the two people she hated most would unite against her.

She said as much to Varia when her massage had begun.

'It doesn't matter what they do.' Varia said sagaciously. 'You will defeat Nastasen, and then Sorina. You are the best.'

'And that is how it must be.' Lysandra fairly undulated as the Roman girl's skilled fingers kneaded the tension from her. 'I *must* face Nastasen, Varia, I must.'

'Why don't we just have him executed for…' she trailed off. 'For what he did.'

'We?' Lysandra arched an eyebrow, quietly amused at the girl. Varia remained silent, working her way down her legs. 'I do not

400

want him executed, Varia. I want my revenge. Athene will be at my side and I shall defeat him. But more than this: when I win, it will strike a blow of terror into Sorina's heart. And…' She paused, wondering if she should reveal her innermost thoughts to the girl. It was shameful, but she suddenly felt the need to confide in someone. 'And,' she said at length, 'it is more important that I will know.'

'Turn over,' Varia said. She applied the unguent to Lysandra's thighs and continued. 'What do you mean?'

'I am not sure that I can win against Sorina,' she said quietly. 'Despite it all, I am not as confident as I should be. We have much to fight for and, though I am certain of my skills, I know that her will to win is as strong as my own. I am the younger, the stronger, but she is the *Gladiatrix Prima*. Never defeated. Her experience may tell.'

'Don't be silly,' Varia chided. 'She's all used up. You will win.'

'The point is,' Lysandra ignored Varia's blind optimism, 'that if I defeat Nastasen, I will have no doubt in my mind that I will go on to beat *her*. It is necessary that I face him for this reason above all. He is my catalyst. To win against him is the ultimate prize, Varia. After that Sorina will be a mere formality. In here.' She tapped her head.

'I don't know why you are making such a fuss.' Varia shrugged. 'He's as good as dead, Lysandra. There has never been a gladiatrix like you. You are the best that there has ever been.'

'Of course,' Lysandra responded, more from habit than real conviction. 'I am being foolish.' The words, however, were imbued with a confidence she did not feel.

LI

'What you are doing is wrong,' Catuvolcos said, wiping the foam from his mouth.

'No, what *you* are doing is wrong,' Sorina bristled. 'Training with *her.*'

'She will need help to face Nastasen,' Catuvolcos said earnestly. 'Only I am anywhere near as strong as he.'

'This is true, but in aiding her, you could hasten my defeat. You are making her stronger and faster – this is the result of training against a man's strength. So it is *your* actions that forced me to train with Nastasen. I must have all the advantages she has if I am to kill her.'

'Maybe.' He handed her the beer sack. 'But that isn't the real reason, is it? You're training with him to unsettle her.'

'That too,' Sorina said. 'And why not? She is trying her mind games with me. She will learn that I am long enough in the tooth not to be affected by this sort of thing. I think her game has been turned about.'

Catuvolcos did not reply to that. 'You could find other men to train with?' he protested. 'There are plenty of gladiators who would help you.'

'I know. But it will be Nastasen, for those reasons we spoke of.'

'He raped her, Sorina. You lose honour in what you do.'

Sorina fixed him with her chestnut-coloured eyes. 'Honour, Catuvolcos? It has died in this place. It died with Eirianwen. Perhaps it died when I was made a slave. Honour will be satisfied when Lysandra is dead and Eirianwen is avenged. That is all that matters.'

'You think Eirianwen would approve of this, Sorina?' Catuvolcos did not hide his exasperation. 'Like it or not, she loved Lysandra!'

'And I loved her,' Sorina flared. 'She was like my own daughter, Catuvolcos, and a part of me died with her. You cannot know how I feel. I struck the blow, but her blood is not on my hands. *Lysandra...*' The name dripped with a hatred Catuvolcos found chilling. 'Lysandra. It is always her. Before she came we were at least happy, if happiness can be found in such a place. You and I were close yet – and let us not lie to one another – our friendship is not what it once was. Eirianwen was alive. All was as it should be. Even Nastasen,' she threw up her hands. 'For years he had been at the *ludus*. Never had he laid a hand on any of us. He was cruel for sure, but he was no rapist. But Lysandra drove him to it. She is a witch. She brings death and hatred where she walks. She beguiles with her false austerity then wantonly displays her body, claiming it is natural to be so. But we know how she snared you. Balbus panders to her whims and even Stick, of all people, has a place in his heart for her. He *likes* her. And Stick likes no one. There is magic in what she does, Catuvolcos, and none of it good. I will kill her for the better of all.'

'You're insane in hatred, woman. You will not beat her, for you hate too much. It has clouded your mind...'

Sorina surged upwards, her face close to his. 'Don't say that!' she screamed. 'Don't say it, Catuvolcos. I will destroy her, I will cut her down. I will bathe in her blood!'

Despite himself, Catuvolcos took a step back at the maniacal fervour in Sorina's eyes. Saddened, he turned away.

'Catuvolcos.' Halting, he looked back. Slowly, deliberately, Sorina spat on the ground between them. 'Go to her, then. We are finished, you and I.'

'We were finished a long time ago,' he said softly. 'Sorina is dead. She, like honour, died with Eirianwen, and I only see it now. She has not seen it herself.'

'And Catuvolcos is dead to Sorina.' She did not wait for a response but stalked off, burning with fury.

Attalus yawned. The Macedonian was weary, and yet his guard duty had only just begun. It was, he thought, a good job, and he was lucky to work for Balbus. The pay was decent, the job safe. Certainly safer than taking the Legionary's oath, more secure than patrolling the streets as one of the *urbanae*, which in its turn offered its own dangers. However, there were some parts of the job that were less than savoury. He glanced at the cell door, knowing that the giant, Nastasen, slept within. An evil bastard, Attalus thought. Admittedly, that Lysandra was a stroppy one but nobody deserved what the Nubian had dished out. Guarding the door alone, so close to the giant savage gave Attalus the chills.

Lysandra was becoming quite the love of the crowds, the Macedonian mused. He recalled that it was he who had spoken to her first and she had mocked his accented Latin. He should have known even back then that she was something different from the rest. If any mere woman could defeat a strong man, it was Lysandra. She had bigger balls than most of the guards, that was certain.

He chuckled at that, but then was unable even to cry out as strong hands gripped his head and, with appalling suddenness, the wall loomed up in his eyes. There was sickening pain as his skull crunched into the unyielding stone. He tried to struggle but again his head was smacked into the wall. Attalus felt his legs go, and then there was nothingness.

Nastasen blinked into wakefulness as the torchlight from the cata-combs fell upon him. 'What's going on?' he mumbled, brushing the sleep from his eyes. 'What are you doing here?' he asked, swinging his legs from the cot, his face splitting into a grin. 'Come to keep me warm?'

The sword thrust took him straight in the chest. He cried out in shock and pain as the fire of agony engulfed him. Huge gouts of blood erupted from the wound and he slumped back on the cot, a stunned expression of horror on his face. Holding up his hands, he called for help but the entreaty became a scream as the gladius whistled downwards, biting into his meaty forearm. Again the weapon fell, cutting his face, blow after blow raining upon him, butchering him where he lay.

Nastasen shrieked frantically for help, his strength gone. The walls of the cell were coated in his blood, the stink of his shit rising from between his legs. The skin of his arms hung about in bloody tatters as the attacker stepped in.

'Why?' he whispered, blood bubbling on his thick lips.

'Because I must win,' came the response. The gladius swung again, catching him on the side of the neck, spraying blood and ichor into the air. The severed head clattered across the floor, Nastasen's final expression one of open-mouthed horror.

'... And because you are a pig.'

The room was awash with blood. Despite the chill of the early morning, flies had, with their unerring sense for such things, found their way into the cell and had already begun feasting upon Nastasen's corpse.

'Jupiter's sake!' Balbus hissed, running a hand over his thin-ning hair. 'What a mess.' Despite the fact that he was well used to the sight of blood, the carnage that had taken place in the cell was sickening. Nastasen's body had been butchered with barbaric ferocity.

'He had it coming,' Stick said, crouching by the mutilated corpse. 'It's not like anyone is going to be weeping at his loss.'

'That's not the point, Stick.' Balbus was more resigned than annoyed. 'We can't have this sort of thing.'

'Who do you think did it?' asked Catuvolcos.

Stick turned about and got to his feet. Unflappable as ever, the scrawny Parthian spat on the floor. 'Look at the state of him! It doesn't take Archimedes to work it out. Obviously our Spartan decided to end her bout with the bastard ahead of schedule.'

'Lysandra wouldn't do such a thing!' Catuvolcos protested.

'No?' Balbus broke in. 'We all know what he did to her. Gods on Olympus, if anyone deserved to die in such a way, it was Nastasen.'

'That's what I mean,' Catuvolcos said thoughtfully. 'If Lysandra was going to do away with him, she would not act in such a frenzied way. You know what she's like,' he went on. 'She would have just stuck her blade in him and left.'

'Who knows how she thinks,' Balbus muttered. 'Of course, Attalus doesn't remember a thing. One moment he was watching the door, the next,' he snapped his fingers, 'he was out like a candle. I should have him whipped for dereliction of duty, but I can't help but think we are well rid of Nastasen.' That was the truth, he thought to himself. Though he had given in to Lysandra's wishes, he could not help but be relieved that the fight she wanted so desperately could not now take place. Despite her assurances, in his heart he believed that she would have been hard pressed to match the black giant.

He turned to the guards who were lurking in the corridor beyond. 'Clean this shit up and have it burned. You two.' He indicated Stick and Catuvolcos, 'We must at least question Lysandra.

I cannot have her thinking she can just murder someone and get away with it. Bad for discipline,' he added.

In the early hours, Lysandra had finally fallen into a deep, exhausted sleep. Her slumber was broken when the door to her cell crashed open. Furious, she snapped into full wakefulness, her eyes focusing on the shocked faces of Stick, Catuvolcos and Balbus, all crammed into her doorway.

'What is the meaning of this!' she shouted. 'Am I an animal to be gawped at while sleeping?' She broke off. 'Why am I all wet?' Even as she spoke, Lysandra lifted up her arms, which to her felt damp and tacky.

They were slick with blood. Stunned, her eyes lowered to see her blanket soaked crimson. And there, staring at her, its tongue horribly swollen and protruding was the severed head of Nastasen. Horrified, she screamed and leapt from the bed, throwing herself as far away from the ghastly trophy as the confines of the cell would allow. The head rolled obscenely from the cot, its strange wiry hair tangling about it.

Lysandra screamed again, her eyes wide with terror.

'Get her out of here!' Balbus shouted.

Catuvolcos rushed forwards and shepherded the blood-mired gladiatrix from the room.

LII

Lysandra was sickened. That she was used to killing, accustomed to the sight of a body falling at her feet, could not have prepared her for the shock of seeing the disembodied head staring at her, almost accusing. That she had reacted so in public also galled her. She should have shown more control, she berated herself, but the queasy feeling in her gut would not abate, nor would the shaking of her bloody hands.

Catuvolcos had been the soul of concern, leading her to the bathhouse where he sluiced her down with warm water from the pool.

'I am quite fine, Catuvolcos,' she told him. 'You are being a mother hen. It was merely a shock that is all.'

His reddish eyebrows furrowed as he peered at her. 'You are all right?'

'Yes, of course,' she snapped, the lie making the response harsher than she intended. 'I have already told you so.'

Catuvolcos handed her a tunic. 'You didn't do this?'

Lysandra's eyes blazed as she prepared to launch into a tirade against the trainer, but she held her tongue. She suddenly realised how the situation must look. 'No, I did not.' She forced her temper in. 'Though I can imagine that it is thought that I did.'

'Balbus assumed so. I spoke in your defence, though,' he added.

'As well you might. Such a barbarity is beneath me, Catuvolcos. I would not stoop to murder in the dark. My bout with the Nubian meant too much to me to end it by assassination...' she stopped suddenly, her face flushing red.

'Lysandra...'

'That bitch!' The hissed exclamation was laced with rage and hatred. 'That conniving, gutless bitch!'

'What are you talking about?' Catuvolcos's voice bounced around the walls of the bathhouse.

'Sorina,' Lysandra raged, beginning to pace up and down. 'It all makes sense. She *knew* how much this bout meant to me. She knew it! Damn that woman. Damn her to Hades!'

'I don't understand.'

'It is all so clear! This is why she trained with him, Catuvolcos, do you not see? She did so to gain his trust, so that she might approach him with ease! She has robbed me of my revenge.' Tears welled up in her eyes. Furious, she wiped them away, her cheeks burning. That she recognised Sorina had played her own mind game against her did not lessen the ploy's success. How could she have known? 'I'm going to have this out with her!' she stormed, making to move past Catuvolcos, but he pushed her back. 'Get out of my way!' she demanded. 'Or I will move you myself.'

'Lysandra!' He used the trainer's voice, the voice of instruction and, for a moment, it gave her pause. Years of ingrained obedience did their work. 'Think about what you are doing. If you go and confront her now, awry and with tears on your face, she will know she has gotten to you! Think, girl!' He smacked his palm to the side of his head. 'Will you let her win so easily?'

'But Nastasen was mine, my tool to beat her,' Lysandra almost wailed.

'And she has taken it from you, as well she might!' Catuvolcos face reddened. 'You began the mind games with her and she has proven herself to be too canny for you. She is, by her own mouth, long in the tooth, Lysandra, and you are still a girl – to *her*,' he amended quickly. 'You are the one that speaks of tactics and cleverness in battle, are you not? Do you think it is good strategy to show your enemy that she has gained an advantage? That her ploy has worked?'

'No, but this is different.' Lysandra sniffed, and wiped her nose.

'It is no different!' he stormed. 'No different. Why am I telling you this? You know these things. By confronting her now, you hand her advantage. Show her that her ploy has no effect on you. Besides…' He calmed somewhat. 'You didn't need Nastasen to defeat her, Lysandra. You have the beating of her, and she knows it.'

'I am not sure. I thought that if I beat Nastasen, then I could easily defeat *her*. I am not sure that I can match her, Catuvolcos. I have told this only to Varia. Nastasen's death meant everything to me. Not only for what he did to me… but for what seeing me kill him would do to her. I needed to show her…' Lysandra trailed off. 'She is *Gladiatrix Prima*. I am afraid to lose.'

Catuvolcos blinked, seemingly shocked by her admission. 'Look,' he said heavily. 'I know that your fight with Nastasen meant a lot to you. For many reasons. But they are gone now. He is dead, and he died hard, Lysandra. Believe me – I saw the body. Sorina may be driven by hatred of you, but she has no love for any violator of women. She cut him up badly – worse than you would have done, in fact. He went to his gods in agony.'

Lysandra compressed her lips for a moment. 'He was mine to kill,' she said quietly.

'Perhaps so. But Sorina has taken that from you to hurt you. She is shrewd, and she knew of your need to face him, to prove yourself. She knew that if… when… you beat him, your mind would be sound to face her. So she took your certainty from you. But what does that tell you?'

'It tells me that she has outthought me. This is what I feared.' Lysandra sat heavily on a stone bench, resting her forehead in her hands. 'I am younger and stronger than she; I am the superior fighter. Yet she knows many tricks, many strategies. More than my years have given me.'

'It tells you that?' Catuvolcos sat beside her and rested his hand on her shoulder. 'It does not tell me so, Lysandra. It tells me that she is the one who is afraid of you.' She saw him smile sadly as she looked up. 'She is driven to this because she knows that when you face each other you will not stop until she is dead. In the arena, there is always a chance, a chance for the *missio*, a chance that you will come out alive. In this bout, there is no hope of that. One of you will die and she believes it will be her.'

'I am not convinced,' Lysandra said, but inside there was a stirring of hope.

'I am. Look, Lysa, she was once my friend. But this war between the two of you has driven her mad. She spat on the ground between us, you know. We are ended as kin. I told her she is dead to me and has been so for a long time.'

'She is as unsettled as I?'

'More so. For though you cannot take away her experience and her skill, she has lost her focus on what is real and what is not. She has driven herself mad. Too many years in the arena, too many years as a slave, and,' he paused looking straight into Lysandra's eyes, 'Eirianwen's death weighs heavy upon her soul.'

'And mine,' she broke in bitterly. 'She took her from me, Catuvolcos.'

'Aye, that is true. But in the killing she died too. Put your hatred aside for a moment and you will see it as plainly as I do. Clear as daylight. You two are from different worlds, Lysandra. What you of the middle sea seek to build is an aberration to Sorina. Order and straight roads, walls of stone – these are not things of the Tribes. To Sorina these things are evil. You, with

411

your Hellenic ways, represent everything that she hates. When Eirianwen gave her heart to you, she turned her face from the Tribe. Sorina loved her fiercely, but to see her with you…' He stopped suddenly, and Lysandra realised that the memories must be as bitter to him as they were to her. 'Can you not see that, to her way of thinking, she thrust a blade into the guts of her own daughter, Lysa? Can you not imagine what it did to her? To the Tribes, to be a kinslayer is the worst thing. Yet, this she did, for she feared that your love would corrupt Eirianwen, and then spread amongst the rest of us… we *barbarians*,' he said, no rancour in his voice. 'It pushed her over the edge,' he went on. 'I was too blinded by other things at that time to see it happening, and when I did it was too late. I tell you these things, not because I betray her, but because death will be a release for her. She was Clan Chief, an owner of horses, a great woman. And what is she now? A murderess. A slave, with her hopes broken, her sister-daughter dead by her own hand…' He trailed off, lapsing into silence for long moments. When he spoke again his voice was quiet and sombre. 'She is afraid of you, Lysandra. She is afraid to die, but her life is over. Face her in the arena. Give her release.'

Lysandra let the words wash over her in a gentle tide. She closed her eyes, reflecting upon them. She could not, as Catuvolcos had urged, put aside her hatred for Sorina. Too many things had happened, too many to simply forgive. 'I must think,' she said, her voice raw. Abruptly, she got to her feet and strode from the bathhouse, walking towards the arena. It was quiet and still, the only sound the soft hiss of the wind stirring the sand.

In her mind's eye, she could see the ravening mob screaming as their favourites fought and died on the self-same sand beneath her feet. She recalled her first bout, against the Gaulish woman with the straw-coloured hair. Her journey to Balbus's *ludus* with Hildreth and the Germans and the warrior woman's kindness to her in those first days. But Hildreth was dead now – she glanced to the centre of the arena – killed in this very place with her own blade. Here too, Penelope had fallen, her vitals pierced; was it not she and Danae who were with the ribald fisher girl at the last? And Danae herself, gentle, kind Danae, killed by Sorina, killed to spite Lysandra.

Lysandra squatted down, her black hair hanging about her face. And Eirianwen. Beautiful Eirianwen, her love. She felt tears spring hot to her eyes, her throat aching. She looked up, seeing through a blurred veil, Eirianwen, her hand reaching out to her, covered in blood. Lysandra looked down at her own hands, so recently drenched scarlet. The vision caused a lurch in her heart, a heart she tried to turn to stone.

It could have all been so different. If not for Sorina's hatred. If not for her own selfishness. She could have prevented Eirianwen's death, by denying herself the warm comfort of her embrace. She, in her need, was as responsible for Eirianwen's fall as was Sorina who struck the blow. She could have, *should* have turned away but had been ruled by her heart. All the years in the *agoge*, all the discipline, all the training. All for naught, for she could not save the one thing she had come to love.

'Weeping for your black man?' A shadow fell across her, the cracked, hated voice at once recognisable as Sorina's. 'I killed him, you know. Killed him as I will kill you.'

Lysandra wiped the tears from her eyes, and rose slowly. She found it strange that she felt no shame in showing the older woman that she suffered.

'What's the matter, girl?' Sorina sneered at her. 'Has it all gotten too much for you? Your little game has failed, Spartan. And you are more the fool for thinking that you could play it with me. I have seen your like before, and will see many more after your passing. You are nothing. I look forward to butchering you as I butchered him.'

Lysandra shook her head. 'You think it matters, Sorina? You

413

think it matters to me that you killed him? It did, but no longer. He was but a stepping-stone between us. I thought to prove to you that I was the better woman by slaying him in the arena. You sought to stop that from happening and have succeeded. What now remains between us? Eirianwen is gone. Nastasen is gone. It is just you and I. Here,' she gestured to the arena all about them, 'here is where you were made, and I was cast. There is little of the priestess that came to this place two years ago. There is nothing of the Clan Chief left in you, old woman. What are we then but two gladiatrices, two who must fight to the death?'

'You are afraid and seek to distract me with soft words,' Sorina hissed. 'Nothing will stop me from bathing in your blood, Spartan whore, nothing – for what you have brought me to, I will kill you.'

'I did not bring you to anything, Sorina. We, both of us, brought ourselves. And because of it, Eirianwen is dead. I can never forgive you, though I share some of the guilt. But you struck her down. And for that killing, that alone, you will die by my hand.'

There was nothing else to say. They stood for a few moments, staring at each other. Lysandra felt empty. For despite all the guilt, all the mistakes, all the losses, she found that there was no understanding in her, no forgiveness. She saw before her a broken woman, twisted and hateful. And in that moment, the desire to strike her down burned hot in her breast.

She broke the stare and turned away, feeling the wrathful gaze of Sorina searing her spine. It would, she knew, be over soon.

One way or the other.

LIII

An unforeseeable accident?' Frontinus bristled, his watery eyes boring into Balbus, who shifted from foot to foot under the gaze.

'As I said, sir, I could not have foreseen it.' The *lanista* had thought it prudent to bring the news of Nastasen's demise to Frontinus straight away. There was, he reasoned, little point in delaying matters.

'A most convenient turn of events.' This from the Spaniard, Trajanus. Balbus thought of those from the Iberian peninsular as little more than barbarians, but this one at least carried himself like a Roman, his Latin faultless. Balbus supposed that he was of Roman parentage. 'I knew that this woman of yours, this Spartan, would stand no chance against a male warrior,' Trajanus continued in a pedantic tone. 'I would suggest that perhaps someone has realised the folly of their idealism and has circumvented any losses they may had a-betting.' At this, he cast a sidelong glance towards Frontinus, and Balbus noted the old man's scowl.

The *lanista* cleared his throat. 'No, my lord, that is not the case, I can assure you. It is my belief that the killing was a personal matter, between slaves.' He took on just the right look of resigned regret. Better to side with Frontinus who would remain in Halicarnassus long after the Spaniard had departed. 'The bout between Achillia and Nastasen was not yet public knowledge. If any side bets have occurred, they could only have been between yourselves, as no one else knew the bout was scheduled.'

Trajanus sniffed disdainfully, his air that of a man who had been fleeced. 'You've apprehended the killer?'

'Unfortunately, no,' Balbus lied quickly. 'There were many who had cause to despise Nastasen and, truth be known, no one will speak out. I know that there are methods of extracting information but so many slaves could have done this. Then again, it could have been a guard... an arena employee...' he trailed off. 'I simply cannot know who did this.' He paused, spreading his hands. 'I am sorry if this sordid affair has disrupted any honourable wager between you. I assure you that nothing underhand has gone on and you may of course investigate the murder if you wish.' He kept his face neutral, hoping that his bluff would not be called. To offer them the chance to look into the matter would, he hoped, dissuade them. He felt his sphincter twitch as Trajanus made to speak, but Frontinus opened his mouth first.

'No need for that, good Balbus,' he said. 'I know well that you are an honourable man. I realise that your offer is made in good spirit, but I feel that it is rather beneath men of our rank to go scrabbling for details in the death of mere slaves.'

Balbus could have kissed him for that. Even if Trajanus now wished to delve he could not, without revealing himself as the lesser, pettier man. 'Of course, sir. Foolish of me to offer but, as you say, it was in good faith. Despite all our precautions these things do happen, I'm afraid.'

'Yes, quite.' Frontinus waved a dismissive hand. With much bowing, Balbus retreated, thoroughly relieved. Again, he could not help but think that this game was getting too much for him.

A younger man may well have enjoyed the trials, the risks, the highs and the lows. But for him there was merely the sense of relief, mingled with an almost overwhelming tiredness.

The games wore on, their passing lost to Lysandra. The Carian countryside blurred as she ran, her mind fixed only on putting one foot in front of the other. Fitness, stamina, strength, discipline and skill; these were her watchwords. Each day came and went, obscure in their similarity. Mile upon mile passed beneath her feet, countless cuts and thrusts with the *rudis* as she sparred.

She felt herself growing stronger, her muscles tightening under the punishing regimen. There were no longer women good enough to face her, so she was forced to bribe the male gladiators with her savings in order to train.

For Lysandra, there was nothing but pain, sweat and toil.

And Sorina.

'Come on, Sorina, pull!' Teuta urged as the Amazon hauled herself up on the chin bar, the tanned arms bulging. 'Legs!' she shouted, and was well pleased as Sorina lifted her legs with seeming effortlessness. 'Thirty leg-raises! Go!'

Silently, the *Gladiatrix Prima* complied.

Lysandra's wooden swords blurred as she attacked the wiry Ethiopian. The man was fast, moving quickly to evade her blows and counter with those of his own. But even as they moved, his features shifted, becoming those of Sorina's. With a scream, Lysandra weaved in, her swords a spider's web of violence. She did not even see which of her blows had struck him, knocking him senseless.

Sorina also found that no woman could match her in training. Circling her adversary, her face was fierce and feral, her movements

417

fluid and, if the swords were real, deadly. Her lithe opponent wa good.

But not good enough. Deftly, she stepped inside the man guard and scissored her swords at his throat.

'Get me another one,' she snapped at the watching Teuta.

'Ninety-six, ninety-seven, ninety-eight…' Thebe counted out th repetitions as Lysandra performed her push-ups. Alongside then the little slave, Varia, gamely attempted to keep up. 'Ninety-nin one hundred! Good, Lysandra, good.'

Her body drenched in sweat, arms trembling, Lysandra gritte her teeth. 'Fifty more,' she hissed.

The sandbag shook and bled grit as Sorina pummelled it, he fists smacking into the canvas sacking with hot venom. Eac blow sent a juddering satisfaction thorough her body, as sh pictured the coldly beautiful face of the Spartan pulping unde her fists.

The men watching guffawed with glee as the big German glad iator crashed to the ground, spitting blood. Lysandra stood ove him, her shoulders heaving with exertion. Furious, the Germa surged to his feet, swinging angry blows at the agile Spartan Where she could not evade, Lysandra parried. Where she coul not parry she struck back.

Her foot lashed out, catching the warrior straight between th legs. Clutching himself, the man collapsed to his knees, then o to his side as his compatriots jeered.

Lysandra glanced at them and allowed herself a rare smile.

The months passed, each day as before, both women honin; themselves to their peak. In her youth, Sorina had felt herse. strong; but with Lysandra to drive her on, her body reached level

418

she did not think herself capable of. For her part, Lysandra, even with all the training of the *agoge*, knew that she too was at her best. Never before had she been as skilled.

The last night was upon them. It had come abruptly, a sudden end to all the preparations that had dominated their lives for so long.

Lysandra put down her swords and watched Sorina as she laid a last, huge blow into the suspended sandbag. Across the training area their eyes met. In that moment, time seemed to stop. For they knew that come the following eve, one of them would lie dead. It was a comfort to both of them.

LIV

'Are you sure?' Thebe eyed Lysandra critically. 'It's so beautiful, though.'

'I am sure.' The two women, accompanied by Varia, were in Lysandra's cell. Above them, they could hear the rhythmic thrum of the crowd, the muted howls of the mob.

'It's never bothered you before.'

'This is different,' Lysandra snapped.

Thebe shrugged. 'Very well then.' She took hold of Lysandra's hair, and with bronze scissors, cut a huge hank of it away. The raven tress fell to the floor, where it was gathered by Varia. 'I'll make it short,' she said. 'But you aren't going out there bald, Lysandra.'

'Short is good enough,' the Spartan muttered. 'Just get on with it.'

'You are ready for this, Sorina.' Teuta gently massaged the muscles on the Amazon's shoulders, keeping them loose. 'All your life, you have been a warrior, from swaddling to saddle, to this place here. You have always been the best, Clan Chief. That you hate your enemy honours the gods; that your enemy is Lysandra is

420

nothing. She is just another body, another victim to your blade. You will strike her down.'

'I am sure of it,' Sorina murmured.

Trajanus applauded politely as a Carian gladiatrix dispatched her foe on command. He turned to Frontinus. 'I must say, Governor, that I am impressed. These games have been a delightful elucidation. It is my opinion, that, whilst these women that you so espouse are a titillating addition, they lack the strength and skill of *proper* gladiators.'

Frontinus shrugged, and his response was somewhat lofty. 'The mob seems to enjoy both equally.' He gestured to the sea of faces about them. 'Do you not think?'

Trajanus nodded disdainfully. 'I cannot help but agree. But it must be said that these performing women you have here are indeed superior to anything we have in Rome.' The time for hedging and veiled competition was over. 'I think the Emperor will be well pleased with next year's spectacle if it comes anywhere close to this one. I shall tell him this is so,' he said with finality.

Frontinus winked. 'You've yet to see our best,' he said. 'But I thank you.'

Trajanus motioned for Diocles to pour for them. 'Think nothing of it, my friend,' he said. With that, he turned his eyes back to the sands.

Lysandra was alone. She had Thebe oil her, and sent both her and Varia away. Before long, she would be under the eyes of the multitudes, but for now she needed solitude. She glanced at the small statuette of Athene above her bunk. The unmoving ivory features seemed to be fixed in an enigmatic half-smile.

'Be with me tonight,' she whispered.

She ran a hand ruefully through her shorn hair. In Hellas it was the mark of mourning and she realised that, if she was victorious, she would mourn. For if Sorina fell, there would be no cause for which to fight. She would have proven, beyond all doubt that she was superior. That she was Spartan. That she was the best.

But thereafter? There would always be others like her, she realised. Always another who wished to prove that she could beat the best. In the end, she knew that when Sorina fell, she herself would become her.

Gladiatrix Prima. The one to defeat.

To be in this place was her destiny, as Telemachus had said. Thinking of the Athenian priest made her smile. She wondered briefly if he was out there, amidst the ravening mob, come to watch her in this greatest of trials. Somehow, she knew that he was.

Sorina regarded herself in the bronze mirror. There was no mark of age upon her. Clad only in the *subligaculum*, she saw her breasts were prouder and firmer than they had been in years. Muscles stood out on her stomach, chiselled as if she were a Roman statue.

She too was alone with her thoughts. She felt the weight that had burdened her since Eirianwen's death lift. The curse of the Morrigan, that the beautiful Druid's daughter predicted so long ago, had passed. Looking back, she realised that she had indeed become maddened with hatred. Obsessed with it. It had set her apart, branded her indelibly. But now she felt that the madness had gone.

Only the hate remained. She would allow it to burn within her this one last day. Till Lysandra had fallen. Then she would let go of it and have her peace. This, she knew, would be her last battle, even if she had to maim herself to escape the arena. Balbus would have no say in it. Choice, at last, would be hers.

'It's time.'

She glanced up, to see the blocky form of Titus in her doorway.

'Centurion!' A smile sprang to her lips, unbidden. 'I thought you were at the *ludus*.'

'I was,' he said. 'But I could not miss this, Sorina. Much has been said and done these past months. I came to wish you luck. Both of you,' he added. 'The best will win, and that is all you should want and hope for.'

'Then I shall win.' She got to her feet. 'Let us go.'

Lysandra moved towards the light. Around her, the bustle in the passageways ceased as she passed by. Her friends were there, as were Balbus, Stick and Catuvolcos. The Gaul, she noted, had brought Doris with him. By them stood Telemachus, come to see her as she knew he would. She wondered why they had all come to her side of the arena, when she felt movement close by her.

Titus emerged from the gloom, flanked by Sorina. Like herself, the Dacian was nude save for the loincloth, her body oiled and gleaming in the torch light. She tensed, but the older woman made no aggressive move, her eyes blank and focused.

Titus steered Sorina to Lysandra's side, and pointed her in the direction of the Gate of Life. 'This,' he said, placing his hands their shoulders, 'is as it should be. Luck to you both.' He shoved gently, and both women moved forward, their feet in step.

The tunnel vibrated with the roar of the crowd, so familiar to them both, yet this time so different. As one they moved towards the light, the vestiges of Lysandra and Sorina falling away from them. The gate cranked open, bathing them in the cacophony of an expectant mob. The beast ranged around them, ravenous for the feast that was to come.

As they stepped in to the light, the mob howled with lust at the sight of them. Lysandra and Sorina remained within – it was just Amazona and Achillia now.

LV

ysandra had never heard them so loud. The sound was deafening, washing over the sands like Poseidon's tempest, shaking the teeth in her skull. A *herinarri* rushed up and placed the two swords in her hands. Across from her, another did the same for Sorina. The two women raised their weapons and the crowd screamed in a vicious frenzy.

Lysandra spun her swords twice, and stretched her neck from side to side before dropping into her fighting stance, the left blade held out at an angle, the right drawn back to guard her body. Sorina responded in kind, her lead sword held out, the right held at an angle above her head.

The noise of the crowd faded, till Lysandra was aware only of the sound of her breath, the beating of her heart, and even the soft hiss of the wind upon the sands. She clenched her toes, feeling the grains bunch beneath them, and breathed out sharply through her nose. This done, she stepped forward towards her enemy.

Sorina did not circle, nor did she step back. Her step matched Lysandra's; as they came into range of each other's weapons, they paused, their eyes meeting over the dully gleaming iron. For a heartbeat they stared thus.

With a cry, Lysandra attacked.

Her blades flashed out, screaming towards Sorina, but the older woman blocked and countered, her iron seeking Lysandra's flesh; Lysandra intercepted, and the duel continued, swords shining in the torchlight.

There was no respite, the combat unceasing. Strike after strike was met and countered, each woman striving to outmatch the other. Sweat broke out over Lysandra's body, mingling with the oil as she lashed out at Sorina. But the older woman moved impossibly fast, her swords always answering her own. Sorina pushed back, wrenching initiative from Lysandra, her blades swirling in an iron tide of fury.

Sorina spun about and Lysandra struck forward, but she had not counted on the Amazon's ruse; the spin was not to cut, but to kick and Sorina's trailing leg smashed into Lysandra's side knocking her off balance. The crowd screamed a mixture of delight and dismay as she stumbled. Like a tigress, Sorina raked in, her blades slicing down. Lysandra was forced to roll away, coating her sweat slick body in sand.

Sorina growled triumphantly and pressed on. Furious, Lysandra rushed in to meet her and the song of iron on iron rang loud as the two women cut at each other. Locked in combat they circled, blows landing closer and closer to their mark. Lysandra stepped in, crowding her opponent. Thinking quickly, she collapsed her guard, striking out with her elbow, catching Sorina with a glancing blow. It was enough and as the Amazon blinked in shock, Lysandra's blade slashed across her chest, opening a bloody wound beneath her breasts.

She felt a hot surge of elation at the sight of Sorina's blood and cut across again, this time slicing her across the stomach. Sorina staggered back, a look of stunned pain etched on her features. She had her! Lysandra moved in to finish the tottering Amazon, raising her blades to end, once and for all, the enmity between them.

It was then that Sorina struck. Even as Lysandra moved, she realised that the canny Dacian's plight was a ruse, but was powerless to stop the sword that sought her. It was all she could do to twist frantically away, letting the blade that would have gutted her carve a bloody seam in her ribs. She felt the stinging pain as cut met sweat, followed by the searing burn as the true extent of the injury was registered in her mind.

There is no pain, she told herself. *Discipline is stronger than pain.* The two women eyed each other, shoulders lifting in exertion. At an unspoken agreement, they stepped together once again, their blood running freely. The staccato song of metal against metal rang loud in their ears, accompanied by their grunts of effort and the now distant cadence of the mob. In this blur of aggression, hits were struck, minor yet strength-sapping cuts that threatened to exhaust them both. Scored in blood and filthy sand, they strove on, their hatred for each other and their will to win pushing them beyond all limits of endurance.

Sorina's blades spun in dual attack and, though Lysandra deflected one of them, she hissed in pain as the second bit into her left shoulder, spraying blood across her face, into her hair. Gritting her teeth savagely, Sorina tried to saw her weapon into the bone, her chestnut-coloured eyes burning with fury. Sick with agony, Lysandra felt her knees giving way. She dropped the sword on her injured side and grasped Sorina, throwing her weight into her.

They crashed to the sands, rolling on top of each other. Somewhere in the tangle their swords were knocked from their hands, skittering away as each sought to hold her opponent and deny her the advantage. Bereft of weaponry, they rained blows upon each other, smashing the flesh of their hated enemy. Surging, Lysandra heaved the older woman away and they both rose to their feet, each taking up the unarmed stance. Lysandra saw spots in front of her eyes as exhaustion did its insidious work upon her; but in her heart, she knew that Sorina was as tired as she. If she could not cut her down, she would beat her to death with her fists.

But it was Sorina who struck first, a long, looping overhand blow that crashed into Lysandra's cheekbone with the force of a hammer, splitting her skin. Furious, she hit back, slamming her palm into the old warrior's nose. Sorina gagged as bone and cartilage shattered under the force, cloying red fluid exploding across her face. Fists raised, Lysandra drove in but, in her haste, she did not see Sorina's striking foot. The blow caught her in the lower stomach, and she doubled over in time for her head to meet the hard bone of the Amazon's knee.

Light exploded before her eyes as the strike slammed into her forehead. Her vision tilted upwards, the lean image of Sorina, then the blur of the crowd, and finally the night blue of the sky as she crashed onto her back. Almost vomiting from pain, she saw the blurred form of Sorina rushing to finish her but, with a last desperate effort, she raised her own leg, catching her foe in the pit of the stomach. Grasping Sorina's shoulders, she heaved, and the older woman's rush continued on, propelled over Lysandra by this wrestler's move.

Sorina skidded across the sand, leaving a bloody mire in her wake as Lysandra rolled, trying to rise. She found that her left side was blind, her eye swollen shut by the Dacian's earlier blow. Heaving, she scrambled to her feet but her knees gave in and she fell forward, exhaustion seeping through her. She screamed at herself to get up, but her body would not obey.

Sorina had rolled onto her front, arms straining to lift her face from the sand. With titanic effort she struggled to a kneeling position, her body trembling from fatigue. Lysandra saw that the Dacian's legs could not carry her; gritting her teeth, she crawled towards her.

It was bestial; on hands and knees, they struggled to meet each other, colliding like pillars of a falling temple. Skill was lost to them now. Lysandra hit out, snapping Sorina's head back, who responded in kind. Blow was traded for blow, will alone keeping them conscious. Leaning against each other, their hands found each other's throats. As their eyes met, slowly, inexorably, they both began to apply pressure, each seeking to see the spark of life die in the other's eyes before she too gave in to death.

Trajanus was on his feet, screaming his encouragement to the fighters. It was most un-Roman, but he could not help himself. He was awed by their skill, their courage. When their weapons were lost to them, he thought the bout over but, to his astonishment, these women sought to batter each other to death. He had never seen the like. He had witnessed many gladiatorial contests, but never had he seen such vehemence, such will to win.

As they crawled to each other, he was already moving. Grasping the oaken box from by his seat, he rushed from the place of honour towards the sands.

Lysandra could see Sorina's eyes glazing, even as her own brain screamed for lack of oxygen. Her own strength was almost gone, but just a few more moments, and the Amazon would die. Eirianwen would be avenged.

Strong hands grasped her shoulders, dragging her away even as Sorina was pulled from her grasp. Howling and clawing with the last of their energies, the women sought to free themselves from the hands that held them, but to no avail.

'No!' Lysandra screamed. 'No!'

Trajanus stepped between the two battered women, held firmly by the *harenarii*. The crowd had lapsed into silence at this unprecedented act.

'Raise them up,' he said quietly to the arena attendants. Then, he raised his voice, the solid timbre echoing throughout the arena:

'People of Halicarnassus! I am Marcus Ulpinus Trajanus, Senator of Rome, advisor and friend to the Divine Emperor. Hear me well. Much is spoken of the great Flavian Amphitheatre and the spectacles staged there. I have been there. I have seen them with my own two eyes. But I tell you all, before the gods, never before have I witnessed such a display. Never before have I been so honoured to see a battle such as this. You have shared this honour with me.' He paused, and regarded the exhausted combatants. 'These two... women... have provided such a fight that will echo throughout the ages.' He opened the oaken box and drew forth two palm leaves, forged of solid gold. 'To the *victrix* goes the palm leaf,' he shouted, pressing the metal to their numbed fingers. 'They have done enough,' he continued. 'As they have honoured us, so it is in my power to honour them. I, Marcus Ulpinus Trajanus, Senator of Rome, do grant Amazona and Achillia their freedom. May they take a wooden sword from this place, never to fight again if they so choose it.'

The mob screamed its assent and then began chanting the Senator's name. Leaning close to the battered warriors, Trajanus shook his head. 'I have never seen anything like it,' he whispered. 'May the gods go with you both.'

The gladiatrices were lead away.

But this time, it was to their own Gates.

LVI

They had all come to see her as she lay on the surgeon's palate: Catuvolcos and Doris, Thebe, Stick and Titus, Telemachus and, of course, the adoring Varia.

Lysandra mumbled her thanks, aware only of her own pain and the bitter taste of failure. Despite it all, all the training, all the preparation, all the desire, she had failed. Sorina lived.

The gift of Trajanus was a hollow one; for though she was now nominally free, she knew that in her heart she could never be so. Not whilst Sorina lived. Tears of frustration welled in her eyes when her visitors had left. In the silent darkness of the surgery, she wept. Wept for her failure.

'Lysandra.'

It was Balbus. He hovered by the door for a few moments before sitting by her side.

'Lucius Balbus,' she acknowledged.

'What you did today…' He trailed off, looking at his hands, thumb working over thumb. 'What you and Sorina did has never been seen before. Not here. Not in Rome. Did you know that they are going to make a frieze of your fight? Amazona and Achillia, immortalised forever in stone. What a thing.' He shook

430

his head. 'This has never been done for women before,' he added, 'nor do I think it will happen again. You two are the best that there will ever be.'

Lysandra tried to compress her lips but the pain merely caused her to grimace. 'I failed. I was not good enough to kill her.'

Balbus shrugged. 'You are free now. What does it matter?'

Lysandra raised herself up slowly. She opened her mouth to explain but found she had no words. How could Balbus feel what she had felt? How could he know that freedom was empty without Sorina's death? Without Eirianwen. 'I suppose you are right,' she said after a while.

The *lanista* cleared his throat. 'What will you do now?'

Lysandra almost smiled at that. Typical of Balbus to always be thinking about his purse. With his two best fighters freed, he could never again hope to receive the gates and interest of the past two years. His dream of staging the grand battle for Domitian's birthday was over for, without her, she knew it would turn into farce. Balbus knew her too well. She could not and would not abandon those women already trained. She could not leave Thebe and Varia alone, bereft of her leadership.

'I shall stay with you,' she said quietly. 'This is what I am now, Balbus.'

'I thought this would be so.' His voice sounded strangely thick, as if a hard, dry crust was lodged in his throat. 'But it will not be with me,' he added softly. 'These past two years, with you, Sorina and, aye, Eirianwen, have taught me that I am getting too old for this game. It's all...' He trailed off, gesturing with his hands. 'It's all too much.'

'You are to retire?' Despite herself, Lysandra was stunned.

'Oh, yes. Eros and I shall go to Greece, where our situation with each other will not be frowned upon. Hellas, I mean,' he amended, and was rewarded by a wan smile. 'Of course, that leaves the matter of my *ludus*. I have spoken with Titus, Stick and

Catuvolcos on this, and they agree – it truly has become the *Ludus Lysandra*. Thus, I leave my school in your hands for you to do with it as you see fit. The women are now truly your responsibility. You can free them all, fight your battle or even sell the place. Or you could remain in the arena, though I hope you do not. He sighed. 'You have taught me much about myself. This is the only gift I can give you.' He leant forward, and kissed her softly on the forehead. He rose and went to the door. 'Goodbye, Lysandra of Sparta,' he said, and was gone.

There was only silence in the room then. Lysandra felt tears spring to her eyes as the enormity of Balbus's gift washed over her. What could she do? She had once said to Frontinus that she would not return to Sparta to become a priestess once more. That part of her was dead.

All that remained was the gladiatrix.

EPILOGUE

THE DACIAN BORDER – ONE YEAR LATER

Marcus Sabinus cowered in terror beneath the bodies. A legionary for less than two years, he had never seen a battle before and the reality was sickening. Men and horses cut down, or shot full of arrows.

They had come at sundown, raging over the marching camp like a tempest, scaling the walls, their shrill terrifying cries mingling with the crackle of flames and the screams of dying Romans. Such numbers they had were beyond counting. The gate breached, they had poured in, mounted warriors, terrible to behold.

The battle lost, he had sought to save his own skin, diving for cover amongst the dead. Then the screaming had begun anew, as the victors tortured their captives, maiming them, unmanning them, burning them. Marcus had soiled himself in terror and was unashamed, praying to all the gods on Olympus that he would survive. He prayed to his dead mother and father to spare him. He did not want to die.

Rough hands scrabbled at the bodies above him, dragging them away. He screamed frantically, trying to escape. But they were all over him, tearing the *lorica* from his body, pulling his tunic from him.

'Please,' he babbled, 'please don't kill me.' Fresh shit ran down his legs when he beheld them, these wild barbarians with only death in their eyes. Chattering in their vile tongue, they shoved him through the desolation that was once the marching camp. All around him the impaled bodies of legionaries rode on stout pikes, some of them still shrieking their death agonies.

It was then he realised that the attackers – all of them – were women. He had heard tell of the Dacian Amazons, but had laughed the stories off as fanciful tales. Yet here were the camp-fire yarns made horrific truth.

One, obviously their leader, approached. She was tall on her horse, bathed in the hellish light of the burning fort. Fresh scalps, Roman scalps, dangled from her saddle. Her sword was bloody, her quiver empty.

'Roman,' she said in Latin, her chestnut-coloured eyes boring into his own. 'Only you of your kin will leave this place alive, but not because I am merciful. Look around you. Etch the suffering of your comrades into your mind. This then, is the fate of all Romans who cross into my homeland. Find your kin. Tell them what has taken place here. Tell them that Sorina of Dacia has made good her promise once made to a Spartan. Tell the Romans that I have returned to take back what is mine. Do you understand me, Legionary?'

Marcus nodded meakly, his entire body trembling.

'We go!' the Amazon shouted, rearing her horse about. Her Sisters cried out their keening war cry and the thunder of hooves filled the camp as they rode, shrieking into the night.

AUTHOR'S NOTES

ladiatrix is a work of fiction and should be read as such – I make no pretence at classical scholarship – but the background to the story has its basis in fact.

That women fought in the arenas of the Roman Empire is irrefutable. Several ancient writers make references to the gladiatrix in their commentaries. Seutonius, for instance, tells us that: *Domitian presented many extravagant entertainments in the Colosseum and the Circus. Besides the usual two-horse chariot races, he staged a couple of battles, one for infantry, the other for cavalry; a sea-fight in the amphitheatre; wild-beast hunts; gladiatorial shows by torchlight in which women as well as men took part'*

In the arena spectacles, the afternoon and evening was the time of the main event, the gladiatorial combats. Fighting 'by torchlight' is evidence that these female bouts were taken in all seriousness by Domitian, though it must be said that the women's combats never superseded the male gladiators in interest or importance. One can draw an analogy with modern-day football. The women's game has its core of fans, but the sport remains dominated by the men – thus it was in the gladiatorial events.

Aside from the commentaries of ancient writers, the most

enduring piece of evidence of the gladiatrix is a stele found in Halicarnassus during the nineteenth century.

It shows two gladiatrices facing each other in a fighting stance, both heavily armed and the inscription at the bottom of the stele tells us indisputably that both combatants are female – they are named Amazon and Achillia, the latter being the feminine form of 'Achilles' and, of course, our word 'Amazon' is derived from the Ancient Greek lexicon to describe the fearsome warrior women of legend.

Inscribed above the combatants is the Greek word 'apelythesan,' referring to their honourable retirement from the games. From this, we can garner that 'Amazon' and 'Achillia' (these were almost certainly stage names) must have won their freedom by excellence in the arena.

In this novel, I have tried to give the mysterious women of the Halicarnassus stele a story, a tale that would have prompted their contemporaries to celebrate a *female* combat by inscribing it in stone. It would have been fairly time consuming and undoubtedly expensive to have such a work commissioned, so the fight between these two gladiatrices must really have been a spectacular and memorable encounter.

As much as possible, I have tried to weave the fiction of *Gladiatrix* into the known facts of classical history:

Sextus Julius Frontinus was indeed the governor of Asia, around 85-86 AD, during the reign of Domitian, and it was Frontinus who was famed for putting down the rebellious Silurian tribes of Wales during his tenure in Britannia. Later in his career he was to serve in Dacia.

Marcus Ulpinus Trajanus, the emissary and eventual gladiatrix aficionado of our story, would ultimately become Emperor of Rome, marking his place in history with his campaign against the Dacians.

The Spartan princess Archidamia, who is referenced in this

novel by the priest, Telemachus, was also a real person. During the Pyrrhus's invasion of Sparta, she – according to Plutarch in his *Lives* – '*came into the (Spartan) senate with a sword in her hand*' and went on to lead the women of the city in digging trenches in defence of the city. It has been expounded (and this is on Wikipedia, so it must be true) that she was 'captain of a group of women warriors.'

As I have it, the Spartans created a quasi-military religious order based on Archidamia's actions and our protagonist, Lysandra, is a product of this sect. This is a fiction: there is no evidence to suggest that the Spartans, as liberal as they were in their attitudes towards women, created any such Order. However, given their highly militarised and religious society, I did not think it would be too much of a stretch to imagine that they had.

Though I have tried to stay as close to the facts as we know them to be, as with all novels, some licence has been employed to heighten the drama. This aside, if there are any historical errors, the fault lies entirely at my door (or keyboard) and I can only apologise.

ACKNOWLEDGEMENTS

My thanks to:

Barry Robinson and Fiona Skene, test readers extraordinaire who both gave me courage and belief to keep going with the book.

Svenja Grosser for her expert review and recommendations, Catherine Colegrove for her help with the Latin translations and Alistair Leslie for his support with the promotional material.

Graham and Liz Ashford, Emma Heath, John Morgan and Alisa Vanlint of the Ludus Gladiatorius, and Dave and Lindsay Richardson of Legio Secunda Augusta – to whom I will always be know as 'AWOL.'

Ilan Eshkeri who risked the wrath of his publishers to send me the beautiful music that so inspired me whilst I was writing *Gladiatrix*. Without his work, I would not have been able to imagine and write down the scenes herein. His music certainly is the soundtrack to this novel.

Doug Watts of the Jacqui Bennett Writer's Bureau who taught me a whole lot about point of view and that if 1st century gladiatrices could hope for 'benevolent editors,' 21st century writers certainly cannot.

Ed Handyside, my publisher and the most wonderful editor a writer could hope to work with. I'm very grateful to Ed who is most directly responsible for *Gladiatrix* making it to the bookshops.

Donna Gillespie who has been for many years and continues to be an inspiration to me. Her great, great work *'The Light Bearer'* made me want to be a writer – reading it was a life-changing experience for me, and as I have said to her on many occasions, without Auriane there would never have been a Lysandra. Now, Donna has that in writing!

And finally, to my beautiful and long-suffering wife, Sally, who has put up with my writing-induced despair, the fact that I locked myself away in the spare room for weeks at a time and who has endured endless hours of 'The History Channel' which must have been an ordeal. To her, most of all, my heartfelt thanks. Her love and support is everything to me.

Russell Whitfield, March 2008

Another great read from Myrmidon Books...

The Painted Messiah by Craig Smith

A legend persists that, after the 'scourging', Pilate commanded that his victim be painted from life. Somewhere, the painting survives, the only true image of Christ, granting the gift of ever-lasting life to whoever possesses it.

Kate Kenyon, the wealthy young widow of an English aristocrat, has an addiction to mortal risk. She feeds it by engaging in the armed robbery of priceless artefacts with her accomplice and lover Ethan Brand. Their latest target is a priceless 'Byzantine' icon hidden in the tower of a chateau by Lake Lucerne. So far they have never had to shoot anyone. This time will be different.

Thomas Malloy is a retired CIA man looking for his first lucra-tive freelance assignment. His chance comes with a presidential favour to a rich but ailing televangelist. Malloy's task seems simple enough: pick up the preacher's newly acquired painting from a Zurich bank and get it to the airport. But, once in Switzerland, Malloy's old friend, the enigmatic Contessa Claudia de Medici tries to warn him off his mission.

Sir Julian Corbeau is an international criminal holed up in Switzerland to avoid US extradition proceedings. He is also the sadistic head of the modern Knights Templar. He *had* the painting and now he desperately wants it back and swears to wreak a bloody revenge upon those who stole it.

As the contenders vie for possession the bullets fly, the body count rises and the secrets of the portrait gradually unfold.

'I got paper friction burns on my fingers and pressure sores elsewhere because I could barely move until I'd finished it. Things were so tense that at several points I had to remind myself to breathe.'
Dovegreyreader's literary blog

'A marvellously thrilling book… the distinction between villain and hero is constantly blurred… a most enthralling story.'
Paul Doherty, author of the Hugh Corbett mysteries

'… a rattling good yarn. Fast paced, exciting and very very filmic.'
Random Jottings of a Book and Opera Lover

ISBN: 978-1-905802-15-9